ELIZA WAITE

ELIZA WAITE

∽

A Novel

ASHLEY E. SWEENEY

Ashley G. Sweeney
· 2016 ·

SHE WRITES PRESS

Published 2016
Printed in the United States of America
ISBN: 978-1-63152-058-7
Library of Congress Control Number: 2015955781

Book design by Stacey Aaronson
Map design by Jay Eckert

For information, address:
She Writes Press
1563 Solano Ave #546
Berkeley, CA 94707

She Writes Press is a division of SparkPoint Studio, LLC.

To Michael,
who first took me
to Cypress Island

PROLOGUE

❦

MARCH 7, 1898

*E*liza spies the slim piece of card stock turned facedown in the mire, a perfectly formed rectangle lying on top of the slurry of mud and dung. Ordinarily, Eliza does not stop to pick up stray pieces of paper, especially in the center of a bustling city street. But here, crossing First Street at King in Seattle, Eliza raises her skirt above her ankles and bends over at the waist. She retrieves the card stock in her raw, chapped fingers.

"Git outta my way, missus!"

A spray of sludge splatters Eliza's traveling skirt as she narrowly avoids a team of horses barreling down King Street. Hungry, nearly broke, and now without passage to Alaska for another week, Eliza prays the item in her hand might be a voucher for a cut rate at one of Pioneer Square's less squalid hotels.

She turns the slip over in her hand and squints to read the fine print: *Contract to transport at sea, not transferable, one-way passage only, second class;* stamped *SS Ketchikan; March 9, 1898.*

Eliza catches her breath.

Two days from now!

Eliza keeps her head lowered, half-thinking the owner of the ticket will appear like a magician and rip this slice of gold from her grasp. Eliza steps up to the wooden planked sidewalk and leans against a clapboard storefront to catch her breath. She adjusts her spectacles and reads slowly. Her eyes do not deceive her, and no one pays her any mind. She wipes the card stock with her handkerchief and slips it into her handbag.

A bonafide ticket, not a used stub or a receipt!

✀

WITH ONLY FORTY-FIVE DOLLARS IN HER CHANGE PURSE, free passage to Alaska saves Eliza half her worldly worth. On any other day, Eliza might try to find the rightful owner of the ticket.

Not today.

Earlier in the morning, Eliza had stood for two hours on a snaking line to the ticket booth.

"That's it, folks. All sold out for Monday's boat north."

Only ten people in front of her, and the ticket window slammed shut. A scuffle in the line resulted in wayward gunshots fired into the cloud-filled sky, loud swearing, and fisticuffs.

One cannot be too careful, here in the midst of this madness.

Last night Eliza slept sitting up at Northern Pacific Station. She shivered in her threadbare coat and pulled fingerless gloves full over her fists. She begged for a few precious hours of sleep.

Maybe I can afford a real hotel for a couple of nights now that I've found a ticket north.

Eliza gathers her satchel close. She spends the remainder of the day parsing out quarters, the first for a hot bun with sausage and a coffee, and another for a pair of woolen gloves with fingers. She peruses the storefronts: Yukon Supply Co., Palmer Bros., Miner's Emporium. She sees her reflection in the plate glass window of Cooper and Levy, Pioneer Outfitters, and hardly recognizes herself.

I look like a man. Well, maybe all's the better for it.

She passes storefront after storefront. Notices plastered on plate glass windows advise traveling women to buy large trousseaus of traveling gear and accoutrements for life in Alaska, including fur robes and coats, "Arctic" stockings, woolen underdrawers, and wool-lined mitts. Such luxuries lie far out of Eliza's reach. What she needs she will have to buy in Skagway once she opens her bakery. Jacob's threadbare coat, her off-sized boots, and her spanking new gloves will have to see her through.

Eliza meanders toward the wharf, a frightening mass of merchandise and men. She strains to pick out the *Ketchikan*, a weary stern-wheeler with a massive stack in its center. Upon closer inspection, the craft looks worse for wear, its weathered wooden hull pocked with dings and patched-over gashes, its railings worn to dulled steel, and gunwales peeling paint.

This will be my home.

A shrill whistle pierces the afternoon air. Men pour from the docks toward Pioneer Square.

"Watch out, lady! You need new glasses?"

Eliza bristles. *No man from Missoura would dare speak to a woman so harshly.*

"Lookin' for a jolly, Carrot Top?"

Or so brazenly.

"Who's you lookin' fer, Ma'am? Yer mister?"

A husband? Eliza thinks. *Those days are long past.*

Eliza circles back up King Street and crosses over to Second. She inquires at The Northern Hotel and then continues up past Jackson and Washington streets toward Yesler Way. She inquires at two more establishments before she finds a bed for two nights.

On the first night at the Alliance Boarding House for Women Eliza does not have a roommate, and sinks into a delirious sleep. On the second night she shares a single bed with a fashionable girl from Oslo who looks to be shy of twenty and barely speaks English.

"I go to Klondike, too!" the woman says. "My husband, he there. My name Greta, Greta Torgersen. T-O-R-G . . ."

Eliza does not understand the rest of the woman's story, although she catches some familiar words: New York, Chicago, and Seattle, pronounced more like "Sattle." Eliza assumes her bedmate traveled across the West by rail, like she did, many years earlier. Of the woman's future, Eliza cannot piece together a coherent story.

First, Eliza thinks that maybe Greta Torgersen does not have a husband, but means to find a husband in the Far North. There are stories of one hundred men to one woman in Alaska. But then Eliza second-guesses herself. Other stories reveal that many women traveling to the Klondike pose as actresses as a cover for lewd behavior.

That would explain no wedding band. And the provocative underdrawers! No, this Norwegian beauty does not mean to take a husband at all.

The obvious language barrier clouds Eliza's understanding of the woman's situation. Greta pulls out a new map of Alaska Territory, and traces the inked trail from Skagway to Dawson with her finger. Eliza cannot comprehend traveling over what must be a towering mountain pass and then five hundred additional miles into the heart of the Yukon. Eliza fears the journey to Skagway alone will prove difficult enough. She shakes her head.

"I'm sorry, I don't understand," Eliza says.

Eliza sits and peels off her boots.

Does this plucky Norwegian think she can navigate the mountains of Alaska in her fancy boots?

"All the best wishes to you, though. Do you have a ticket yet?"

Eliza holds her breath.

"I go to Klondike, too! My husband, he there."

Greta points again to the map and stabs the small dot marked Dawson with her pointer finger. Eliza drops the subject.

Eliza excuses herself and undresses behind the thin curtain in the corner of the cramped room. She removes her soiled traveling clothes and changes into her one nightdress. She hears Greta changing and muttering in unintelligible Norwegian. Eliza waits until Greta sounds the all clear. Eliza slides into the uncomfortable bed beside Greta and murmurs a good night. With a bit of maneuvering, Eliza turns her back to her bedmate. She slips her change purse between her slender breasts and clutches it tight. She then rearranges Jacob's coat so that it covers her midsection. She drifts into a restless sleep.

The next morning Eliza wakes early. Greta is still asleep and snores lightly in the poor excuse for a bed they had shared. Eliza dresses quietly and lets herself out into the dark hallway. She does not look back. She holds her traveling bag close to her side as she navigates Seattle's streets toward the harbor. Early morning sounds from the hectic waterfront grow louder as she approaches the wharves.

Sailing's at eight. I have a little more than an hour until I am on my way north. Am I really going to the Klondike? Alone?

Eliza stops at a corner store and buys a warm bun and coffee.

"Make that two, sir."

Eliza quaffs down the coffee and stuffs the warm buns into the deep outer pocket of Jacob's coat. She approaches the entry marked *Northern Steamship Co.* She keeps her hand on the cool bone handle of her hunting knife sheathed in the coat's inner pocket. A burly prospector just ahead of her blocks her view of the vessel. Eliza can hardly stomach the stench from the man's filthy oilskins.

Has he never had a bath?

At a quarter to seven the gangway of the *Ketchikan* clatters down to admit the first of the passengers. As the line inches forward, the weak spring sun rises over the Cascade Mountains and casts first light over Elliott Bay. Eliza feels the press of passengers behind her. She plods up the gangway and waits her turn to board.

Eliza holds her breath as the steward grabs her ticket. A second passes, then two.

"Wait your turn there, buster," the steward barks to the rush of passengers behind Eliza.

"We've got people trying to board who ain't got the right tickets. Just give me a damn minute here."

Eliza's heart *thumps* in her chest. The steward eyes the ticket, looks down at Eliza. She stands immobile under his scrutiny. She does not meet his gaze. He checks the ticket again, and punches it through.

He lets out a loud belch.

"On your way, then, Ma'am."

PART ONE

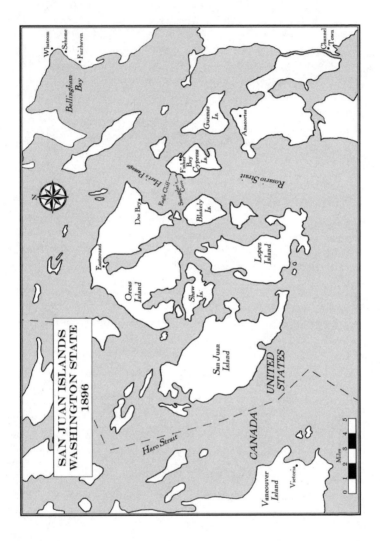

SAN JUAN ISLANDS
WASHINGTON STATE
1896

I

⁕

SEPTEMBER 1, 1896

Cloudy, first fall chill. Deer in garden again.

Need to mend fences.

ood fences make good neighbors," her aunt used to say. Eliza examines her muddied property and stifles a snort. There are no neighbors, no cheery *hellos* or help at harvest time, no shared secrets or meals offered at the door when grief steals joy clean away. No, her neighbors are all gone from this windswept island plagued with relentless autumn rains that close in on the coming darkness.

I do not know if I can endure another winter here, especially after what happened last year.

Eliza removes her nightclothes and rushes into her undergarments, woolen skirt, muslin blouse, and thick socks. She gathers up her skirt, and pushes out through the cabin's rickety door, inhaling wood smoke and counting her memories, both blessings and curses.

She clucks her tongue at Merlin and pegs out her linens. She clips the length of a worn bed sheet on a clothesline that stretches between two rough-hewn posts on the leeward side of the cabin. With her right hand, she frees another wooden clothespin from her chapped lips. She secures the flapping end of the wet sheet and pins it taut.

My hands were smooth back then, and my fingernails clean, when I monogrammed my trousseau with the letters E, and W, and then the unfamiliar S, inscribed larger in the center of the monogram.

Merlin ruffles his mottled owl feathers and screeches. His haunting *hoo-aw, hoo-aw* reverberates in measured waves off the massive basalt cliff face that rises seven hundred feet behind the cabin. Eliza had found the owl last month, wounded, beneath a nearby fir. She sat on the stoop and watched him. The owl tried many times to lift his heavy body off the ground, to no avail. Eliza watched him again on the second day. Midmorning she tossed him a live field mouse that she snared in her ingenious trap. The owl looked up at Eliza after ingesting the rodent. His eyes bored through her. The next day Eliza moved closer to the owl, and again fed him a live mouse, the rodent dangling from its snaky tail. On the third day, Eliza took a long stick and gently prodded it beneath the owl's talons. He grasped the stick and Eliza raised him to a low fir branch.

"Don't you look like a wise old man. I'll call you Merlin."

Today Merlin squawks in anticipation of his breakfast.

"I'll have to work a little harder to get you a morsel. I didn't get a mouse today."

Eliza drops a handful of clothespins into her basket and hunts beneath a cluster of sword ferns. She sees a brownish-gold leg under a feathered frond and lunges to capture it. She closes her fist over the slimed creature and offers it to Merlin. She looks away as Merlin scoops the frog from her palm. She wipes her hand on her skirt and pegs out the remaining linens.

Her woven basket holds limp and faded striped dishtowels, a shabby blue blanket, and her second set of well-worn undergarments. The barest ray of autumn sun slants through Douglas firs, cedars, and Madrones. A stiff westerly whips the sheets and towels and underthings: *flap, slap*, a short pause, followed by another sharp *flap, slap*, like salt-laden ghosts dancing in mime. With some wind and a little luck, the clothes might be dry by noon. Eliza hears the low *chugga-chugga* of a steamer plying the pass west toward San Juan Island.

No one's coming to Cypress anymore.

Indian John had left two months ago, and wasn't expected again until spring: moon of the digging time.

And no one else lives on Cypress anymore, except Tuttle. Of course unless Mad Virgil and his deaf son still live up near Eagle Cliff.

Sometimes Eliza thinks she sees a shadow, or feels a presence of another human being in the vicinity of the cabin. She knows she must be mistaken. There is no one else left on the island. She squints, looks out over the pass toward Orcas, and follows the steamer's path until it fades into the low-lying fog.

A heron passes low over Hart's Pass between Cypress and Orcas islands, its cry disrupting Merlin's sense of territory. Merlin rearranges himself, and watches the heron's slow, rhythmic wing beats with stoic eyes. His injured wing precludes any chase; his limp left appendage hangs low, a wounded soldier. He emits another haunting *hoo-aw*. Merlin observes all manner of winged birds with stoic intensity: black oystercatcher, rock sandpiper, long-billed dowitcher, black-bellied plover. At present he cannot fly any more than a mouse can fly.

Gunmetal clouds peer over Orcas, and Eliza shivers in her coarse clothes, the only sweater she owns wrapped around her thin frame tight as a bandage. A distant buoy clangs, its sonorous *gong, gong* muffled by the wind. She wipes away damp sweat.

Must be nine o'clock by now.

Hasn't had a clock for nearly three years now, since Jacob's pocket watch stopped at four-nineteen one afternoon. Just stopped.

"Even a broken clock is right twice per day," her aunt used to say.

Time is now irrelevant, or four-nineteen, simple as that. Instead of relying on a broken pocket watch, Eliza lives by the tides and the seasons. Winter and spring. Summer and fall. Neap tides and spring tides. Ebb tides and flood tides.

Eliza marvels at the flood tide's force. What seems the whole of the Pacific Ocean surges east through the Strait of Juan de Fuca twice each day, like clockwork. Cold grey-green waters race through myriad passes, boil over reefs hidden below the surface, and churn around islands and headlands. Water rushes past San Juan, Shaw, and Lopez islands, then around the horseshoe of Orcas, and finally on toward Blakely, Decatur, and Cypress. Day and night. Night and day.

Must be a jealous moon! And mighty!

Eliza's high tide marker runs the length of the mossy cove: a mass of driftwood, kelp, and foam whose sour smell dissipates in the weak sunlight. Its smell reminds Eliza of mildew mixed with rot. The low tide marker sits sixty feet offshore, a lonely glacial rock; its upended corner emerges from the strait when the tide dips to its lowest low. Today the rock lies submerged and the current gallops over its gnarly head.

Eliza's cabin stands just short of seventy-five yards from high water at Smuggler's Cove, its windward side facing Orcas three nautical miles north across Hart's Pass. Potter's Creek flows into the little rounded cove at the west edge of the property and emerges through a dense copse of Madrones. Her small plot of flat ground is bounded to the east, at the rear of the cabin, by the formidable Eagle Cliff. Wayward trunks of peeling red Madrones gash out of the cliff's base and sneak up the face, their roots imbedded into improbable cracks and fissures in the basalt. In spite of its exposure to north winds, the cabin warms perceptively as the morning gains momentum. The wood cookstove gobbles a never-ending supply of spitting alder and popping fir. Eliza hitches up her skirt as she mounts the crooked stoop. She pulls the cabin door open and deposits the empty basket on the kitchen table. The sweet scent of wood smoke embeds itself into her clothing.

Eliza stretches down to scratch her leg. Three large sores ooze under her socks on her right shin; they are nasty and pungent, and invite scratching. That she had tripped over the axe and sprawled in the mud irks her.

Typical, Eliza thinks. *How many times have I tripped over my own feet?*

Eliza remembers another scene as if it had happened just yesterday, although she had been sixteen at the time, and not nearing thirty.

"Mother! It's Eliza! Clumsy mule, she's fallen again."

Eliza had lain crumpled at the bottom of the grand staircase at their parents' home in Columbia. Her collarbone snapped, clean and quick. She winced from the pain.

"Help me up, Mae," she said. "Before Mother comes down."

Mae had bent over and helped Eliza to her feet. Mae adjusted her shirtwaist and led Eliza gingerly to the bench in the grand foyer.

"Mother! Come quick!"

Mae had disappeared up the stairway like a gazelle: effortless, weightless. Eliza sat on the bench for a quarter-hour before her mother appeared at the top of the stairway and sashayed gracefully down the winding staircase to the entry. Several moments later the front bell gonged, and Dr. Watts blew through the entry.

"My darling Harriet, what you go through," Watts had

said. Eliza's mother shuddered, her handkerchief butted up to the bottom of her nose. Watts examined Eliza's collarbone and tweaked the bone with his fingers. Eliza smarted.

"Can't expect a girl who wears size ten boots to walk daintily," her mother had said. "Can't seem to keep on her feet, this one. I don't know what's to become of her."

"God may forgive sins, but awkwardness has no forgiveness in heaven or earth," Watts said.

He's misquoting Emerson, Eliza had thought. *I hate him.*

Eliza buries that scene to the rear of her consciousness and scratches the foul infection crusting on her leg. She dreads another fever, another winter.

I'll be needing figwort.

She pulls her heavy black woolens over the sores and glances toward the closet. As for Sunday boots, Eliza has no need of Sunday boots on Cypress. They sit side by side in the cabin's only closet, unused, like two spinsters waiting for an invitation to dance. Aware of a sudden movement, Eliza catches her reflection in the cracked mirror on the closet door.

She is not a handsome woman. In this regard, she agrees with her sisters Mae and Margaret: *I am the ugly duckling.*

At five-foot nine-inches, her feet alone measure a solid size ten. Large green eyes peer out from a long ovoid face, and appear magnified with her rimmed spectacles. Her unruly copper hair is pulled tight into a low bun; wisps escape around her ears and down the nape of her neck. Eliza's frame supports small breasts and an even smaller waist. Her hips, large in proportion to her measurements, give Eliza an elongated pear shape. Dainty, prim, delicate, or petite—these words never attach themselves to Eliza. These words cause men to defer to the weaker of her sex, and choose the lovely ones. No, she is not a handsome woman.

She closes her eyes, and sinks slowly onto the narrow bed frame she once shared with Jacob. Jonathan's picture stares out at Eliza from its small frame on her bed stand. Eliza emits a gut sigh, one that starts from her depths and punches its way up to her heart.

Jonathan!

Light rain courses down the kitchen windowpane, in cadence with the *plink, plink* of the raindrops on the stovepipe. Eliza sits, reminded of grief's power.

ᗢ

BEFORE THE EPIDEMIC THERE HAD BEEN A STORE, AND A POST office, and a cannery, and a school. And—of course—a church. On those long ago Sundays, Eliza had squirmed each time Jacob mounted the stairs to the simple wooden pulpit at First Methodist on tiny Cypress Island, his pompousness preceding him. Eliza sat stiffly in the front pew with Jonathan close beside her. Jonathan's delicate hands held hers and his small brown leather boots dangled over the front lip of the wooden bench. If she tries hard enough, Eliza can still hear Jonathan's warbling voice stumbling over the words of the ancient hymns.

After Sunday services, Eliza and Ida Lawson had poured weak coffee into china cups at opposite ends of the cloth-covered table in the basement of the church. They adjusted the china cups, filling in spaces when others were served. They checked the sugar bowls. They rearranged the teaspoons, and placed them symmetrically. They exchanged glances and shared private conversations in between parishioners.

Did you hear the foreman killed a Chinaman over at Atlas Cannery?

Another parishioner would interrupt. Pleasantries. Then another interruption. More pleasantries.

Did you see Sly Chapman walking Adelaide Winters home from school on Wednesday?

There was always scuttlebutt about the townsfolk, or the trappers, or the fishermen, or the loggers. And always about the Chinamen. In the kitchen, Eliza and Ida would mimic the Chinamen, taking small steps and bowing to each other. They stifled their laughter. Only once had they had an awkward and guarded conversation about the intimacies of marriage.

But those days are long past. Now all Eliza has is a heap of gravestones to visit.

⌒⌒

ELIZA STANDS AND STEADIES HERSELF NOW. HER LEG THROBS, in cadence with her heartbeat. Jacob's woolen jacket scratches her wrists as she unrolls fingerless gloves over her rough hands. She pulls Jacob's boots up and over her woolens, and winces as the leather constricts the sores. She dismisses the thought of tetanus.

Jacob's boots haven't warmed yet, but her heavy wool socks will be drenched by the time she returns from the cemetery, steaming almost when she takes them off. She pulls on Jacob's filthy brown slouch hat, tugging the edges down low over her brow. Clutching her skirts, and careful not to slip on the undergrowth, Eliza leaves the damp laundry on the line and starts up the mossy embankment to the edge of the deep cedar forest. She dives into the brush with heavy footfalls. Dense with matted underbrush, the trail narrows about three hundred yards from the cabin.

If I had a machete, it would be so much simpler.

Eliza tromps past Potter's Pond and takes the western path toward the vestige of Fisher Bay. Eliza passes Tuttle's cabin on this way, a two-mile trip she makes at least once per month when she visits Jonathan's gravesite. When Tuttle's home, Eliza stops to call. The two don't talk much; they just sit on Tuttle's rotting porch and drink tea. Eliza's never been inside his cabin, nor does she have any compunction to do so.

Besides, it wouldn't be right, being a widow.

She always brings Tuttle a sweet treat, a half dozen muffins or half a pie. Today Tuttle isn't home, and Eliza leaves a wrapped package on his porch: Ida's Coffee Cake.

ᐧᐩᐧᐩᐧᐩᐧᐩᐧᐩᐧᐩ

IDA'S COFFEE CAKE

This is one of the best of plain cakes,
and is very easily made.

Take one teacup of strong coffee infusion, one teacup
molasses, one teacup sugar, one-half teacup butter, one
egg, and one teaspoonful saleratus.

Add pinch of salt.

Add spice and raisins to suit the taste, and enough
flour to make a reasonably thick batter.

Bake rather slowly in tin pans lined
with buttered paper.

Top with cinnamon sugar and serve warm.

ᐧᐩᐧᐩᐧᐩᐧᐩᐧᐩᐧᐩ

THE FIRES THAT RAVAGED FISHER BAY HAVE ERASED ANY known landmark, except for the stones, some toppled now and in disrepair. A few cedar stumps, hollowed in the center, remain on the barren landscape. A dense carpet of moss and wild strawberry tangles with salal and bracken fern, and new vegetation grows in the places that once housed the small town.

The autumn fog hangs impregnated with a lingering scent of smoke, a sweet, sickly smell that envelops Eliza as she kneels at Jonathan's grave. She delays there, and lets her mind roam back to happier times of her heart.

⸙

ON THE DAY THAT THE TRAVELING PHOTOGRAPHER, ONE MR. Nelson of Whatcom, had arrived at Cypress to take the annual school photograph the year before Jonathan died, Jonathan was absent from class. He had succumbed yet again to another ear infection, and lay on the blue brocade divan in the parlor with his tin soldiers making battle on the coverlet. When a knock came, Eliza opened the parsonage door to find a strange gentleman on her front porch mid-day.

"William Nelson at your service, Ma'am."

The stranger proffered a card to Eliza. She noticed the now familiar insignia of a hooded camera on the ivory embossed card. She thought that a family portrait might be in order, but of course Jacob would never consent to such frippery.

"Miss Winters sent me, seeing as your young'un's feeling poorly," he had said. "I just took a photograph of the class over at the school."

Nelson cocked his head in the direction of Fisher Bay School, three short blocks from the parsonage.

Eliza had thought then of Jonathan's schoolmates: the younger girls Novella and Jane, and the older girls Henny and Dorcas (*Sweet Dorcas!*); and the boys, eight-year-old Ellis, nine-year-old Floyd, and the not-so-innocent German twins, Otto and Heinrich. She was sorry Jonathan missed the annual school picture.

"Miss Winters thought you and the reverend might want a

portrait taken of your boy, as long as I was here. Of course I'd do you the pleasure, and for only twenty-five cents."

Eliza knew she should request Jacob's permission, but hesitated to disturb him as he practiced his sermon in the draughty church next door. Of course, it would be imprudent to let a strange man into the parlor without her husband at home, but Jacob was less than one hundred yards away, and would not want to be bothered. Jonathan lurked behind Eliza's full skirt and peered out at the short man on the stoop.

"Of course. What do you say, Jonathan? Shall we attempt a photograph?"

The boy looked up at Eliza with questioning eyes.

Eliza ushered the man in, past the boy and the entry, and into the overstuffed parlor. Nelson proceeded to remove his cumbersome equipment from his overland case. The boy watched.

Eliza settled Jonathan onto a straight-backed dining chair. He wore a sky blue sweater, with a wide white lapel at the collar, and worn brown knickers. His white socks poked above his brown boots, and his feet didn't reach the floor. Eliza laced up Jonathan's boots while bending over his slender frame. She talked Jonathan through the process, and he smiled into the lens with a shy smile, his hands in his lap and his feet crossed at the ankles. He clutched his worn brown bunny, its body thin from lost stuffing. In the end, after the flash and the smoke, and with great flourish, Mr. Nelson emerged from under the black curtain to exclaim that he had not only taken a remarkable resemblance of the boy, but one that would surely fetch fifty cents, if the good reverend and his missus lived in Whatcom.

Eliza thanked him, and removed a twenty-five cent piece from a box on the pump organ.

"When shall we expect to see this extraordinary likeness?"

"In about three weeks, Ma'am. I'll send it along with the photograph of the class. Miss Winters will surely deliver it upon arrival. Miss Winters—now there's a looker."

Nelson whistled through his teeth.

"Oh, excuse me, Ma'am, but I couldn't help noticing that Miss Winters didn't wear a wedding band."

Eliza ignored the comment.

As Mr. Nelson walked down the front pathway, Jacob had slammed the side door.

"And who was that hooligan?"

"Just a salesman. I shooed him away."

"Just as well. Don't need any shysters in town. I had hoped we'd left them behind in Seattle."

Jacob bristled then, and Eliza knew he remembered the event that brought him shame and consternation, and one that must be often revisited, but never spoken of again.

After nine days on the overland route from St. Louis to Seattle, Jacob had been accosted as he, Eliza, and Jonathan disembarked the train at Northern Pacific Station in Seattle. In the chaos and cacophony of the moment, Jacob was removed of his billfold, and in it, all the cash Eliza's father had paid Jacob to remove Eliza and her bastard son from St. Charles. It had been too easy for Jacob to accept the elder Waite's offer.

One thousand dollars free and clear.

A ticket and a future.

Gone.

Their pockets were empty.

If it wasn't for the pin money Eliza had sewn into her coat hem, the young couple would have had to resort to the kindness of strangers, perhaps even begging for their fare to reach their outpost on Cypress Island. At their meager lodgings at the Mayflower Hotel, Eliza picked open the seams of her coat and offered up her savings to her husband, twenty-five dollars to the penny.

"It's all we have, Jacob. Just enough to pay for our lodgings and garner the fare. We'll make our way to Cypress tomorrow and announce to the congregation that our funds have been stolen. Surely in their Christian mercy they will come to our assistance."

Jacob had scowled at his wife of less than one month, as if their predicament was wholly her fault.

"We will pay them back in time, Jacob. That is a certainty. For tonight, we'll eat the last of the kippers."

Eliza recalled Jonathan's quizzical look that night at the Mayflower, unsure of the surroundings, or the import of the situation, but putting full trust in his mother. The same look repeated itself when Jonathan looked up at his mother after Mr. Nelson's departure.

"But Mama," Jonathan said.

"But Mama, nothing, young man. Back to the divan, where you belong."

Her voice had been stern, but when she turned to Jonathan, she winked at him, a sure sign that this was just another secret between them, and one they didn't dare share with Jacob.

⌒

ON THE WAY HOME FROM THE CEMETERY, ELIZA TAKES A circuitous route around the pond in search of figwort. She ducks her head, and a low swoop of fir branches brushes her leather hat. A deluge of slender needles imbeds itself in the loose tendrils of her hair. She rests one hand on the fir's furrowed bark and removes Jacob's hat. She shakes her hair loose, a cascade of fir needles unloosed with one swift motion and a wild unruly mane of copper hair fanning out from her face. She stuffs the hat into the creel, and tucks the edges under the basket's lip. She reaches down to smooth her skirt, and untangles feathery spines of figwort.

"My grandmother, medicine woman," Indian John had said, on one of his earlier visits to Cypress. He had pointed to the weed-like figwort that grew in feathered clumps on the island. "Dig for root, and then boil. Use for sores."

Indian John taught Eliza to make infusions, ointments, compresses, and tinctures for any manner of ailment: wild lettuce for insomnia, peppermint for indigestion, stinging nettle for mosquito bites, yarrow for sore throat. She watched Indian John mimic applying a poultice with wide, dark hands, and smoothing the invisible edges down.

It was only last winter that Eliza thought she would die after succumbing to a fever brought on by another wound, a deep gash from a fallen tree that sheared the flesh of her right shoulder straight off. She pawed through the snow to find figwort and shivered in near delirium for three days and three nights until the fever broke.

Today she gathers the hardy plant and inhales its woody aroma. As she stoops over, she spies a clump of dark mushrooms near the base of a fir. She moves closer, drawn by the musky smell that emanates from the collar of the fungus. She inspects a wedge of black chanterelles and collects a handful from the bases of their stems. She places them carefully in the creel and flips the lid shut. A dragonfly buzzes near her ear, and she swats it away.

She rubs her leg again, and favors it.

Damn nuisance, she thinks. *Thank God for figwort.*

As Eliza skirts Potter's Pond, she listens keenly to the forest. The island echoes silence; there are no more whistles from the cannery or bells tolling from the school. There are no sounds except for the screech of gulls or the high-pitched shriek of bald eagles, the croak of frogs or insistent whirr of dragonfly wings. Or when Eliza talks to Merlin or whistles under her breath. Now that's something that ladies can't do, as a rule—whistle, that is. But no one can hear Eliza, and she doesn't care if they can. She lives like a man; she can damn well whistle like one.

∽

2

September 19, 1896

Sunny. Out of coffee.

Eliza checks the bucket she uses as a mouse catcher. A small field mouse runs in circles around the bottom of the wooden pail. The spinning wooden dowel fitted across the bucket's upper rim is still fully coated with thick grease. Eliza hears the dull *thud* of mice at night as they attempt to navigate the dowel and slip to the bottom of the container. She's awakened not so much by the *thud* as the inevitable *squeak* after the rodent hits the pail's floor.

It's as fruitless as trying to walk on a grease-slathered log, Eliza thinks. *Poor mouse. Just wanted a taste of butter. Well I would too, if I was that hungry. But Merlin will be pleased.*

Eliza moves the bucket from its nightly place behind the Acme to a spot near the cabin's front door. She stokes the fire beneath the rusting cookstove and places the blackened coffee pot on the Acme's rear burner. She stretches coffee grounds by using them two- or three-fold. She savors every drop, slurping the last of the thin black liquid down to the dregs. Today, her coffee is unusually weak, and tasteless.

Thank God today's a supply run.

Eliza checks the sky. It's three nautical miles north to Doe Bay on Orcas Island, an easy row on a turnaround tide. If Eliza lived on the southern tip of Cypress, it would be much closer to row to Anacortes, which she tried once, and failed. And even though she can see towering Mount Baker on the mainland on cool, clear days, rowing to Whatcom or Sehome or Fairhaven ten miles to the east is asking for trouble. Too many ships lost, too many times.

She remembers past headlines from the Puget Sound Mail:

"Wreck at Rocky Point," "Explosion on the Josephine," "Loss of the Steamship Tacoma."

No, rowing to Whatcom is out of the question.

Eliza pulls an Indian basket out from under her bed. Nestled in the basket are ten pairs of off-white mittens. Eliza keeps her hands busy on dark evenings in the cabin, knit-one, purl-one, knit-one, purl-one, as the kerosene lamp flickers in eerie patterns on the slatted walls.

"Idle hands breed trouble," her aunt used to say.

Out of boredom, or guilt, Eliza used to knit copious amounts of mittens for the Methodist Women's League and sent the boxes off island. Now she sells her inventory, and the sales contribute to her pin money, that paltry amount of legal tender that a woman can call her own. Sometimes Eliza weaves two strands of yarn into the mittens, and sometimes three. In desperate times, Eliza's mittens do not make a matched pair. Her supply relies on the wool sheared and carded on Orcas. She remembers when buying a matched skein was not of issue, like the year she made mittens for all of Jonathan's school-mates. She had knit red and green mittens, some with little white snowmen and white snowflakes that popped out on the dark background. She had dangled the mittens in the air, tall Henny and the German twins jumping above the rest of the students to grab for their favorite color.

Before she leaves, Eliza pulls Jacob's coat over her traveling clothes and picks up the mouse by its long, twitching tail. Now that Merlin's wing is all but healed, days go by without sight of him. And then, quiet as the mice he craves, he's back.

If he's here today, he'll get this morsel. If not, this poor little creature will go free.

Eliza rounds the corner of the cabin and spies Merlin on his perch.

"Here you are, my friend."

She drops the rodent at Merlin's feet. He pins it with his massive claw and bends to devour it. Eliza does not watch. She totes the basket to the water's edge and returns up the beach to right the dory.

To move the *Peapod* from above the tide's highest reach requires strength and resolve. Eliza keeps the dory under a generous canopy of cedar branches at the upper end of the beach, perpendicular to the shore. The dory rests upside down, perched at the bow on a log and tied to an even larger log uphill at the edge of the woods by a sturdy line. From one side, Eliza strains to right the boat on the rocky beachfront. She heaves the heavy craft over with a dull *thump* on the rocky sand and swings the bow end around. Here she pauses and breathes heavily. Pulling the *Peapod* toward the water line requires small, quick bursts of energy, and after five or six minutes, the dory reaches the lapping waters of the cove and eases bow first into the chill water.

Eliza lifts the basket into the *Peapod* and pushes the dory beyond the water's edge. Eliza steps over the transom, one woolen leg ahead of the other, careful not to let her boots

leech salt water. She sets the oars into the rounded oarlocks
and settles in to row.

The morning could not be more beautiful, Eliza thinks. *The way
the sun sparkles on the strait, like a thousand diamonds cast into the sea.*

It matters little if Eliza hurries or not today. The difference between the high tide and the low tide is imperceptible.
The *Peapod*, thirteen feet long and dory-hulled, plies the strait
easily, the oars timed in six-second strokes. Eliza's arms have
grown strong. She has learned the tides and the currents, and
reads the weather by the sky. Rowing to Doe Bay is a two-hour
journey, sometimes less when timed right, like today. Eliza licks
her lips, salt a familiar friend. Of other friends, Eliza cannot
count one still alive.

On her approach to Orcas, Eliza veers the *Peapod*'s port-
side to the floating wooden dock, using the wind and the
current as aides to a smooth landing. She lashes the lines to
the oversized wooden cleats and gathers the basketful of mittens
under her arm as she steps to the dock. She is careful as she
ascends the slippery ladder, one arm hugging the basket and
the other managing the rungs. Several wagons block the gangway,
but Eliza weaves her way through teams of whinnying horses,
their heads bobbing up and down in anticipation of a command.

"Good girl."

Eliza pats a brown-eyed mare tied to one of three hitching
posts in front of the Doe Bay Store. The white clapboard
general store, a mere eighteen-by-forty-feet square, contains a
plethora of goods: woolens, candles, soaps, hardware supplies,
and kerosene; and sundries: sugar, flour, molasses, tea, and
tobacco, all stacked tightly from counter to ceiling. Mingled
smells meet Eliza at the door—fresh brewed coffee, cinnamon,
yeast, licorice. She nods to Old Steiner and places her mitten
basket on a shelf behind the register.

"I've got that book that youse ordered," Old Steiner says. "It's right here."

He bends over slowly to retrieve a bound book under the counter.

"And it looks like it'll take youse awhile to finish it!"

Eliza smiles and takes the book in her hands: *Tom Grogan*, F. Hopkinson Smith's latest.

Not to be outdone by any city librarian, Eliza orders new novels as soon as she reads of their publication. This year she has ordered Thomas Hardy's tragic *Tess of the D'Urbervilles* and R. L. Stevenson's *The Strange Case of Dr. Jekyll and Mr. Hyde*.

Eliza opens the front flap of *Tom Grogan*.

To think that a woman could take on the persona of a man! And what she could do with it! What nerve!

Old Steiner plunks down a stack of yellowing newspapers beside the basket. Eliza almost salivates thinking of all the nights she'll spend catching up on the news of the world before the well-read pages become eventual fire-starters. She places the thick novel on top of the yellowed stack. She eyes the pigeon-holed cabinet behind the counter to see if any mail has made its way to Orcas with her name inscribed on the envelope. Today there's a thin package of church bulletins from Geneva Methodist Church in Whatcom and *The Old Farmers Almanac, 1897*. There is never a letter from home.

Eliza scans the aisles of the Doe Bay Store.

Where is Old Jennie?

No one bothers with the issue that Jennie is first generation Coast Salish, and Old Steiner, white. Eliza's father would have something to say about the common law arrangement; her more-than-Queen-Victoria-Victorian mother would also weigh in with severe disapproval.

None of that matters in the West, Eliza thinks.

Eliza pours herself a steaming cup of coffee, complete with fresh cream and a heaping spoonful of sugar.

Ambrosia of the gods!

Without a steady supply of milk, Eliza is accustomed to drinking her coffee black, or with the scantest amount of tinned milk. The coffee warms her hands as she meanders up and down the four narrow aisles of the grocery.

Eliza glances at magazines on Old Steiner's back shelf, and looks for a couple to add to her reading list. In last month's *Harper's Bazaar*, Eliza read with great interest of the travels of a Mrs. George Nelson, lately of New York, whose trip to the Orient via the South Pacific afforded her a glimpse into exotic aboriginal cultures. Seven thousand miles. One way. The extent of Eliza's travels measures three short miles, door to door.

Eliza browses through a dated issue of *The Ladies Home Journal*, and thumbs the pages quickly for recipes.

I must attempt a meringue. Oh yes! I need eggs.

Her eyes scan other magazines, a recent *Vogue* cover. Her interest piques at the sight of the familiar name, Kate Chopin.

Mrs. Chopin!

Scoffed in polite society in Columbia and St. Charles, Mrs. Chopin had roused crowds of forward-thinking women in St. Louis and beyond with her radical thinking. Eliza read secretly of Chopin's *"feminisme"* leanings when she stayed with her aunt during her confinement in St. Charles.

Such scandalous thoughts! That women can have opinions! And vote!

Eliza feels a chill run up her spine. She slips the slim, seductive issue into the deep pocket of Jacob's coat.

Eliza lingers in the aisles, and adds small items to her basket. When she finishes her shopping, Eliza places her provisions on the front counter.

"I've been thinkin'," Old Steiner says, "that maybe youse like to borrow more'n one book, or maybe a stack of magazines, seein' as youse don't come 'round too often."

Eliza blushes, toying with the magazine's thin spine in her coat pocket.

"Why, how kind of you," Eliza replies, her face hot. "I'll think on that."

"Youse can take as many as youse would like, my dear girl, as many as youse would like."

Eliza notices that Old Steiner's back curves in a perfect "C."

Before long he'll need some help at the store, Eliza thinks, *or have to pass it on.*

Old Steiner hands Eliza an envelope with ten crisp bills inside.

"Your mitten money."

Eliza extracts a thin dime out of her change purse, and places it nonchalantly on the counter, next to the register, when Old Steiner turns his head to greet a new customer. In this manner, she pays for the magazine lodged in her coat pocket. She knows she will not return it. Her take for the day: ten dollars, minus two dollars and forty cents for foodstuffs, and minus ten cents for the magazine. Another seven dollars and fifty cents to write in the ledger. There is no bank anymore where she can deposit cash so Eliza keeps her bills and change stashed in her Sunday boots in her closet.

"How's Jennie?" Eliza asks, changing the subject. Her cheeks drain slowly.

"Ah, she's poorly, right poorly. I had to bring her to Whatcom last week. I miss her bad, that I do."

He shuffles around the counter, his weepy eyes moist.

"Now, git on with youse. Gonna make an old man cry, youse is."

Eliza reaches the cabin after a pleasant afternoon row on a small ebb tide. Merlin is not on his familiar perch. Eliza looks for him in the fir branches behind the cabin, but if he is there, he is well concealed. After toting her meager supplies to the cabin and dragging the *Peapod* up the beach to secure it, she's too tired to make supper. She rummages through the pantry and settles on a jar of canned chow-chow and leftover corn fritters, hard around the edges.

ᑯᕐᑲᑯᕐᑲᑯᕐᑲᑯᕐᑲᑯᕐᑲ

CORN FRITTERS

One quart of grated corn, three eggs, the yolks and whites beaten separately, two crackers.

Beat corn, yolks, and crackers thoroughly.

Add pinch of salt.

Beat whites stiff, fold in just before frying.

Add more crackers if needed.

Have ready in a skillet butter and lard drippings in equal proportions. It should be hot, but not burning. Drop the mixture by the teaspoonful into the hot fat and brown upon both sides.

Be very watchful lest they burn.

ᑯᕐᑲᑯᕐᑲᑯᕐᑲᑯᕐᑲᑯᕐᑲ

SOON AFTER SUPPER, ELIZA UNDRESSES AND CLIMBS UNDER her grey flannel blanket. She cracks open the issue of *Vogue.* She begins to read Kate Chopin's "The Story of an Hour."

There was something coming to her and she was waiting for it, fearfully. What was it? She did not know; it was too subtle and elusive to name. But she felt it, creeping out of the sky, reaching toward her through the sounds, the scents, the color that filled the air.

Two short pages. Eliza reads and rereads the story. The words crowd her mind, and she wishes she could read more. Her mind swims with renegade thought. Eliza wonders how many other stories Mrs. Chopin has written. Although Eliza lives at the edge of the known world, she feels a new kinship, if only on the page.

It is as if I dwell in the antechambers of another's heart, and breathe in synchrony with it!

Eliza considers Mrs. Chopin's central character, one Mrs. Mallard, who has heard that very day that her husband has been killed in an unfortunate accident. Eliza weighs the pros and cons of Mrs. Mallard's plight.

Mrs. Mallard is now a sudden widow, and no longer bound by the constraints of a loveless marriage. In this way, Mrs. Mallard is a free woman.

What a woman could do, and be, without a man! Just like in Hopkinson's novel!

She thinks long on the concepts of liberty and entrapment, and wonders if living as she does on Cypress results in freedom or its contrapositive.

But constraints still bind women, Eliza thinks, *both inside and outside the home. We do not have a voice in household affairs! We cannot even vote!*

She longs to talk to Mrs. Mallard, even though Mrs. Mallard lives only in an imaginary world, and only on paper, in the folds of a popular women's magazine. Eliza settles her way deeper under the blanket. She warms to the mattress and keeps still so as not to invite a chill. The last of her embers chars to ash. She is too warm by now to get up and stoke the dying fire. She lies awake deep into the night.

3

SEPTEMBER 21, 1896

Monday again.

ONDAYS, launder. Tote three washtubs of water from
Potter's Creek. Boil water, enough to fill one of
three washtubs two-thirds full. Fill the other two washtubs with
cold water and place them nearby. Sort laundry. First,
underthings. Then blouses, sheets, towels. Last, skirt, socks,
rags. Plunge clothing into the hot water tub and rub each indi-
vidual piece on the washboard, adding soap. Repeat. Remove
clean items from first washtub and plunge into first rinse
washtub. Wring clothing thoroughly. Plunge clothing into
second rinse washtub. Wring out clothes again and hang them
to dry immediately on a clothesline.

For eight months of the year, the clothesline stretches
inside the cabin; in July, August, September, and October,
outside. Eliza's hands are raw and chapped most of the year,
her Vaseline Camphor Ice tin worth its weight in gold. She
rubs the camphor into her joints and in the cracks between her
fingers. She picks at her fingernails, and keeps them short.

❧

TUESDAYS, gather and chop wood, hopes and fears bundled like so much kindling, and burned as fast. Alder and fir. Fir and alder.

Cypress teems with timber. Eliza cannot fell a tree by herself, and relies on deadfalls. Eliza carries her axe, a wedge, and an unwieldy crosscut saw, its heavy *boing boing boing* echoing over her shoulder. She looks for trees up to fifteen inches in diameter, roughly the length from her fingertips to her elbow. She trims the dead branches with an axe; the branches snap with loud cracks and fall to the forest floor. Then she crosscuts the free end, starting at the narrower tip of the tree, with a steady back and forth, until her arms ache. When she cuts four full rounds, Eliza loads the logs onto a canvas travois and hauls the cargo back to the cabin.

Cedar shakes missing on the north side of the house cause the greatest concern. Eliza retrieves a shake wedge from the lean-to, and hews ragged roof shakes from old cedar blocks left behind the cabin. Her hands chap in the dampness, and she cuts the fingers off her Sunday gloves to work in the cold. Up the ladder, leaning forward on the pitched roof, Eliza carefully tucks and overlaps the shakes to the roof in as even a pattern as she can, given her precarious perch, and nails the shakes down. The rhythm of the hammer helps to pound out the frustrations of living in this friendless place. Every year the roof has caved a bit more. Last year Eliza had awoken to a near deluge one nasty November night and it was all she had in her to rouse herself to patch the roof once again. She wondered at that point—and again of late—if she has the energy to spend another winter on Cypress.

∽

WEDNESDAYS, plant, weed, put up stores. A well-worn path leads to Eliza's garden plot a quarter-mile west of the cabin. After rounding the head, the geography of the San Juan Islands opens into a wider expanse; through the narrow slot of Peavine Pass between Blakely and Obstruction islands, Eliza can make out the faint silhouettes of Shaw, Lopez, and San Juan Island beyond. Eliza tramps to the plot in all manner of weather, and carries a well-worn hoe, a woven basket, and her trowel, the latter a gift from her aunt upon her departure from St. Charles.

"Trouble springs from idleness," her aunt said, as she pushed the trowel into Eliza's hands.

No china, no silver, no linens. A trowel.

The garden space, near twenty-by-twenty square, possesses the darkest soil Eliza's ever seen. The plot is bound on all four sides by a crude fence, deer-proof in the sense that deer are not hardy learners, and try, day by day, season by season, to nose through the slats to munch at the edges of the bounty. Spring brings peas, onions, new carrots, and leeks; summer, all the beans—green, waxed, fava; autumn, potato, squash, corn, and yams; and winter, the gleanings before the ground lays fallow.

Eliza kneels in the dark, loamy soil. It's the closest she comes to praying anymore. The earth feels cool between her fingers. She works the trowel down the rows. Grubs surface and burrow their way back under ground. A worm slithers up Eliza's wrist. She flicks it away, bends to her task, pitches small rocks, and pulls errant weeds. She unwraps the paper packet of carrot seeds, small, slender, brown, a hundred to a pinch. She sprinkles a conservative amount of seeds per row, six rows in all. She tamps the soil down and imprints the dirt with gentle finger taps. She stands and straightens then, and stretches her back by bending backwards at the waist. She holds the clumsy pose for a few seconds and then regains her posture, hands on hips. She brushes dirt from her skirt in sudden movements, kneels again. Now for beans.

Eliza totes basketfuls of produce through mud or dust and spends long Wednesday nights in late summers and early fall canning and putting up stores. It's a messy affair. Some nights, innards of tomatoes slide down her forearms and boiling water pops out to scald her skin as she lowers the Mason jars into the roiling water bath. Other nights, it's the aroma of garlic and dill as the tang of marinating pickles pervades her senses.

❧

THURSDAYS, mend and iron.

Tedious chores.

And watching for the Thursday boat. A long spout of steam always drags behind the *Jubilee*, a white wake in the sky. Sometimes the strait fogs over and Eliza can barely hear the steamer. But like the Scriptures say, *now faith is being sure of what we hope for and certain of what we do not see.* Eliza is not one to cheat Scripture, and so marks each day religiously in *The Old Farmers Almanac.*

On Thursdays when she sees or hears the *Jubilee* chug past, she self-checks as to the date. On the rare occurrence that the *Jubilee* is detained by weather or mechanical problems, Eliza questions her record keeping. She marks off the day nonetheless, with a small black tick on the crowded pages of the almanac.

Just because I can't see it, doesn't mean it's not true, she tells herself.

Eliza envisions the mail boat docking at Doe Bay, and wonders what headlines she's missed. She yearns to read the *Puget Sound Mail*. She calculates that it's at least two more weeks until she'll hold the inky sheets in her hand and squint late into the night, reading. Eliza finds it amazing that one actually knows what is happening in New York and San Francisco, let alone in London, England or Paris, France. But no one, save Merlin, knows what happens in her small corner of the world. That is between Eliza and the wind.

❧

FRIDAYS. By the end of the week, Eliza craves meat. She salivates when she thinks of supper.

I can almost taste it.

Eliza digs the rocky island shore for butter clams and steamer clams. She wades knee-deep in the cove and spears unsuspecting Dungeness crab. At slack tide she rows to the bull-kelp bed five hundred feet offshore, and settles in to jig for lingcod or the occasional rockfish. She dredges the bottom of the reef with an abalone lure set close to a sharpened hook. It's sometimes a fruitless and maddening scavenger hunt, but most times she scores a bounty.

Today she dresses for the weather, and prepares for her pursuit. She rows to the bull-kelp bed and sets her hook. Waits. Waits some more. Over the years she's learned the art of patience.

And then the slight tug followed by a sure snag, a four- or five-minute wrestle to the surface, and a sometimes-awkward landing. She lets the lingcod slip from her hands to wriggle in the belly of the *Peapod*. She knows enough to club the fish square on its enormous head. She's been lucky today, and her gift from the sea lays lifeless at her feet. She doesn't ask for more than her share.

Eliza drags the *Peapod* above the tide line. She leans over the transom and grabs the cod, and lugs her catch to a flat top of a stump at the high water line.

Half this fish is head.

She lays the fish on its side and wedges her left hand under the gills to grasp it. With her right hand she draws a long, thin knife through its skin downward to slice the meaty filet away from the backbone. Then she flips the carcass over and filets the second side of the fish. She discards the skeleton to the squealing delight of the hovering gulls, and carries the fleshy meat to the cabin. Her fingers ache. The sweet smell of lingcod sautéing in her cast iron skillet fulfills Eliza's craving. She eats the entire filet.

∽

SATURDAYS. *Oh, if only every day could be Saturday.*

Eliza loves the sound of the wooden spoon hitting the enamel bowl as she folds ingredients into a sweet or savory mix. On Saturdays, she bakes muffins, or cakes. Pies or doughnuts. Sometimes cookies, scones, biscuits, or bars. She uses new recipes, old recipes, or off-the-cuff recipes, all mixed together with scads of butter and flour. Well-used slips of scrap paper crowd her recipe file. Of all of her recipes, her favorite, gingerbread.

ᘓᘔᘓᘔᘓᘔᘓᘔᘓᘔᘓᘔ

GINGERBREAD

*Mix in a large basin one teacup molasses, butter, size
of an egg, one-half teacup sugar, one teaspoonful each
ginger, cinnamon, cloves.*

Add pinch of salt.

*Add to this one-half teacup sour milk, in it one
teaspoonful saleratus.*

Beat in two teacups flour.

Leave overnight.

*Bake one hour in greased and floured square pan, or
until knife comes clean.*

ᘓᘔᘓᘔᘓᘔᘓᘔᘓᘔᘓᘔ

∽

SUNDAYS, Eliza adheres to Scripture. It is most deservedly the
day—*Amen!*—of rest.

4

◌⁊◌

OCTOBER 8, 1896

Down with the curse.

At her time of the month, Eliza takes one day off from chores, as her menses flow heavy. She mixes a tincture of white deadnettle and rubs the salve on her abdomen. Since Jonathan's birth, her insides have sloughed off violently, a message that Eliza records in her mother heart.

No, she thinks, *there will not be another child. And today*—she mentally scans the calendar—*would be Jonathan's birthday.*

Jonathan sank away slowly, unlike Jacob, who succumbed in the first weeks of the smallpox epidemic. At first, Jacob's nagging backache and fever hadn't aroused suspicion. A few days later, flat, red spots appeared on his face, and spread within days to his hands and forearms. Jacob wore his sleeves long. Eliza noticed pustules on Jacob's back on Sunday after church.

"Let me make a salve for you," she had said.

"Away from me, woman! I don't need your salve. And see to it that you don't fetch the doctor. The Lord will heal me."

He was dead the next Wednesday.

When Eliza noticed two small spots on Jonathan's thin shoulder blades several days later, she panicked.

"Is there nothing to be done?" she had pleaded with the doctor.

A blank stare answered her question.

Within three days, Jonathan's body was smothered in raised red bumps. The doctor said the pox ravaged the inside of a body in grave fashion, creating sores throughout a person's digestive tracts. Jonathan's bloody stools evidenced this, and foretold the end.

Eliza dabbed Jonathan's feverish forehead with a damp cool cloth that she wrung out by the half hour from a basin at the side of his bed. She was careful not to tear open the scabs on his face as she bathed his shivering body. He looked to Eliza with fright.

"I'm here beside you, my sweet boy. Just close your eyes. Mama's here."

Eliza had sat by Jonathan's side as he writhed in feverish restlessness. The last morning Jonathan was alive, he slipped in and out of consciousness. It was all Eliza could do not to crumble in grief. She stroked Jonathan's sweaty curls, a slow, gentle caress, repetitively. She memorized again every feature of his delicate face, how his nose curved slightly upwards at the end, and how his bow-like mouth pursed when he breathed. The shallowness of Jonathan's breathing signaled his imminent passing. Eliza waited in both anticipation and agony for each breath. When no more breaths came, she sat and willed another breath to come. A minute passed, no breath. Two minutes. Three. Eliza buried her head in the covers that consumed her child and sobbed.

When Jonathan's small body stilled, a neighbor had to pry Eliza's fingers from Jonathan's body. There were fifty-eight deaths that month, a full third of the island's population. At Jacob's hasty burial, Eliza felt numb; at Ida's burial and at the burial of Jonathan's classmates, she began to fill with an anger she didn't know existed. After Jonathan slipped into death, Eliza's rage reached its apex, and she was inconsolable. She did not sleep for three days.

Eliza had leaned on Sly Chapman's arm after Jonathan's burial, as the pair walked stiffly on the gravelly path behind First Methodist away from Jonathan's grave. Fresh mounds interspersed with fresh stumps dotted the graveyard. A fine mist gave way to large droplets, then heavy rain. Eliza felt as if her head was encased in wool. She could not focus, or think. She dragged behind Chapman and stopped then, immovable. She could not put one foot in front of the other. It mattered little that her coat soaked though to her underclothes.

Chapman turned to face Eliza and pulled her by the arm.

"Nothing left to do but burn Fisher Bay down, Mrs. Stamper, the cannery and the store and the school. The church, too. Got to erase any remnant of the pox. No one's staying behind, least of all women."

Eliza had been rendered deaf and dumb, the allotment of the aggrieved. All of her energy centered on breathing: one breath in, one breath out. She stumbled behind the church as if comatose. Sly's words sounded muffled, and reached Eliza's ear in the form of a hollow echo. Eliza hadn't any energy to answer, or to comment. Her eyes focused on the rocky earth below her feet, the earth that swallowed up Jonathan whole.

"The Richardsons left this morning, and eight or ten stragglers. Adelaide's chomping at the bit, going to Fairhaven, we are, and you're more than welcome to join us. We're likely the last ones out. And talk is, Wednesday's the last boat coming. No one's coming to Cypress anymore.

"There's nothing here for you, Mrs. Stamper. If you stay here you'll end up like that old bat who used to live over at Smuggler's Cove, riding out winters on this God-forsaken island on your own. And you heard what happened to her."

"Mr. Chapman, please, you must indulge me. I need just one more night here. There are things . . ." Eliza trailed off, her eyes moist.

She took a moment and cleared her throat.

"Things I will need, and time to gather them. I promise you by tomorrow night I will set the rectory on fire, and burn the ravages of the pox. You must trust me on this. I plan to stay at the old cabin at Smuggler's Cove, at least for the next while."

Chapman turned to face Eliza as the two watched First Methodist crumble to ashes next door.

"Can't say that I agree with your decision, Mrs. Stamper. Haunted, that place is. Wouldn't want none of my womenfolk staying there, that's for certain. If you're intent on staying, I'll offer you my little boat. A dory, she is. The *Peapod*. You'll find her under the old wharf, belly down.

"There's but two or three others staying, that's the honest truth. Just Tuttle, that old coot, and Mad Virgil and his boy up near Eagle Cliff, can't think of anyone else who'd want to stay, after everything. This may be your last chance to come along. Will you at least think on it?"

But Eliza could not leave Jonathan alone on the island, even though he was dead.

When the last of the islanders left Cypress the next day, Eliza made two trips from Fisher Bay in the *Peapod*, rowing one nautical mile north and west along Cypress Island's rocky eastern coastline to Smuggler's Cove.

On her first trip, Eliza gathered items from the empty

shell of the rectory. She rummaged through vacant rooms for items that could be of value to her, and not fouled with the pox. Most of what she took with her she found in the rectory's kitchen. She collected canned food, two cooking pots, one fry pan, an almost complete set of knives, a whetting stone, an oil lamp, as many tins of lamp oil as she could find, and the last of the tinned milk.

Eliza lingered in the kitchen after packing the items into two sturdy boxes. She peeled the kitchen chair along the rough plank floor and sat at the table where she had breakfasted many mornings with Jacob and Jonathan. She put her elbows on the table and rested her head in her upturned hands. She studied a thick stack of handwritten recipes, and let some of them slip to the floor. The rest of them she packed into a compact recipe file box secured with twine. She felt a sharp *pang* in her heart.

That's all I can handle on this first trip. I'll row back later for the rest of the supplies.

Eliza exited the front door of the parsonage and shuffled down the front steps of Number Four Church Street with the first of the two boxes. She hefted the box and walked two blocks to the where the *Peapod* sat waiting. She then returned for the second box. On the third trip from the rectory she dragged her three brooding hens behind her. She loaded the dory with the two boxes of provisions and the hens. The hens squawked in their makeshift coop, the latter tied hastily with several lengths of rope to the front bench seat of the dory. Then she set to row.

Eliza returned three hours later to retrieve her overland trunk. The only other item she added to the weight of her load was a wooden ladder she found on the western edge of the Patterson place. As she lugged the ladder toward the launching dock, she saw a glint of gold in the rubble. She bent over and retrieved a coin. This led to a nearly fruitless hour of bending and gathering, picking through mounds of charred debris. Her hands were covered with soot by the time she foraged a pewter candlestick and a metal basket, in which she placed her booty: bobbins, barrettes, and a charred coffee pot. Exhausted after the day's rowing and scavenging, Eliza dragged her overland trunk two blocks to the launch site, and heaved the trunk over the transom. It landed with a *thud* in the dory's belly.

It's all I've got left, she had thought, *a few books and a photograph, a meager amount of clothing and personal effects, and my recipe file. Nothing more.*

Eliza walked one last time through the rectory, removing drapes and curtains from their rods, and gathering linens to set ablaze. At first, she carefully unhooked her bedside curtains from their clips and folded them, along with her bedding, into a neat pile. She became more careless as she moved from room to room. By the time she reached the parlor, she tore the damask drapes from their rods with a *snap*. The drapes ripped into strips of faded finery. Eliza mounded the cottons and damasks in a pyre in the rectory's doorway.

Her fury reached a zenith by the time she stepped out onto the front porch. Her heart beat heavily. She flicked the flint, once, twice, and lit the end of a pointed branch. She blew on the tip until the smoke jumped to flame. Eliza held the stick for several minutes to be sure the flame would not extinguish easily. She tossed the lighted stick toward the open entry. The stick landed just inside the rectory door, to the left of the credenza on the Oriental rug, the very same spot Mr. Nelson of Whatcom had stood when he had doffed his hat before taking the only photograph of Jonathan that she now possessed.

Eliza stood for the first quarter-hour and watched her home disintegrate before her eyes, at first slowly, the smoldering linens leaping into flame and licking up the rectory walls, and then the cracking and popping of wood beams collapsing and plummeting to the floor. When the fire had gained momentum, Eliza stepped backwards away from the heat. Smoke had begun to envelop the structure and was wafting out of every crevice: doors, windows, and chimney. She watched silently as the inferno chomped through the first story and up into the second story. The smell of burning wood and metal and rubber overpowered her. She covered her nostrils with a handkerchief.

In less than an hour, a tremendous *whoosh* swept through the rectory. In the succeeding moments, her home collapsed under the invisible strain. In the aftermath, a flurry of embers floated in the slate grey sky like tiny lanterns. A light drizzle ensured that the blaze would die a certain death.

Like my family. Like so many others.

Eliza walked by the burned shells of her neighbors' homes, the Patterson's and the Lawson's, their chimneys the last reminder of the lives that they had inhabited there. Eliza lingered no more than she thought appropriate. She rowed away from Fisher Bay for the last time, her home burned clear to the ground.

That an old woman had lived in the cabin Eliza now occupied and had survived by her own wits had encouraged Eliza, but did nothing to assuage the tyranny of the immediate: the roof of the cabin leaked, several of the window panes were cracked, and the chinks in the siding allowed the cold northerly to blow through.

When Eliza finally reached the cabin, she heaved the unwieldy trunk up and out of the *Peapod*. She maneuvered the crate up the cabin's uneven stairs and returned to pull the dory above the high tide line. She collapsed on the single frame cot without eating supper.

This will be my home.

During the night, a loud crack and subsequent crash startled Eliza from a dreamless sleep. A rogue limb had reached its long slender fingers deep into the cabin and rain seeped in around the new gash in the cabin's roof. Eliza mounted one of the two high-backed chairs left behind in the cabin, and stretched as high as she could to tack the corners of her grey blanket to the sagging roof. In the near darkness, she worked as if by Braille, her only light the weak streams of light from a waning moon. The blanket served as a poor bandage over the gash, but what else could she do? It was dark and cold, and Eliza lacked both the skills and materials to fix the leak. She also lacked any other means to stay warm, other than wearing Jacob's coat to bed. She shivered and wrapped the oversized coat around her.

Not long after dawn, Eliza stoked the woodstove from a ragged stack of kindling piled to the left of the stove, near the cabin door. She threw on Jacob's coat and collected three eggs from the chicken coop. As the fire roared to life, Eliza set the table for one, measured coffee in a scant cupful, and scrambled eggs with salt and pepper.

I must have a routine here, she had thought. *Or else I am never going to survive this.*

༼༽

THE RAGS ELIZA USES FOR MENSTRUAL PADS BULK UP UNDER her nightclothes. The sweet smell emanating from beneath thick flannel reminds Eliza of many days lying about and reading in her floral room in Columbia when her menses flowed. How she had loved *Little Women* and *Little Men*. She visited the Columbia Free Library every three weeks, and walked home with an armload of classics to devour. Her father blamed reading for Eliza's poor eyesight.

"Old Four-Eyes, that's what you are," he had said. "And that dreadful hair you've got. Why can't you be more like Margaret, or Mae? You'll never marry, that's for certain."

Isaiah Waite had repeatedly said that Eliza was as large and clumsy as a mule, "and not a looker." And he had always decried that Eliza had a mouth on her. He often wondered if Eliza was in fact his child, but his wife was most certainly a virgin when they had married. Eliza was what he called a bookworm, and from all observations, had no interest in fashion or hairstyles or going out in society. As far as Isaiah Waite was concerned, his eldest daughter was bound to be a spinster.

Eliza passes hours reading; she does not notice clotted blood seeping through the rags and onto her nightclothes. Of course there had been indoor plumbing in Columbia, not the outhouse Eliza is forced to use behind the cabin here on Cypress.

Eliza rarely uses the outdoor privy behind the cabin, preferring to use the chipped ceramic chamber pot under her bed. Sometimes the chamber pot is so cold, or so full, that Eliza is forced to go outside, but instead of tramping to the rickety privy behind the house, she just squats on the leeward side of the stoop and pees outside. During her menses, Eliza trudges to the outhouse, drops her used rags in a crude bucket just inside the privy and swaddles herself in new rags. The smell overpowers her. Eliza thanks God that there are no bears on Cypress Island. Eliza has heard that bears are attracted to the smell of fresh blood. If she lived on the mainland, upriver in the valleys of the Skagit, the Nooksack, or the Stillagua-mish, bears, eager for blood, might well surround her cabin. She shudders at the thought.

Back inside the meager warmth of the austere cabin, Eliza boils water for tea and whips up Johnny Cake to assuage her discomfort. She omits the egg. There are no chickens anymore. Eliza was forced to eat them, one by one.

ᏣᏂᏣᏂᏣᏂᏣᏂᏣᏂ

JOHNNY CAKE

Take two scant teacups of cornmeal, one teacup of flour, one teacup of soured milk, one egg, one-half teacup butter, one tablespoonful of molasses, and a teaspoonful of saleratus dissolved in a thimbleful of water; mix thoroughly.

Add pinch of salt.

Moisten with sufficient sweet milk to cause the batter to spread in the pan.

Bake quickly in a cast iron pan in a well-heated oven.

Serve with butter and honey.

ᏣᏂᏣᏂᏣᏂᏣᏂᏣᏂ

ELIZA RUBS HER CHAPPED HANDS WITH OINTMENT AS SHE waits for the kettle to whistle. As she works the grease into her fingers, she takes care to rub warmth back into her cold hands. She thinks of Jonathan's cold body.

What of the trumpets, Eliza thinks. *Where is the glory of heaven, anyway?*

Eliza wrestles with the Christian view of death and—*God forbid!*—heresy. She wants to believe that Jonathan resides in heaven, as the Scriptures promise, but she is haunted by the image of a tiny pine box six feet underground, and in it, a young boy clawing for a way out and back to her. On glum days like this, Eliza grapples with the notion of leaving Cypress behind, its daily existence too difficult, and the memories more difficult still. But the invisible cord that binds her to Cypress is taut.

"It's an ill wind that blows no good," her aunt used to say.

Outside the cabin, the wind jerks violently, and buckets of rain pound on the roof on the grey October afternoon. Although Eliza relishes the opportunity to take a single day off from chores, her insides continue to rebel against her body. She maneuvers into a more comfortable position and reaches for her tea. She stares through the uncurtained window above the chipped enamel sink and cannot see through the dense fog that descends over Cypress. Every shade of grey colors the landscape, from steely clouds that conceal the daylight to the vague cinereous mound of Orcas rising out of the dusky sea.

Eliza burrows deeper into her covers and closes her eyes. Even with her eyes closed, Eliza travels through visible scrims, one after another, and the outline of life continues to blur. She wonders how—*and why?*—she avoided the pox. Everyone she knew, everyone she loved, had succumbed to the ravages of the disease.

Maybe I am left here to die.

Out of habit more than intent, Eliza follows the daily readings in the Methodist Bible lectionary, its tattered pages worn from so much use. Tonight's reading offers little comfort.

My God, my God, why hast Thou forsaken me?

Psalm Twenty-Two reverberates in her mind. She knows the lines of the psalm by heart.

Why art Thou so far from helping me, from the words of my groaning?

On a dark and drear day at the cabin like this, Eliza feeds the fire. Does obligatory chores. Eats sparsely. Drinks nettle tea. Naps. Reads.

O my God, I cry by day, but Thou dost not answer; and by night, but find no rest.

The October wind whips around the cabin, and howls forlornly. Eliza listens to the gusts through the trees. A low whistle weaves between the high fir branches. Eliza hears a groan, and then a snap. For a moment she cowers, but no new limbs crash through the patched roof.

Eliza misses Jonathan more than ever before. She aches to read to him, mend his socks, make his supper. She longs to brush his dark curls, iron his rounded collars, walk him to school. And today, to make him a birthday cake.

A birthday cake!

But now he is gone, like the rest of them all.

Be not far from me, for trouble is near, and there is no one to help.

Winter, cold winter, worms its way into her soul.

5

DECEMBER 31, 1896

New Year's Eve. Sunny, very cold.
Do yearly accounts. Bake Mother's fruitcake.

*E*liza rifles through her recipe file until she finds the card marked, "Mother's Fruitcake."

New Year's traditions die a hard death, she thinks.

MOTHER'S FRUITCAKE

One teacup of butter, two of brown sugar, one of molasses, one of strong coffee, four and one-half of flour; four eggs; two teaspoonfuls of saleratus, two of cinnamon, two of cloves, two of mace; one pound of raisins, one pound of currants, one-quarter pound of citron.

Be careful to cut paper for each loaf pan before putting in the mixture.

Bake in layers and put together with icing.

Leave out the currants if you like.

ELIZA POUNDS THE BUTTER AND SUGAR WITH A VENGEANCE, her long memory her companion. It is mid-day, New Year's Eve, and just before the loaf folds into the baking pan, Eliza reaches into the small canvas pouch that houses the last of her precious currants. As the fruitcake bakes in the old Acme, smells of cloves and mace permeate the cabin. Eliza sits with her coffee and stares out the window above the dry sink. Mounds of bowls, spoons, and cups fill the sink to overflowing. Eliza needs to fetch more water from the creek to boil and finish the last of the week's dishes. But she doesn't move at the sug-gestion. Instead she dredges up memories of long New Year's Eves past. The memories are spiked with emotion, and full.

How I loved to dress up!

From her earliest memory, Eliza had peeped over the stair rails as her parents welcomed in another new year in the company of family and friends. Out of all the dates in the calendar year, Eliza loved New Year's Eve best. Champagne flowed and uniformed housemaids served *hors d'oeuvres* on silver platters. The women wore fancy gowns and the men, black tie. The event of the season in Columbia, Missouri unfolded as Isaiah and Harriet Waite toasted the New Year with a houseful of guests. Isaiah Waite, boisterous at the quietest of times, roared at the men's jokes and flirted brazenly with their wives. At exactly midnight, guests piled outside and each chose a gaudy Chinese sparkler, which they lit and twirled in the frosty night, making wishes and promises bound to be broken. The last year she lived at home, Eliza partook in the festivities, her younger sisters posted on the stair. Mae twisted her blond curls and pouted. Margaret played *"peek-a-boo"* with no one in particular through the stair rails.

How I loved that first taste of champagne!

The first sip of champagne that passed Eliza's lips had

startled her. The effervescent bubbles gurgled down her throat as her eyes opened wide. She almost dribbled some of the contents of the long, slender glass from the corners of her newly rouged lips and onto her ball gown. Her mother had fussed for nearly an hour to prepare Eliza for the party.

"It's high time you joined society, Eliza. I just don't know how you will ever meet a suitable man if you never want to attend the parties."

Eliza fidgeted in front of the delicate glass propped up on her mother's vanity table. The magenta dress her mother had had made for her was ill-fitting at best. The material hovered just above Eliza's small breasts and a large gap buckled between the satin fabric and Eliza's bustline. Her mother stood behind her and curled the tendril ends of Eliza's rusty colored hair.

"Well, tonight will be a test. It's the first time you'll wear your hair up, like this. Here, don't put the rouge on like that, let me help you. Have you never paid any attention to your toilette? I must say, I should be at my wits' end by about now where you are concerned. Now if only Mae was old enough . . ."

Harriet hurried to the water closet and returned with a handful of soft rags.

"Here, roll these rags up. No, Eliza, like this."

Her mother fashioned a small rag roll with her bird-like hands. Without asking, she plunged her hands into Eliza's bodice and plumped up Eliza's breasts with the rag cushions. Eliza looked in the glass again and hardly recognized herself. Her mother took a long draw of champagne from a crystal flute.

"Take this, Eliza. Drink it. Don't look at me that way, just drink it."

How I loved to dance!

"May I have this dance?"

Eliza had looked up into the face she knew so well. Uncle

Gideon had been a fixture in the Waite household every summer, the older brother the girls never had. And he was most certainly Eliza's very first crush.

It was Uncle Gideon who had first taken Eliza and her sisters fishing, clasping his large hands over theirs as they learned to bait a barbed hook. He raced with the girls in the backyard and descended into a heap at the end of lawn, three girls clawing their way over his sweaty torso. He also told the most fabulous stories to them at night, frightening tales of pirates and stowaways. The girls had rushed to the stair whenever Uncle Gideon had arrived, with fistfuls of anticipation of antics and adventures to come. But Eliza had not seen much of her uncle that year as he studied for the bar. And Eliza detected chilliness when he arrived earlier in the day.

"Gideon's just a ladies' man," her mother had lamented as she fixed Eliza's hair.

"You mark my words; all the young women will be clamoring for just one dance with the junior Mr. Waite. I hear he studies law religiously during the day, well, he'd have to, he's got no mind for studies. And what he does at night is not a topic for polite conversation. If it wasn't for your father's urging, he would never stoop so low as to accept an invitation to this home anymore."

Eliza had ignored her mother's steely gaze as Gideon swept Eliza around the dance floor. Eliza felt honored that her uncle thought to dance with her before the New Year rang in. She smiled up at Gideon. Chances like this did not present themselves to Eliza very often. Her heart accelerated as she flew in circles in Gideon's arms. His flesh was warm, and his touch, exhilarating. Of course Eliza knew her infatuation with her uncle would never come to more than moments like this, and she relished each dip and turn. Eliza felt safe in Gideon's embrace.

At the conclusion of the piece, Eliza saw her mother whisper to her father.

"Last dance, ladies and gents," Isaiah Waite announced.

Isaiah Waite took his time as he approached Eliza and took her hand. He dismissed his younger brother and held Eliza at an arm's length. The orchestra dove into the finale, a lively tune that Eliza did not recognize. Isaiah Waite and Eliza danced in silence. Eliza matched Isaiah's height, but instead of seeking her father's averted eyes, Eliza looked past her father's shoulder to the others whirling in the hall. It was with a tinge of jealousy that she saw Gideon guide Judge Garrett's daughter toward the open portico and move into the night.

How I hate thinking of New Year's Eve now . . .

An hour later, after festivities had died down and weary partygoers had disappeared into the cool New Year's night, Eliza sank into her bedcovers. She was nowhere near sleep.

She replayed the scene of the evening in slow and deliberate detail.

Maybe this going out into society is not all that disappointing a prospect, she had thought. *I could perhaps be persuaded to go out more often. Especially if I can dance like I danced with Uncle Gideon!*

Eliza heard footfalls in the hallway outside her bedroom and heard the doorjamb squeak. She squinted.

Father?

A figure entered her bedroom, his face obscured and backlit by the weak hall light. Eliza sat up in bed and pulled the bed sheets up and over her nightdress.

"Shhh . . . no, don't. It's just me, Gideon."

By the time he reached her bedside, his trousers were unbuttoned. Gideon covered Eliza's mouth as he lunged down on her, stifling her screams. He smelled of dank whiskey and cigars.

Eliza batted at her uncle as he lifted up her nightdress and roughly pulled at her underdrawers. In the struggle, Eliza felt Gideon's fingers pry deeply into her private parts. She tried to raise her upper body in an attempt to escape his grasp. Gideon pushed Eliza down with one arm and pinned her to the mattress. He used his legs to part hers and left her vulnerable to his advances. Eliza had no recourse except to bite her uncle hard on the neck as he mounted her. Surprised, and dazed, he slapped Eliza hard across the face and then pushed as hard as he could toward fulfillment. A slick stream dribbled onto the mattress as Eliza lay motionless. She glared at Gideon in the semi-darkness.

"You bastard."

The next morning at breakfast, Isaiah Waite sliced a gluttonous piece of his wife's prized fruitcake, and proceeded to eat and drink noisily as he creased the morning paper in two.

Isaiah Waite laughed easily at his brother's jokes and the duo all but ignored Eliza and her sisters, who ate quietly at the table. Mrs. Waite had claimed the female hysteria and didn't come down to eat; instead she ordered tea and dry toast delivered to her heavily curtained room. Eliza's throat was dry and the sting of Gideon's slap had prickled a deep red.

No one asked why Eliza's face reddened in the shape of a large man's handprint. No one asked why Gideon Waite wore a high collar at breakfast.

Three months later, after repeatedly missing her monthly menses, and as a supreme embarrassment to her mother, Eliza removed to her spinster aunt's in St. Charles. She feared for her sisters, and pleaded with her mother to send the girls along with her to St. Charles. But Mrs. Isaiah Waite would not hear of it. The girls would stay in Columbia. Only Eliza would go.

"A guilty conscience needs no accuser," her aunt had said,

as she ushered Eliza into the outmoded guest room above the parlor in the dark, cavernous house in St. Charles.

Eliza lived in St. Charles with her old maiden aunt the entirety of her six-month confinement. Neither her mother nor her sisters paid any visits. After Jonathan's difficult birth, Eliza remained at her aunt's for a year afterward, only going out on Sundays to accompany her aunt to church. Again, there were no visitors.

Every Sunday, at precisely fifteen minutes to eleven, a carriage appeared at her aunt's front door. Eliza waited as her aunt gingerly maneuvered her way up the short step and then up to the even more precarious long step before tiptoeing over the rim and into the chassis. Her aunt flipped her cape behind her as she settled into the cushioned interior. Eliza lumbered up beside her aunt and sat uncomfortably in her Sunday dress and Sunday boots. Her aunt smoothed her severe serge skirt with delicate calfskin gloved fingers. Her aunt did not make eye contact, preferring to gaze out from her perch at the walkers making their way to St. Charles First Methodist Church on the corner of Fifth and Clay streets.

"A person is known by the company he keeps," her aunt had said.

Eliza and her aunt had nothing in common; their days were spent in relative silence. Sunday afternoons were the longest of days. After the church service, a cold lunch. And then a long afternoon, as Jonathan slept for hours after Sunday morning spent with the Scottish nursemaid. Eliza spent her days reading. She read every word of the newspaper, or books from her aunt's miserable library, or the rare magazine.

The St. Louis Star Republican arrived on the doorstop each morning, early. Eliza breathed in the news. Jane Addams had opened a settlement house in Chicago, and Frank Lloyd

Wright had recently finished his long-awaited studio in the same city. Mark Twain had released his newest, *A Connecticut Yankee in King Arthur's Court.* Benjamin Harrison had been elected president, and a slew of states petitioned to be added to the Union: South Dakota, North Dakota, Montana, and Washington. Suffragettes dominated the headlines. The first vote on women's suffrage had been defeated just two years earlier in the United States Senate. Eliza wondered when the next vote on suffrage would be held.

It can't be long now. It's time we had the vote.

Eliza dared not talk to her aunt about political matters, and kept her opinions guarded. A flurry of excitement rose in Eliza's gut when she read of the growing women's movement. When she read of a rally in St. Louis, headlined by a Mrs. Kate Chopin—*"a woman of forward thinking"*—Eliza ached to go. She yearned to wear a yellow pin from the National American Woman Suffrage Association, and to join in the throng of women of similar sentiment, but to obtain a pin or travel to St. Louis in her condition and in her position was next to impossible.

A year after Jonathan's birth, Isaiah Waite brokered a fool-proof marriage deal with the junior minister at St. Charles First Methodist, one Jacob Stamper. Isaiah's brother Gideon was pledged by this time to marry the lovely Cynthia Garrett, daughter of the retiring county judge, and Isaiah needed to erase Eliza's scandal from the family in order for his plans to foment. Although he did not know for certain that Gideon was the cause of Eliza's predicament, he could think of no other suitor who would have been attracted to Eliza. Harriet spelled out the timing of Eliza's confinement in no uncertain terms, and Isaiah Waite could not deny the connection. So Isaiah Waite withdrew a handsome sum from his bank account and traveled to St. Charles by train. The monetary amount he offered Jacob could not be matched anywhere in Missouri, and it afforded Jacob the chance to follow a dream of moving west. Jacob took the money gladly.

The wedding, a quiet affair, took place in August. Isaiah and his sister acted as witnesses. After the ceremony, the foursome ate cold roast beef, cabbage salad, and beets, with a thimbleful of sherry.

"To think that these women, these 'suffragettes' as they call themselves, think they can access the vote is plainly preposterous," Isaiah Waite had said, looking past Eliza toward his sister and then, with a wink, to Jacob, who sat on a tufted chair near Eliza in her aunt's dim Victorian parlor. "A woman has no right to vote."

Eliza's aunt nodded primly and sipped her tea.

"But it's only fair, Papa," Eliza broke into the conversation. "We have every right to vote! Mrs. Stanton wrote the Declaration of Sentiments more than forty years ago. Both women and men signed the document demanding equality. And our founding fathers themselves wrote that all men are created equal."

Isaiah Waite turned slowly and glared at Eliza.

"That is correct: all *men* are created equal. There is no mention of the word, '*woman*.' And as for Mrs. Stanton and those other addle-headed crones, what would a woman have to say that her husband could not say for her, little lass?"

Jacob smiled at Isaiah, in gentleman's unspoken agreement. Eliza's face reddened.

"To think women should vote," Isaiah said. "Talk about ridiculous!"

When it came time for Isaiah Waite to take his leave, he stood and shook Jacob's hand. He dismissed his daughter with an offhand wave.

"'An undutiful daughter will prove an unmanageable wife.' She's all yours to deal with now, my fine man. Good luck's all I can say."

Isaiah Waite ignored Jonathan completely. Seeing Jonathan in the flesh reminded Isaiah that deeds do indeed have consequences, and he intended to pull Gideon aside at his earliest convenience and demand repayment. Isaiah Waite thought his brother a fool. But with Gideon's promising marriage to the young Miss Garrett, Isaiah knew his own path to a judgeship lay clear. By year's end, Isaiah Waite would certainly sit in robes in Columbia.

Jacob had married Eliza under duress. The fact that she already had a child—and out of wedlock—reeked of scandal. And she had opinions. That fact alone would have driven Jacob away under normal circumstances. It was also well known that a minister's wife should be chaste and meek. She should also be prim and pleasant to look at. Eliza failed on all accounts. But one thousand dollars sealed the bargain. Jacob wanted nothing more than to flee St. Charles society and pastor a fledgling congregation in the far reaches of the country. There he could be something, be someone. His prospects in St. Charles were limited. Who looked up to a man who stood no more than five-and-a-half feet tall, was balding, and whose voice still squeaked when excited? Isaiah Waite's bankroll offered Jacob the opportunity to fulfill his dream. Taking Eliza was part of the bargain.

Jacob gave Eliza a mirror on their wedding day.

"Try to take more care with your appearance, Eliza. It is only fitting that you do so."

Eliza did not have a wedding gift for Jacob.

Jacob never asked Eliza who fathered the child. He did not want to know the sordid details. He imagined that Eliza conceded to the sex act out of force, but he did not let his mind wander further. The thought of Eliza with another man disgusted him. She was marked and brazen. But Eliza would have lied if he had asked. She would never divulge Jonathan's father's identity; it rankled her daily to remember her uncle's hot breath.

"I hope you don't expect me to sit at home and entertain visitors all day once we arrive at your posting," Eliza had said to Jacob later on the night of their quiet wedding. "I've got other pursuits and of course the upbringing and education of the child."

Jacob raised his hand and slapped Eliza square on the cheek.

"You'll do as I say," he had seethed.

Eliza's steely eyes glared at Jacob with hatred. Jacob's slap stung even more than her uncle's slap.

"No, I won't, Jacob," she countered. "You can rely on me to play your minister's wife in public, but God save your soul if you treat me like a whipped dog at home. I'll leave you in a second, Jacob. Mark my words."

Jacob froze. He knew that a minister's wife leaving her husband would be even more scandalous than his marrying a woman with a child. The latter could be explained, especially the farther from St. Charles the couple traveled west. By the time they reached Cypress Island in the new state of Washington, no one would know that the boy wasn't his. Jonathan even looked like Jacob—small, and wiry. But the similarities ended there.

Eliza revolted at the thought of sleeping with Jacob, but the sex act in marriage was Eliza's ticket out of Missouri. In the marriage bed on her wedding night, Eliza lay lifeless as Jacob mounted her. It was a price to pay. She would be glad to move as far away as Jacob's wanderlust stretched, even to the farthest shores of the United States. Every mile between Eliza and her father, his damnable brother, her mother, and her wretched aunt counted as a blessed mile. She would miss Margaret and Mae, in her own way. She would write to them, maybe post a letter from Nebraska or Utah.

Jonathan sat perched on Eliza's lap and gazed wide-eyed out the smudged parlor car windows as the Stamper family traveled west, one thousand dollars to their name.

Topeka. North Platte. Cheyenne.

Extraordinary vistas flashed by, punctuated with loud whistle stops. The *ca-clack, ca-clack, ca-clack* of the train powering west thrummed into Eliza's psyche. Even as she slept sitting up, her head resting against the grimy windowpane, Eliza felt the train's rumble in her whole body. She shuddered and changed position, Jonathan moving to fit the lanky curvature of her belly.

When the train pulled into Laramie, Wyoming, people of every color and nationality boarded and de-boarded.

The whole country's moving west. Like a magnet.

Eliza heard languages foreign to her ears—guttural German, lilting Italian, and indistinguishable Polish, replete with consonants tripping over the tongue. She marveled at strange accents, especially the startling Cockney. She nodded politely to other women, unrelated sisters on the one-way journey.

Salt Lake City. Pocatello. La Grande.

When she could wait no longer to use the parlor car's privy, she extricated Jonathan from her lap and sat him next to Jacob. Jacob disregarded the boy. Jonathan looked at Eliza and she read in his eyes the entreaty to accompany her.

"Mama will be right back. Here, Mama will read to you, in just a minute."

She pressed a copy of *Aesop's Fables* in Jonathan's hands and patted his dark curls. She walked in the direction of the train toward the front of the parlor car. Eliza noticed a shy young couple among the parlor car's travelers as she wended her way to the small privy. They held hands and talked with their heads bowed close together.

How happy they look!

Eliza felt jealous for the first time in several years. The train lurched and Eliza stumbled and pitched forward. She caught herself by reaching for a seat back and unavoidably brushed the corner of the young man's hat.

"Excuse me, sir, for my clumsiness. Beg your pardon."

Eliza did her business in the privacy of the train's water closet, and straightened her hat. Her traveling costume looked rumpled, three days into the journey. She peered into the mirror and studied her face.

You're so clumsy.

Careful to pick her way back to her seat, Eliza grasped the edge of each seat so as not to trip and sprawl in the parlor car. The young couple averted their gaze. She put their evident happiness out of her mind.

No use thinking about happiness.

Later, as a minister's wife, Eliza missed the raucous festivities of the approaching new year, as after midnight services, a chaste coffee hour offered congregants the opportunity to wish each other a good night before worship services the very next morning.

"Why can't we at least have Chinese sparklers, Jacob? Is it truly unbiblical to enjoy a night of revelry?"

"There will be no sparklers. Period."

After the epidemic, Eliza didn't have the heart for revelry. So, again, there were no Chinese sparklers on New Year's Eve for all the long succeeding years.

❧

ELIZA REALIZES IT IS NEARLY DARK AND SHE HASN'T LEFT THE house. *The dirty dishes will have to wait another day.* She pours a generous dram of whiskey, savoring the sweet, languorous way it flows through her veins and invites sleep. New Year's Eve is the one day of the year Eliza imbibes. She slices a piece of fruitcake and calls it supper. Then she walks around the cabin with no destination in mind, and makes three turns around the wintry interior before she pours a second dram. A familiar thickness envelops her brain. *So many memories. Some dear, some wretched.*

Eliza stares at the ceiling, her memories disappearing as twilight dims into darkness. She tamps down the wick on the oil lamp.

Eliza dreams wildly in the night. The pictures that race through her head are at once vivid and then shadowed, filled with both unfamiliar and familiar faces and places. She tosses in her sleep, not settling into dreamless slumber until dawn reaches its chill fingers through chinks in the cabin. She wakens not long after to the *caw, caw* of the early rising gulls. Eliza is groggy from the whiskey. She remains in bed listening to the steady lap of the waves. When she cannot stay in bed another minute longer before getting up to use the chamber pot, Eliza sits up and stretches her arms over her head.

Another year over, another year begun.

6

JANUARY 1, 1897

New Year's Day. Sunny, cold again. Fish for supper.

ew Year's Day dawns crisp and clear, a beautiful
Friday morning with a light northerly wind. Eliza
steps out of the cabin and into the frosted morning to greet
the New Year. She looks for Merlin. Eliza never knows when
Merlin will come or go, but she perks up when she sees him.
This morning he sits on his post and turns his stout neck to
stare at her.

"Happy New Year, my friend!"

The cold stings her face, and she wraps her woolen scarf
tighter around her chin and neck. Eliza follows the upward
slope of the beach toward the *Peapod* as the weak winter sun
hangs on the horizon. She overturns the dory and drags it to
the shore.

What a fine day for fishing!

After breakfast Eliza plans to row to the reef off the
western point of Cypress at slack tide and jig for lingcod. Eliza
picks her way along the seaweed-slathered beach. She tests the
temperature of the ice-crusted water with her fingertips.

To think some brave souls dare to take the Polar Bear Plunge each New Year's Day!

Eliza swears under her steaming breath and frozen crystals form on her woolen scarf.

Colder than a witch's tit!

Eliza doesn't dare strip down at all in the wintertime, just sponge bathes, and hastily at that. In a rare moment of serendipity, Eliza kicks at the water with her booted toes. The frothy seaweed rises and falls in an icy green pattern. She half skips, half runs the length of the small beach.

"Happy New Year!" Eliza yells to the world.

Every new year stretches out before Eliza like a promise: a promise of new crops and new recipes, of new stories and new books. She mentally scans the calendar, twelve new months ahead. Each new year closes the door on her grief just a little bit more, a slow ebbing of heartache, like the tide.

Jonathan would be nine this year. He would be reading and climbing trees and playing soldier in the woods. He would be growing taller and asking more questions and figuring sums. He would be gathering firewood and learning to whittle and running with his friends.

At the curve of the cove, Eliza wheels around to continue her serendipitous jaunt. The sun catches in the corner of her eye and she whips her head around to face west. She feels a momentary dizziness, and staggers forward. She suffers from aural migraines, and sees the telltale zigzags form at the peripheral edge of her vision. She trips and falls, as if in slow motion.

Eliza wakes, dazed, half in and half out of the freezing water.

Have I slipped? Or fainted? And how long have I been laying here?

A burning chill rises up her legs. From a visceral place in

her consciousness, Eliza realizes she sits in several inches of icy seawater. Even in a fog, she knows if she doesn't strip down at once she risks severe chills. She turns to get up and feels a gnawing pain in her left ankle. Looking down, Eliza sees her foot turned askew. In less than a second she knows it's broken; the bulge of her ankle mounts toward the surface of her bruising skin. She nearly faints from the unsightly wound. She flails in an effort to stand, and slips again on the dense, matted seaweed. She crawls forward and stretches for a stick of driftwood to hoist herself, and uses the driftwood as a cane. It takes all of her effort to reach a standing position.

Eliza drags her left leg behind her. In an awkward series of limps and hops, she reaches the cabin. She mounts the cabin's uneven steps one step at a time. She gasps for air. The pain overwhelms her. She hobbles across the small room and sits shivering at the edge of her narrow bed frame.

Eliza struggles to remove her dress and strips to her damp undergarments. The feat of changing out of the undergarments and into her second dress appears impossible. She draws the grey wool blanket from the bed and wraps it tightly around her shivering body. On her way out the cabin door she throws Jacob's coat over the blanket. Without thinking about the tide or the wind, Eliza shoves the *Peapod* to the water's edge and steps inside, dragging her left leg over the lip. A stabbing pain shoots up her leg and she emits a stifled scream. No one can hear her.

Eliza sets her course toward Doe Bay. In and out of consciousness, Eliza makes slow progress, Doe Bay now in the near distance.

Not long now, until help.

Eliza winces and cries out in pain. She feels woozy. The oars, buckled into oarlocks, lie askew. After a minute, she reaches for the oars and begins to row again. The discomfort in her foot throbs through her whole body. It takes all of Eliza's mental strength to row. Her head feels foggy and black spots appear in front of her eyes. Her migraine forces the pain out of her leg and the sum total of her misery explodes in her head. Out of her spotty vision, she sees Doe Bay, and she strains to calculate her approach. It is at that moment that Eliza recognizes the shape of a small skiff rowing straight toward her. She squints as a stranger approaches the *Peapod* and lashes his skiff to hers. She thinks it all a mirage. But then a voice.

"The name's Steiner, Miss. Alphaeus Steiner. Let me help."

The wind picks up as Alphaeus Steiner maneuvers the two boats to the Doe Bay dock. He juggles the bow and stern lines and lashes the skiff and the dory tight. He extricates the tall woman from the bowels of the boat, where she lies crumpled. He rearranges her tattered coat around her near-naked body and carries the woman's limp, drenched form up the scrubby path to his uncle's lodgings above the store. Her body is as light and lithe as a child's. Her auburn hair cascades down her shoulders and covers her breasts. Her muscled upper arms and toned thighs are taut to the touch. Her waist narrows to reveal full hips.

Steiner yells to his uncle as he pushes the front door open with his foot. Old Steiner meets Alphaeus at the bottom of the stair.

"What the . . ."

"Get out of the way, Pops. This woman needs help, and straightaway. I found her drifting just offshore. Know her?"

"That I do, I do. It's the widow, Mrs. Stamper, from Cypress."

"Well, what the hell are you standing there for?"

"Youse git her upstairs and outta those clothes. I'll ride to Doc Thatcher's and be back as soon as I can. At least youse didn't dredge up one of those Chinamen. Old Ben Ure from over on the mainland has been known to wrap 'em up in burlap bags and toss 'em overboard if the customs men come near. Quite a few dead Chinamen have washed up on these shores."

Alphaeus tries not to stare at Eliza's nakedness as he undresses her in his upstairs bedroom. Eliza groans imperceptibly as Alphaeus manages to fit her into one of Jennie's old nightdresses he finds in the top dresser drawer. He knows he shouldn't be seeing her like this, but there's no woman within a mile of the store, especially on a holiday, and it's of the utmost importance to change the woman out of her coarse and wet clothing.

The sight of a naked female always arouses Alphaeus. But this is somehow different. He treats Eliza with careful hands, as if she might break if he mishandles her. Her left leg lies in an awkward position; a bone bulges under the skin just above the ankle. She mumbles incoherently.

Alphaeus checks out the front window. On New Year's Day finding the doctor might take longer than usual. Doc Thatcher might be out on an early call, or taking a constitution. He might be off island, or entertaining company. For now, the task falls to Alphaeus to keep the young woman comfortable until help arrives.

The bright winter sun reflects off the water and nearly blinds him; when he turns back to face Eliza, his vision blackens with sunspots. He waits a moment for the uneven lines to dissipate. The woman breathes shallowly, with sudden gasps. Her face winces in pain although she lies unconscious. Alphaeus rearranges the covers and sits in the hard-backed chair beside the bed.

He examines her features. She is nothing like other women he's attracted to, but he is intrigued with her, and her story. And here on this bright New Year's Day, this strange woman rests in his bed, asleep to the world. No one, save his near-senile uncle, knows where she is, and for this fraction of a moment in time, the role of sole caretaker falls to him alone.

Alphaeus cannot remember a time when a woman has really needed him. Maybe Pearly, yes, but that was different. That was lust, but love? Many times Alphaeus kicked himself for never asking Pearly's hand in marriage. They could have carved a life out in the west together. After all, they were cut from the same cloth. He could have provided for Pearly and she, in turn, could have provided more than Alphaeus ever imagined a woman could provide a man. But that was thirty long years ago. He has never met anyone like Pearly again, even though he's slept with countless whores from Chicago to Seattle.

Alphaeus swears under his breath. Sometimes not even whores can bring him to climax anymore. The last prostitute he'd called on in Seattle couldn't bring him to fulfillment so instead he hocked a huge garnet red-hot off her hand. He thought the arrangement a fair trade on his investment.

Alphaeus listens for the door; the only sound the *tick tock tick* of the clock in the entryway. Many minutes pass, the long arm of the minute hand moving like a sloth. Alphaeus remains in the hard-backed chair.

Three-thirty.

Three forty-five.

Four o'clock straight up.

As the day dims, Steiner rearranges himself on the chair.

Four-fifteen.

Four-thirty.

Four forty-five.

He stares at the sleeping woman until daylight fades from her face. His thoughts range from the innocent to the obscene. There Alphaeus stops short. He might be a man of base desires, but he is not a monster. And there is something different about this woman. He reaches over and touches her pale face.

For only the second time in his life, Steiner wonders if this is how a wife might look, sleeping like an angel, with her hair splayed out around her face like a fan.

7

*A*s he sits at Eliza's bedside, Steiner unravels his past. The years melt away as he loses himself in the memories. He does not think about his childhood. He worked his way west, first on the railroad and then as a barkeep in Seattle, before he went to Orcas to visit his lame uncle. Old Steiner's Jennie couldn't tend the counter anymore, and the little general store at Doe Bay needed more than one shopkeeper. In exchange for his nephew coming to Orcas, Old Steiner bribed Steiner with the promise that the store would soon be his. Old Steiner didn't have a son, and the son of his dead brother was the closest thing to having a son that he would ever know.

The bribe worked, and Steiner returned by steamer in late fall. Orcas Island was nothing like Seattle. The Great Depression of 1893 had left that burgeoning city damaged and dulled. And Orcas certainly was not like the hell-on-wheels towns he experienced on the route west while working on the railroad. Plus, if his luck held out, no one would find him here. Orcas was a near paradise of lofted hills, ample apple orchards, and small livestock farms, and filled with simple folk who minded their own business when they weren't minding everyone else's.

The railroad had brought Steiner west.

A Union Pacific man, he had thought. *I've found my place.*

The work had been exhausting: twelve hours per day, six days a week, month after month of hard manual labor. Thousands of men worked at a speed that a beaver would envy, crating shovels, picks, plows, and scrapers west. On the lead team, surveyors assessed the landscape and drove indicators in the hardpan to mark the rail route. On the second team, Steiner worked with other Huns and Coloreds and massive teams of oxen to place wooden cross ties on the surveyed grade. Flat cars filled with rails and supplies followed just behind Steiner's crew, and the hard-driven spike drivers— Micks and Chinks, mostly—laid the rails, their spike mauls pounding six-inch iron barbs into the wooden cross ties to hold the iron rails in place. In this way, the caterpillar inched forward, repeating the process over and over again, six or seven miles a day depending on weather, or Indians, or lack of supplies.

The crew landed in a new town each payday. Some of them were little more than tent towns—muddied hellholes really—and they epitomized a sense of place in the loosest sense of the word. They were all hastily built and rebuilt main streets lined with canvas tents, makeshift storefronts, and windowless shanties, and they all looked exactly alike. It was like a game of leapfrog, Steiner thought; the rails moved west, and the tent towns moved west just ahead of them. But Steiner didn't care. Each tent town offered every distraction he could ever want: bartenders, gamblers, shopkeepers, prostitutes.

The goal, like the carrot in front of the horse, was Promontory Point, Utah, the place the Union Pacific would meet the Central Pacific line and create the first U.S. overland rail route. By the time the Union Pacific reached Utah, Steiner had been laboring next to other German, Irish, Chinese, and black-skinned drifters who allowed themselves the indignity of working a month for thirty dollars' pay. He was one of thousands of men who walked across the west.

Steiner had other reasons for continuing his journey west. Pearly topped the list. Her lusty body enveloped Steiner many nights, first in Omaha, then in Ogallala and Laramie, as the boomtowns busted up following the railway west. After that, Steiner thought he might try his luck in Seattle. He had an old uncle in those parts if he ran out of money. Or he might go to San Francisco. There might still be gold up in the Placer Valley. And there was always Mexico.

Steiner kept to himself. He rarely talked to other workers, preferring to stay out of the daily fray. One day was much like the rest: hot, sweaty, and exhausting. Now three miles from Benton, a mirage of pleasures, Steiner stopped for a moment and rested on his pick. He would have Pearly tonight. If he was lucky, he might even have her twice.

Mike O'Malley, the crew boss, knocked Steiner on the back of the head with a huge hand. Steiner was momentarily stunned, and his gut reaction was to throw a punch. He wheeled around and then thought better of it. Trouble with the crew boss meant trouble every day. He reeled his anger in.

"Get yourself back to work, you lazy sod," O'Malley said. "I got my eyes on you, now, you worthless Hun."

Steiner bristled with hatred.

Damn Mick.

Steiner worked faster than almost any man, and was nearly as strong. Only a few of the Coloreds worked faster, and none of the Chinamen. As for strength, there was one gigantic German who could lift a rail spur on his own, but he was nearly a freak of nature. Steiner glared at O'Malley and decided to distance himself from the foreman. He had gotten into trouble in Chicago by reacting too quickly to a slur and barely got out alive.

The Micks are the worst, he thought, *all that Hail Mary-ing on a Sunday and living the life of the devil the six other days of the week.*

Steiner knew the system, and he resolved to let his anger simmer rather than blow. Good thing they were only three miles to payday and a much-deserved day off. And Steiner didn't want to chance any possibility that he wouldn't see Pearly. Thinking of her face, the way her neck opened the way to her cleavage . . . he stiffened and raised his pick up over his head and dug into the last few hours of work for the day.

Steiner's crew arrived in Benton at dusk, and the dust that remained in their wake settled into every crevice of their bodies. Lights flickered inside hastily erected tents and saloon doors opened to reveal the first of the railway workers, no doubt the Irish foreman and his cronies, boisterous and unruly. Benton was reconstructed from its predecessor, town after town the same, and with the same unsavory characters.

There was money to be spent. The thought of a shot of whiskey and a game of cards won over the need to see Pearly right away. Steiner would end his evening with her, not begin it. The Whistling Dog Saloon offered the quickest respite. Steiner usually frequented Belle of the West, but he saw O'Malley enter that establishment, and didn't want to fraternize with his superiors. Not a night for chance.

A large gilded mirror hung above the bar at the Whistling Dog, and shelves of liquor lined the wall. The reconstituted bar—dismantled piece by piece as towns moved west just ahead of the railway—showed its wear and tear, from water stains to bullet holes. Steiner pulled up a stool and ordered a whiskey. The sweet poison flowed down his parched throat like satin. A warm glow lay like a mantle on his filthy shoulders.

He had another, and then another, feeling warm and empowered. He listened to the barkeep and to the men on nearby stools. He heard a good joke, and laughed under his breath. He ordered a fourth whiskey.

He felt himself aroused looking at the women of the night straddling other men in the bar hall. The one closest to him looked past her client's shoulder and licked her red lips sensuously at Steiner.

Damn the cards, he thought; *Pearly's waiting. And if she's not here, I'll take my pick of any of these other women here tonight. Maybe two of them.*

Steiner paid his bill and pushed through the saloon doors. He headed to Mrs. Smith's Boarding House, a long block north of the Whistling Dog. The streets were dark but lively. Groups of drunken men sparred and stragglers arrived by horseback and on foot. Early winter soaked into his bones, and he pulled his pea coat closer.

Steiner continued to be aroused as he thought of the last time he had lain with Pearly in a hastily built bordello in Laramie.

"Here, my love," she had whispered in his ear, as she soaped up his long, lithe body in the deep claw-foot bathtub.

"Come into the bath with me," he had said.

Pearly had focused on Steiner's stubbled face and did not break eye contact. She let her red satin robe slide to the floor; her lush black hair cascaded down her white body. Her body was a visual wonderland of curves, beginning at her full, porcelain breasts, and following downward to a tiny waist and curved hips. And there, beneath her navel, a bushful of black hair covering her vulva. She sank down on top of him, maneuvering his hardness inside of her. She washed his chest slowly with castile soap. He held her narrow shoulders with rough hands and panted as she rode him straddled; a warm delicious pleasure overlapped his senses. They lay in the warm water together clasped in an embrace. Steiner didn't speak; neither did Pearly. They knew nothing about the other except what transpired in their bed and bath, and for both of them that was enough.

"You are my reward," Steiner had said. "It's been twenty days of hard labor since I've had you last."

Pearly had smiled, and bit her bottom lip.

Steiner rounded the corner at the edge of Benton and entered a dim shanty. Mrs. Smith reclined on a frayed red divan in the anteroom. The room bathed in a red glow from two flickering gas lamps. No one else was about; all the hall doors were closed. The subdued light cast eerie shadows on the gaudy curtains.

Mrs. Smith rose to greet Steiner.

"Mr. Steiner! Such a surprise! We weren't expecting you until much later."

She moved toward the hallway and barricaded herself between the narrow door jam and Steiner.

"I've come directly. Where's Pearly?"

Mrs. Smith held her ground. She smelled Steiner's breath and knew he was drunk.

"Why, she is indisposed at the moment, Mr. Steiner. Perhaps you can come back in an hour."

Steiner's ire crept slowly up his neck into his ruddy cheeks. Fueled by the whiskey, he pushed Mrs. Smith away and burst through the first door on the left. He knew exactly where Pearly was and what she was doing.

"Mr. Steiner, please . . ."

Mrs. Smith pulled on Steiner's coat and he pushed her away again.

The door opened to a sight that Steiner crowded out of his mind every time he thought of Pearly. She lay splayed on the coverlet, breasts heaving, and enjoying the attentions of a client, whose mouth was buried in her vulva. Mike O'Malley.

Steiner reacted without thinking. He reached for an armchair next to the bed, and lifted it up and over his shoulder with a swift motion. The heavy armchair came to full height before he slammed it down with full force. A loud *crack* of wood filled the room as the chair landed square on O'Malley's skull. The man slumped down between Pearly's legs and lay motionless. Pearly screamed.

"You filthy whore!" Steiner had roared. "You bloody filthy whore!"

Mrs. Smith moved to protect Pearly in the face of Steiner's anger.

"Steiner!"

Pearly screamed again.

"Don't!"

Steiner shook Pearly with brute force. He raised his hand toward her and the blow glanced off of Mrs. Smith's forehead. Both women looked momentarily stunned. Pearly collapsed backwards on the pillow. Mrs. Smith wiped blood from her forehead and lunged toward Steiner. Several clients from other rooms gathered in the doorway, including another Union Pacific man, one whom Steiner recognized as one of O'Malley's cronies.

"What the hell are you doing, Steiner?" the man had said. He reached for Steiner and Steiner bullied him off.

"Get out of my way."

Steiner burst through the gathering crowd and continued out into the night. He saw nothing but blood, and the hot rage of the fire that burned the image of Pearly and O'Malley into his mind. He roared out of the makeshift bordello and caught his breath in the frigid night air. O'Malley's horse stood tied to the front post. Steiner untied him, and mounted him in one swift motion. Steiner knew he could be hanged for stealing a horse. But what would it matter? They'd hang him first for murder. His blood boiled, his head hurt. The horse, nervous under the new rider, shook his mane and whinnied. Steiner dug his heels into its sides and turned the anxious beast west and out of Benton. Only darkness lay ahead.

❦

STEINER LOOKS AGAIN AT THE SLEEPING WOMAN SNORING lightly in the bed beside his chair. He shakes his head.

Better to put all that behind me, he thinks.

Just past six o'clock, Steiner hears the back door to the Doe Bay Store bang open. Voices grow louder as his uncle and the doctor reach the stair. The stairs creak under the men's weight as they ascend the treads. Steiner bends closer, and traces the woman's face again with his finger.

❦

8

January 6, 1897

Eliza wakes in a strange bed, her eyes blurry, and her memory gauzy.

How did I come to be here?

The unfamiliar room fills with weak winter sun; two overstuffed chairs in front of a large bay window look south over the strait. The grey and green paisley pattern reminds Eliza of her aunt's stuffy guest bedroom in St. Charles. On the sturdy dresser next to the bed she spies an enamel washbasin and pitcher. Eliza touches the nubby chenille, a light green to match the wallpaper.

A real bed. A real room. A real house.

A dull stabbing pain in her left leg assaults her senses, and Eliza sinks into the pillow and crawls backwards in her mind to reconstruct events.

I slipped and broke my foot, and then I rowed to Orcas for help. Crossing Hart's Pass was hazy at best.

She hears a faint bustling downstairs and tries to remember where she is, and why.

Was there a man? Or was that a figment of my imagination? And how did I end up in a strange bed in a strange room in a strange house, my left leg encased in rough plaster?

"Ah, Mrs. Stamper, youse finally awake," a male voice sounds from the doorway. Eliza turns her head. She recognizes Old Steiner's voice and the blurry outline of his form, near-sighted as she is, and without her spectacles.

"Mr. Steiner! How . . ."

"I know, my dear. Terrible shame. That ankle of yours was broke almost right through the skin. Doc Thatcher said it was the worst he'd seen. But I reckon you don't remember much. The doc's been mighty generous with that laudanum."

Old Steiner shuffles closer to the bed, and Eliza draws up the covers to her neckline. She realizes with acute embarrass-ment that someone has changed her clothing; she now wears a long cotton nightdress meant for a much smaller woman.

Old Jennie!

"If it weren't for my nephew, I don't know rightly if you'd have come through. He spotted youse out in the strait, a-driftin', and on New Year's Day! Most people would have been sleepin' it off, as they say. Good thing it was daylight, or you'd have been a goner."

Eliza strains for words, but words do not come.

"It's alright, now, don't worry yourself. Youse welcome here for as long as it takes, don't nevermind. My nephew, Alph —Alphaeus, that's his Christian name—is helpin' me with the store now. He's the one who found youse. He'll be up directly. I'm sorry that Jennie ain't here to help youse along. Youse just gotta bear with us old bachelors."

"Thank you ever so much. Can I trouble you to ask what day is it?"

"It's the sixth of January, Ma'am. Day of the Magi, if I remember from my Sunday School days."

Six days!

Eliza has slept on and off through six days, without

memory. Her mind floods with questions, but she is too tired to think. She drifts in and out of sleep. When she wakes next, she hears two male voices, as if muffled by dense fog. Eliza makes out Doc Thatcher's low baritone.

"It'll be two, three weeks before she'll be able to walk, even on flat ground. I don't reckon she'll be ready to go back to Cypress and live on her own anytime soon. Plus, it'll be weeks before she weans off the laudanum."

Eliza does not recognize the second voice.

"Why does she live there like that, and alone? My uncle said there's maybe a handful of people still there, what after the epidemic and all. He said Mrs. Stamper must be a stubborn one, not wanting to leave her dead child there."

"I don't ask questions. Guess she's got a right as any to do as she pleases. It wouldn't be for me, that's for sure, and besides I wouldn't have any clientele!"

The men laugh. Their backs face Eliza and she scoots uncomfortably to a sitting position in the four-poster bed. Again, she draws the covers high to her neckline.

"Doc Thatcher! Many thanks to you, and to you . . ."

She trails off.

The men stand and take several steps closer to the bed. Thatcher places his large hand on the bedpost. The other man —*who is he?*—comes around to the side of the bed, but keeps his distance.

"The name's Alphaeus Steiner, Ma'am. I'm the one who brought you here. You were near delirious when I found you. I hope you don't mind my putting you up here in my bedroom. I'm not inconvenienced if that's what you're thinking. I've slept on pallets and bare ground more nights than I care to remember. The cot in the kitchen is plenty comfortable for me, and warm."

Eliza squints toward the pair, and realizes the younger of the two men is the man who rescued her from the strait. There is no mistaking him. Alphaeus Steiner possesses a strong face, with penetrating blue eyes, a substantial nose, and long, white teeth. His unkempt sandy hair falls unevenly over his ears, and he wears the stubble of a beard. He is undoubtedly the most handsome man Eliza has ever seen, with or without glasses. Her cheeks flame. She shifts in the bed and winces from the pain in her leg.

"Better get you some more of that medication," Thatcher says. "Thank God Alphaeus spotted you out there on the strait, Mrs. Stamper. Another hour, and you would've been sleeping with Poseidon, as they say. Count your blessings, young lady."

Thatcher spoons a dark liquid onto a teaspoon and offers it to Eliza. She swallows and sinks again into the pillow. Thinking will have to wait. Overcome with drowsiness, Eliza cannot join one coherent thought to another. She has no choice. The drug runs rampant through her veins and sentences her to another deep and dreamless sleep.

Eliza anticipates Alphaeus's visits. A steady footfall on the wooden stairway signals his imminent arrival to the bedroom. He dishes up the most delicious, although simple, meals: full breakfasts, hearty lunches, and for supper, soups: julienne, white vegetable, pea.

Alphaeus wears dark corduroy trousers and white linen shirts, covered with a long white apron tied in the back. His hair hangs low, over his eyes, as he bends to deposit a simple wooden tray. Eliza admires the way he swings his hair out from his eyes and back behind his ears as he steps back and away from the bed. Large veins protrude from his forearms.

He is ever so strong.

Eliza notes a smell of alcohol on Steiner's breath, even in the morning. But Eliza is not one to damn; men are men, and that is that. She thanks him and watches as he turns to leave the room. She wishes he would stay to talk, but knows that customers and chores top his list. She turns her attention to the contents of the tray and digs straight into her breakfast, a steaming potato omelet and potato biscuits.

"You must share the recipe for these delectable potato biscuits!" she calls after Steiner.

Eliza devours each meal like a hawk. Over the course of her recuperation, a full month plus a day, she gains a full six pounds.

ᑳᑐᑳᑐᑳᑐᑳᑐᑳᑐ

POTATO BISCUITS

Three good-sized potatoes boiled and mashed fine, one tablespoonful sugar, one-half pint boiling water. Add pinch of salt.

When cool, add one tablespoon yeast dissolved in one-quarter teacup warm water with pinch of sugar or drop of honey, then add three and one-half teacups flour to knead; knead for fifteen-to-twenty minutes and set it to rise again before baking.

After rising, if needed, add sufficient flour until desired consistency.

Roll into three-inch balls and set to rise again on greased baking sheet. Bake until golden.

ᑳᑐᑳᑐᑳᑐᑳᑐᑳᑐ

THE POTATOES ELIZA UNEARTHS FROM HER GARDEN PLOT ARE often hard and pocked. To make a mash for herself, she needs three or four of the small, deformed root vegetables, carefully peeled and quartered before the boil. She often nicks her rough fingers and draws blood, and brings the injured knuckle to her mouth and sucks it clean. The potatoes on Orcas taste soft and creamy, no doubt because they are mixed with a generous amount of milk, a luxury Eliza does not have on Cypress.

Before bed each night, Steiner brings Eliza a large cup of warm, steaming cocoa. Eliza loves cocoa even more than coffee. Steiner sits on one of the armchairs he has dragged nearer to the bed. He knows it is highly unusual that he attend to a woman—a single woman, he now knows after conversations with his uncle—but out of necessity, he is the one attached to the detail. Doc Thatcher comes by just once per week now, and Old Steiner can barely make it up the creaky stairs to bed and has, of late, taken to sleeping on the cot in the kitchen. This situation allows Steiner the use of the other upstairs bedroom across the landing from the room Eliza occupies. Many nights Steiner mentally calculates that Eliza sleeps not five or six yards from his bed.

Steiner remains until Eliza drains her cocoa. She delays finishing the last sweet drop. She swirls the cup and leaves a scant mouthful to drink later. He hopes she will start a conversation. Steiner and his uncle don't have much to talk about. Feed prices. Supply runs. Or talking about customers. Conversations with Eliza are more meaningful and evenings mark the only time they spend more than a few minutes trading pleasantries.

"You were born in Pennsylvania? I hear the Quaker State is truly beautiful," Eliza says. "I cannot say that with authority, as I have not been to Pennsylvania. But there is no doubt that there is much beauty in this wide country of ours. You must have seen so for yourself when you came out by train."

Eliza catches Steiner off guard at the mention of the railroad.

"Indeed, Ma'am. This country's full up with sweeping beauty. I, too, was taken by the mountains. The Rockies, that is. Worked the railroad. Long, tiring work. But that was many years ago. Of course, there are no mountains of that magnitude in Pennsylvania."

"Nor in Missoura!" Eliza says, pronouncing her home state like a local. "Missoura's flat like a pancake. I think I shall never go back there."

"I traveled through Missouri, once," Steiner says. "You might say I've been traveling most of my life, from Ohio through the Middle West. Once it gets in your blood—traveling, I mean—well, it's hard to think of stopping. I wonder if I'll be able to put down roots here."

"I thought you'd be here for a long while now that you're helping your uncle with the store."

Eliza trails off, and looks away from Steiner.

"What of your family?" Steiner begins, all at once regretting that he mentioned the word, "family." He winces.

"My family is all but dead to me," Eliza says. Eliza does not mention her dead husband or dead son.

"My father is deceased, and my mother and sisters have all but disappeared from my life. I haven't had a letter from them in more than two years. I don't even know if they are still in Columbia; perhaps they are now in St. Charles. The last letter I had from my sister was postmarked from there—St. Charles, that is—informing me of our father's death, by his own hand. It is shameful to think of it."

Steiner wonders how Eliza's father had ended his life, but declines to ask. Eliza takes Steiner's silence as the question he wished to pose.

"He hung himself, if you are wondering. My mother and

sisters were away in St. Charles, and received the message by courier. Seems he did not get a judgeship he anticipated."

In a moment of compassion, Steiner's hand reaches for Eliza's. Her eyes widen as she feels the shock, electric. She pulls her hand back. She hasn't felt the touch of a man in so many years.

"Pardon me, Ma'am," Steiner stumbles.

Eliza places the cup on the tray next to the bed and deflects his overture. She turns away from Steiner so that he cannot see her flushed face.

"Excuse me, but I am so very tired."

"'Night, Ma'am."

Steiner gathers up the tray and exits the room in silence. He kicks himself for mentioning family to Eliza. The subject obviously caused Eliza distress; that he could see plainly. Steiner undresses and lies on the bed in the adjacent room. He hears Eliza's gentle breathing through the wall. His heart pumps wildly in his chest and he wills his heart to slow.

He wonders if the time has come to settle down. His uncle has handed him the perfect opportunity. He and Eliza could set up house and shop in Doe Bay, and maybe start another family. Steiner knows Eliza in a more intimate way than he has ever known any woman before, save the coupling. From what he has gleaned from many conversations, she can cook and bake and tend house and garden. And he enjoys her company, and the forthright flow of her words and hands that punctuate the air as she speaks. He hungers for their time together, more and more.

After a quarter-hour, restless, Alphaeus gets up and peers into Eliza's room. He is tempted to sit by the bed again as Eliza drowns into sleep. Her breathing regulates, slow and bottomless. He resists the urge to stay, to touch her just once again.

He wonders if he has finally found his bride.

9

⌒

Sunny. Healing nicely. Reading volumes.

liza spends her days reading and napping. She asks Alphaeus to bring her magazines from the store, in hopes of finding more stories by Mrs. Chopin, or reading of far-flung adventures. She devours yellowed newspapers in hopes of finding new recipes or reading of the growing women's suffrage movement. Legislators in Washington State have entertained several attempts to franchise women. The votes to date fall short for needed passage.

I can't even leave this bed, she thinks. *Not even to do my business. This is the most distasteful part of the arrangement.*

But Alphaeus does not flinch as he empties Eliza's chamber pot. The subject is not spoken of, nor acknowledged. Eliza feels stronger by the day.

Soon I can go back home.

Alphaeus brings stacks of *Harper's Bazaar*, *Vogue*, and *The Ladies Home Journal* to Eliza and deposits them on her nightstand. He thumbs through the publications as he takes the stairs two at a time. Stories. Recipes. Advertisements. Alphaeus finds the advertisements most interesting: ads for kitchen aids and products, and the more titillating ads touting brassieres and female powders.

Eliza finds numerous articles by Mrs. Chopin, and reads them again and again: "The Father of Desiree's Baby," "Ripe Figs," "Dr. Chevalier's Lie." She relates to the woman abed in the aptly named story, "The Recovery."

She was a woman of thirty-five, possessing something of youthfulness. It was not the bloom, the softness, nor delicacy of coloring which had once been hers; those were all gone. It lurked rather in the expression of her sensitive face, which was at once appealing, pathetic, confiding.

For fifteen years she had lived in darkness with closed lids. By one of those seeming miracles of science, and by slow and gradual stages, the light had been restored to her. Now, for the first time in many years, she opened her eyes . . .

And how beautiful was the world from her open window!

Eliza adjusts her spectacles and strains to take in the whole vista from her vantage point on Steiner's bed. If she could only get a bit closer to the window she would see a sweeping view of Hart's Pass south toward Cypress. If only she could stand, she could almost see her cabin.

Some days fly; others drag. On weekdays and the ever-busy Saturdays, Eliza overhears a bustle of activity. She listens for conversations outside the window, or the whinnying of horses and the short clipped commands of their masters. She marks another week when she hears the *chugga chugga chugga* of the *Jubilee*, and its long horn signaling its approach to the dock on Thursdays. Helpless in her condition, Eliza remains unable to get up, unable to fully see or hear the world continuing at its normal pace.

One morning during the third week of her restless recovery, Eliza hears a loud *crash* downstairs followed by a scuffle.

"Trouble follows youse, boy."

She hears Old Steiner, his voice raised beyond its usual limits.

"And what the hell are you going to do about it, old man? Do you think I want to be here?"

Eliza hears feet shuffling and then a *whoomph*.

"What do youse think youse doin', beatin' up on an old man?"

"Get out of my way, Pops. I'll clean it up. You're helpless as a nanny goat."

"Don't youse go shootin' your mouth off at me, boy. I'm the one brought you up here to these parts and I can let youse go anytime."

"Gladly! Just might light a shuck one of these days and be gone, just like that."

Once, twice, and then again, Eliza hears Alphaeus raise his voice toward his uncle. Eliza cannot reconcile her discomfort. Eliza wonders how a man can be so gruff one moment, and so kind the next. The fact that Alphaeus caters to Eliza yet is brash toward his uncle renders Alphaeus disingenuous. She's reminded of the Robert Louis Stevenson novel she read just a year ago. That one man could possess two distinct personalities frightens her, like Dr. Jekyll and his alter ego, Mr. Hyde. She resolves to keep her distance from Alphaeus, at least as much as she can in her compromised condition.

After three weeks confined to the bed, Eliza begins a long, laborious walk around the bedroom, first using the bed to steady her, and over time, using a cane to pick her way to the bay window and back. She also makes her way to the make-shift privy behind the bedroom door and covers the basin with a towel after she eliminates. She reddens, picturing Alphaeus disposing of her waste.

By the fourth week she navigates the stairs to the main floor slowly, her right leg leading. She practices going up and down the stairs when Old Steiner and Alphaeus are busy in the store. When she can manage the stairs both up and down handily, she makes her decision. On the first morning in February, Eliza wakes early, packs her meager belongings into a makeshift bundle, and descends the stairs one step at a time, favoring her left ankle. Eliza will not outstay her welcome at Doe Bay.

"Doc Thatcher says youse almost good as new."

Old Steiner and Eliza sit at the dining table and attack plates of steaming scrambled eggs, fried potatoes, and bacon. Eliza savors each bite.

"I want to apologize 'bout all that fuss the other mornin'."

Old Steiner drops his knife on his near empty plate.

"'Scuse, me, Ma'am. Youse see, my nephew and I don't see eye to eye, youse might say. He had it rough, he did, growin' up an orphan boy. My brother's wife, she died when Alph was just a boy, youse see, and my brother—God rest his soul—couldn't care for the rascal. Alph was sent off to one of those boy's homes, somewheres up Michigan way, if'n I remember right. From what I hear, those places ain't fit for the likes of children. I'm afraid Alph's been fightin' since he were a young'un."

"Don't mention it."

Alphaeus walks by the back window without looking into the kitchen. Eliza feels the hair on the back of her neck prickle. She feels a familiar flush creep into her cheeks.

"I'd be a fool not to. I think my nephew's grown sweet on youse, and there's more'n a few skeletons hiding in his closet, if'n you know what I mean."

Eliza takes Old Steiner's comment with a grain of salt.

Sweet on me? No. Alphaeus did what any Christian man would do, attending to an injured and helpless female. And who in his right mind would be attracted to someone whose slop he disposed of? No. Alphaeus is not sweet on me. And I most certainly am not sweet on him.

She dismisses Old Steiner's remarks as quickly as she wolfs down her breakfast.

No time to think on such nonsense.

After the meal, Eliza takes Old Steiner's arm and walks out through the front door of the Doe Bay Store and left to the end of the tender dock. Alphaeus stands at the end of the dock, his apron flapping in the wind. He bends over the *Peapod*, packed with extra supplies and a sure surprise—a nanny goat —tied and harnessed to the front bench seat of the skiff. He braces the goat while Eliza steps over the transom and settles herself into the dory.

"Thought you'd like fresh milk, now that you're used to it."

Alphaeus winks at Eliza.

And who am I to disagree, seeing as I have devoured mug after steaming mug of cocoa each night?

Eliza is anxious to push off. Old Steiner's confessions of Alphaeus's intentions nag at the edges of her mind. Alphaeus lingers, arranging Eliza's belongings so the weight distributes evenly in the boat.

"I'd be happy to follow you, at least through the pass."

"No, no need, but thank you, Mr. Steiner. I am more than capable, especially now."

Eliza tamps her left leg on the bottom of the dory to reinforce her statement.

"I would feel more comfortable knowing you had made it home safely."

"Really, no need. But thank you again."

Eliza diverts her gaze and mentally assesses her cargo, the

goat dazed and fear-stricken lashed sideways in the bow. The goat bleats a mournful cry and Eliza pats its quivering head.

"Looks like I'll be having company now," Eliza says. She quickly realizes that perhaps Alphaeus will interpret her comment as an invitation to visit. She regrets saying anything.

"Well, off you go, then. I'll come looking after you in a few weeks' time."

Alphaeus unties the lines and casts Eliza off.

Three short miles until I'm home.

Alphaeus watches Eliza row, stroke after stroke, away from Doe Bay. The dock is littered with mounds of supplies and it'll be after dark before he's through unloading, stacking, and sorting. As much as he desires to follow Eliza today, he's nailed down a foolproof plan, one that has knit together slowly and seamlessly over the past month. He fingers the garnet in his trouser pocket.

Steiner turns heel, up the ragged planks away from the water. He's tempted to look backwards to see Eliza, but doesn't. He strides up the dock and around to the back of the store. He heaves a large flour sack over his shoulder and kicks the back door open. He hefts the load to the row of drygoods and plops the sack to the floor. He lifts the heavy wooden lid of the flour bin and funnels a steady stream of grain into the near empty container, wafts of white steaming off the top of the newly formed powdery pyramid. He remembers the moist oatmeal raisin cookies his mother laid out for him after school, three to a plate, when he was six or seven. He had dunked the warm cookies into a full glass of warm milk, still with froth. His mother had been beautiful, with slender, cool hands.

He shuts the lid with a heavy *thump*. A small amount of flour has escaped the bin and circled the barrel like a halo. Steiner reaches for a thick stiff-bristled broom, not the thin-handled shop broom propped by the counter. A sliver imbeds itself into his large palm.

"Damn it!"

He kicks the flour barrel then, steel toe to iron casing. A drift of white escapes the seams of the barrel. He swears again, and leaves the mess. His boot prints remain, shadowed in white behind him on the pocked fir floors.

❧

10

MARCH 11, 1897

Overcast. Spring shoots up. Socks need mending.

Eliza sees Steiner long before he reaches Smuggler's Cove, his skiff bracing the stiff spring tide as he approaches the shore. She knows why he is coming, and she panics. The thought of accepting his inevitable proposition frightens her to the core. She has only shared one man's marriage bed, and the prospect of being naked again with a man chills her blood. Jacob's sudden absence from her life closed her down, and even the thought of being with Steiner —or any man for that matter—puts her off. All that sweating and moaning and grunting. No, she doesn't want to face all of that. She does not want to face Steiner. She finds a pencil and scrawls a hasty note.

Steiner rows steadily toward the exposed cove, his strokes even and measured. When Steiner arrives on shore, he does not see Eliza anywhere on the property. Her cabin door is shut and there is no sound of life in the small yard except for the feeble protest from her shaggy goat. He wonders where she could be this early in the morning. He feels for the garnet ring in his pocket. He calculates that by day's end the ring will reside on the fourth finger of Eliza's left hand, and he intends to consummate the engagement on the spot. When he washed his private parts this morning, he hardened at the thought.

When he rounds the west side of the rude structure, he notices a slip of paper tacked to the cabin door. He pulls the ivory stationery off the cabin door and unfolds it.

Go away.

Nothing else, not even a complete sentence. He holds the paper in his left hand and feels again for the ring in his trouser pocket with his right hand. He stands for a moment and considers his options. He tries the door of the cabin. Eliza's door is wedged shut.

"Mrs. Stamper!"

No one answers. The goat whinnies and shies away from his voice. Again he shouts Eliza's name, and not even the goat notices the second time. He paces the periphery of the cabin, anxious. After five minutes—he checks his pocket watch—he returns to his skiff to retrieve the box of supplies. He slams his fist on the door, swearing under his breath. He calls once more for Eliza and leaves the box on her uneven front stoop.

Eliza sits in the corner closet with her knees drawn up to her chest and her head bent low. Her heart pumps cold blood. She shivers. Her left leg begins to cramp and she moves her foot in silent circles. She hopes that terror isn't audible.

Eliza guesses Steiner's been drinking already, and before ten o'clock in the morning. Men and drink prove a deadly combination, this Eliza knows. Her only regret is that she hadn't the strength to push Gideon away. But of course then there would not have been Jonathan . . .

Steiner plods around the cabin one last time, nursing a cigar. The cigar smoke wafts in through the missing chinks in the closet's outer wall. Eliza stifles a cough. She hears a familiar sound, and realizes Steiner's pissing on the corner of the house just inches from where she sits cramped in the confines of the closet. Within seconds, she hears a loud *whoomph* and a loud whinny escapes from the goat. Eliza puts her hand over her mouth.

"Bitch," he yells.

The goat bleats mournfully. Steiner saunters around the property and considers plowing through the cabin door. It would not be difficult to do; he had done so countless times before. He thinks for a moment that perhaps Eliza is hiding from him inside the cabin. He thinks again, and convinces himself that the message cannot be for him.

Steiner shrugs and turns toward the cove, his back to the cabin. The sky has darkened. Steiner knows he needs to beat the flood tide. He stomps the mud off of his boots in the shallows and pushes off the beach. He hops into the skiff and settles in to row.

When she hears no trace of Steiner, Eliza emerges from the closet and crawls toward the door. She stops to listen for any semblance of movement. She slowly unfolds herself first to a kneeling position, and then to a low crouch. She peeks out the small window above the sink. From her vantage point, she can barely make out the skiff as Steiner rows back to Orcas. Her leg throbs from being cramped in the closet. She stands and shakes her leg. She realizes her whole body shakes, involuntarily. She needs to pee.

When Steiner disappears from sight, Eliza nudges open the cabin door and squats to relieve herself. She then inspects the contents of the box on the stoop. Her note lies crumpled on the ground.

Nestled on top of the other supplies, and wrapped individually in sheets of brown paper, are three ripe pears. Eliza slowly unwraps one pear, turning the plump piece of fruit in her hand and squeezing to check its ripeness. She sinks her teeth into the juicy pulp.

Heaven on earth!

She savors the pear, and juice dribbles down her chin. She eats right down to the seeded core. She gnaws at the core until there is nothing left but the hardened shell of the seedpod. Beneath the pears Eliza finds, in no particular order, a casing of dried sausage, a jar of sourdough starter, a sack of chopped walnuts, a shoulder of pork, two tins of sardines, six eggs, a packet of thin rye crisps, two vials each of cinnamon and cardamom, and, at the bottom of the box, a package of crystallized ginger.

Such luxuries!

She feels guilty consuming these delicacies because she rebuffed Steiner, but her lust for the provisions knows no boundaries.

Lining the bottom of the box Eliza unfolds three weeks' worth of newspapers. A large envelope is attached to the side of the box. On its front side, in a large masculine hand: "Stamper." With trembling hands, she removes the envelope from the side of the box and turns it over in her hand. She can only imagine what message lies inside, especially attached to a box of forbidden fruit. If there had been a note inside at one time, there is not one now. She peers into the depths of the envelope, and feels carefully in each of the corners of its dark abyss. She comes up empty.

"Let it be so."

Eliza makes good use of the remainder of the pears. She bakes a sweet, yet savory, pear crumble before retiring for the night. Its inviting aroma causes Eliza to burn the tip of her finger as she scoops out a taste.

"Dash it all!"

She shakes her finger and rushes to the counter. She plunges her whole right hand into a jar of cold water and lets it rest there until the throbbing subsides.

ᑯᑊᑐᑯᑊᑐᑯᑊᑐᑯᑊᑐᑯᑊᑐ

PEAR CRUMBLE

Mix one and one-half teacups rolled oats, one-half teacup chopped walnuts, one-half teacup brown sugar, one-third teacup flour, and one-half teaspoonful cinnamon, and set aside for topping.

Peel and slice two to three pears and mix with one-half teacup maple syrup, a large handful of raisins, a scant one-quarter teacup flour, and sprinkle of crystallized ginger, if you have so.

Place in baking dish and divide topping evenly over pear mixture.

Bake until golden.

While crumble is still hot, fold topping into filling and let sit for an hour or more before serving.

Can be eaten cold for breakfast, like oatmeal.

ᑯᑊᑐᑯᑊᑐᑯᑊᑐᑯᑊᑐᑯᑊᑐ

ELIZA DREAMS OF STEINER THAT NIGHT. SHE PICTURES HIS LONG, lithe body walking toward the cabin where she had hid just this morning in the cabin's corner closet, squashed between the wall and her Sunday boots. In her dream, Eliza pictures a different scenario. She runs out to greet Steiner; he gathers her up and wheels her around in arms. She becomes dizzy with the joy of it, and laughs out loud. The laugh wakes her from her dream, and Eliza chastens herself for entertaining these thoughts, even in her subconscious. Old Steiner had warned Eliza about his nephew.

March turns into April. Steiner does not return. Eliza waits longer than usual to row to Doe Bay. In the meantime, Eliza plants her garden and salivates when she thinks of all the canning she'll put up later this summer. Soups run a clear favorite—easy to can and with a long shelf life. Eliza figures she can live on soup if needed. She puts up twenty quarts at least each year. Eliza reaches for the last of her stores on the plank shelf, rearranging the last two jars. But she feels a distance between what her hands do and what her heart nags her to do.

During the day, Eliza tries to put Steiner out of her mind as soon as he appears. It is a battle, though, because she sees him in everyday chores: digging clams near the edge of the cove, his broad shoulders bent; rowing her dory to the kelp beds, his veins protruding from his strong forearms; patching her roof, his lanky legs ascending the ladder one rung at a time. She pictures him in her home, helping her with everyday tasks. The only place Eliza does not entertain thoughts of Steiner is next to her in her narrow bed. But he lurks there, just under the surface of the everyday, and every day he is there.

There's more'n a few skeletons hiding in his closet, if'n you know what I mean.

He is surely a Jekyll and Hyde, Eliza thinks. *Even though I've seen the way he treats his uncle—and my goat!—he has been ever so kind to me.*

After a while, Eliza gives up the battle and lets Steiner in, but only as a ghost companion. She finds it easier to have him there in absentia than to battle her desire. And she knows of course he isn't really there, *so what's the harm?*

II

⌒

JULY 3, 1897

Sunny. Off to fair.

ome get these here frankfurters! Hot off the grill!"
Eliza recognizes the voice. Old Steiner, his heavy white
apron splattered with grease, hawks what looks like a giant
sausage in the air. Tantalizing smells that emanate from his
Bavarian-style booth intoxicate Eliza's senses. She has walked
as fast as she might to get to the judging barn on time, feeling
every inch of the ten miles from Doe Bay to Eastsound
wearing her Sunday boots. She is famished. Eliza relents to the
odor of the sausage, and the saliva-inducing taste of real meat.
She tips back her straw hat that shades the beating summer
sun and approaches the booth. She lowers her heavy basket.

Old Steiner's nephew stands at the rear of the booth
tending wieners. Steiner removes another fat sausage from the
grill and places it into a folded bun encased in white butcher
paper. He slathers fresh sauerkraut on the wiener and hands
the steaming package to his uncle. Sweat drips from his
forehead. Flies buzz around his head and he swats them away.
He turns back to the grill. The sizzle spits grease onto his

apron and he turns his head away from the billowing smoke. He does not see her.

Eliza eyes the prices of the various sausages and draws a quarter from her small purse.

"Why, Mrs. Stamper! So good to see youse up and about! Here, this one's on me. Put yer quarter away."

Alphaeus spins around and stares at Eliza's face. She does not look away.

Eliza bites into the foot-long frank. A dribble of sauerkraut escapes her lips and she reaches for her handkerchief. She does not break Steiner's gaze.

"Mmmm, this is wonderful."

"Somethin' my Ma used to make," Old Steiner says. "I read that now youse gotta pay fifty cents for one of these in Chicago. They had 'em at the World's Fair there a couple of years back. If Ma knew about that, she'd have shook her head. Fifty whole cents!"

"Out of the way, Pops."

Alphaeus Steiner wipes his hands on his apron and comes around to the front of the booth.

"Mrs. Stamper."

He emphasizes the declaration. Steiner regards Eliza closely, her mouth full of sizzling sausage. He notices her ungloved hands, the way her lips part as she chews, slight beads of perspiration in that delicate space between her collarbones. He motions for Eliza to follow him. He picks up her basket and strides ahead of her toward rough-hewn picnic tables in the shade. He selects one nearest the base of a sprawling willow. Eliza hesitates. She balances the unwieldy and dripping frankfurter and picks her way to the table.

"Here, little lady, try your hand at ring toss!"

Eliza slips by the carnival worker and joins Steiner. Steiner leans against the table. His legs are splayed wide, one foot propped on the picnic table bench and the other foot planted on the ground. He reaches to touch Eliza's shoulder as she sits on the bench and then lowers himself to sit beside her. Eliza does not flinch at his touch.

"Quite a lovely day."

Eliza straightens her town skirt. She perches at the edge of the rough board facing out and puts only a small distance between herself and Steiner. She wipes damp perspiration with her handkerchief and surveys the fairgrounds. She is very aware of his proximity, and smells his sweat. Her town boots peek from beneath the hem of her skirt. Steiner looks at Eliza's ankles. He remembers what she looks like naked.

"How's the ankle? All set?"

"Healing well, thanks to you."

A sudden *crash* directly in front of Eliza and Steiner disrupts their conversation. A runaway wheel tumbles over a root and comes to rest by Eliza's feet. A boy, nine or ten, appears in the next second. He wears blue shorts and a rumpled muslin shirt. He carries a large stick. Eliza starts to rise, but Steiner holds her back, his hand pressing into her shoulder. Eliza stays on the bench.

"Having a little trouble, son?"

The boy nods and reaches for the wheel. Steiner helps the boy to right the wheel and steadies it.

"Might want to try to run just a tad faster this time."

The boy doesn't look up, but nods to Steiner's waist and continues on, the wheel wobbling as he guides its path. Eliza thinks of Jonathan. Her face clouds over.

A girl, probably closer to six, and a full head shorter than her brother, reaches Eliza just as her brother starts off again. She tries to keep up with her brother, and the wheel, to no avail. She whimpers as she runs by, and the sash of her once-crisp pink dress trails behind her like a kite. Eliza feels a rush of compassion.

"The little girl, the one in the pink lawn? I used to have hair that long. My sister Mae would always braid my hair into plaits, like this."

Eliza mimics the motion with her bare hands, braiding the air. Steiner laughs, and desires to take her hand. He stops short. Flies are thick, and bothersome. Eliza is parched. She swats at a fly and dabs her forehead again with her handkerchief; it must be close to ninety degrees, a rarity for the islands, even in the summer.

"Rumor has it that all the hotel rooms in Eastsound are booked for the night," Steiner says.

"And I can see why! Never have I seen so many people at the fair, and I've been coming to the Orcas Fair for going on six, maybe seven, years now. Must be people from as far away as Whatcom."

"Heard tell that there's expeditions today to the top of Mount Constitution, with a swim afterwards at Orcas Lake. Must say, sounds like a heck of a way to spend a day like today."

Eliza does not answer right away.

"Why, that sounds heavenly. I haven't been swimming in ever so long. Too blame cold most days."

The pair sits for several minutes more, taking in the unfolding scene, a buzz of voices around them. Eliza notices a ladybug inching its way up Steiner's arm. She feels a burp rising in her throat, and turns to the side to suppress it. She covers her mouth and then replaces her handkerchief in her purse.

"I've been thinking, Mrs. Stamper."

Steiner clears his throat and takes Eliza's hand without asking.

"I hope you don't think me impertinent for saying, but it must get mighty lonely out there on Cypress, being alone, I mean. Have you ever thought of throwing in the whole kit and caboodle over there, and coming to Orcas to live?"

Eliza smells the familiar tang of whiskey on Steiner's breath, and remembers his visit to Smuggler's Cove. Eliza's mind fills with the cacophony around her, and she feels dizzy in the heat. If this is a proposal, Eliza is not prepared to answer Steiner, at least not directly, or without thought. She doubts her feelings, and does not answer.

Instead, she focuses on the sea of faces around her. She does not recognize anyone in the swelling crowd. Families stroll by, mothers fanning themselves and trying to keep youngsters in tow as they head for the carnival games. Some of the children eat ice cream, streams of chocolate and strawberry cascading onto their fancy clothes. A group of men lingers in the shade near Steiner and Eliza, trading farm stories. Their laughter peppers the humid air. Most of the men wear shirt-sleeves without jackets, and some do not wear hats. Eliza notices a young couple walking leisurely, arm in arm, sharing a sack of popcorn. Most of the fairgoers do not hurry. Some head toward the agricultural barns, others toward the judging barns.

The judging barns!

"I really need to excuse myself, Mr. Steiner. I've got to get to the judging barn and then I need to walk back . . ."

"Nonsense! No one leaves before the fireworks! I'll take you back in the wagon later tonight, and you're welcome to stay at the store tonight; and no talk about walking, not in those fancy boots. Hey, Pops, I'm going to help Mrs. Stamper here."

Old Steiner waves his hand and smiles. Eliza has no say in

the matter. Steiner picks up Eliza's basket and offers his other arm to Eliza. Not one to be rude, Eliza ties her straw hat on again and proceeds to walk arm in arm with Steiner to the judging barn. Local islanders nod to the couple. Several of the locals bend their heads together as they watch the pair.

She, a widow! And he an attractive, likeable, and very eligible bachelor!

Eliza knows winds of gossip swirl around the fairgrounds.

"Character is higher than intellect," her aunt used to say.

Eliza bristles to think of her character besmirched. Steiner guides Eliza through various booths and onto a patch of grass. They do not talk.

"Now showing in rings one and two, sheep and swine!"

When they reach the judging barn, Eliza withdraws her arm and takes her basket from Steiner.

"I think I'm on my own now."

I couldn't get here fast enough, she thinks.

She puts her basket down on the judging table and signs the register. Her six blackberry scones await judging, and she is almost late. Two matronly women have begun sampling the baked goods. They each carry a clipboard and a pencil. One is tall and gangly, the other short and plump. Eliza thinks them a mismatched pair. The matrons sample a bite, confer, jot down comments. Eliza rushes to place her goods at the far end of the plank table. She squeezes her entry between others and positions her plate to the forefront.

ᘒᘓᘒᘓᘒᘓᘒᘓᘒ

BLACKBERRY SCONES

Take two teacups flour, one tablespoonful saleratus,
three tablespoonfuls sugar and mix well.

Add pinch of salt.

Cut six tablespoonfuls cold butter and fold in until mixture resembles pea-sized chunks.

Add one tin evaporated milk and mix gently.

Lastly, add one teacup fresh blackberries. Pour into well-greased iron skillet and bake until golden.

Cut into eight pie slices and serve warm with cream, or cold with butter.

⌢ᗡ⌢ᗡ⌢ᗡ⌢ᗡ⌢ᗡ⌢ᗡ⌢ᗡ

ELIZA COUNTS FOUR OTHER SCONE ENTRIES, EIGHT PIES, eleven plates of cookies, and five elaborate cakes, one with a bride and groom atop a barnyard themed wedding cake.

Clever, she thinks. *Very clever.*

Familiar smells reach Eliza's nose: the strong scent of vanilla, the sweet aroma of iced sugar. Eliza relaxes. She's comfortable for the first time in the past half hour.

Steiner meanders around the baked goods table and winks at Eliza. She ignores his advances and focuses in the dimmer light on the bustle of activity in the judging barn. She scans the other entry tables: vegetables, fruits, herbs, preserves, floral arrangements, youth exhibits. She does not look behind her for Steiner.

When she hears Steiner approach, she hopes that he will not touch her.

"Must be the only fella in this hall."

Eliza stiffens and does not make eye contact. She finds herself annoyed by Steiner. She dismisses any thought of continuing the conversation with him, at least not today.

I have no time to think about moving to Orcas. That's just plain nonsense.

"Yes, well, you should probably be getting back to the

frankfurters. And thanks again, but no bother getting me back to Doe Bay. I'm going to be here in the judging barn for the next hour and in any case, I'll be heading back to Cypress today. If I'm lucky I'll hitch a ride on one of the wagons heading out to Doe Bay before nightfall."

"Have it your way."

Steiner tips his hat to Eliza and turns heel.

I don't care if he thinks me insufferable. I just have too many questions about his character. And now a proposal! I have a blue ribbon to win here. That's what I'm thinking about today.

Eliza spends the next hour wandering around the judging barn, keeping one eye on the matrons as they near closer to the scones. She mentally judges the floral arrangements to pass the time, admiring elaborate displays of summer flowers and the simplest of nosegays. She awards an imaginary blue ribbon to a commodious display of dahlias, their sturdy petals folding in on themselves in a dazzling array of oranges and yellows. Eliza remembers the urns of flowers her mother ordered each year for galas, and wonders how her parents could have afforded such luxuries.

The matrons now stand squarely in front of the scones. They taste a competitor's selection, nod, and scribble notes on their pads. Eliza watches from behind the dahlias as one of the matrons, the shorter one with thick spectacles, lifts one of her scones and takes a small bite. The matron savors the bite and hands the remains of the scone to her counterpart. Eliza waits for what seems like many minutes as the matrons discuss among themselves the merits of her baking skills.

Another blue ribbon would be wonderful, Eliza thinks. *That's the problem with winning blue every year. My standards cannot get any higher.*

As Eliza waits, she walks to the far side of the judging

barn, its whole north side devoted to handiwork, and the requisite entries of needlecraft and quilts. This category is the most popular, by far, estimating the number of entries and the space that the category requires. Eliza is drawn to the center-piece quilt, a large Irish Chain hanging prominently on the far wall, its blues and pinks and greens weaving squares on an ivory background. A large blue ribbon adorns the Irish Chain. She glances behind her to see if the matrons have begun awarding ribbons on the baked good table.

Could they be any slower?

Two other admirable quilts hang near the Irish, a variation of the popular Log Cabin design in colorful reds and blues, and another, an intricate Exploding Star, pieced in contrasting shades of green. The Log Cabin has garnered the third, its white ribbon a far cry to the Irish's blue ribbon. The Exploding Star boasts the red, and not at all shyly. A gaggle of women surrounds the Exploding Star, and Eliza joins them to examine the fine stitch work.

The difference between the blue and the red ribbon is almost indis-tinguishable in this case, Eliza thinks. *I hope it's not this close for me.*

Eliza knows she will never garner a ribbon of any color in the quilting department. She remembers her first attempts at needlework, uneven stitches ripped out again and again. To pass the time, Eliza ambles through dresses and children's clothing displayed from wooden hangers, some with blue ribbons, and others with red or white. She studies the knitting and crocheting, and marvels at the intricate stitchery. She knows it can't be long now, to know her fate.

When Eliza dares to turn back to the baked goods, she smiles. Her hand flies to her mouth and she covers her pleasure. The ribbon is large.

And blue.

12

⌒⌒

AUGUST 24, 1897

Sunny, unseasonably warm. Beets and corn ready.

s'Qwe-Mit arrives at the cove early one morning, late August, moon of the salal berry. No fanfare, just the smooth lines of his dugout canoe plying the pass. Eliza sees him curve the point in his hand-hewn dugout, his striking figure upright. He lifts one hand in salutation and guides the canoe to the shore. He makes a silent landing. From the belly of the canoe, he lifts a huge burlap bag filled with dried salmon. Eliza tastes the salt before it reaches her tongue.

Squaw Candy!

She nearly salivates as she meets Indian John on the shore.

"This. For you," he says. Eliza reaches out to take the rough burlap. She smells smoked salmon through the coarse fabric.

"And flapjacks for you," Eliza says. Eliza has saved six jars of berry jams for Indian John. Eliza laughs when she thinks of how much jam he slathers on her pancakes. She thinks he would probably eat the jam by the spoonful from the jar, if he didn't think it would offend Eliza, or if he had a spoon.

Ts'Qwe-Mit offloads his pack and disappears into the woods west of the cabin. He re-emerges a half hour later, clad in a loose shirt and deerskin leggings. Around his waist he wears a leather belt, from which hangs a large hunting knife. The first time Eliza saw Indian John, she was frightened of him. But he sensed her timidity and threw down the knife on the ground.

"*Syaya*," he said, "*Friend.*"

That was all.

A tentative and unlikely friendship grew over time, and always over flapjacks. No matter how large the stack Eliza served, Indian John ate them all, to the last morsel. After the meal, in broken English, and always punctuated with bold, and sometimes startling, hand gestures, Indian John related stories of the mischievous Raven, and how he tricked humans into believing whatever he wanted them to believe. He told Eliza about Orca, and how when whales breach the surface they are in fact lost souls coming to visit their relatives. On each subsequent visit, Eliza had learned stories of Deer or Raccoon, Salmon or Eagle.

Eliza understood that Indian John's people lived on nearby Samish Island. Eliza deduced this fact after many conversations and interpreting a series of crude maps drawn in the sand of the cove. Indian John had marked Samish Island with a large "x." But Indian John made multiple "x" marks in the sand, some to indicate small islands along Hale Passage, and some on spits of land as far north as the Canadian border. A large island drawn on the beach represented Vancouver Island, a two day journey west. Indian John pointed to all the "x" marks in the sand and then repeatedly pointed both north and west. Eliza wondered if the native people had many residences, and if so, why they seemed to travel constantly. Eliza didn't know if Indian John had an actual dwelling, or multiple dwellings, or more. Or maybe "home" traveled with them. She couldn't visualize a life always on the move. It was unsettling to her.

"I have five sisters," Indian John had said one evening. "No brothers. None. But many cousins and uncles to show me the ways."

Eliza had never seen any of Indian John's sisters, but she pictured them in her mind: strong, dark, and inexplicably beautiful. The only Indian woman she had ever met was Old Jennie, but she was old and wrinkled. Of course Eliza had seen many Indians from afar on her westward journey by train. But she had Jacob and Jonathan then, and didn't strive to meet any redskins. Her father had said to avoid Indians at all costs, and to always carry a gun.

"Never trust a savage," her father had said. "And never meet one unless you are on the right side of the trigger. There's no good Indian unless he's a dead one."

Eliza wondered how her father knew of savages, or if in fact he had ever encountered a savage face to face, or if he talked behind inflated confidence or hearsay, and its associated discrimination. There was so much Eliza did not know about her father, and now he was dead—like, in his own words, all good Indians.

Jacob had carried a small pistol in his overland luggage, which Eliza used for target practice soon after she moved to the cabin. Now the pistol rests unused and useless in Eliza's bedside drawer. There is no need for a gun on Cypress, and nothing to shoot.

Indian John disappears for the remainder of the day. Eliza does not know where he goes or what he does. She fills her days with baking, and copying out well-worn recipe cards. She mixes up a large batch of pancake batter and lets it sit covered by the window.

࿓࿓࿓࿓࿓࿓࿓

FLAPJACKS

Beat up three eggs and a quart of milk;
make it up into a batter with flour.
Add pinch of salt.
Work batter into a fine thickness and perfectly smooth.
Clean your frying pan thoroughly, and put into it a
good lump of dripping or butter; when it is hot pour in
a cupful of batter, and let it run all over of an equal
thickness; shake the pan frequently that the batter may
not stick, and when you think it is done on one side (a
slight bubbling may occur), toss it over; if you cannot,
turn it with a slice, and when both are of a nice light
brown, lay it on a dish before the fire; sprinkle sugar
over it, and so do the rest.
They should be eaten directly, or they will become heavy.
For a special treat, add fresh blueberries to the recipe.
Do not overfold the batter if adding berries, however,
as the batter will become discolored and unappetizing
and must then be fed to the dogs.

࿓࿓࿓࿓࿓࿓࿓

NEAR DARK, INDIAN JOHN COMES AGAIN TO THE CABIN. ELIZA hears a slight rustling and opens the cabin door. Indian John sits on a stump a few yards away. She hands him a large stack of flapjacks that she has had warming on the stovetop and sits quietly on the uneven stoop while he eats. When he finishes, he wipes his mouth with a rough swipe of his bare hand. He places the empty plate at his feet and nods to Eliza.

"I tell you story," he begins. "Tonight, about Moon."

Eliza settles into a more comfortable position.

One never knows how long these stories can be, she thinks.

Indian John begins.

"Two sisters camp on prairie, dig camas bulbs. Older sister fall asleep in dark. Younger sister wish that two stars in night sky come to them as husbands. Sisters wake up in Sky World. Star husbands visit sisters. Very soon, older sister has son, Star Child. But sisters miss home, far away. They dig in Sky World's prairie, and break through ground. They see home of childhood and many peoples there. Sisters weave ladder of roots, go down again to home. Great feasts honor sisters. During feast, Star Child carried away by Dog Salmon People. Star Child cast away; he become Moon."

Eliza looks up at the moon, nearly full, and bright. She feels a sharp pang.

Star Child, carried away by Dog Salmon People.

Eliza stifles a cry and looks away from the moon. She studies her clasped hands in her lap. Try as she might, Eliza cannot accept that Jonathan is reduced to dust and ashes.

Eliza allows herself a breach of Christian dogma and looks up again at the moon, partially covered by a passing cloud. She affixes her eyes on the moon and the numerous stars that dot the night sky: Orion, Ursa Major, and Polaris.

Maybe the moon, and every star, is a child taken too early from its mother's arms. It matters not how the child was taken, she thinks. *No, there is no mother whose grief can be erased, dulled maybe by time and circumstance, but never gone. The moon is my reminder.*

Eliza begins to cry, reclines against the doorjamb, and removes her spectacles. The stars, just moments before pin-point clear, now congeal together in a watery haze. She breathes in deeply, and holds her breath for as long as she can, bathing in the moonlight, inhaling the stars.

❧

Ts'Qwe-Mit gets up without a sound and leaves Eliza. He retreats to the woods just west of the cabin, his footfalls imperceptible to human ears. He had set up a rough camp along the creek many times before, on multiple trips to the island. He makes a low bow to the earth, and then settles onto a coverlet. Although he hardly ever sleeps, Ts'Qwe-Mit closes his eyes and remembers the first time he had come to Cypress, well before any white man stepped foot on the island, when he was just ten.

It was on Cypress Island that Ts'Qwe-Mit had spent his first week alone, as a man. He was skinny and nervous, and only ten years old. When his uncles paddled Ts'Qwe-Mit to this very island and left him here to fend for himself for seven long days, he wore only the clothes on his back and carried the large hunting knife that he still wears close, all these years later, honed finer year after year. When he had first stepped foot on the island, it was late summer, time of long moons, time when salmon journeyed home.

On the first night, Ts'Qwe-Mit had fashioned a crude shelter out of cedar boughs and moss. He added to the shelter the next day. He starved for the first two days until his hunger stabbed his insides like a dagger. He spent the majority of the third day trying to catch one of the salmon milling in the deeper waters of the cove. He looked with envy at the eagles swooping down to the strait and rising with glittering prey in their talons.

"I must be like eagle," Ts'Qwe-Mit had said aloud. "I must be quick and stealthy."

Ts'Qwe-Mit had searched the ground for a sturdy dead fallen branch, one that was not too thick to hone, but one that would not break easily. He had seen his uncles split and hone twigs to fashion prongs for spears; he must do the same if he hoped to spear a salmon. Ts'Qwe-Mit honed three short twigs into sharp prongs; he whittled until the points drew blood. Then he searched for a sturdy piece of ironwood. He found a stand of ironwood along a little-used path and snapped a larger branch in two. It took a fair amount of strength to sever the branch. He cut the branch to a length roughly the measurement of his arm.

Ts'Qwe-Mit held the ironwood branch upright in his small hand, and with his other hand he unraveled a strand of cedar bark from his belt. Then he carefully lashed the three endpoints of the smaller prongs with cedar strands to the tip of the ironwood. A slight slip of his knife pierced his skin. Ts'Qwe-Mit left his blood on the spear's tip and handle.

He waded into the cool water up to his knees. For a minute or two, the water in the cove tingled his skin and he shuffled, hopping from one foot to the other to acclimate to the frigid water. After a few minutes, his legs warmed with numbness, and he waited for his catch, as still and patient as a heron. Any sudden movement would frighten the salmon away as it entered the mouth of the stream.

The sun had neared its zenith before Ts'Qwe-Mit landed a Chief, the largest of all the salmon. The salmon appeared from the corner of Ts'Qwe-Mit's sight, and wriggled into the shallows. In that split-second, Ts'Qwe-Mit pinned his prey to the rocky bottom with his makeshift spear. His branch cracked in two with the force of the thrust and Ts'Qwe-Mit lunged for the spear that held his dinner. He could taste the sweet pink meat already.

His first salmon! Ts'Qwe-Mit remembered to thank Swimmer for its gift; his elders had taught him that Swimmer was sacred, and he must honor Swimmer's spirit. Ts'Qwe-Mit clubbed the salmon's head with a fist-sized rock. He could only club the salmon once; if he clubbed it twice, he would kill its soul.

Swimmer, I thank you because I am still alive at the season when you come to our good place . . .

The salmon lay lifeless in his hands, blood streaming from its gills. In haste, Ts'Qwe-Mit fileted the salmon on the banks of the cove, its innards spilling pink and black and oyster colors back into the sea. Ts'Qwe-Mit prepared the fish in the old ways and ate ravenously, fish oil coursing down his neck and arms.

Ts'Qwe-Mit knew well the ritual of returning Swimmer to the sea. He sat at the edge of the cove and wove a simple pouch from the remaining cedar strands hanging loose from his belt. He carefully placed pieces of the carcass into the pouch and threw Swimmer back into the strait. Ts'Qwe-Mit then shed his sparse clothing and dived in headfirst, a boy-salmon ceremoniously sending Swimmer away from the cove.

Swimmer, now go home and tell your friends that you had good luck on account of coming here . . . now call after your father and your mother, and uncles and aunts, and elder brothers and sisters to come to me also . . .

By the fourth day, Ts'Qwe-Mit, fueled with protein and emboldened by his catch, had ventured farther from the cove. A long, ill-used path lay near the base of the monstrous cliff. Ts'Qwe-Mit recognized squirrel dung and set out to make a bloodier catch. He wove in and out of thimbleberry branches, his skin roughened by the brambles. The path ended at an outcropping halfway up the cliff. Eagles soared above, and again Ts'Qwe-Mit felt their power. He resolved to reach the top of the cliff by the end of the day.

Near nightfall, Ts'Qwe-Mit managed to scramble up the back side of the rock face, one foot at a time. He took in the sight of numerous islands and distant mountains. He would travel to all of these places someday. Ts'Qwe-Mit stood at the edge of the cliff and imagined he could soar. He offered a deep, guttural cry of praise. There was nothing he could not do.

The sun set in brilliance. Every color in the Creator's paint box widened across the western sky. Ts'Qwe-Mit sat at the cliff's edge and dreamed of his future, and the life he would need to embrace as a leader of his peoples. He had forgotten his hunger. He now hungered for other things, some seen, but mostly unseen. He knew it was time to put away childish pursuits. This he felt ready to do.

He had spent the next two days exploring the island, a boy-turned-man, eating snared squirrel, pilfered duck eggs, and berries. When his uncles returned for him, they did not see a trace of him at the cove. They fanned out to search for their young nephew, perhaps hiding in a tree trunk trying to keep warm. He was only ten years old, after all. It was when they heard a piercing cry from above that they shielded their eyes upward to see their nephew, his torso exposed to the elements and his arms outstretched, dipping and soaring like many eagles floating just yards in front of him. They thought he would fling himself into the air, so close he was to the edge, perched to fly from the top of Eagle Cliff.

⚯

THE NEXT MORNING, ELIZA WAKES JUST AFTER DAWN. SHE mixes a new batch of pancakes with goat's milk and the last of her fresh eggs. Not long after sunrise, Indian John appears silently at her door.

"Just a moment more."

She flips the last of the hotcakes and brings out another steaming golden stack. Indian John accepts the gift solemnly and returns to the stump. He eats silently, eyes down. Eliza sits again on the stoop and warms her hands around her tin coffee mug. Indian John does not drink coffee. No matter the protestations, Eliza cannot get him to drink the steaming black gold. After awhile, she stops offering him coffee, leaving the best of the morning to her alone.

When Indian John finishes his breakfast, he walks to the stream to rinse Eliza's plate. He cups a handful of clear, cold water to drink. His profile, more noble than savage, strikes Eliza as very handsome. She has never before thought in this vein. It would be considered unladylike to even entertain the thought in Columbia. For a half-second, Eliza allows herself to appreciate Indian John's strong, muscled torso. She flushes at her thoughts.

"Right, then," she says, as she rises and steps up into the cabin. On the table Eliza has six canning jars filled to the brim with raspberry, boysenberry, and marionberry jam. Although the cost of the jars is five cents on the dollar, Eliza does not begrudge Indian John for not returning the empty jars. What she gains from his friendship is worth far more than thirty cents per visit.

"Will you see your sisters next?"

"I traveled with one sister," Ts'Qwe-Mit answers. "I will see other sisters soon."

He points toward the west.

"I wish you Godspeed," Eliza says, and realizes her Christian statement might not make sense to Indian John.

"And Godspeed to you," he says in return. He bows to Eliza and disappears into the woods. In less than ten minutes,

Indian John drags his canoe to the water's edge. He loads his bedroll and empty burlap and raises his deep voice to the heavens:

əstigʷicid čəd, xaʔxaʔ šəq siʔab, ʔə ti qa adsʔabadəb.

I am thankful to you, Holy Creator, for your many gifts.

ʔutigʷicid čəd ʔə ti adskʷaxʷad ʔi ti adsʔušəbic, ʔi ti adsʔušəbid ti dʔaciɬtalbixʷ.

I thank you for your help and your taking pity on me, and on my people.

Ts'Qwe-Mit continues the chant as he steps into the canoe and casts off. His strong brown back ripples as he chants. Eliza feels privy to a secret and solemn event, and retreats to the cabin. She dislikes goodbyes. Goodbyes often mean death.

As Indian John paddles west, Eliza hears the echo of his chants ricocheting off Eagle Cliff. When she glances up, she sees a shadow on the cliff, but because of her near sightedness, she cannot be sure what it is that she sees. She squints and shades her eyes. Eliza hasn't seen Mad Virgil or his deaf son for more than two years. Mad Virgil could well be dead by now, she thinks.

But if it is the deaf child, how can he hear Ts'Qwe-Mit's chants? Maybe he feels the vibration of the sound and runs to see its source, or maybe he isn't deaf after all.

Eliza walks the scant quarter mile west to her garden plot, passing Indian John's campsite on the way. His smell lingers, and his voice. When Eliza reaches the garden, Indian John disappears around the island's northwestern shore. Eliza kneels in the soft, dark soil and weeds between the rows. She unearths the first of the potatoes and the last of the carrots. She checks the tassels of the corn, and feels the fleshy body of the cob. The corn is ready.

That means buttered cobs! Cornbread! Indian corn pudding!

⌒⌒⌒⌒⌒⌒⌒

INDIAN CORN PUDDING

Pour quart of boiling milk in half-pint of cornmeal,
stirring it all the time.

Add pinch of salt.

Beat up three or four eggs, and when the batter is
nearly cold stir them into it.

Put the pudding into a cloth or tin mold and boil for
two hours.

Serve with cream, butter, syrup, or any other sauce
such as you please, if you have any. Blackberry sauce is
most pleasing.

⌒⌒⌒⌒⌒⌒⌒

SEVERAL HOURS LATER, ELIZA RETURNS DIRTY AND FULL OF LATE summer sweat from a full afternoon in the garden. She glances again up at the cliff. The cliff stands empty. Indian John is now six hours into his paddle to Vancouver Island, and no echo of his visit remains. A stiff breeze blows through Eliza's hair, and her wild copper braid comes undone at the edges. She can't help thinking about the shadow she had seen earlier in the day. Eliza resolves to hike up to the top of the cliff, when she can find the time. It is late August, and Eliza has much to do. Her table is covered with vegetables of every conceivable color and size. The earth has done its work; now it's Eliza's turn. A savory Scotch Broth simmers on the back burner as Eliza cuts and chops vegetables for canned soups. It isn't until after midnight that Eliza collapses into her lumpy bed and into a long-awaited sleep.

Fall approaches quickly, stealing summer away once again. Eliza begins to wear woolen leggings under her skirts, although some days she has to shed them by late afternoon. The evenings bring a distinct chill, and Eliza wonders when Indian John will come again. Seeing Indian John stirred something inside Eliza, something visceral, and gnawing. It is then that she realizes that it has been almost a week since she has thought of Steiner.

Maybe, she thinks, *my resolve has eroded.*

It's not that I am giving up, or giving in, I am just giving over, like Eagle Cliff, exposed each day to ravages of weather and tide, changing subtly until I am not recognizable from who I was before.

That's it! I am like the cliff, at times hard and unmovable. But I am not the same! Something has happened in my heart, a slow imperceptible erosion of will, but not of spirit.

Or maybe I am no longer as picky as I once was. I might do worse than hitch up with Steiner and make a go of it at the Doe Bay Store. He's a good twenty years my senior, but he hasn't lost any of his vitality. Yes, I think I will set my sights on Mr. Alphaeus Steiner.

Eliza examines herself in the small mirror Jacob gave her on their wedding day. The crack in the mirror's face courses a jagged line across her cheek. She feels for her cheek instinctively and realizes her face does not contain a trace of the scar. She moves closer to the mirror, removes her spectacles, and gazes at her reflection. There is no doubt. Eliza is intact.

13

SEPTEMBER 18, 1897

Overcast. Low on sugar, flour, eggs.

*E*liza gauges her mood by the weather, and she often laughs at herself because of it. The weather in Washington leaves much room for improvement.

Why not live in a tropical paradise where every day dawns splendidly?

Eliza reads about such magical places in the various women's magazines, and she can but imagine them, faraway locales with exotic names like Bora Bora, a near-heaven in the South Pacific, or St. Croix, a sultry wonderland in the Caribbean Sea. But the argument runs aground, especially in summer, and often in September, when the San Juan Islands bloom as a paradise, with a plethora of salmon and clams and mussels and oysters, all for the taking, and rich, black soil that yields every variety of vegetable and berry. The creek streams clear and cold, and twilight lingers deep into the evening, often past ten o'clock, when the night sky bruises a purplish grey.

If anything is missing, missing at all, she thinks, *it is a man.*

Eliza is not surprised to see Steiner rowing toward Smuggler's Cove the following Saturday, as if by design. Her arms, covered with flour, fly to untie her stained apron. She throws the apron under the sink, and pulls the curtain closed. She peeks out the window through a slight opening.

He will be here in five minutes.

She hurries out of her soiled skirt and changes into her second skirt and a fresh blouse. She straightens up the cabin, a ten-minute tidy, she calls it, but she has now less than five minutes to do so. Steiner runs aground on the beach, his skiff grinding into the small stones that line the cove. Eliza hears the distinctive *scrape, scrape* as Steiner heaves the skiff up the beach. She checks herself in the cracked mirror, moves to the side to see herself fully. She smoothes her skirt, her hastily pinned bun.

Am I ready for this?

She straightens up, moves toward the cabin's front entry, and opens the rickety door. She stands on the uneven stoop, her eyes wide.

Steiner stops a few yards from the waterline. They stare at one other, an elongated second.

Steiner tops his hat, then strides toward the cabin. Eliza descends the crooked steps and meets him halfway between the shoreline and her home. Her steps are sure, and rapid. Steiner opens his arms to enfold Eliza. Without hesitation, Eliza walks headlong into the embrace. They stand enclosed in each other's arms, the beating of Eliza's heart evident through her blouse, a quickened *th-thump, th-thump.*

Eliza feels unfamiliar warmth. She smells Steiner's body, his familiar whiskey-laced breath. Her mind explodes with excitement and fear. After a full minute of the wordless embrace, Eliza starts to disentangle herself. Steiner stops her, turns her face upwards and bends down to offer his lips. Eliza turns her head just as his lips brush the corner of her mouth, an awkward exchange of breath and saliva.

"I've been waiting for this day," Steiner says.

"Will you come in for tea? I have blackberry scones hot out of the oven. Please, come."

Eliza turns toward the cabin. Steiner follows Eliza closer than before. He notices her wide hips swaying as she mounts the stairs. He glances at her ankles as she lifts her skirt to cross the threshold. He catches his breath, steps over the doorsill. He closes the door behind him. His arousal mounts, but he sits at the offered chair, wobbly under his full weight.

Eliza busies herself with the tea, filling the kettle, reaching for two bone china cups from the highest shelf above the counter, pouring milk into a white enamel pitcher. Steiner sits at the wooden table, removes his coat, and surveys the sparse interior: a closet, a mirror, a bedside table, a bed. He appraises Eliza as her back is turned, her hips, her waist, her shoulders, and as she turns to face him, her slender neck, arms, breasts. He feels another rush of arousal.

"I heard you garnered the blue at the Orcas Fair."

"Why, yes, how did you know?"

"Small talk at the store, we hear it all. Don't know if you heard that Old Jennie passed."

Eliza scrapes the second chair out from its space under the small table and sits across from Steiner. He notices tears welling in her eyes.

"When?"

"Last week Tuesday. My uncle went to Whatcom, stayed two days there to make all the arrangements, and then stayed a few days more. Went upriver to be with her people, Nooksacks, I believe. I've been tied to the store, or I would have come sooner."

He hesitates, and their eyes meet across the table.

"You know the reason I'm here, Mrs. Stamper."

Steiner reaches into his coat pocket and feels for the brown box. He extracts the box and places it on the table in front of Eliza.

"Here."

Eliza stares at the box. She looks at Steiner, looks at the box again. The kettle whistles on the stove and Eliza startles. She looks again at Steiner, then gets up, pours tea. She brings the tea to the table, this time not making eye contact. Returns for the milk, and spoons. Sits again, her right hand shaking. She reaches for the small box and holds it in her hand.

"Why, Mr. Steiner. I don't know what to say."

Eliza feels each of the four sharp corners before she opens the box. A small gap reveals the surprise inside. She cocks her head to the left and looks closely as she pries the box open. Her eyes flare wide as the box snaps fully open. Inside, a large garnet ring sits propped on a small off-white cushion. Two dainty diamonds on either side offset the rectangular red gemstone. A thin gold band circles the stones. Eliza stares at the ring and then looks over the tea things toward Steiner.

"You need to say yes, that's what you need to say."

Steiner rises and moves to the opposite side of the table. He stands behind Eliza, his hands on her slender shoulders. He desires to move his hands toward her collarbone and down over her small breasts. She moves her hands to her shoulders and he holds her shaking hands.

"It's been ever so long."

He strokes her hands, and feels an unusual tenderness, like he might feel toward a child.

"Please say you'll think about it."

She nods, silently. He kneels beside Eliza's chair, and slowly lowers his head onto her lap. Eliza's hand hovers over Steiner's head. She wills her shaking hand to move downwards. She feels a rush of warmth as her fingers descend into his freshly washed hair. She strokes his head. They sit this way, in silence, for the next half-hour. Their teacups remain full, and turn cold.

14

SEPTEMBER 19, 1897

Change of heart.

The next morning filtered sun peeks through wispy cirrus clouds. Eliza rakes the shore for odd bits, and finds, from the corner of her eye, a well-worn agate.

Could it be a moonstone?

Its iridescence sets it apart from the worn grey stones lining the salt-crusted shore. She squats to pick it up, noting its weight and perfect shape, almost that of a heart. She turns the stone over and over in her palm. Eliza lifts the moonstone up to the sun and peers through. Its clarity amazes Eliza; she rotates the specimen slowly and puts it up to her eye again.

Seeing the world through a moonstone, now that is a different perspective, she thinks. *The edges are blurred and yet the center is clear.*

She places the moonstone in her apron pocket, and feels its smoothness through the coarse fabric. She looks over the pass toward Doe Bay, and caresses the worn stone.

The center is clear.

She places her find on the kitchen windowsill, between a chambered nautilus and a double whelk. The moonstone glistens like a prism. Eliza stands at the window and looks again toward Doe Bay. She replays the scene of the day before over and over in her head.

Please say you'll think about it.

She can still feel Steiner's strong arms locked around her waist and pulling her tight toward him as he kissed her long and deep before leaving. Their rendezvous fulfilled her more than she allowed herself to say aloud. She had panted afterwards.

Eliza gathers her picnic items and her walking stick fashioned from an old piece of driftwood. She knows where the pathway to the top of Eagle Cliff begins but has never ventured farther on the path. She thinks perhaps the climb is too strenuous for her, but she wills herself to try.

After all, I am a new woman, she thinks.

She packs a supper of dried sausage, day-old apple fritters, and a small jug of tea. She pines for a lemon to float in her tea and lemon rind for the fritters.

ᑕᓄᑕᓄᑕᓄᑕᓄ

APPLE FRITTERS

Cut apples into rounds as thin as possible, cut out the cores, pare away the skins, put them in a dish, pour over them a glassful of brandy, and sprinkle sugar and grated lemon rind over them;
let them soak in this for an hour.

Half fill a good-sized saucepan with drippings. Make it quite hot, and when it is still and a blue smoke rises from it, dip each apple slice separately into a batter of one teacup flour, one and one-half teaspoonfuls saleratus, three tablespoonfuls sugar, one-quarter teaspoonful salt, one egg, beaten, and one-third teacup milk, and lower each one quickly into the fat; after one minute, turn it over lightly with a fork.

*When the fritter is crisp and lightly brown it is done
enough. Put on paper to free it from grease; sprinkle
with sugar and serve.*

᚛ᚑᚉᚑᚉᚑᚉᚑᚉᚑ

ELIZA USES HER GLOVED HANDS TO BEAT BACK THE BRAMBLES
that meet her at face level. For the first half hour, she fights
through thick forest underbrush, her arms in constant motion.
A few of the branches snap back at her face, and she knows
she will not emerge from the thicket unscathed. When Eliza
rounds the first bend, she sees the strait through a filter of
salal and fern. She estimates that she is approximately one-
third the way up the rear side of the cliff. She still does not
know if she will reach the topmost level of the massive rock
face.

Eliza stops for moment and wipes her brow. Her climbing
costume would garner snickers in polite company; she wears a
long shirt of Jacob's buckled around her waist and her woolen
leggings, minus the skirt. Over the leggings she wears Jacob's
boots. His creel holds Eliza's lunch. She laughs at herself.

A gentlewoman I am not!

"I'm game for this," she whispers. Her left ankle feels
strong and she pushes through the underbrush carefully. A slip
this close to the edge of the cliff could be fatal. The path
inches around the front side of the precipice. Eliza keeps her
eyes on the path and challenges herself not to look down, at
least not yet. Her heart beats heavily in her chest.

Not one hundred yards beyond, the path dives again into
the woods. Eliza feels enveloped by the denser wood, and
relieved, safer in the wood than near the face. Again, Eliza
talks herself into continuing. The sun is not yet high in the sky;
she judges that she has walked for about two hours. In a

clearing, Eliza sits and eats part of her supper as sustenance. The sausage is tough but flavorful and the sweet apple fritter boosts her energy. She drinks half of her tea and covers the jug. The rest of the tea will be cool before Eliza reaches the top of the cliff, and she will need to parcel it out during the climb.

By mid-day, Eliza emerges from the wood and sees before her a long rocky plateau that slopes steadily toward the summit, and before it, a field of low grasses punctuated by out-crops of smooth rounded rock. The riotous purples of camas and hook-spur violets vie with the gentle yellows of buttercup. Brilliant reds of sorrel and Indian paintbrush juxtapose with the loamy greens of saxifrage. And in and among the rainbow of color, Eliza spies tiny blue-eyed Marys and remains of columbine.

Although her legs wobble from the strain, Eliza continues toward the top of Eagle Cliff. True to its name, eagle nests are tucked into upper branches of fir and hemlock snags. Three eagles soar just off the edge, hanging on air. Eliza fills with awe looking out over the strait below. She can see forever: a mosaic of all shapes and sizes of islands, snow-peaked moun-tains, sparkling blue-grey water, and cloudless blue sky. This is as close to heaven as Eliza has ever come.

Eliza calculates the geography from her memory of maps plastered on the walls of the store at Doe Bay. Squarely in front of her, looming Mount Constitution dominates the eastern neck of Orcas. From this vantage point, Eliza can almost jump to Doe Bay across Hart's Pass. To the northwest, she sees mound after mound of islands stretching up into the Canadian Gulf Islands. Eliza gauges it must be more than fifty miles to the ragged tops of the Canadian mountains on faraway Vancouver Island. She turns her head away from the sun to the northeast, and sees glacier-draped Mount Baker east of Whatcom.

A rush of adrenaline swarms through Eliza's veins. She wonders what Steiner is doing today. She pictures him at the store, greeting customers, hauling loads, walking the wharf. She wonders if he thinks of her.

Please say you'll think about it.

She knows what her answer will be. Especially after the way they had held on to one another.

She sits not too close to the cliff's edge and finishes the last of her tea. She reclines on the moss-covered granite under the full noonday sun. She removes her spectacles. The sun's warmth permeates her skin and warms down to her bones. Even with her eyes closed, a rosy glow saturates her vision.

I will be a married woman again.

Mrs. Alphaeus Steiner. Eliza Steiner, to any friends.

And my initials will remain: EWS.

She laughs aloud. The monogram on her trousseau will not change.

Eliza conjures Steiner's features from beneath her eyelids. She lingers on his face, with its strong jaw line and piercing eyes, and then on his sandy hair, with its thick, long ends. She feels his imaginary shoulders and the muscled mass of his arms. She finds herself aroused thinking of his lean and powerful body rising to meet her own. She dismisses any reservations.

Eliza hears a vague sound and opens her eyes. She replaces her spectacles and scans every corner of the exposed cliff. Of course Mad Virgil and his son never lived on top of the cliff; if they lived in its proximity, they probably lived in the eastern wood from which Eliza had recently emerged. Although quite alone, Eliza has an eerie feeling that she is not.

She notes slight, imperceptible movement. Birds. Wind. Insects. Dust. That is all. She reclines again and naps for half an hour. She wakes refreshed and eats the remainder of her supper. She wishes she had more tea. On a whim, Eliza leaves a wrapped apple fritter on a stump.

The route down goes much quicker than the journey up. Eliza is buoyed by the excursion. She has made up her mind about Steiner. She enters the small clearing by the cabin, dusty and weary, but happy.

She hears Merlin squawking before she reaches her stoop.

"What's the fuss about? Mind your manners!"

When she opens the door of the cabin, Eliza gasps. Her linens are stripped from her bed, her blanket gone. Eliza furrows her eyebrows and assesses the room. She looks from one corner to the next to see if anything else is missing.

On first glance, nothing else is out of place. On closer inspection, Eliza sees the bedside table tilting toward the bed, its short top drawer pulled out. She rushes to the table, pulls the drawer off of its runners and peers inside. Jacob's gun is gone. Like that. She opens and closes the drawer several times to see if her eyes deceive her.

She freezes and turns carefully around to see if anyone is hiding in the small closet or under the bed. She gives a stifled scream and her hand rushes to her mouth. Eliza spins around and realizes all the apple fritters on the table are gone, and she panics that other foodstuffs might also be missing. Her pantry door stands ajar. Empty shelves: one, two, three, four. All empty. She grabs a large kitchen knife and stands like a sentry at the kitchen table, her eyes roving back and forth over the scene. She picks her way around the cabin, first peering under the bed, and then with a flourish opening the small closet door and standing back with the knife poised to enter into the darkness. There is no one inside. She bends to check if her Sunday boots are still there. They are.

At least my pin money is safe!

There is no sign of a footstep on the dust by the cabin door.

Who could it be? And why?

It would not be Steiner, this Eliza knows for certain. And it would not be Indian John, or Tuttle. By process of elimination, Eliza assumes that it must have been Mad Virgil, or maybe his son, ransacking her cabin while she walked to the top of the cliff. But the facts do not add up. She would have certainly heard footfalls or caught a glimpse of someone on her trek up or down the cliff. And they had not bothered Eliza in all these years. She sits on the front stoop and looks carefully in each direction. Her stomach lurches.

Eliza sleeps with her clothes on, the large kitchen knife at her side. Her mind wanders frantically. She cannot get warm, even with Jacob's coat as a blanket. A new blanket will be a pricy purchase the next time she rows to Doe Bay. Not to mention foodstuffs. Eliza's uneasiness grows knowing Jacob's gun is gone.

When dawn breaks, Eliza unfolds herself out of bed and straightens up the cabin. She opens the bedside table drawer to see if Jacob's gun has mysteriously reappeared, or if she has missed it in her thorough search. She talks to herself as she walks the small perimeter of the cabin. *It must have been Mad Virgil's boy*, she thinks. *No grown man would have ransacked the cabin. It had to be the boy, desperate for food, desperate for shelter.*

For three weeks, Eliza makes it a habit to climb to the top of Eagle Cliff twice per week. The fall weather turns colder as October circles into November. She rows to Doe Bay for necessities, including a new blanket. She is disappointed that Steiner is gone for the day. The question is still on the table, although Steiner had re-pocketed the ring. Eliza can feel the weight of the garnet on her hand already.

I'm ready to give him my answer.

She looks toward Doe Bay every morning, looking for any trace of Steiner's skiff rowing her way.

Surely Old Steiner told him I came by. Surely he'll come again soon.

In the ensuing days, Eliza climbs the cliff a dozen times. On her first trip, she leaves a small bundle of dried salmon. She figures if the boy didn't spy the package first, field mice or raccoons would find it, and gnaw at it until they retrieved its contents. She would be able to tell by the condition of the package who—or what—had nibbled the gift. To Eliza's surprise—and hesitant delight—the parcel is nowhere to be found on her next foray. She hurries home and bakes ginger snaps to take to the boy. The next day the cookies are gone.

ᏣᏂᏣᏂᏣᏂᏣᏂ

GINGER SNAPS

Mix one scant tablespoonful of fresh ginger, or dried ginger if you prefer a subtler taste, and a teacup of butter.

Add a pint of molasses.

Boil these together for three minutes—no longer—then add a teaspoonful of saleratus and a quarter-teaspoonful of powdered alum. Set aside to cool.

When cold, work in enough flour to make stiff dough.

Roll out very thin, cut small, and bake crisp and brown. Top with sugar.

Keep in a cool, dry place, and they will remain fresh and crisp a long time.

ᏣᏂᏣᏂᏣᏂᏣᏂ

A LONG FALL OF GIFT GIVING BEGINS, AND THE JOY OF GIFT giving replaces Eliza's melancholy. *Why doesn't Steiner come again?*

She aches for his body and his conversation, his presence and his help.

Eliza creates reasons to go to Doe Bay, but once and then again—the last time rowing in inclement weather that she should have avoided, her clothes saturated and her arms spent —Steiner is not at the store. Gone to Whatcom on a supply run. Over in Eastsound. Eliza is troubled, but nonetheless has reason to get up and out. Even on the days of her menses, Eliza does not linger long under her blanket. Her ragbag had also gone missing in the burglary, so she is forced to rip one of her two remaining bedsheets into the necessaries.

The temperature continues to plummet as November's icy fingers reach Cypress Island.

Another winter.

Eliza watches ice crystals form on her single-paned windows. Some days, the ice crust never disappears. Darkness falls earlier, and soon the path to the cliff becomes too treacherous to navigate. With great regret Eliza admits that she cannot mount the summit again until spring. Fog is thick and the pathway slick underfoot. She continues to leave bundles in the lower wood. Again and again, the bundles disappear.

Eliza redoubles her efforts to find the boy. She takes to staying as late as she can near the brambled pathway and going out again at dawn, in hopes of helping the orphan. She sprinkles fresh dirt around the cache, in hopes of tracing his footprint. Eliza forms a hazy plan, in which she takes in the boy and mothers him.

He will need sensible clothing and sturdy boots. Schooling and Bible training. A mother. She wonders how big he has grown.

Eliza names him Samuel, the Hebrew meaning *"God Hears."* She regrets that she doesn't know Samuel's given name, if in fact he has one. Perhaps his father just called him "Boy" or "Son," or perhaps no name at all, if the boy couldn't hear. But if Samuel himself can't hear, Eliza believes that God has given Samuel an extra sense, one that replaces sound with fine-tuned intuition.

Eliza slowly plans a future with the boy. There is no doubt that they will have to leave Cypress and move to Orcas Island, where the boy could be educated and apprenticed. Samuel would of course need another father figure in his life. Eliza fixates on Steiner, and wonders if his intentions toward her remain. She has not seen him for nearly six weeks. Of course Eliza cannot count on the fact that Steiner will agree to her plan, cannot gauge whether the addition of a child—and not his own—will alter his feelings or decisions.

But this does not dissuade Eliza. She resolves to take Samuel off island. Where Steiner figures in the plan is now secondary, or tertiary. Samuel remains Eliza's first priority. But none of her plans can come to fruition without the boy. She needs to find him first.

15

NOVEMBER 20, 1897

Sunny. Cold. To Fisher Bay.

On the twentieth of November, a bright and cold Saturday, Eliza walks to Tuttle's, six blueberry muffins and a jar of blackberry mush in her basket. She will ask Tuttle directly what he knows of the boy. Maybe Samuel had come to Tuttle's also and stolen what he needed, items a man might need, like a razor or an axe.

ᒡᔆᒡᔆᒡᔆᒡᔆ

BLACKBERRY MUSH

*Two quarts of ripe berries, a half-quart of boiling
water, two teacups of white sugar.*

*Boil slowly five minutes, then thicken with flour until
all lumps are incorporated and cook a few minutes
longer.*

*Put into a greased mold to cool and serve with cream,
or use as spread for muffins.*

ᒡᔆᒡᔆᒡᔆᒡᔆ

ELIZA IS FRUSTRATED WITH HER EFFORTS. SHE IS SURE THE boy is now toying with her. He must know that Eliza is the one who leaves all the goods for him. He had rummaged through her cabin, after all, so he knows who she is and where she lives, even though they have never formally met. The only recollection Eliza has of the boy is when he would accompany his father to town, and Eliza would see the ragamuffin child trail behind his father's rough and coarse woolen coat that dragged in the mud behind him as he shuffled, silently, toward the docks. Mad Virgil and his boy went off island twice per year, but Eliza did not know where they traveled, or why.

Mad Virgil did not attend Sunday services. The one time that Jacob had approached the man, Mad Virgil had ranted at Jacob. He mouthed senseless words, and spittle ran from the corner of his whiskered mouth. Jacob felt he had done his Christian duty in attempting to converse with the man; after the rebuff, Jacob ignored the wild-haired character, opting to invest his skills and services elsewhere. There were ruffians who lived near the docks who needed salvation, not to mention loggers and trappers who grazed the island bare.

"I will not be demeaned," Jacob had said to Eliza one morning as he sipped coffee in the anteroom of the parsonage as she dusted the spare furniture.

"As it is written in Deuteronomy, *'The Lord will smite those with curses, confusion, and rebuke, until they are destroyed, because they have forsaken Me.'*"

"It is the West, Jacob." Eliza had replied. "Perhaps the Lord needs to work harder to turn their hearts from stone."

"Hmmm, *'Hearts from Stone,'* that's a good working title for a sermon. Thank you, Eliza. You have good ideas from time to time. Now excuse me. I must attend to more important matters."

❦

ELIZA ROUNDS THE CORNER OF TUTTLE'S CABIN AND SEES TUTTLE chopping wood behind his crude shanty. His beard all but occludes his face. A pile of cedar logs lays akimbo in a semi-circle around his feet. He stops mid-chop, his axe high above his head.

"Ah, Mrs. Stamper. A sight for sore eyes."

He lowers the axe to his side.

"You are too kind, Mr. Tuttle. You must not see many women if you are able to say so truthfully."

Tuttle comes forward to accept the parcel Eliza offers from her basket. A ruddy nose and deep-set eyes are all that Eliza can make out through the mat of hair that covers his face, neck, and upper arms. Tuttle's mouth all but disappears beneath a tangle of black.

"Shall we have tea?" Tuttle asks, as a formality.

Eliza sits upright on a hard chair on Tuttle's porch as he goes inside to prepare the tea. Eliza looks toward what had once been the thriving town of Fisher Bay, and chances to remember what it had been like to live in town, back when there was a town in which to live.

❦

ELIZA HAD WALKED THE SHORT TWO BLOCKS EAST ON CHURCH Street to the general store most afternoons when Fisher Bay rumbled and bustled with activity, before the epidemic. On the waterfront, to the right of the now dilapidated dock, the Fisher Bay Store offered drygoods and, on Wednesdays, fresh produce and meats. Eliza made it a habit to stop in at the store each day before she continued on to the post office.

When the *Pamela Jean* chugged away from the dock on Wednesday afternoons, bellowing steam with a loud cough from a monstrous engine and emitting a long whistle from the captain's perch, the vessel's leaving signaled a run on the store. Eliza learned this fact quickly. Wednesday afternoons were the mid-week social event on Cypress, as women and men frequented the store to pick over the week's meat and fresh produce. By closing time on Wednesdays, it was "slim pickin's" as Ida used to say. If wives and single men wanted any pork or beef, or the rare treat of fresh asparagus or peaches from east of the Cascade Mountains in late summer, they had better visit the store on a Wednesday afternoon, and sooner as much as later. Eliza only missed one Wednesday, when she fell ill from influenza, soon after their arrival to Cypress. That meatless week caused friction in her household, and garnered snide comments from Jacob when Eliza served Welsh Rarebit with quince jelly for Sunday dinner.

Jacob had left the table when Eliza put the meal before him. She had no appetite and left the plate where she set it down. The plate remained on the table for a full twenty-four hours, until the dish congealed. Eliza removed it at Monday supper, and placed Indian corn pudding in front of Jacob. Jonathan heaved a mouthful of the dish into his rosebud mouth. Eliza felt greatly restored to health, and mother and son ate with great relish; Jacob picked at the edges and reluctantly ate his portion. They lived through Tuesday—egg salad with mixed greens, with tapioca for dessert. On Wednesday, after the supply run—*and thanks be to God!*—there were pork chops; on Thursday, oxtail soup; and Friday, roast mutton. To everyone's great relief, meat graced the table and normalcy returned to Number Four Church Street.

✐

TUTTLE EMERGES WITH THE TEA, SERVED IN CHIPPED TEACUPS. Eliza always drinks from the yellow cup with the rose pattern; Tuttle uses the green one rimmed with gold leaf, with a large white band encircling the cup just under the lip. They sip politely and share a blueberry muffin. Neither of them talks of the past.

"Mighty good, Ma'am," Tuttle says. "I must say, I miss home cookin'."

Eliza doesn't know if Tuttle refers to the muffins, or is asking for something much more.

Does he wish for me to make him more than the occasional sweet treat? Is he fishing for an invitation to dinner?

With horror, Eliza wonders if Tuttle refers to something else entirely, something vaguely marital.

She deflects her gaze. She instead peers past Tuttle's ruddy, bearded face to the spot where the church once stood. There is little trace of First Methodist; no trace of the hand-hewn pews, no trace of Jacob's forced piety, no trace of a thumb-worn hymnal. All that is left is a charred pile of wood and ash. She changes the subject.

"I've been wondering, of late, if you've seen the boy, the deaf boy, Virgil Cooper's son."

She turns to face Tuttle straight on.

Tuttle puts his cup down on the makeshift table near his knee.

"You mean that half-breed and his boy? Why, they left here more than a few months ago, Ma'am, didn't I tell you? Or maybe I ain't seen you since then. And since I've seen you last I've found myself a lady friend, you might say."

Eliza starts to answer, but her thoughts jumble.

The boy is gone?

"No, I don't remember you telling me, no."

Eliza's mind races. Her brow furrows and she winces. The blanket. The gun. The bundles of foodstuffs. She feels confused and disconnected from her present state as she balances a delicate teacup on her flannelled knee.

"They hitched along with Indian John. Don't know where they ended up. Heard tell that there's gold up in the Klondike. Somewhere up Alaska way. Mountains of gold, and all for the taking. I have half a mind to go chase the stuff myself. I don't expect the others will be back now. Boy's almost a man by now, between grass and hay, I'd reckon. You should have seen how much he growed, maybe a foot or more."

Tuttle uses his large hands to indicate how much the boy had grown.

All color drains from Eliza's face.

Put teacup down.

Straighten skirt.

Step, one, two, three paces.

Descend first step.

Descend second step.

Descend third step.

Eliza walks deliberately toward the cabin. By the time she reaches Smuggler's Cove, Eliza's emotions have welled up past crying, and she emits a loud soulful wail.

No, Jonathan is not here anymore. And neither is Samuel!

Eliza grieves for Samuel and for her grand plan. She grieves for all the lost moments of this fall, and last fall, and the fall before that. She grieves for all the knowing, and the not knowing.

And what of Steiner?

Eliza prays to God long into the night.

Heavenly Father, only You know the plans You have made for me. I look to You and Your wisdom to direct my steps.

Eliza wakes mid-sleep with perspiration dripping off her forehead in sheets. Eliza does not feel right in the head. She sits up and swears, and for the first time in her life takes the Lord's name in vain.

"God-damn it! God-damn it all!"

In a motion so swift she cannot remember with clarity, she rises from the mattress and strips down until she stands naked in the darkness of the cabin. She raises the back of her wrist to her forehead. Her temple burns, as does the whole length of her torso. She sheds her nightclothes in one movement, rips them off her damp breasts and bottom. Any shred of cloth that touches her skin deepens the wound. Her entire being feels as if on fire. Sweat pours down her pale body, droplets collecting at her feet. A wave of nausea and vertigo washes over Eliza and she reaches for the bed frame to steady herself. Spots dance before her eyes.

I am burning alive.

Eliza fights nausea as she bends over and pulls on Jacob's boots over her raw feet. She stamps her boots, once, twice, on the wooden slats of the cabin floor. Only then does Eliza open the door to the cabin, fully naked to the dark world.

To this day, the next quarter-hour still lingers at the edge of Eliza's consciousness, as if at any moment she might return to the near-certain madness of unbridled grief, the night she ran through the woods on the north end of Cypress Island, dodging dense stands of fir and alder, railing against God and the world, swearing and screaming, living at the edge of sanity, welcoming the lash from the brambles and branches that stung her fragile skin, regretting her life and all that inhabited it, raging against death and delusion, and forgetting the evident fact that she was alone, and naked to the world, singed deep to the core.

Without thinking of the obvious consequences, Eliza runs into the strait and throws herself into the dark foam.

Weightless, slanted, down through the green, a shimmering moon dims as Eliza falls away from the light. She must have hit her head, because the world bruises purple, and the light refracts in hues of violet and blood.

No one will speak my name after today. It will always be, "that day," or "the accident," or, more often than not, "the drowning." Just like the crazy woman who lived here before me. No one will find my body.

In that moment between death and life, that split second before the flame is extinguished and all that is left is the smoke, Eliza rises to the surface and takes in one last breath, a deep full inhale before the nothing. She sinks then toward the sea floor.

The water burns her skin, even more than the air. She is suspended between one hell and another. From somewhere deep inside, Eliza claws to the surface and gasps for breath. Her limbs are heavy as lead as she makes for the shore.

She wakes in the dark, drenched, in shallow water. Near freezing seawater laps at her sallow skin. As she rises into full consciousness, a tremble wracks her frame.

I am still alive.

She drags her bruised and bloodied body out of the shallow waters of Smuggler's Cove, peeling Jacob's sea-filled boots off her beached-white feet. She throws the boots up the beach where they land with a dull *thunk*, and she runs for the cover of the cabin, her soft feet torn by shards of mussel and clam shells. The cabin's shadow looms large as she approaches, and she feels her way up the stoop like a blind man.

She races into Jacob's coat and sits square in front of the

cookstove on the three-legged stool, feeding the dying embers of the Acme a steady supply of kindling. Her fingers feel removed from her arms, her arms removed from her body. Her body now feels colder than she has ever experienced.

In a matter of minutes, in imperceptible increments, a wave of warmth creeps up her sleeves toward her heart, and with it, a soothing stream of forgiveness, and relief.

16

⌒

DECEMBER 6, 1897

Advent. Waiting.

On the sixth of December, Eliza realizes that the Advent season is upon the world, that time of waiting for Christmas.

Waiting. All I am doing is waiting.

She tries to put Samuel behind her. Wonders who ransacked the cabin. Who stole the foodstuffs. Who accepted all the gifts.

Who? Who? Who?

She pens letter after letter to Steiner. All end up in the Acme.

December drags on more than usual. Eliza spends evenings knitting a long green scarf for Steiner. She is careful not to make any mistakes.

Two days before Christmas, Eliza rows to Doe Bay. She spends extra time on her appearance. She irons her better blouse, fusses with her bun. In an act of rare femininity, she laces on her Sunday boots. When she is fully dressed, she examines her profile in the cracked mirror, turning slowly to view her slender physique from each angle. She layers gloves and covers herself with Jacob's coat. Steiner's finished scarf is wrapped in brown paper and tied with twine. The message on the card stock reads: *To keep you warm, Eliza.*

The *Peapod* waits at the shoreline, small frigid waves lapping its sides. She takes her small purse, nothing else.

Today there is nothing to buy, nothing at all, she thinks. *Today is a day for giving.*

She knows from a deep space within that a mere fraction of a second will decide her future, that intangible second between being forever single or forever yoked. Her heart beats in anticipation, each beat mirroring her oar strokes.

Today I will accept Steiner.

The Doe Bay Store bustles with activity, a hum of voices evident before Eliza opens the well-worn wooden door.

"There's gold just sitting in the rivers, all for the taking!"

"Can't be, Miller, you're joshing us."

"No, it's right true. Heard it from my brother. He was on the docks when the *Portland* came in last July. Hit the jackpot, they did, boys, a man name of George Carmack and his half-breed brother-in-law Skookum Jim. Didn't you read the papers?"

Eliza inches into the store. A group of men surrounds the counter. The intoxicating smell of coffee pervades the interior, this mixed with tobacco and sweat. She cranes her neck to see to whom the men direct their conversation. To her slight disappointment, Old Steiner stands behind the counter.

"Heard tell there's thousands itching to go north," Old Steiner says. "'Klondike Fever,' I believe it's called."

"Yesiree, old man. My brother dropped everything and got the last boat up. Sent me word by post. Money's on it that I'll be following as soon as the spring thaw. And it's not just me. All kinds of people are heading up there—and not just miners and shopkeepers. There are even some women heading up to

Alaska. Actresses they call themselves—*ahem*—well, you know what that mean, boys."

The men snigger.

Alphaeus bursts through the back door and stomps in, his boots thumping the wooden floorboards with heavy footfalls. He carries three large crates, and his face is obscured from view. Eliza's heart quickens. His boots, his trousers, his apron.

Him.

She moves to the far aisle and watches Alphaeus as he approaches the counter. From this angle, she sees his strong profile, his cheeks now covered with a rusty beard. His hair hangs low over his shoulders and hides his eyes. He lowers from the waist and dumps the crates on the floorboards.

"Congratulations, you whippersnapper, you!"

Eliza moves toward the rear of the store to get a better angle. She stops by the flour bins and pretends to read the labels: buckwheat, cornmeal. She longs to run straight into Steiner's arms, but knows the time for that is not far off. She smiles inside, and feels his invisible weight. She clutches the brown paper package in her hands.

One of the men slaps Steiner on the back, and Steiner's hair sways forward. Eliza is fixated on Steiner's every move.

"Why, thanks, can't say that she deserves me."

"Couldn't meet a nicer gal, old boy. Sweetest thing on Orcas."

Another man steps forward.

"You're a lucky man, Steiner. Isn't a girl a hundred miles from here who beats the likes of Jane Hemple."

"Not only lucky, I'm the luckiest man on the face of the earth."

Eliza reddens, freezes in place. Her knees shake as she maneuvers toward the rear of the store.

Jane Hemple?

The commotion at the front of the shop diverts attention from her movements. She steals quickly toward the back door and then out, and closes the door without sound. She rounds the far side of the clapboard building and makes a near run for the *Peapod*. Her eyes are moist. She runs a gloved hand over her eyes up and underneath her spectacles. She clambers into the dory and unhitches the lines. In between sobs she rows away from Doe Bay.

Halfway across the strait, she tosses the green scarf into the swirling current and watches it drown.

What a fool I am.

~

IN THE DIM LIGHT OF THE OIL LAMP, ELIZA ROCKS BACK AND forth on the edge of her three-legged stool in front of the stove.

Stampeders, shopkeepers, actresses, whores.

She wonders if she is up to the journey.

And why not? I've homesteaded alone on Cypress for three years now. But I am not a stampeder. And certainly not an actress nor a whore. What about a shopkeeper or a cook?

Eliza stares at the Acme.

Maybe a baker? That could be my ticket to success.

She runs the conversation around her brain, over and over again. She talks aloud to drown other thoughts that well up from the deep.

Sweetest thing on Orcas. You're a lucky man. Lucky man, indeed.

Who? Eliza thinks. *When? How?*

She berates herself, and hits her knee repeatedly.

Why didn't I see this coming?

She hates to admit to herself that Steiner's lengthy absence belied another reason for not returning to her.

I waited too long! I missed my chance!

The words reverberate until she is deafened by the sounds. She tries to put Steiner out of her mind. But that is as futile as ignoring the wind.

His boots. His trousers. His apron.

His hair, his face, his eyes.

His body, his arms, his legs.

Please tell me you'll think about it . . .

☙

17

MARCH 2, 1898

Rain, cool. Check ledger. Pack up.

s soon as the hard frost passes, spring thrusts timid shoots through the frosted ground. Eliza trudges the goat through the thicket toward Tuttle's, a crude travois bumping along behind her.

To waste even one onion just wouldn't be right.

On the pallet she drags pantry stores, canned fruits and vegetables, and two loaves of gingerbread. The goat whinnies up the craggy path. It is slow going. When she finally reaches Tuttle's it is after noon and the lot stands empty.

Maybe better that way, she thinks. *Goodbyes are not my strong suit.*

But she doesn't want to leave the goods on the porch where they could be scavenged by rodents or raccoons. She opens Tuttle's cabin door slightly and peers inside. It smells of sweat and rot. Instead of hurrying to unload the supplies and leave, Eliza allows her eyes to adjust to the dimness. Of course she has never been inside the cabin.

All's the better for it, too.

What she sees surprises her, and almost makes her blush.

On the bed, not ten feet from where she stands, a woman sleeps soundly on a rough cot against the side wall. The woman —*is she an Indian woman?*—is completely naked. Her skin is tawny and waist-long black hair conceals part of her face. Her ample breasts heave in, out, and the blanket—*my blanket!*— that covers only a modicum of her nakedness rises and falls with her breathing. Eliza's heart quickens.

How long has this woman been on the island? And where did she come from?

Eliza's mind races. No women have lived on Cypress for more than three years. Eliza's eyes adjust to the limited light. She observes the sleeping woman's features.

Yes, she is most certainly an Indian woman! And a beauty! What is she doing here with Tuttle?

Eliza thinks back to her conversations with Indian John.

Hadn't he said his sister had traveled with him? Could it really be Indian John's sister?

Eliza remembers the end of her conversation with Tuttle, the day she left his cabin without speaking.

I've found myself a lady friend, you might say.

Eliza shudders.

How could I have missed the clues?

She leaves her questions along with her provisions on Tuttle's porch. She ties the goat to a post and hurries away. The goat whinnies a mournful bleat. From the corner of her eye, Eliza sees her rag basket under the porch. Her eyes widen.

Was this woman the phantom on the cliff? The one I thought might be Samuel? Was she the one who ransacked my cabin, and made off with my foodstuffs, my blanket, and Jacob's gun? And what of all the bundles —the dried salmon and the cookies?

A cruel joke, Eliza thinks. *Just like in Tom Grogan. To take on the persona of a man, and get away with it.*

Early the next morning, Eliza eats the last of a cold fish cake she saved for breakfast and packs five items into her satchel: her town boots, Jonathan's photograph, her recipe file, her ledger, and the moonstone. She does not pack her Bible.

Eliza pulls on her woolen trousers underneath her traveling skirt, buttons up her best cotton blouse, and dons her fisherman's sweater and Jacob's coat. She has nearly twenty-five dollars tucked into her belt pouch, and a hunting knife attached to her belt. She laces up her town boots and looks around the cabin one last time.

She leaves the cabin immaculate, everything in its place and ready for any wayfarer—a fisherman, maybe, or a trapper —who would happen upon the cove, down to clean linens on the feather bed and her well-thumbed Bible. If a transient stopped at the cabin, he might guess that a woman had lived there at one time, even though he might never guess as to why. Eliza thinks about leaving a note, but decides against it. The traveler would be comforted only by the eleventh verse of the twenty-ninth chapter of the book of Jeremiah, underlined in a steady hand in the Bible open on the table:

"For I know the plans that I think toward you, saith the Lord, thoughts of peace, and not of evil, to give you hope and a future."

Eliza sweeps the floor for the last time, and places the worn broom in its spot behind the cabin door. She pulls the door snugly behind her and sits on the uneven stoop. She heaves on her Wellington boots and looks out over the cove that she knows so well. She looks for Merlin. She is happy to see him perched in a nearby fir.

"Come on, boy," Eliza clucks to Merlin. "It's time for you and me to get on alone."

Eliza raises her arms and waves them in Merlin's direction.

"That's it. Go."

Merlin ruffles his wings and beats the air in a slow *thwump, thwump*. He rises a few inches from the branch and settles back down again, looking left and right with fierce beady eyes. With a surge of energy, he lifts himself up and off the fir and flaps his spotty wings. And then he is off.

Eliza leaves on the flood tide, rowing north and east toward Whatcom. It will be a long row, and she is glad she ate fish for breakfast.

First to Whatcom, and then Seattle. And then north to the Klondike it is.

The morning is fair, with little breeze. Eliza rows in rhythmic time to the beating of her heart. The waves lick the sleek dory as she pulls on the oars, the repetition calming. After a while, she feels in rhythm with the current, and it pulls her farther and farther from the cove. Eliza squints as she searches the sky for Merlin. He must have disappeared into a stand of cedar lining Eagle Cliff.

Eliza draws in a sharp breath. Mrs. Chopin's words could not have been truer:

There was something coming to her and she was waiting for it, fearfully. What was it?

She did not know; it was too subtle and elusive to name. But she felt it, creeping out of the sky, reaching toward her through the sounds, the scents, the color that filled the air . . . when she abandoned herself, a little whispered word escaped her slightly parted lips. She said it over and over under her breath: "free, free, free!"

The concept rattles Eliza. No, she has never been truly free. She has been yoked to her father, and then to her husband, and then to Jonathan. Even after Jonathan's death, Eliza has not been fully free; she has been chained by an invisible cord that has held her fast, and tied her to Cypress.

Has Cypress been a prison, or merely a resting place?

Eliza puzzles at the thought. She knows with certainty that internal stirrings have led her to leave her humble home. *Freedom has a price,* she thinks, *and that price is courage and uncertainty.* The thought empowers her. *For the first time in my twenty-eight years, I am free to make a decision on my own, unshackled from any man.*

The spring breeze refreshes her, and she draws the oars through the water, once, twice, again. For the first half-hour Eliza watches the receding shoreline, Eagle Cliff a sheer and formidable icon. Like wind and water eroding the shore, the cliff grows smaller and smaller as she puts distance between the *Peapod* and the cove, Eagle Cliff first the size of a massive, striated rock, a heavy slab that hangs precariously to the side of the hillside poised to crash into the strait, and then a much smaller stone, like one of the thousands of grey and white dappled ones that line the shores of every cove on Cypress. Finally, and most noticeably, she thinks, the cliff recedes to no more than a pebble: small, grey, and insignificant, without beginning, or end.

PART TWO

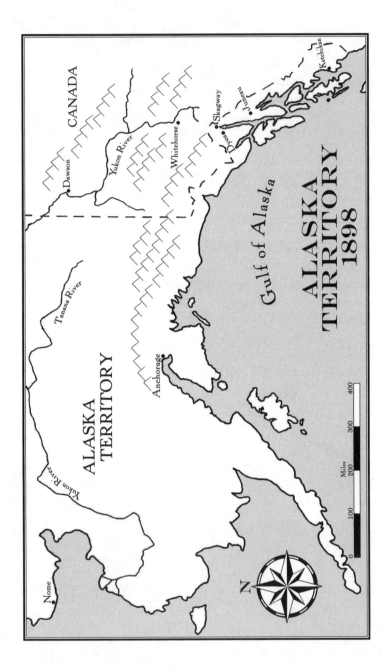

18

March 9, 1898

Partly sunny, cool. North to the Klondike.

Eliza marks each step on the forward deck. She finds herself a spot at the port rail, and stares back over the smoky city of Seattle. Eliza licks her chapped lips and tastes salt. She balls her fists to keep warm and stamps her feet on the planked deck. She blends into the crowd and observes her fellow passengers, who *clang clang clang* up the gangway of the *SS Ketchikan* in droves.

The dapper men wear sack coats with matching waistcoats and trousers, and knee-length overcoats, trimmed with finest fur. The more fashionable among the men wear their hair short and sport pointed beards with no moustache, and top hats. Few top hats line the railings, however, as the majority of men on board wear the trappings of a woodsman, and carry their belongings close: picks, shovels, saws, rifles, and mining pans hanging hurdy-gurdy from their backs. A loud chorus of male voices overwhelms the groaning of the ship.

The society women wear heavily corseted traveling gowns, with the new leg o'mutton sleeves that balloon down to a tight wristlet. These stylish voyagers seem out of place, especially with their outlandish hats, some with ostrich feathers or dulled eyes of fox. The sporting women, on the other hand, wear tailored menswear, with high-collared blouses and skirts above the ankle, and expose the lower half of the leg above buttoned boots. Some of these daring women do not wear hats at all. Eliza admires the new look of their hair: soft and wavy, and quite feminine, framing faces and sending tendrils down their necks. Eliza's severe bun and absurd outfit mark her as some other type of woman, amorphous and indistinguishable, perhaps a miner herself.

Eliza does not leave the port rail. As the steamer leaves Elliott Bay and heads north up Puget Sound, Eliza assesses that of the three hundred and some-odd aboard, less than thirty are female. She pulls Jacob's slouch hat down over her face so that only her eyes and nose poke out. She wraps Jacob's coat around her to stave off the wind. She reaches for one of the hot buns in her coat pocket and unwraps it slowly.

The *Ketchikan* plows up the Inside Passage from Seattle to Alaska, and passes layers of islands that mirror Cypress— silhouettes of ghost-like islands receding into dense mist. The vessel overnights at Nanaimo, and takes on additional passengers at Port Hardy. Eliza wonders how another human soul can fit on the already overcrowded steamer.

Below deck, the vessel reeks of human filth, but its stink minimizes on the upper decks. Room in steerage becomes even more cramped as people begin to spread out, and Eliza chooses to sleep sitting up in a corner. She wonders if she will ever be warm again.

One day I will wear a fur coat, and fur boots, and fur-lined mitts. Perhaps the fur will be the common fox, or perhaps the smoothest mink. But tonight I would wear the fur of a great brown bear if it would keep out this chill.

Eliza shivers on the top deck. She moves to the starboard rail, away from the wind. She stamps her feet to keep blood flowing. More than once she sees a pod of orca whales rising out of the sea; their black fins knife through the straits and—if she catches a rare glimpse—flashes of black and white appear in the creases between waves. Eliza gasps when a pair of orca breaches in the near distance. They *slap* the water on re-entry and disappear. Eliza mistakes swift porpoises that race the steamer with juvenile whales. She counts as many as eight or nine of the creatures flitting close to the *Ketchikan.* She leans over the rail to watch them duel the ships's speed and crest its wake. They dart and dip and dive. Eliza becomes annoyed with incessant gulls tailing behind the vessel. Their constant *screech* is deafening. She hums to block out the sound.

The *Ketchikan* chugs up the rugged west coast of British Columbia and refuels in Bella Bella. On approach to harbor there, Eliza squints.

Can it be?

A shuffling brown bear, its nose low to the kelp-strewn shore, lumbers not a hundred yards in the distance. Eliza shudders. She hopes never to meet a bear in close proximity. She imagines its snorting and grunting and almost feels its hot breath.

By the time the ship reaches Prince Rupert, cold climbs through Eliza's sparse clothing and nags at her very bones. She curls her hands into tight circles inside her new gloves and breathes shallowly. Deep breaths hurt her lungs. She develops a cough.

During the day, Eliza eyes her fellow travelers, stacked close as sardines in conversation. She has yet to speak to anyone on the voyage.

"Bad advice is seldom forgotten!" a booming voice

resounds. "Just remember that a fool and his money are soon parted. And there be many fools on this journey."

Eliza turns to see a ragged character holding court on the opposite side of the rail. He looms over all the other would-be miners.

Why, he must be seven feet tall!

The man's head is covered in a mop of wild red hair and his face is all but obliterated by a full beard in a darker shade of red. He wears long suspenders over his sweater and smokes a long-stemmed calabash pipe.

Just like Sherlock Holmes!

The man's thick Scottish accent attracts as much attention as his stature. As if on cue, he crosses the slatted deck to the near rail.

"A nickel will get you the best advice you've ever known," the tall stranger says. His burr elongates the word *"ever."*

"Name's Richardson, Donald Martin Richardson, that is. People call me Shorty. And you'd be?"

"Mrs. Waite."

No other explanation.

"Pleasure's all mine, Mrs. Waite," Shorty says, with a mock low bow. "Pardon me for saying, but from a distance, I thought you were just another *cheechako.* I can see now I was terribly mistaken. We redheads need to stick together."

Eliza laughs aloud.

I might not need to use my hunting knife after all.

But that thought is short lived. According to Shorty, con men and gangsters travel the marine highway to Skagway, ripping money from unsuspecting travelers.

"I'm one of the lucky ones in this crowd of fools," Shorty confides to Eliza. He pronounces "lucky" like *"looky."*

"And what do you mean, sir?"

"Heard of Rabbit Creek? They call it Bonanza now. Hit the mother lode there last summer. Up by Dawson. Yukon Territory. My partners stayed behind while I—*ahem*—settled some business in Seattle. Heading back up there now, the wiser, and the richer."

He winks at Eliza.

"If you don't mind a piece of free advice, Skagway's no town for a woman, unless of course you're one of the sporting girls."

He cocks his head to the left and raises an eyebrow. A pair of modish young women stands not five feet away on the leeward deck. One girl has unbuttoned her blouse to reveal ample cleavage, despite the chilled air. She fingers a locket in the deep crevice of her bosom. Eliza notices the lack of a wedding band.

"But there's a fortune to be made, in more ways than one. And I like you. I'll see to it that you don't get snookered. There's another woman in Skagway on her own—has a passel of boys, she does—Harriet Pullen's her name. Best pie maker in Skagway. She's hoping to open a hotel, she is. I believe there's room in our town for a few honest women."

Shorty winks again at Eliza.

"Now, you'll pardon me. I've got a few nickels to earn. Some men get rich from the digging; others get rich off the diggers."

Shorty turns to snooker the men nearest him on the rail, and pinches the vogue woman on her ample ass as he passes. She lets out a high-pitched giggle and wiggles her backside at him.

Shorty's grand tales of thievery and corruption in Skagway and nearby Dyea draw an audience.

"Nothing like firsthand information, boys."

Crowds flock around Shorty for stories and advice during

daylight hours on the ship's crowded deck. The circus continues in the saloon late into the night. Shorty's purse grows with every new nugget of information that he shares.

"So here's what you'll need, boys. Every Klondiker heading over the pass needs a ton of supplies, and I don't mean that figuratively.

"You'll need heavy woolens, flannels, buck mitts, and moccasins. Blanket rolls and mackinaws. Mosquito netting and camphor. Add to this: navy beans, bacon, rolled oats, and flour. Coffee, tea, condensed milk, and vinegar. Potatoes. Onions. Mustard and pepper. It's not for the faint of heart, boys. You'll get turned back at the Canadian border if you don't have the supplies. Don't think I mean it? I've seen plenty turned away.

"That'll cost you a nickel, partner. I don't give advice gratis! Thanks, and yes, thanks. And you, sir? Yes, a nickel."

Eliza learns that first the miners must trudge up the "Golden Staircase" at Chilkoot Pass outside of Dyea, a single-file human stream of gold seekers who climb an ice stairway to an elevation of three thousand feet. Most miners make the ascent up the ice stairs at Chilkoot near forty times, carrying an average of fifty pounds per climb. They deposit their goods in hapless piles at the summit and then skid down the pass to retrieve another load of goods. This initiation rite cannot be avoided; if a miner does not have the requisite two thousand pounds of survival gear to see him through the quest, he risks being turned away by the Canadian border agents before reaching Dawson.

"It's a circus up there. Of course one can hire a packer at a price of one penny per pound, but often the packers ditch you if another miner offers a higher fee," Shorty continues. "I'll find me a Tlinget; they're the fastest. And I'll pay the going price plus a penny more."

Eliza does the sums in her head. First, one needs to get all his or her supplies to the top of Chilkoot Pass. That could take over a week. But that feat represents less than one-tenth of the distance to the mother lode.

The faint of heart must turn back, or freeze to death. Or starve! Or —God forbid!—perish or go mad.

∽

SHORTY SHARES HIS KNOWLEDGE WITH ELIZA FOR FREE.

"I got one piece of advice for you that's the most important of all. Don't get mixed up with the likes of Jefferson Randolph Smith. He's a filthy, good-for-nothing crook. Used to work for him, but not anymore.

"He's known as Soapy. Soapy Smith. He's a conniver and blowhard. And he's trying to turn Skagway into his own little kingdom. Take it from me, he ain't doing it the honest way. He'll try to befriend you, and then he'll stick a knife in your back when you've barely turned your head."

Shorty mimics a jab.

"You know the old saying, *'An open Foe may prove a curse, but a pretended Friend is worse.'* Well, that's Soapy Smith in a wee nutshell."

Shorty extends the word, *"wee."* The lanky Scot pulls a folded newspaper from the chest pocket of his mammoth fur coat, and his stubbed second finger points to an editorial dated last week in the *Portland Oregonian:*

"Skagway and Dyea have more liars per square mile than can be raked up in any 1,000-mile area elsewhere . . ."

"Just remember that, little missy. Can't trust a soul. Watch your steps, watch your words, and watch your purse, that's my best advice to you. They'll bilk your soul if they can."

Eliza feels a flush rise to her cheeks.

Who of us is immune from this madness?

Eliza begins to doubt her decision to travel north, but that thought turns from likely to ludicrous; to return to Seattle now she would have to jump ship and swim. The waters that swirl around Cypress reach fifty degrees at the height of the summer. With floating ice in the Inside Passage, Eliza guesses the water here hovers closer to freezing. Even the rain pelts down in freezing rivulets, falling in grey sheets from the ceiling of the sky down to the ever-greyer sea. Eight days of fine mist cause Eliza's hair to escape the confines of its bun. Not even Jacob's hat can keep wisps of her coarse copper hair from escaping.

On approach to Juneau, Eliza feels she can almost touch green velvety moss anchored on exposed rocks at the entrance to Stephens Passage. She has her first glimpse of a true glacier and trembles at the thought of crossing one. From the deck of the ship she sees a sign: Juneau Bakery.

Not long until I open my own establishment!

Eliza spends her days planning. She draws rough sketches with a pencil, and uses an eraser liberally. She finds comfort in the loud *chugga-chugga-chugga* of the ship's engine. She avoids other passengers, except in the ladies' washroom, where it is impossible to avoid another human being. She eats sparsely. Talks to Shorty when they happen to pass. Reminds herself that the hunting knife will be her surest friend. Pores over her recipes. Makes lists. Bundles Jacob's coat around her. Loses herself in raisins and cinnamon and yeast.

Stray scraps of paper multiply in Eliza's oversized bag. She can almost smell bread rising.

19

MARCH 17, 1898

Heavy snow, freezing cold. Arriving Skagway today.

*E*ight days after disembarking the Seattle waterfront, the *Ketchikan* reaches Skagway at nine o'clock in the morning, its arrival greeted with a late spring snow that all but obliterates the long view toward White Pass. A din of men's voices drowns out the sputtering of the vessel. The ship's long whistle announces their arrival, and an all clear to disembark.

Wharves that jut into the bay are docked full, and the *Ketchikan* tries to shimmy up as close to shore as possible without running aground. Lighters approach the vessel, some manned by whites, and others, Native. Eliza hears the unfamiliar name *Shghagw'ei* in the native Tlinget language. Luggage and trunks pass from hand to hand and masses of men lunge their goods overboard. Eliza watches as several trunks tumble and split open on the slimy mud of the tide flat. High women's voices pierce the lower monotone of men's. Several children run up and down the deck, *like whooping Indians*, Eliza thinks, as they wait for their turn to disembark with their harried parents. Eliza rests momentarily by the starboard rail and memorizes the sights and smells.

This will be my home.

Shorty comes up behind Eliza with a promise to catch up with her later in the day, "after I do a wee bit of business." He points Eliza to a Mrs. Brown's Boarding House on Sixth Avenue.

"Tell Mrs. Brown that I sent you, and she'll find you a room straight off. And see to it that you pay one Lester Edwards, *Esquire* . . ."

At this mention Shorty makes a low bow.

". . . the pleasure of your company, too, Ma'am. He's the land agent here in town, knows places for rent before renters know they're out of their digs."

Shorty pats Eliza's arm.

"Don't worry, I'll be watching out for you, little missy."

Eliza joins the throng of men who slog across the mud flats toward the shore. Selling her wedding ring in Whatcom had proved costly, *swindlers!* She received a trifling fifteen dollars for the ring, to add to another five she received for the *Peapod.* If the forty-five dollars and odd change she has in her change purse cannot start her new career, she knows she'll be back on a southbound boat in a month, with no prospects ahead.

I don't have much. No fur hat, no fur muff, no fur coat.

Her meager change purse is now sewn into the lining of Jacob's coat.

Eliza's satchel contains the bare necessities of a woman's toilette and her second woolen skirt, a cream-colored blouse, a spare pair of stockings, and bloomers. Her town boots. Jonathan's picture safe in its brass frame. The moonstone. A ledger. And of course her precious recipe file, her veritable ticket to gold.

A relentless thirty-foot tide laps in and out of Lynn Canal

every day, which makes disembarking the vessel a slippery affair. Jacob's boots succeed in keeping out the frozen slush as Eliza sloshes through the icy mix of mud and seawater toward the shore. Eliza thinks sardonically that this may be the only positive comment she can utter about Jacob.

His boots hold stay.

The hem of Jacob's coat crusts with wet mud and hangs low to the ground. By the time Eliza reaches the wharf, Jacob's boots resemble a logger's, caked with a half-inch of icy sludge.

Eliza stamps her sopping boots on the wooden wharf, her heels indenting the soft fir. She squints, and gazes the whole length of the long half-mile toward town. False wooden storefronts and the spire of two lone churches form Skagway's pathetic skyline. Acres of mud, stumps, shacks, and shoddy tents fill in the rest of the scene.

More tents than buildings, she thinks. *Tents! In this frigid no man's land!*

A group of young ruffians, not more than ten or eleven years old, clamors for attention at the foot of the wharf. Some hawk newspapers; others jostle to hawk wares. Beneath jaunty hats, the hooligans look thin, and dirty. She will be careful with her purse.

"This here way to Mr. Simpson's! Boots and the like for fair prices!"

"Read all about it! Avalanche kills miners on Chilkoot Trail! Survivors tell story!"

Eliza stands in the sodden spring of Skagway, snow stinging her brow. Upon disembarking, Eliza Waite is known only to have come from points south, a recent widow without children. She means to open a bakery, her references being a woman. By way of comparison, Skagway already boasts more than forty beer parlors and boarding houses doing a booming business for thousands of men traveling through the portal. And the town is barely a year old.

Eliza maneuvers through the mob of boys and men and walks up the muddied street toward Mrs. Brown's Boarding House.

"Over here, mister! Only twenty five cents for a shave at Klondike Lil's!"

"News flash! More gold found in Miner's Creek. Pokes worth millions!"

The tallest of the boys wears short worsted pants and scuffed brown leather shoes with no socks. His cap hides a mop of curly dark hair. His eyes flash as he darts from passenger to passenger. He pushes a smaller boy toward the offloading passengers. The smaller boy winces. The taller boy stamps his heel on the toes of the smaller boy, and the smaller boy howls. The taller boy moves on to another of his charges, hawking papers high above his head. Several passengers stop to extract a coin for the local rag. Most keep walking. Eliza glances over the tops of the boys' heads and averts her gaze.

Jonathan would be near their age now.

Blinding snow renders it difficult to find the way as Eliza walks north up Broadway from the wharf. She stops to catch her breath and to wipe her spectacles.

In the near distance she reads: Burkhard House, Pill Box Drug Co., Royal Laundry.

Biting cold burns her lungs, and ice-cased snowflakes freeze her cheeks. She wonders again if this grand adventure is a grand mistake. All around her a tide of men surges into town. She wonders if their thoughts echo her own.

One thing for sure, she thinks, *after I find Mrs. Brown's, I certainly need to purchase a warmer coat.*

Up Broadway toward Sixth Avenue, Eliza peeks into

storefronts, establishments, and hotels: Getz and Donovon Packers, Joseph B. Meyers Cigars and Tobacco, Hotel Mondamin.

What I would do for a hot meal!

When Eliza turns left from Broadway onto Sixth, away from the wind, she sees with great relief a two-story wooden building on the south side of the muddied side street engraved with large white block letters: Mrs. Brown's Boarding House.

Eliza stops, catches her breath again. She notices detail of the wooden structure, from its form to its function. Thick green brocade drapes frame the inside of the windows that border each side of the doorway, and refuse a glimpse into its interior. A single step up from the crude wooden boardwalk, Eliza opens the heavy wooden door, its *cre-e-eak* her entrance.

"Morning," comes a voice, perhaps from behind an ornate desk by the stairwell. Eliza dusts the snow from her overcoat and smiles.

A real house.

The carpeted parlor dredges long-locked memories, this room the most elegant she's seen since leaving her aunt's in St. Charles. A large woodstove stands in the parlor's rear left corner, and emits a steady blast of warmth, its door slightly ajar. A large green divan sits close to the stove; its carved arms support elaborate woolen throw blankets with sensuous fringes reaching down toward the floor. A smaller green brocaded loveseat is positioned at a right angle to the divan, its back to those who enter the parlor. Rich tapestries overlap on the wooden flooring, and several small tables and armchairs dot the right side of the room. Lace and lamps. Fringe and furs. The soft glow of a single oil lamp on the desk beckons to Eliza, *come.*

"A Mr. Richardson directed me to you," Eliza begins,

although she doesn't see anyone to whom to direct her comments.

"Shorty! Seems everyone around these parts knows Shorty!"

A stylish woman of a certain age with the new soft and wavy hairstyle Eliza recently admired appears from behind the oak desk with a duster in her hands.

"Yes, we met on the *Ketchikan* . . . we've just docked, maybe an hour ago."

"He's back, is he? Well, well. Won't be long before he's at the door. Now what can I do for you? You'll be needing a room for the night?"

"I'm thinking for a few nights, maybe a few weeks, if you've got a room to spare."

"For a friend of Shorty's, there's always room," the woman says. "My name's Pearly, Pearly Brown, landlady of this here establishment. And you would be?"

Two small bedrooms occupy the first floor of the boarding house, one sparse room on either side of the parlor. Just behind the parlor, a large claw-foot tub sits surrounded by a heavy green damask curtain.

"Bathtub's used most nights, sometimes three and four times over," Pearly says. "We've got people coming and going every day. Most of them men. Never seen so many men in one place. Yesterday I turned away five, six men—two in one hour alone—and that hurts the pocketbook. Sent some of 'em over to the Mondamin, and others over to Paradise Alley, I did. I need to build myself a hotel."

At the top of the stairwell, Pearly motions to the front room to the left of the stairwell. A partially opened door reveals the most opulent bedroom Eliza has ever seen.

"You'll be my neighbor, here, in the blue room," Pearly says, opening the door to the rear bedroom. "Fifty cents a night, a quarter more for a bath. Might be willing to dicker on the price if you're staying longer."

In addition to a large feather bed flanked on both sides with oak side tables, the room houses a polished maple vanity table and large full length mirror. Cornflower blue paper covers the walls from floor to ceiling, and the rear window's ivory and blue flowered drapes blanket out the cold. Two carpets overlap at the foot of the full-sized bedstead.

"There's pitifully few of you traveling women," Pearly says. "I'm glad for the company. We get some real corkers, let me tell you. Why, just last week we took in the most curious woman—signed the register only as one J.T. Cummins—took a double take, I did, thought she masqueraded as a man. She stayed just one night, and did not bathe. Imagine that. Crazy woman left before I woke and left only two quarters on the nightstand. And that's the God's honest truth."

Pearly turns her attention back over her shoulder and points to the right of the stairwell.

"Those are Rose's and Cilla's rooms. They're what I call enterprising young women. Ladies of the night, some call 'em. Not me. They're sweet as kittens in the day, but fierce as tigers in the night, if you know what I mean."

Eliza catches a glimpse of herself in the large ornate gilt mirror at the top of the landing, and blushes.

Am I renting a room in a bordello?

But she is too exhausted and too dirty to care. All she can think of is luxuriating in a hot bath after eight days aboard the *Ketchikan.*

Pearly reads Eliza's desperate thoughts like a mystic.

"Now you get out of those filthy rags and get yourself into the bath directly. I'll fetch you a couple of towels and a robe. You look like you need an hour to yourself to just soak."

After spending a full hour in the bath, Eliza changes into her woolen skirt and spare blouse. To Eliza's surprise and delight, Jacob's boots sit polished outside her bedroom door. Eliza pulls the boots over her thick woolen stockings and gathers her satchel. There is no evidence of Pearly as Eliza descends the stairs and lets herself out the door of the boarding house. She turns to look up to the second story windows. The curtains hang still.

Eliza trudges through frozen mire to find Lester Edwards, Esq. just around the corner of Broadway and Sixth. She walks up to Seventh, and then Eighth. She finds the law office of Lester Edwards, Esq. and lets herself in the modest storefront.

If everyone in Skagway knows Shorty, then perhaps I'm about to meet a valuable friend in this Mr. Edwards. If anyone knows where to rent space for the bakery, Shorty says it's got to be him.

Later that night, inviting sleep, Eliza hears steady footfalls on the stairwell. In the two weeks she boards at Mrs. Brown's the footfalls become a regularity, a steady stream of men at all hours of evening and night.

Rose, just over five feet tall, has found herself a comfortable niche at Mrs. Brown's. Men cannot resist Rose's ruddy complexion and voluptuous mouth, and her even more voluptuous frame. One can hear Rose at all hours, sometimes her low guttural bellow and at other times a stream of profanities that can be heard from the parlor.

"Quite the mouth on my Rose," Pearly says. "Would make a preacher blush. She's what I call seasoned. Maybe twenty-five, if I do my sums right."

Rose's whole body shakes when she laughs, and her jet black curls sway in the air as she throws her head back and roars. Rose's greatest characteristic, Eliza notes, is her complete non-judgment of any man or woman. Rose loves life, and it seems, from the list of clients she keeps in a small leather bound book attached to her waistband, men.

Cilla, on the other hand, a waif of a girl, cannot be more than nineteen as far as Eliza can judge. Cilla bears a continual pout, and stands aside the doorway of the boarding house like a sentinel, smoking thin cigarettes and watching the world stream by. She stands almost as tall as Eliza and levels her gaze at Eliza as well as every other customer entering or leaving the establishment. Cilla looks much like the now famous Gibson Girl, whose lovely face graces the pages of the ladies' magazines in the front parlor. Eliza much prefers to talk to Rose in passing than Cilla, although Cilla's constant presence at the doorway encourages Eliza to seek a new look. Eliza knows if she is to open a new establishment herself, she will need to appeal to her mostly male clientele.

Men are fickle, this Eliza knows all too well.

If I lure them in once, they'll be steady customers.

And Eliza knows once anyone tastes the sweet buns she offers, there will be a line out her door as well, albeit for a much different reason than the men who frequent Pearly's.

Eliza assesses her situation. She knows she must move quickly with her plans to open the café or she risks the reputation of being associated as one of Mrs. Brown's "girls." Of greater import, the forty-five dollars she possessed when she left Seattle has dwindled to sixteen. Her lease on the small café runs four dollars per week, paid in advance, plus another four for rent in eventual lodgings, and she owes Pearly seven. She pays a dollar each morning for egg pie and coffee at The Empire Café, and goes hungry the rest of the day. Eliza traverses the length of Skagway and peers into the storefronts. In addition to The Empire Café, Eliza counts three other bakeries: The Home, The German, and The Denver. Eliza cannot afford to frequent any of the bakeries regularly, except to survey the surroundings and make mental notes.

The Home Bakery caters to a late crowd. The German, well, I can't understand the proprietor. What's a Nussecken or a Bratapfel anyway? And the Denver . . . well, their muffins taste like cardboard.

Eliza counts and recounts her mere sixteen dollars, dollar by dollar and coin by coin. With that paltry amount, she needs to buy rudimentary supplies to start up: flour and yeast and coffee. Prices for goods alone skyrocket the further north one travels.

Highway robbery! And I need a sign made. A nice one at that. I can see it now. But what shall I call it? The Moonstone! Yes, The Moon-stone Café.

Eliza borrows cash from Shorty. She marks it on a new page in her ledger, under the initials: MC. Eliza targets the fifteenth of April as her opening day.

But what to wear for the day-in, day-out drudgery of baking? And what to wear when buying goods and tending to other business in this San Francisco of the north? She admires how Pearly, Rose, and Cilla present themselves to the public, despite the fact that the elder of the three is a madam and the younger two are likely prostitutes. Eliza has not paid mind to fashion for so long that she chides herself for vain thoughts.

But I need to join them, in looks anyway.

∽

"COME IN," PEARLY SAYS. HER BEDROOM DOOR GAPES AJAR. Eliza has been in Skagway for a week now, and she knows from the bottom of her gut there is no going back. She hesitates after she knocks, but pushes through the door to Pearly's opulent boudoir.

Wide swaths of rich brown brocade fabric circle Pearly's high four-poster bed. Layers of thick coverlets and gold-fringed pillows invite reclining there. The walls, a lighter cocoa color than the bed curtains, display mirrors of varying shapes and sizes, all framed in ornate gold. A large tufted divan sits positioned in front of the upstairs bay window, the window's casings also of the brown brocade, and tied back with gold tassels. A thick bear skin rug lounges at the end of the bed. Pearly sits in her nightdress on a plush bench in front of a large dressing table, sweeping her hair up into its elaborate style. Eliza focuses on the bearskin.

"I've been wondering if you could help," Eliza begins.

She pauses before continuing.

"It's just that I don't know the first thing about hairstyles. Or fashion."

Eliza blushes as she admits this self-evident fact.

"Why, of course, my dear! I wondered when you'd ever ask."

Two hours later, Eliza looks at her reflection and stifles a short cry. Her waist length rust-colored hair, first washed in a basin and then coated with egg yolks before the final rinse and towel dry, lays in wavy pleats on the crown of her head, with the remainder gathered up in a soft chignon at the nape of her neck. Eliza hardly recognizes herself, and squints to see herself even closer.

A long silence ensues as Eliza sits glued to the dressing table bench. Pearly busies herself cleaning up the mess they've made, and then pauses before her armoire and selects four day dresses. She spreads the dresses on the coverlets.

"Pick one, my dear. We will see about having another made for you at the end of the week."

Eliza chooses a pale blue day gown with an empire sash of

brown velvet. The square neckline seems risqué, but Eliza does not complain. She slips into the day dress while Pearly gathers the jumble of towels bunched on the floor. The gown, sized for a buxom woman several inches shorter than Eliza, falls lower on Eliza's chest than she's ever allowed, and reaches above her ankles. Eliza feels exposed. She returns to the dressing table and lowers herself onto the bench. She cannot help but stare at her reflection.

Pearly laughs. "That, my dear, is what we do."

"I haven't worn a gown since I was nineteen," Eliza says. "And that was near ten years ago."

She bites her lip; she has resolved not to reveal anything about her past. Of her heritage, hometown, and history, Eliza has decided to wipe the slate clean. Her grand plan relies on this fact. She must reinvent herself to survive in this new world.

"And why ever not, Lizzie?" Pearly asks. "Don't they wear gowns in San Francisco?"

Eliza scrambles for words. No one has ever called her Lizzie before. And she knows she's caught in a lie.

"Of course, but as a minister's wife . . ."

"Ah, now I see. You needn't say another word."

Eliza breathes out, and with the breath, her anxiety fades. Pearly bends over and gathers more towels into her arms.

"Did you love him, your husband?" Pearly asks. Her voice sounds muffled; she speaks from behind a mound of still damp towels.

Words catch in Eliza's throat; she can only dole out the barest details to be true to her promise to herself.

"I suppose not," Eliza says. "But it's nothing I've ever spoken about. To anyone."

Pearly tosses the towels into a basket by the dressing table and sits down on the bench next to Eliza.

"I was in love once," Pearly says. "He was ace-high, would have tied myself to him in an instant. And quite a lover, too."

Eliza reddens at the mention of a lover.

A lover. What a concept! And quite a lover, too.

"I met him back in '69, near thirty long years ago. He was a real looker, a Union Pacific man from Chicago. A bit offish. Met him in Nebraska, of all places.

"Funny thing, I never told him that I loved him, and he never told me that he loved me. But if that wasn't love, I don't know what love is."

Eliza has never had such an intimate discussion with any other woman, not even Ida. There were some topics never discussed, even between married women. But why not? Hadn't she challenged her own father about women having a voice? And didn't she talk like a man, to herself at least?

"What happened?"

Eliza surprises herself with the asking.

Now Pearly waits before answering.

"We had a falling out, you might say. It was sudden."

Pearly lapses into the past, her eyes clouded and distant.

"*'A man in a passion rides a mad horse.'* I've often wondered what became of him, but it couldn't have been good. You see, he killed a man, and I was a witness."

Eliza's eyes widen at Pearly's statement. Eliza knows that Pearly has what her aunt would call a "colorful past." That euphemism dredges up many unladylike qualities, and ones not talked about in polite company.

But murder! That is a topic best left to saloons and newspapers. Then again, Eliza reminds herself, *this is Alaska.*

She makes another note to herself: *Nothing here will surprise me ever again.*

"There is another Benjamin Franklin saying, the one

about judging others. Oh yes: *'He that would live in peace and at ease, must not speak all he knows, nor judge all he sees.'"*

Pearly does not respond. She continues to stare past Eliza in the mirror. Eliza tries to meet Pearly's gaze, but is unable to wake Pearly from her reverie.

"Yes," Pearly says, after what seems to Eliza an eternity.

"I often wonder what became of Steiner."

‍⁀‍

20

APRIL 1, 1898

Day of Fools. Send letter to Mother soon.

The next morning Eliza wakes early. She burrows in her soft mattress and spins the details backwards and forwards in her mind. Nebraska, the railroad, Chicago, the span of years—it all makes sense. After stitching the details together, the coincidence, she thinks, is uncanny, but nevertheless, real.

Eliza rests in her downy bed, devising a plan. She won't mention Steiner right away to Pearly; this she knows for certain. Plus, there's the slight possibility that the Steiner Pearly described is not the Steiner Eliza knows. Steiner is a common German name, and many Germans traveled west. If the time proves right, Eliza will delve deeper into Steiner's identity, asking Pearly pointed questions under the guise of innocence. But that day will have to wait. And despite her protestations to the obvious, Eliza cannot say with utmost certainty that the man is one and the same.

Eliza rouses from her bed, and her reflection again startles her.

What a transformation! It's as if a magician conjured up a beautiful woman in the place of a plain Jane!

She hardly recognizes herself. She needs to study the intricate hairstyle and practice over and over again to achieve the same result. Eliza remembers in detail her conversation just the day before with Pearly.

The mention of Steiner had thrown her off. She mulls Pearly's words over in her head.

And quite a lover, too!

Eliza tries to push Steiner from her mind.

She thinks again of the thin shred of circumstance that pointed her away from pursuing Steiner's bold advances that long-ago day when he last visited her cabin. She had refused his final pleading to consummate the engagement. He had left in a hurry, and took the garnet with him.

There's more'n a few skeletons hiding in his closet, if'n you know what I mean. No, I need to find my own way, and if along the rugged pathway I meet a man who fulfills my longings, so be it.

She stands long and lean in front of the full-length mirror and studies the updo from every angle. She turns to the right, and then the left, and then looks back over her shoulder, like the Gibson Girl in the ladies' magazines. Eliza, never one for vanity, determines to make the effort. Besides, she likes what she sees, a confident, attractive woman about to strike gold.

She descends the stairs to the parlor. No one is about. She gazes into the various storefronts on the two blocks to the Empire Café. She sits at a table close to the window and orders the usual.

In an hour, I will sign the papers leasing the café.

Eliza can't believe her luck. She almost pinches herself. For a second time in two weeks, providence has shined its beacon on her, first with the found ticket for her passage north, and now again.

"Fortune's smiling on you," Edwards says. "Hasn't been but a week since these doors were shuttered. Owners headed north to Dawson, didn't take more than what they could carry on their backs. Plan to cook in a tent, they do."

He shakes his head as he tells Eliza the story.

The café's location, between Fifth and Sixth streets, right on Broadway, couldn't be better for foot traffic. What little Eliza knows of New York's Broadway from newspapers makes her laugh; Skagway's Broadway is nothing more than a wide muddied street lined with hastily built boardwalks and false storefronts. But she doesn't complain.

The layout of the establishment pleases Eliza. In the front room, a large planked counter runs almost the full length of the bakery's western wall, and behind the counter, shelves of varying heights and depths line the wooden walls. Eliza calculates the space. She will display her cakes and breads and pies on the shelves behind the counter; cookies and doughnuts will fit in small wicker baskets on the worn wooden counter. Six tables and eighteen mismatched chairs sit empty in the front room of the café waiting for customers. Two chairs wobble when Eliza tests them for stability.

"Can't have the customers falling on their backsides," Eliza says. She checks her tongue. She almost says "asses." Eliza scrapes the chairs to the side of the room near the counter. She will see about fixing the wobbly legs before she opens for business.

Lester Edwards, Esq. shows Eliza the kitchen, a cramped anteroom several steps behind the counter and hidden from view from the front room by a cloth curtain strung above the door jamb. A single rear door exits to the alleyway. The kitchen contains not one, but two cookstoves, and a center pine table, worn at the edges. An assortment of kitchenware and utensils had been left helter-skelter in the kitchen when the previous tenants up and left in a hurry. Mouse droppings populate the top of the table.

"I'll take it," Eliza says.

Edwards pats Eliza's behind. She moves two steps to the left.

Ass.

"Might have one more enticement to help sweeten the deal," Edwards says. "The previous tenants left in such a hurry they went and left all their furnishings upstairs in their lodgings."

Edwards cocks his head in the direction of the upstairs apartment.

"Give it to you for a song, little lady, a song."

Eliza lets Lester Edwards, Esq. go first up the rickety wooden stairs to the second floor. She eyes the room from the doorway. She does not feel comfortable being alone with her prospective landlord.

The lodgings are quite small, but outfitted with a suitable pot-bellied stove, bed, bed stand, desk, and oversized chair. The only drawback Eliza notices is that one cannot access the upstairs apartment from the bakery itself. To get to the lodgings, one would need to walk out the bakery's back door into the space that borders Jap Alley or exit the front door of the café and walk around to the back of the building by traversing a cramped space between crude buildings.

"An extra four dollars per week, you say?"

An ample woodpile lays stacked at the building's rear.

"And will you be supplying the wood for the stoves?"

"For a lady such as yourself, I'd be obliged," Edwards says. "It'll be an extra dollar and a half per week, though. To keep the cordwood split and stacked, that is. You'll have to arrange for a boy to haul the wood inside."

Eliza lets that comment pass. She can split and stack. And her arms are as strong as any boy's.

Lines of rough outhouses cram the alleyway. Eliza decides to purchase a small lock for the one directly across the alley from the back door of The Moonstone Café. She has put up with enough inconveniences over the past three years, but this one shred of privacy must remain hers and hers alone in this world of wild and rowdy men.

Eliza pays Edwards and makes an excuse to take her leave. She walks two short blocks to Taylor's Drygoods to price provisions. First, vinegar and rags. Next, a large coffee pot. The vinegar and rags don't strap her purse; the coffee pot sets her back, and strips her meager finances to the bone. But her most powerful weapon is her recipe file, and she guards the file with her life, carrying the file, as well as her small purse, with her at all times.

Shorty had warned Eliza that thieving was rampant. Eliza cannot risk her recipe file landing in dirty hands. She reviews her precious recipes in her mind, culling out ones too dear or too time consuming. She needs recipes that are cheap and fast, like quick breads, doughnuts. And of course, breads, cookies, sweet buns. Just the basics. She wonders if luxuries like bananas reach Skagway. Otherwise, nut breads will have to do.

ᑯᑊᑐᑯᑊᑐᑯᑊᑐᑯᑊᑐ

BANANA NUT BREAD

Cream butter, size of three large eggs, and one and
one-half teacups sugar; add three eggs, one at a time.
Add two mashed overripe bananas and mix thoroughly.

In separate bowl, mix a generous three teacups flour
with two teaspoonfuls saleratus.
Add pinch of salt.
Add dry ingredients and one teacup soured cream in
intervals to dry mixture.
Add a handful of nuts, preferably shelled walnut,
if you choose.
Pour into greased baking pan and bake until golden.
The bread is dense, and filling.

꙰꙰꙰꙰꙰꙰꙰

ELIZA SPENDS TWO DAYS SCRUBBING THE MOONSTONE CAFÉ from top to bottom, front to back. She begins in the front room and works her way to the rear of the shop. She scrapes the small round wooden tables to one side of the front room and stacks the chairs atop the tables. With a long-handled duster she wipes down the walls from ceiling to floor, and then climbs a sturdy ladder to wash the walls with vinegar and water. Rivulets of vinegar water run down her forearms and into her hair.

I smell like a pickle!

When the walls shine, Eliza turns her attention to the tables and chairs. The tables show wear, and several are inscribed with initials and dates carved with dull pocketknives. She runs her fingers across the letters and dates, *EJM, 11/1/97*, and another *Jas. T. Thompson*. She wipes the tables clean and repeats the process with the multi-colored chairs. Last, she runs the vinegar-soaked rags around the whole of the wooden floor, crawling on her hands and knees to reach every corner of the front room. When she finishes the task, she stands full height and cleans her spectacles on the edge of her apron.

I've got myself a café.

On the third day, and after Eliza is pleased with the results of her labors, she walks to Taylor's Drygoods and opens the creaky wooden door. A bell tinkles as she enters. She has twenty dollars of borrowed money in her purse. Shorty seems to know when Eliza's purse is running low.

"A wee bit to get you going, little missy. No hurry to make the return."

Familiar smells greet her at the door: coffee, yeast, and licorice. Eliza measures out twenty cups of flour and dumps the flour into two cloth sacks. She secures the tops of the sacks with rough twine. She moves down the aisle and next scoops out ten pounds of sugar and then smaller sacks of saleratus, salt, and yeast. She digs a metal scoop into the raisin bin and extracts two small shovelfuls of golden raisins. Eliza places her goods on the counter and returns to the back of the shop for butter, eggs, and milk, housed in the ice room at the rear of the establishment.

She pays a boy to deliver the goods.

"Come to the back door, do you hear? I'll not have deliveries to the front."

The boy arrives forty minutes later with her groceries on a worn travois.

"That's it, then," Eliza says after the boy unloads copious sacks and packages and *plops* them onto her kitchen worktable.

"Come back tomorrow and I'll have a doughnut for you."

ᑲᓍᑲᓍᑲᓍᑲᓍᑲᓍ

GLAZED DOUGHNUTS

*In medium bowl, mix one-quarter teacup sugar and
one and one-quarter teacups warm milk, add three
teaspoonfuls yeast and allow mixture to sit until yeast
starts to ferment.*

In second bowl, beat two large eggs and add in one and one-quarter teacups melted butter, whisk constantly.

Add egg/butter mixture to sugar/milk/yeast mixture.

In third bowl, mix four teacups flour and pinch of salt; slowly incorporate into mixture. Mix vigorously for five minutes.

Place dough in lightly oiled bowl, cover with muslin tea towel and let set overnight in cool, dark spot. The next morning, move to warm spot, let rise for two hours. Turn out dough on to floured surface and roll out to finger width.

Use small teacup to cut out doughnuts, and shot glass to cut center holes. Remove center holes and transfer doughnuts and center holes to floured baking sheet. Cover doughnuts lightly with muslin tea towels and let rise again for two hours.

Drop doughnuts into pot filled with lard. Doughnuts will float and expand. Use metal spatula to flip doughnuts and remove from lard when doughnuts crisp. Remove to newspaper to cool.

Repeat with center holes.

Glaze with confectioner's sugar dissolved in vanilla and a dropful of warm milk.

༺ᄼᄽᄼᄽᄼᄽᄼᄽ༻

ON HER FIRST DAY OF BUSINESS, FRIDAY THE FIFTEENTH OF April, Eliza sells out before noon. A crush of clients devours her delicacies. She wonders how she can possibly bake more in one day. Instead, she adjusts her expectations.

Looks like more doughnuts. And more cookies! I will have to work like a dog here. And it won't be long until I need to hire some counter help.

Later that evening, even though she is bone-tired and her eyes ache, Eliza pens a letter home.

Dear Mother,

You must forgive me for the long silence. It will no doubt surprise you to hear that I have decamped from lonely Cypress Island and have joined the throng north to Alaska. Surely you have heard of the rush of men (and a few women) who have traveled to Alaska in search of gold.

Alaska is just as you might think, very cold, even in the spring, and sparsely populated. The wildlife in these environs would astound you. Why, black bears roam the streets and rattle in the trash bins at night. But I will not trouble you with this information. It would be difficult to imagine a bear walking down the streets of Columbia, so I might as well be talking nonsense.

I have opened a bakery here, just this very day. I let a wooden storefront in the center of Skagway, not six blocks from the wharves. You must tell Margaret and Mae that there are a hundred men to every woman here. Neither Margaret nor Mae is ever in want of attention, I would think. Has Mae married as yet? And what of Margaret? I long for news of them.

I've got a repertoire of baked goods that seems to appeal to the miners. In addition to pies and breads and cakes, I have fashioned a recipe heavy laden with nuts and currants (when I can purchase them) that I'm calling the Miner's Snickerdoodle. Why, on my first day of business today the goodies flew off my shelves! I am in want of more kitchen utensils and enamel bowls. If only I had a place to purchase such. The shelves at the hardware are stocked with implements for the miner's life, not the housewife's life. Not that I am a housewife, but it would be like Christmas if I saw even a fraction of the bowls and utensils that are available at any hardware shop anywhere but here.

But I go on too long! I wanted you to know of my circumstance, and send my love, etc. etc. etc. to Margaret and Mae. I can be reached at: E. Waite (you may be surprised to read that I have assumed our family name again), c/o The Moonstone Café, Skagway, Alaska.

Yours truly, in familial love,
Eliza

JUNE 8, 1898

Cloudy. Cool. Coffee prices skyrocketing.

Bells and whistles. Hoof beats, hammers, hawkers. A constant murmur of voices, and bawdy laughter. For one so attuned to only the sounds of nature, Skagway bursts upon Eliza's senses like a runaway train. For the first couple of months, Eliza can't help but notice the incessant noise. She is surrounded by men. Not one familiar face enters The Moonstone Café. Every now and again she half expects to see Steiner, or Indian John, or even Mad Virgil and Samuel in Skagway, but every face is new.

Some men crawl and others race through Skagway. Some take their time to refresh appetites for women and vittles before heading up White Pass toward the Yukon. Others barely stop to piss. Business is brisk. By early June, Skagway boasts more than four hundred merchants: bankers, barbers, blacksmiths, and builders. Dentists, doctors, and drygoods. Hotels, nineteen in all. Launderers. Meat markets, and even a musical instrument maker. Outfitters on every corner. Painters, photographers. Saloons, sometimes two to a corner. Tobacconists: a polite cover for whorehouses.

Why, there are more whorehouses in this town than I can count.

Eliza works fourteen hours per day. Breads, cakes, and cookies fly off the shelves. She hardly has time to sleep before waking up at dawn to start over. Her hands are strong and smooth.

The railroad men have now arrived in Skagway, with plans to build the new White Pass and Yukon Railroad right up the middle of Broadway, north and over the mountain pass toward the interior. The furor has turned the muddied, crowded street into an even muddier and more crowded thoroughfare. The incessant sound of sledgehammers, picks, and men yelling out orders renders the atmosphere chaotic. Eliza overhears plenty of grumbles about the new railway slicing through the heart of town, but she keeps her opinions to herself. More men equals more business. Profits swell her bank account, and that is a welcome prospect. She tailors her baked goods accordingly. More cakes, fewer pies. Eliza works in as little vanilla as possible to preserve her precious supply. She breathes in the intoxicating smell as she turns the batter. Vanilla reaches her nose in direct contrast to all the repulsive smells on Skagway streets—ever-present smoke, grease, manure, wet wool, tobacco, exotic Japanese cooking.

"Met Sugi yet?" Pearly asks. "Only madam catering in the Jap trade. They're over at Jap Alley, west of State, between Fifth and Sixth, not far from your place. Certainly you've seen her. I'd love to play with her hair. Voluminous and jet black. And you should see her dresses! She wears the most expensive silks. Can't pin her down, she walks quicker than a polecat. Perfect English, when you chance to talk.

"Talk is the Jap girls perform at the top of the line. Heard it first-hand more than once. I'd love to be a fly on those walls. Might garner some secrets from the Orient. Don't mean to brag, but I've done it a thousand times, and I always want to know new tricks."

Eliza can't fathom pretending to like the sex act, especially with a stranger. But Rose and Cilla work every night, and rarely see the same man twice, unless he's one of the regulars, or "the regs," as Pearly calls them. She rattles off a string of names, some familiar now to Eliza.

"One of the best specimens of the male sex to ever darken my door," Pearly says. "You've seen him, town surveyor, one of the regs. Frank Reid's his name. Can't get enough of Cilla. Hmmmm. Can't get enough of him, if you know what I mean."

Pearly puts her left hand to her groin and gives a quick yank. Eliza blushes, looks down.

Pearly laughs from her gut. Eliza admires Pearly, despite Eliza's indifference to the trade.

"Rose gets stablemen, mostly. And railroad men. Saloon-keepers, too, those that want a little more than what their dancing girls offer. Hell, we had near ten thousand men come through Skagway last year alone. I think Rose knew all but one or two of them."

Rose flaunts her womanhood in ways that amaze Eliza. Eliza admires the way Rose sashays, and the quickness of her ready smile. Cilla looks steely in comparison. Cilla reminds Eliza of the snow-capped mountains lining Skagway's boundaries, silent and regal. Cilla entertains ragged mountain men, fancy-dressed shopkeepers, confidence men, and swindlers peopling Skagway's muddy streets. In contrast to Rose, Eliza has never seen Cilla smile.

Eliza does the math. Every encounter equals two dollars, and with a certain tip, two dollars and fifty cents. With four men per day, a member of the demimonde could earn ten dollars per day, or sixty dollars per week, excepting Sundays.

Sixty dollars per week equals two hundred and forty dollars per month. In Skagway's economy, that sum would never be in doubt. From a purely business standpoint, Eliza calculates the cost of offering her body to men for pleasure. But she knows in her heart of hearts that prostitution would only satisfy men and her pocketbook. Eliza watches the dregs of humanity that lumber up and down the lawless streets, and shudders at the thought of sharing a bed with a stranger.

Eliza does not have a crystal ball, but a gnawing ache inside sidetracks her. *Maybe in this sea of men, one will rise to the top, like cream in a milk bottle,* she thinks. In the meantime, Eliza has hours of baking to go, and a shop full of men waiting for her to open the door at six a.m. sharp.

At the end of the week, Eliza taps on Pearly's door again.

"Don't know where you've drummed up the cash, my dear. But who am I to ask questions?"

Pearly works from a well-worn set of patterns, and adjusts accordingly to each customer. Eliza is by far the tallest woman Pearly has ever sewed for, and probably one of the thinnest. Eliza's bustline is minimal, but Pearly uses tricks she's learned over many years of dressmaking to fill dresses out to a woman's best advantage.

"You may undress behind the curtain. Just leave your bloomers on."

Eliza has never been naked, or nearly naked, in front of a woman before. As she lifts her camisole over her head, she notices that her small nipples harden in the chill. Eliza runs her hand over several sets of fancy bloomers. She has never seen, let alone touched, such finery. She fingers a plush cream-colored robe that hangs on a brass hook behind the curtain's wall. She takes a deep breath before she steps tentatively out from behind the silk curtain.

"Over here," Pearly says, and motions with her head to a round platform in front of a full-length mirror on the far wall. Her lips sport straight pins and in her hands she holds a measuring tape and a small pad and pencil. A pair of scissors and a rough muslin cloth perch on the platform's edge; the muslin drapes in disarray and cascades onto the floor by Pearly's feet. Pearly sticks the straight pins into a pincushion attached to her wrist and eyes Eliza's figure.

"Hmmm," she says, and then, "Yes."

As Pearly works, Eliza examines her near naked body in the full-length mirror. Pearly's hands fly around Eliza's torso and hips, first measuring Eliza's bustline and waist, and after notating the measurements on the pad, pulling the tape tight across Eliza's hips. Eliza stays silent as Pearly registers the measurements and talks to herself. As she works, Pearly's fingers brush Eliza's skin and Eliza feels a tingle up her spine. Eliza stands in her nakedness and begins to feel more comfortable with her body, and with Pearly. But soon she shivers in the late afternoon chill.

After ten minutes, Pearly puts her measuring notions down.

"There. Go and put my robe on to keep warm. We'll look at some material and sketch out some possibilities before you go."

Pearly opens the oversized trunk at the foot of her bed and paws through layers of fabric until she finds a dark flannel. She turns, goes across the room to her dresser, and opens the bottom drawer. The drawer contains yards of cotton sheen fabric in plentiful colors. Pearly studies the stash carefully and draws out a dusky rose-colored piece. She tosses the fabric over her left arm and opens the next drawer above to select matching trim.

"You'll look swell in this color," Pearly says, using one of those newfangled masculine words heard on the streets.

Eliza feels the soft material and eyes the trim.

"This won't be too dear?" she asks. "I've not worn such finery in a long while."

"A woman's got to show off her curves in this place," Pearly says. "Don't worry, the plaid will be dull. But this rose! I have ideas for this dress."

The front door opens, and Pearly looks at the clock on her dressing table. It is just five, and she has other business to which to attend. Eliza dresses quickly as Pearly straightens up the room. As Eliza passes Pearly, Pearly leans in and gives Eliza a peck on the cheek.

Startled, Eliza blushes a deep rose.

"That's the ticket," Pearly says.

"Got to keep those cheeks rouged to match the dress. You'll look like a stunner, Lizzie. Mark my words; you won't recognize yourself when I'm through with you! Why, as soon as this dress is done we should march you right over to Case & Draper's or to E. A. Hegg's for a proper photograph. Never know when a suitor might ask for your portrait. You're quite the looker, my dear. I'd die for that hair."

22

⌒

Rain. Order two new aprons.

*K*ate Chopin!"

Eliza picks up a slim volume from an array of ladies' magazines on Pearly's parlor table and turns it over in her hands.

Pearly looks over from where she stands planted by the foot of the stairs, her hand on the new electric lever that flicks up and down.

"Do you know her?"

Pearly flicks the electric lever up. Parlor lights flash on.

"I've read some of her magazine pieces. Actually, she's from St. Louis, not far from where my people . . ."

Eliza trails off.

Have I said too much? I've not told anyone I'm from Missoura.

Pearly pushes the lever down. The parlor settles into semi-darkness. Pearly doesn't pick up on Eliza's comment.

"Lou brought quite a number of books from Seattle in her luggage. I'm not a reader, but Lou sure is."

"Borrow it?"

"Why, Lizzie, you do amaze me sometimes. I'd never have thought you'd read such radical writings. Full of illicit thoughts, or so I've been told. Lou's finished it already. Left it for me, but I've got no time for reading. You go ahead. Take it."

Pearly flips the lever to the up position again. The parlor illuminates. Eliza tucks the volume in her satchel.

What wonders will this new electric invention open up? Eliza thinks. *It won't be long before kitchens will be electrified. Electric lights! Electric mixers! Maybe even electric ovens!*

Eliza bristles with excitement about this newest luxury, and blushes at other thoughts that race through her mind as she walks back to the Moonstone. *The Awakening.* Eliza likes the sound of the title. And Eliza likes Lou, another of Pearly's girls, now housed in one of the two downstairs rooms at Mrs. Brown's. The "trade," as Pearly calls it, has heated up.

Eliza hears a hushed sob as she closes the heavy parlor door behind her. She looks left, then right.

"Why, Lou!"

"It's nothing, you need not bother."

Lou's head bends forward, her sandy hair unloosed from its barrettes and clips.

"Can I help?"

Lou raises her chin and looks at Eliza from behind blackened eyelids.

"Lou! Whatever has happened?"

"Perils of my line, you might say. Not that you'd know."

Lou descends into low sobs. Rain pummels her hair. Eliza notices Lou's coat is threadbare, and her elbows jut out at right angles as she wipes her swollen eyelids.

"You'd never know about it, you and all you high society ladies. You don't know what it's like to get a walloping from a fella, now do you?"

Eliza reaches for Lou's soaked shoulder. Lou pulls away. "Just leave me alone, will you? I'll take care of myself."

Eliza starts to say something, but refrains.

We are all of us wounded.

Eliza continues up Broadway, careful to raise her skirt above the ankle as she crosses the muddy street. She raises her umbrella high above her head and repositions it to ward off the driving rain. Her hands are cold. She blows warm air on her free hand before switching the umbrella to the other hand. Her boots sink into the mire, and the scent of horse dung clings to the leather long after she brushes the caked mud off later in the day.

Broadway teems with activity, even at this early hour. Eliza crisscrosses the street twice, once to avoid a team of horses dragging a sledge full of railroad equipment, and another to peek into Mr. E. A. Hegg's portrait studio. She determines to make an appointment this week. And she can well afford it. But there's a note on the door: Closed until further notice.

Hmph. I'll check again another time.

She forgets about Lou by the time she reaches the Moonstone.

Eliza devours *The Awakening* later that night, and all in one sitting. She relates to so many of Kate Chopin's heroines. And this Mrs. Pontellier! Eliza resolves to re-read the slim volume again within the week.

And all thanks to Pearly!

Eliza knows Pearly is quite an unlikely friend. Her only other friend had been a devout Methodist. And they had never talked of intimacies.

But Pearly is, dare I say it, a dear friend to me. I wonder how else she will enlighten me.

Eliza anticipates her visits with Pearly at Mrs. Brown's

Boarding House, and never misses a Sunday, the only day of the week that Rose, Cilla, and Lou don't take company.

At first, Eliza had felt uncomfortable gracing the parlor of a bordello with Pearly, but after several months of lonely moonless nights in her lodgings above the Moonstone, Eliza gladly accepted Pearly's offer, and the visits have become a staple on weekend nights, and not just on Sundays anymore.

Eliza knocks at Pearly's door most Friday and Saturday nights now. Shorty swills with the boys, and Pearly craves Eliza's companionship. And Shorty always escorts Eliza home around closing time before going back to Pearly's. It's what Shorty calls "a swell arrangement all around." His Scottish burr elongates the *r's* and his eyebrows arch like a cat's above his deep-set and penetrating eyes. And why would Eliza refuse, when Pearly offers titillating conversation and warming aperitifs?

Eliza dulls to the goings-on in the upstairs bedrooms on Friday and Saturday nights.

Who am I to judge another?

When customers arrive, Eliza bends to her knitting; she avoids eye contact with all but most. A heavy *stomp* on the rear staircase signals a customer departing straight into the alleyway; within a quarter hour an ever-flippant Rose or regal-esque Cilla descends the inner stairway to welcome new clients, whom Pearly has regaled with bawdy stories while plying them with weak whiskey, one dollar per shot. Eliza recognizes many of the regs; they are regs of hers as well.

Men from Soapy's gang make beelines to Rose's and Cilla's rooms, but Eliza never sees Soapy himself.

A real loner, Eliza thinks. *And I've heard tell he has a wife and three children back in St. Louis. So why is he here in Skagway?*

Eliza doesn't have answers to her questions. Soapy avoids

the Moonstone, too, but Eliza knows the answer as to why on that point. Frank Reid and his cronies preside over the Moonstone's front room, and from what Eliza hears, Reid and Smith mix like oil and water.

A scuffle at the Empire Café last week emphasized the fact that tensions are rife. The air bristles with tension, and not a day goes by without an incident. Theft. Graft. Even murder. Eliza stays at the edge of the troubles. She chooses instead to ply men with sugary treats.

Eliza's never spoken to Soapy Smith. She nods to him whenever he passes, and he raises his hat. There are so few women in Skagway that it's no wonder she's noticed, she thinks.

And now that I'm a looker! Eliza chortles. *Me? A looker?!*

"Money and good manners make the gentleman," her aunt used to say.

Her aunt's words ring in her ear, but Eliza thinks this adage shallow.

From what I hear, Jefferson Randolph Smith is no gentleman. He's on the run from something, or someone. I've got a bad feeling about him.

23

JULY 4, 1898

Sunny, warm. Our nation's birthday.
And mine! Parade and picnic today.

"Happy Independence Day all around!"

Eliza hears Shorty's now familiar voice outside the café. Eliza wipes her hands on her soiled apron and unties the muslin strings. She tosses the apron over a chair back and joins Shorty and Pearly on the porch of the Moonstone. She places a plate of small cakes, cookies, and sweet rolls on the bench just outside the front entrance.

"Grand day for a parade," she says, glancing at the cloudless sky. The Fourth of July parade, scheduled to begin at three, is running late. Kids whoop up and down Broadway in anticipation; flags wave lazily in the afternoon breeze. A bunting on the storefront across Broadway barely rustles, its red, white, and blue colors bright and bold. Eliza closes up shop and joins Pearly.

"Sweet roll, anyone?"

In the near distance Jefferson Randolph Smith rides into view. As the self-proclaimed parade marshal, Smith sits tall atop a dappled grey stallion. The horse whinnies under Smith's control, its flared nostrils and bobbing head barely managed. Smith prances down Broadway, and stops every few yards to talk to onlookers. He stops briefly in front of The Moonstone Café and tips his hat to Eliza and Pearly. The moment seems suspended in time. Eliza focuses on Smith's face.

I wonder what his story really is, Eliza thinks. *There is always more to a man than what meets the eye. There's more'n a few skeletons hiding in his closet, if 'n you know what I mean.*

The women nod in return. Shorty rises and makes a mock salute. Smith dips his head in return.

Behind Smith, newsies hawk the daily rag. Eliza hands out cookies and raisin buns to the ruffians as they march by.

"Thank you, Ma'am."

"Mighty thanks!"

"Sweetest buns in Skagway!"

Charlie Adams, the leader of the pack, does a seductive little dance aimed at Pearly.

"Get on with you!" Pearly laughs.

Behind the newsies, The Orphan's League float brings Eliza and Pearly to their feet, and two marching bands draw loud applause to the beat of John Phillip Sousa. A lone cloud blocks the sun for a moment. Eliza puts her hand to her forehead to shield the glare and squints to see who is coming next.

Everyone loves a parade!

"Wish we had a formation of suffragettes marching today. Would love to wear a bright yellow sash and sashay right down the middle of Broadway," Eliza says. "It's been eight long years since the formation of the National American Woman Suffrage Association, and we've only got four states rallied behind the vote so far. We've got a long way to go."

"If you were to march down Broadway today, you'd get sashayed right out of town!" Shorty laughs.

"You wait, Mr. Richardson! One of these days I'll do it! We've got the vote in Colorado and Utah and Idaho already."

"And don't forget Wyoming," Pearly says. "I was there when women first got the vote. Back in '69 that was. Can't believe it's been that long. Rollicking time."

Eliza flashes Pearly a conspiratorial grin.

"If and when Alaska becomes a state, we'll be the first ones out there marching. Me and your lady friend here."

"I have no doubt about that, little missy. No doubt about that at all."

The Alaska Guard, a rag-tag group of Civil War veterans, passes by in solemn formation, a leg missing here, an arm in a perpetual sling there. The mood sombers as the men trickle past. Eliza notices some of the regs along the route.

"Hard life, some of the regs."

John Brook's Packers bring up the rear, and in their wake, the distinct tang of horse manure. Eliza is sorry the parade is over so quickly.

After the parade, for a moment, silence.

Pop! Pop! Pop!

Eliza flinches instinctively.

Gunshots?

She shakes off the sudden chill that has run up her spine. Fireworks are underway, and a town picnic over at Captain Moore's.

"Give me just a second."

Eliza locks up the Moonstone and closes the door behind her. She checks the knob. When she re-emerges on the porch, Shorty is gone.

"Always in a hurry, that man."

Pearly and Eliza walk arm in arm to the picnic, the arc of the sun high in the sky.

"Today is my birthday," Eliza says.

Pearly tightens her grip on Eliza's arm.

"Well, Lawdy Be! Wouldn't you know we've arranged a party for you, right here in li'l ol' Skagway!"

Eliza's resolve melts like a pat of butter when she sees the mountains of food prepared on the buffet: cold roast, potato salad, corn on the cob, and what seems like miles of Harriet Pullen's pies. For once, Eliza is out of the stifling kitchen. Fresh air swirls around her, its scent as fresh as she's ever noticed. She looks toward the Sawtooth Mountains, capped in snow even at the height of summer.

I must walk more often, Eliza thinks. *I must get out into this grand place and explore. Most days I don't get past the kitchen!*

"Look, Lizzie! That's what we kids used to do in Omaha! We just loved the Fourth of July."

Pearly steers Eliza around. In a near field, men and boys pony up for relay races and three-legged races. Eliza notices Mayor Charles Sperry commanding his own conversation with some of her regs, Frank Reid, Si Tanner, and Jesse Murphy. Their demeanor does not match the lightness of the day.

"My turn!"

"No, mine!

Pearly and Eliza laugh as they watch fifteen or twenty children scramble for pennies in a hay pile. Their screams of delight pierce the afternoon air. Two older girls toss beanbags under a maple tree in Captain Moore's front yard. Eliza fills her plate.

"Quite a spread here!"

"The church women outdoing themselves again."

Pearly winks at Eliza.

"You are positively wicked, you know that!"

"Got to keep up my reputation."

Eliza and Pearly walk to a picnic table at the far edge of the lawn and sit. Mayor Sperry mounts an improvised platform and shouts to the group assembled in the yard. Some of the men grumble and walk away from the platform and over to the maple. Pipe and cigarette smoke circle above their heads. A low hum underscores the mayor's impromptu speech.

"Citizens of Skagway! It's my pleasure to welcome you all to this harmonious gathering . . ."

Children scamper through the throng and grab for melting ice cream pops.

". . . and a privilege to welcome the governor of our great territory of Alaska, John Brady, to our little hamlet . . ."

Light applause wafts across the lawn. A group of women has organized a scavenger hunt for the little ones, and a beehive of children scatters. They run across the lawn and around the maple, to the rear of the house, and even under picnic benches before returning, breathless, with treasures of every kind—pinecones, feathers, and maple leaves—before collapsing into a heap.

". . . riches for all . . ."

"Ugh," Pearly says. "Riches for some, maybe less for most. Bunch of malarkey."

Malarkey is one of Pearly's newfangled phrases.

"Why, hello Mrs. Brown."

Shorty plops his plate onto the table and sits next to Pearly. He pinches her backside as he sits.

"You are both wicked. Just wicked," Eliza says.

Pearly collapses in laughter.

". . . and in a few month's time we will be known as a shining city on a hill . . ."

"Yeah, except that we're on the flats," Shorty interrupts.

Men laugh.

". . . and will be the envy of all the world."

Captain Moore moves to the edge of the lawn at the conclusion of the speech. Harriet Pullen, who has been chatting with another woman at the edge of the grandstand, hurries across the lawn to catch up with Moore. She uses an opulent fan to swish away mosquitoes.

Eliza makes eye contact with Moore as the duo passes.

"Thanks ever so much for hosting this grand party," Eliza says.

She directs her comments at Moore and nods to Harriet Pullen, Skagway's copious pie baker.

Can't get too cozy with the competition.

❧

THE NEXT MORNING ELIZA WAKES EARLY AS USUAL, DRESSES, and hurries down to the kitchen. Her routine falls just short of the chaotic, and by six a.m. the humidity in the cramped kitchen rises. Four loaves of bread and two pies sit cooling at the far end of the plank table; small mounds of Miner's Snickerdoodles wait for their turn in the oven.

Charlie Adams pokes his nose through the back door just before opening.

"Go on, don't need any beggars this morning," Eliza says, looking cross.

"I didn't come for any goodies, Ma'am. I have this here for you."

Eliza wipes her hands on her apron and takes the small package proffered from Charlie's dirty hands.

"What?"

"It's from Miss Pearly. She said it's for your birthday."

Charlie turns to leave.

"Wait. I don't have any cookies ready as yet, but you be sure to come back at closing and I'll save a snickerdoodle for you."

Eliza takes a moment to inspect the small package. The wrapping is of the finest quality, a white-on-white pattern encased with a dark pink satin ribbon formed into a full bow. She strokes the smooth satin and hesitates to open the package. Her resolve is weak.

Nestled inside the white box and under a layer of white tissue, a gold locket rests on a small white pillow. Eliza gasps. She has never owned such a fine piece of jewelry. Her wedding ring had been of the cheapest silver, and that she sold happily in Whatcom, although for a pittance. And she never even tried Steiner's garnet. She draws the box closer and notices the delicate filigree. She reaches into the box and picks up the locket, a perfectly shaped heart.

A banging on the front door rouses Eliza from her fixation on the locket. She places the box on a nearby shelf and quickly fastens the locket around her neck. She rushes the full length of the café and unbolts the door. It is six a.m. straight up.

24

July 6, 1898

Market day.

Thick apricot-colored juice spills from the corner of Eliza's mouth. She savors the sweetness. A peach!

She had spied the plump peach at Taylor's earlier that morning, the last in the box. The aroma had tantalized her from an aisle away. Peaches, or plums, or pears made their way to Skagway infrequently.

And the prices!

Eliza remembers many Sunday dinners in her childhood ending with an elaborate peach pie for dessert. The plethora of peaches in Missouri made peach pie mundane. But here, in Skagway, Eliza knows the worth of this type of gold.

What I could make with a peach!

In her lapse, she hears a shuffle. Harriet Pullen bustles up the far aisle, her basket full.

"Mrs. Pullen!"

Eliza maneuvers to the end of the produce aisle and marches toward the peach basket. Mrs. Pullen looks up, adjusts her pince-nez.

"Mrs. Waite. A pleasure."

Eliza moves toward Mrs. Pullen, her rear bumped up against the produce rack.

"A fine afternoon. I often think I should use Taylor's as my home address, seeing as I'm here most every day."

Eliza reaches behind her, blindly feeling for the fuzzed skin.

"Have you been receiving mail here? I haven't seen a letter for you."

"Oh no, of course not."

Why Harriet Pullen knows whether or not she's received a letter is a mystery. Of course no one has seen any letter addressed to Eliza come through in the sacks of mail delivered to this outpost of the world.

"But if I did . . ."

Eliza's fingers feel the familiar downy covering and she clasps her hand around the overripe piece of fruit. She barely squeezes and knows instinctively that the peach is past its prime. In Columbia, she would have passed over this specimen and hunted for another. She pulls her hand closer to her skirt.

"Have you ever seen such a lovely day?"

Eliza tilts her head toward the upper window. Mrs. Pullen follows her gaze. The paned window high above the produce bins is rimmed with soot. With eyes averted, Eliza slips the prized peach into her basket and leaves the licking of her fingers until Mrs. Pullen has moved on.

Happiness knows no bounds, she thinks.

❧

THREE DAYS LATER, THE MOOD IN SKAGWAY CHANGES abruptly. Eliza overhears Frank Reid talking to some of the regs. A new face is among them. She overhears the word "doctor."

A doctor! Isn't he quite the gentleman.

"There's been a heist, boys. And this time, it's a big one. Fellow by the name of Stewart lost his drawers at Jeff Smith's Parlor this morning. Doesn't look like he lost it fair and square."

Reid's profile is grave. Eliza strains to hear more of their conversation. Men scuttle in and out.

"There's trouble brewing," Reid says. "I can feel it. Might need to call a meeting tonight. Put an end to this."

Later that night Eliza sits across from Pearly in the newly electrified parlor of Mrs. Brown's.

Eliza's basket overflows with fingerless mittens for the newly formed Orphan's League. She's talked Jeremiah Taylor of the drygoods business into donating yarn to the ongoing project.

"Can't say no to my favorite customer," Taylor had said. He flashed Eliza a lascivious smile.

"Well, then I'll be asking for more than my share," she had answered. She ignored his lewd comment.

What she didn't tell Mr. Taylor is that some of the donated yarn is siphoned to her underground woolens business. For a dollar and a quarter, any client of Mrs. Brown's can buy a scarf to keep his neck warm after a rendezvous with Rose or Cilla or Lou. Mounds of scarves sit in a basket near the rear stair. They sell like hotcakes.

"Is it true?" Eliza asks. "All this thievery can be traced to Mr. Smith himself?"

"Just another example of that swindling good-for-nothing. If you don't lose your poke playing their shell game, they'll find another way to lighten your load."

Eliza's fingers fly. With her hefty stash, Eliza produces mittens and scarves by the basketful. Time remains a precious commodity in Eliza's schedule, and she parcels out time by rows. Eliza often thinks of Old Steiner when she shops Taylor's, as she bustles through the aisles of flour, sugar, and yeast. She contemplates whether she should write to Old Steiner, and tell him of her whereabouts, and that she is indeed well.

No. Not now. Not now that Steiner figures in the mix.

"Now that's one of the womanly arts at which I can't say I excel," Pearly laughs, as Eliza knits furiously on the divan beside her. Eliza's spectacles fall lower and lower on her nose.

"I've got nimble enough fingers, but knitting! Maybe you can show me how it's done."

"Well, it's got to be an even trade," Eliza says. She raises her eyes from her handiwork to meet Pearly's.

"There are a few of the womanly arts that you mention for which I could use a few lessons. Call it a mutual tutorial."

"Now aren't you the wicked one?"

Eliza hands Pearly two knitting needles and bends over Pearly's shoulder as Pearly casts the yarn on. After two rows, Pearly throws the needles on the floor.

"I don't have time for this nonsense! You are a saint, Lizzie. A real saint. Can't say I've ever met a saint before.

"Wait here. I have something to show you. Something saints don't see, as a rule."

Pearly returns to the parlor. In her hand, she holds a rectangular cardboard box. She flips the end of the box open and a small gadget slides into her palm. She untangles an electric cord and bends down to plug the gadget and its appendage into the new wall socket. The device pulses with lightning fast vibration.

"It's a cure-all. You've heard of the female hysteria?"

Eliza cannot take her eyes off the vibrating machine. She cannot fathom how an appliance can come alive by plugging a cord into an opening in the wall.

"My mother took the treatments, yes. But how did you get a hold of this device? I didn't know you could buy a piece of medical equipment without a license."

The machine buzzes loudly in the parlor. Pearly's cat looks up, yawns, and settles herself into the spot Pearly has just vacated.

"Medical equipment! What a piece of malarkey that is! There's nothing medical about it, unless female hysteria is a disease to be treated! Now, are you telling me that you've never been treated for this so-called hysteria?"

Eliza shakes her head, no.

"And have you never heard of female paroxysm? It's the best treatment for whatever ails you!"

Pearly hands the electrified pulser to Eliza. Eliza's whole hand feels the vibrations. She turns the device over in her hand.

"Bought this machine from Dr. Phillips, I did," Pearly says. "He suggested I buy a used one of his when he ordered a new one. Said I might have some use for it."

The doctor from the café!

Pearly laughs from deep in her belly.

Eliza has never experienced a female paroxysm. She thinks perhaps she will go to Dr. Phillips for a treatment.

Yes, now there's an idea.

The thought arouses a deep longing inside Eliza. Pearly winks at Eliza, and Eliza blushes.

"I know, I know," Pearly says. "But you're helping me with this danged knitting. Least I can do is show you how this little gadget works. You're welcome to borrow it anytime."

Eliza bites her lip. She pushes aside any last vestige of Victorian thinking, her prudish thoughts falling away like the disappearing yarn flying through her fingers.

"Why don't you show me now?" Eliza says.

The unmistakable *ka-pow* of a distant gunshot rings out, a block, perhaps two, to the south. Its report echoes in the street. And then another *ka-pow, ka-pow.*

Without uttering a word, Pearly and Eliza move in tandem to the front window, clutching hands. Eliza's knitting drops in a colored heap on the parlor floor. Pearly bolts the door and pulls Eliza down. The women crouch by the foot of the door, their breathing shallow. Eliza's eyes widen and she stifles a gasp. Pearly puts her fingers to Eliza's lips and indicates silence.

Ka-pow! Ka-pow!

Then men's voices. Yelling. Feet pounding dirt.

A loud *stomp stomp stomp* on the rear stairway signals a customer's hasty retreat. Rose appears at the top of the stair in her robe. She runs down the stairway and joins Pearly and Eliza behind the parlor door. The trio hears footfalls on the wooden sidewalk outside the boarding house, and then a loud *whomp whomp whomp* on the bolted door.

"Pearly! Open up! And make it quick!"

The front door of Mrs. Brown's Boarding House bursts open. The power of the forceful entry knocks Eliza off balance, and she falls to her side, her spectacles thrown from her face. Pearly looks from Shorty and back to Eliza. She rushes to assist Eliza, and registers that something's amiss. She has never seen Shorty with as ashen a face.

Another *stomp stomp stomp* on the rear stairway, and then Cilla appears, her hair loosed.

Shorty towers above the women. His grave face drips with sweat.

"Reid's near dead, and Soapy's more'n dead."

He clears his throat, and stammers.

"Dead, I say. Deader than a doornail."

Shorty strides to the divan and perches on the edge of the velvet frame. He fingers his tattered hat as if a rosary. Pearly and Eliza share a horrified glance, and turn again to Shorty. Cilla slinks down the stair. Rose pulls her robe closer around her full breasts and sits at Shorty's feet.

"Well, go on. Don't leave out a detail."

Lou comes around the corner and stays at the fringe of the parlor. Her gown is torn and her hair disheveled.

"Posse's still down at the Juneau Wharf, some of 'em anyways. There's a lot of confusion."

"Posse? What do you mean, posse?" Pearly asks.

Shorty throws his hat on the carpet near his feet and puts his large hands to his face. He shakes his head from side to side.

"Whole gang of 'em. Reid and Tanner and Murphy were watching the dock. Hard to say who shot who, though, or who fired first. Bullets were flying. It was over so quickly, Soapy coming down the wharf and then the shots. Some say Reid killed Soapy, but from what I saw, might've been Murphy.

"Holy Mother of God! All's I know is Smith's a goner, laid out on the wharf like in his coffin. Dead, he is, stone cold dead. Reid's suffering, and bad. Boys pulled him outta there quick. Shot in the groin."

Shorty winces.

"He's on his way to hospital as we speak. Someone's gone for Doc Phillips. And more certain than not, there's going to be more trouble. I came straight here to warn you ladies. Bolt up the door, Pearly. Quick, now. Go on."

Eliza sits, stunned. Pearly moves quickly and bolts the parlor door shut again. She returns to the divan and takes a place next to Shorty. Pearly takes Shorty's hands in hers. Shorty fumbles for words, his sentences trailing off. Rose looks over her left shoulder toward Cilla, who hasn't moved from the foot of the stair. Cilla's careful countenance cracks ever so slightly. Her bottom lip trembles.

Reid.

It would be hard to mistake Reid. He possessed a fine chiseled face, trimmed black beard, and piercing brown eyes that peered out from below his signature bowler. He wore a long oilskin coat that swung behind him as he strode the streets of Skagway with authority. No wife, no family. Unencumbered. And as close to the law as one could be in a lawless place like this.

If Eliza didn't know firsthand how frequently Reid visited Cilla, she may have looked at him with a keener eye. But Reid never looked twice at Eliza.

Perhaps my breasts are too small, she thinks.

Eliza is no fool. She notices that breasts are a precious commodity in a town like Skagway. A steady stream of men in and out of the Red Onion proves that fact. The Red Onion girls wear their corsets tight, and expose mounds of bare flesh.

"Can't put it all on the table at once," Pearly had said to Eliza when Eliza raised her nerve and asked about the trade. Pearly looks down her nose at the Red Onion girls, and doesn't miss an opportunity to make disparaging remarks about her competition.

"Rose worked the Red Onion before I snagged her," Pearly had said. "And she brought a large clientele with her, now that she has her own room."

Pearly knew a moneymaker when she saw one; after all, she had been a moneymaker herself years ago. When Pearly approached Rose, Rose flipped loyalties in a heartbeat. Pearly boasted that in a matter of days, she transformed Rose from a common whore to a lovely member of the demimonde.

"Sure, men love the grab-and-go girls, Rose, but gentlemen prefer to undress you with their eyes before their hands. And gentlemen have more money to spend, and, mark my words, they come back."

Tonight Rose's cleavage spills out of her robe, and she winds the robe around her buxom frame. Pearly breaks the silence that has descended on the parlor like thick wool.

"Bloody men and their bloody quarrels," Pearly says. "What now, love?"

Shorty settles deeper into the divan and looks up at Pearly from behind heavy eyelids.

"Can't say right away. But all I know is I've got to get this little lady home. It's not a night to be walking the streets of Skagway alone."

Cilla disappears back up the stairway. Rose sits transfixed on the floor. Lou slinks around the corner to her room.

Eliza gathers her shawl. She blows a mock kiss to Pearly and steals out the rear entrance with Shorty. They hurry down the back alleys that crisscross downtown Skagway and avoid the main streets.

"Here, this is for you, little missy."

Shorty places the cool shaft of a small pistol into Eliza's gloved hands.

"I'll be leaving town in the morning for a few months, and I'd feel all the better if you had this pistol for your protection. Might get wild over the next few days and weeks."

Eliza looks at the pistol and back up at Shorty. She bids Shorty goodnight and mounts the back stairs above the Moonstone to her humble lodgings. When she is safely inside, she exhales.

Who knows what flame fans the red-hot blood of Skagway tonight!
Avengers all!

Eliza places the derringer on her bed stand. She shivers as she changes into her thin nightdress. She does not light a lamp, as the July sun offers enough light, even at ten o'clock in the evening. She needs to be up by four a.m. to knead sticky buns and rye loaves before opening tomorrow morning. Conversations all over town will be abuzz about tonight's activities. Eliza mentally scans the faces that frequent the Moonstone most mornings. Some familiar faces will be sorely missed.

She hears herself gasp aloud.

What of Dr. Phillips?

She hopes Dr. Phillips is not caught in the crossfire.

Eliza conjures Phillips's face and how she longs to touch him. She resolves to book her treatments with the young doctor; he would become familiar with Eliza, and she with him. Eliza relaxes her body and thinks of her conversation with Pearly earlier in the evening. She knows it won't be long before she gets up her nerve to ask Pearly to show her the wonders of the little electric-powered machine in the plain cardboard box.

But tonight is not for thoughts such as these, and more ominous thoughts inhabit her dreams, the *ka-pow, ka-pow, ka-pow* of gunshots stuttering and echoing long and deep in the dark spaces between.

25

JULY 9, 1898

Cloudy, cool. Unsettling times.

Shorty leaves before dawn. He doesn't need the obligatory supplies this time around; he holds a claim certificate in his pocket. He makes short work of packing his kit and heading back to Dawson. He stuffs oversized duffel bags and secures them with heavy rope. What he doesn't use he will sell, and for a hefty profit.

"Some men get rich from the digging; others get rich off the diggers," Shorty always said.

"So off he went, just like that. He said it weren't a moment too soon, with Soapy dead and gone."

Pearly relates the story to Eliza. Pearly's eyelids look puffy, and red.

"So he's going to join that crazy mass of humanity trudging north through Alaska again. And all the way to the Canadian Yukon, damn it all."

Eliza wonders what has become of Greta Torgerson, with whom she had shared a bed in Seattle. She wonders if Greta was faint of heart.

Eliza knows that Shorty is not faint of heart. He would assay the masses of men littered about at the top of Chilkoot Pass and forge on from there. But Shorty told her it's many hard miles into the heart of the Yukon: five hundred miles of rough and snow-packed mountain passes, wintry river valleys, and ice-crusted lakes. She's heard it told that thousands of men—and women, too—stumble, scramble, slog, and scratch their way toward gold.

"Only one out of a hundred, no, maybe a thousand, will make it to Dawson," Shorty had confided to Eliza. "Once there, the miners will find all the producing claims taken, and will be lucky just to make it there alive.

"Of course, my gold lays safe underground at the claim. Gotta get back, and the sooner's the better. Carmack's on guard for me, Bonanza Creek, it's called now. Just a stone's throw from Dawson."

Eliza thinks of all that gold locked in the depths of the earth. She realizes now that gold beckons miners with all the cunning of a woman, blinding them with her charms and with the promise of uncovering her secrets buried deep inside.

∽

THE CAFÉ IS EERILY EMPTY. A SUBDUED CHARLIE ADAMS delivers *The Skaguay News* at ten o'clock sharp. Eliza leans on her elbow at the counter and devours the lead article.

"Soapy Smith is dead! Shot through the heart, his cold body lies on a slab at People's undertaking parlors, and the confidence men and bunco steerers which have had their headquarters here for some time, have suddenly taken their departure, the tragic death of their leader having completely unnerved them . . ."

The *tick tick tick* of the clock above the counter echoes in the near empty anteroom. Eliza moves from one task to another, her focus unnerved.

For nearly a week, Skagway waits to hear Reid's fate. Eliza uses the time to clean the café again, beginning this time from the back of the shop toward the front. She cannot stand small talk, and attends to customers when she hears the tinkle of the bell above the door. Business is tentative, and slow.

The following weekend Eliza stays home from her regular visits to Pearly's. She is in no mood for socializing. The next few days drag on, the clock and strangers Eliza's only companions. Charlie Adams loiters at the Moonstone more than ever before, and Eliza packs a brown sack of treats for him every morning.

"Share these, now," she says, as she presses the warm bag into Adams's hands. "And don't you be getting into any trouble, you hear?"

Pearly crashes through the Moonstone's front door on Wednesday. She looks frantic. For a second Eliza worries that the news must be about Shorty.

"Reid's gone. Just gone. I'd swear out loud if I had the heart."

Eliza stares blankly at Pearly. She has no words. She thinks of Cilla and then of Reid's cronies. She looks past Pearly at Reid's empty chair in the anteroom of the café and fixates on the wooden slats that once supported Reid. She looks back at Pearly and wills herself not to cry.

"Damn it to hell."

The few patrons that populate the café turn and face Eliza.

"Yes, you all heard me right. Damn it all to hell."

⧢

THE NEXT DAY PEARLY AND ELIZA DON BLACK AND JOIN THE human parade for a mile east of Skagway for Frank Reid's proper burial. Reid had died a miserable death, nearly two weeks after his fateful altercation with Soapy Smith on the Juneau Company Wharf. The funeral procession is a solemn affair, or at least as solemn an affair as Skagway can posture. A low murmur moves along with the crowd. Pearly's heavily blackened eyes rim again with red.

"Death takes no bribes," her aunt used to say.

Perhaps I should have stayed behind, Eliza thinks.

But no, Reid was one of Eliza's best customers, and his cohorts still frequent the Moonstone. What she offers to the swelling crowd is her mutual respect. She stuffs her sorrow away and follows the procession the mile to Reid's gravesite. By the time Pearly and Eliza reach the crude cemetery, Reid's body has been swallowed by the ground. Eliza hates burials— too many memories of too many burials flood her mind. Dear sweet Ida. Jonathan's classmates. Jacob, and of course Jonathan.

Jonathan!

Eliza and Pearly do not tarry at the cemetery. Pearly and Eliza walk arm-in-arm, murmuring together, and hitch up their black skirts in the oozing mud of the well-worn trail. They dart behind the still-oncoming throng and weave behind the trail toward the hillside. There, in a small, largely un-marked gravesite, lie the remains of Soapy Smith, a hand written wooden sign adorning the bleak gravesite.

"Shame, such a damned shame," Pearly says to Eliza. "But there's a bitter justice after all. Did you see that the brute is buried outside the cemetery boundaries? Fitting, all's I can say."

Eliza and Pearly walk back to town in silence. Eliza returns to the Moonstone, unlocks the heavy wooden door, sits at an empty table. She rests her head on her forearms. After a quarter-hour, she rises, unfolds herself, and makes her way stiffly to the kitchen. She puts the kettle on to boil. The tinkling bell above the café door jingles. Men begin to shuffle in, scrape the chairs across the wooden floor, brood. A pall hangs over the establishment for the rest of the day, hushed murmurs, and more often than not, silence.

The hubbub of the dual deaths resonates for weeks, with swarms of reporters from as far away as Chicago and San Francisco coming to Skagway to cover the tragedy. A large contingent of reporters from the Show-Me state converges in Skagway throughout July. Smith's widow is due in town any day from St. Louis. There are as many stories about the deaths as there are reporters, and after a while, whatever truths there may have been on the evening of the eighth of July are buried as surely under the ground as the rotting bodies of the vigilantes, and it is anyone's opinion as to who indeed played the role of the hero and who played the role of the villain.

Eliza notices the flat accent of a fellow Missourian when she hears it, especially in the pronunciation of the state itself, with the flourish of the short "a" sound at the end of the word, a dead giveaway.

"Hail from Missoura, I do, yes," a voice says, one of a handful of new customers who stops into the Moonstone. "Call St. Louie my home now. Name's Jack Draper, *St. Louis Globe-Democrat*. And you'd be?"

The stranger proffers a card to Eliza by way of introduction.

"My family's from down Columbia way," Eliza says.

This piece of information has not passed her lips since coming to Skagway.

"Haven't been back in near ten year, though."

"You're a long way from Missoura!" Draper bellows.

"Yes, that I am. I'm a long way from Missoura."

Eliza busies herself with pouring coffee and ringing up the sale.

"Lot of folk in town covering the situation," Eliza says. Calling the double murders "the situation" softens the heinous tenor of the subject, and minimizes it. Talk of murders doesn't sit well with Eliza, under any circumstances.

"By chance, did you know the man?"

Draper talks out of the side of his mouth, as if a cigarette should be inserted into the opposite corner of his mustachioed lips.

"Didn't know the man personally, no. But his legend grows every day, if you believe everything you read."

"You mightn't have a story to share, now would you, Ma'am?"

Jack Draper steals a sideways glance at Eliza.

Draper wears his pencil behind his left ear and his ever-ready reporter's notebook protrudes from the hip pocket of his overcoat. He drums up conversation with all the locals, and writes furiously as he sits at a front corner table, sometimes until closing. He spends five days in Skagway, and makes friends on a dime. Eliza talks casually with Draper, but keeps her distance. No need dredging up Missouri memories, or trying to reconnect with her distant past. Business is up to speed, and Eliza wears herself out by day's end.

Wise to keep my ears wide open, Eliza thinks. *One can glean so much more from listening than from talking.*

"Mrs. Waite! I just can't get enough of these here cinnamon buns! How about indulging a fellow's craving for a sweet tooth and giving up your recipe? I'd like it awfully well if my landlady could bake up a batch of these for me some dreary morning come fall.

"No, wait! That's a pun, it is, wait and Waite! I've got me an idea here, Mrs. W!"

He pronounces it "dub-yah."

"I'll promise that you'll see this recipe in print if you'll give it to me. The *Globe-Democrat's* got a new column for the homemakers, "*From the Kitchen of the Missus*," I think it's called. I could post your recipe; maybe call it "*From a Klondike Kitchen.*" Might have quite a following, all those homemakers in St. Louie wondering about who's this Missoura woman up here in this far-flung city baking up the best cinnamon buns in the country."

ᑦᓄᑦᓄᑦᓄᑦᓄᑦᓄ

CINNAMON BUNS

Dissolve three tablespoonfuls yeast and one teaspoonful sugar in one teacup of lukewarm tap water.

Let mixture sit in a warm place until it bubbles up.

In very large mixing bowl, beat two eggs well, then stir
in one teacup sugar, pinch of salt, one generous teacup
shortening, and three teacups warm water, then mix
well and set aside.

Measure twelve teacups flour by lightly spooning into
the teacup and leveling off with a knife.

Add yeast mixture to the egg/shortening mixture and
mix well.

Add ten teacups flour one teacup at a time mixing
with a large wooden spoon until dough is no longer
sticky. Add up to two more teacups of flour if the
dough seems too sticky.

Cover bowl with damp kitchen towel, let rise in warm
place until doubled in bulk. Punch dough down, then
transfer to floured surface and knead lightly.

Wipe out the large bowl and grease it with butter, then
form dough into a ball and put into greased bowl and
turn dough over once.

Cover bowl loosely and let rise again.

On a floured surface, roll dough out in the shape of a rectangle approximately ten inches by fourteen inches, and one-quarter inch thick.

Brush melted butter evenly over the surface of dough.

Sprinkle a generous amount of sugar over the melted butter, then sprinkle a generous amount of ground cinnamon in an even layer over the sugar.

Starting with one of the long sides of the rectangles, tightly roll dough up jelly-roll fashion to form a long "snake." Cut roll crosswise into one-inch pieces.

Place the pieces cut side up very close together in four buttered baking pans. Cover loosely with a damp kitchen towel and let rise until doubled in bulk.

Bake until golden brown.

Makes sixty buns. A half recipe yields thirty buns, and halving does not compromise the recipe.

Prepare icing by mixing confectioners sugar with melted butter, cream, and vanilla until smooth. Top buns with icing and serve warm.

EVEN THOUGH IT'S THE HEIGHT OF THE ALASKAN SUMMER, Skagway shivers in the aftermath of Soapy Smith's death. The entire city council has been forced to resign. No mayor. No town marshal. No police force.

Errant gunshots pierce already common chaos. Eliza keeps her firearm close. She takes to practicing her shot in the kitchen of the café. She loads the derringer with two bullets and clicks the barrel shut. She aims for a crude bull's-eye drawn on thick brown paper affixed to the kitchen wall. She stands firm and fires. Bullets perforate the paper and layer themselves into the thick wooden wall of the cramped kitchen. She misses the center of the target and promises herself she will practice again soon.

No one ever stops in to ask what the ruckus is about.

A somber pall also hovers over Eliza's Sunday night visits to Pearly's.

"Skittish as a new stallion," Pearly says. "I'm as jumpy as one myself. Heard tell that Shorty's not the only one to get outta town. Why, Lester Edwards himself's gone missing, he has, and Frank Pope, the scoundrel. A ne'er-do-well if I ever laid my eyes on one. Shoddy piece of flesh. At this rate, Cilla's going to be lonely nights. All this burying has got me on edge."

Eliza's long-held secret rushes off her tongue.

"I've buried more than my share."

The air spikes with the unsaid.

"Lost my boy, I did. Five years old. The smallpox. Hardest thing I ever did, burying that boy. Lost my husband, too, although I don't think on him much. Fifty-eight people in three weeks, that's the God's honest truth. My boy—Jonathan—and a passel of his schoolmates. And my best friend, Ida. Doesn't seem fair, all this dying."

Pearly rises from her chair. In her stocking feet, she pads noiselessly across the layered tapestries on the parlor floor. She sits close beside Eliza, and strokes Eliza's hair.

Eliza begins to cry.

Eliza's first quiet sobs cause her shoulders to shake in a soft rhythmic pattern: up, down, up, down. Pearly digs her fingers into the mass of wavy copper to massage Eliza's scalp.

Eliza's sobs grow louder. Her shoulders heave upwards as she tries to catch a breath. And then, like a river that surges past an ice floe and unleashes its pent-up fury, great gushes of tears wrack Eliza's lean frame. She chokes on her sobs and falls, exhausted, with her head in Pearly's lap.

A strange calm settles over Eliza as she reclines there. Pearly hums under her breath; any noises that emanate from the streets of Skagway dull into the distance. The two sit in relative silence for the better portion of an hour until the silence cracks open, and the ship's clock on the mantel strikes a sonorous decade of *gongs*, ten o'clock up. As if in a trance, Eliza gazes up at Pearly. Pearly's eyes are moist.

"I had a son, too. Stillborn. Can't say rightly who the father was, but I always like to think it was Steiner's. God, I loved that man."

The mention of Steiner shocks Eliza from her ease. She pushes the thought of Steiner far into the recesses and closes her eyes.

For the first time in the six months since Eliza left Mrs. Brown's Boarding House for her own lodgings, Eliza doesn't go home. She wakes at four a.m. nestled on Pearly's couch, a fringed shawl draped over her. Eliza folds the shawl and straightens her crumpled dress. She slips her boots over her stockings and gathers her satchel. Mrs. Brown's is bathed in a rare moment of quiet.

Eliza meanders through the alleyways toward the Moonstone. She notices for the first time that the burden of Jonathan's memory, from his conception to his difficult birth to his short life, lifts like the smoke that rises above Skagway's spotty skyline.

I am not the only one bearing this grief.

She realizes as she navigates her way through the mud and the manure that everyone must possess a storehouse of grief, here, a smithy opening his heavy rolled door, his weighty, measured movements penance for his suffering, there, a drayer heading to the wharf with his dappled team, his steady *gee* and *haw* marking time against the sure daggers in his heart, and ahead, a barkeep sweeping away his inborn anguish in simple, synchronous *swiffs* after the last of the drinking men headed home.

Yes, we are all of us wounded.

Skagway echoes an eerie silence. No gunshots. No yelling. No sounds except the gulls, ever ravenous and greeting a new day.

Eliza reaches her lodgings and fumbles for her large key. Up at four o'clock each morning in a land where the late summer sun barely sets allows for little sleep. But even though it's summer, dawn remains chilly. Eliza has mastered her hairstyle and, by now, can fashion a swept updo in less than ten minutes. Her working uniform consists of a plaid flannel day dress covered by a large white apron. Every night after work, Eliza shakes the flannel dress out over the back stairway, its remnants of flour snowing off the dress into the purpling night. She hangs the dress by the doorway, where it acts like a curtain over the door's small rectangular window, and keeps in some heat.

Eliza changes and clatters down the back stairway and into the kitchen. She feeds the stove a large armload of cordwood. In an hour flat she'll be roasting and the first of her breads and cakes will be rising in the oven's warmth.

She stirs the sourdough starter and retrieves flour and warm water. Her fingers thaw as she works the dough, a handful of bees slowly adjusting to room temperature, kneading multiple circles of yeast and flour. She wipes her hands on her apron and sets to grind the coffee. Its intoxicating aroma fills the kitchen. She measures the coffee: one, two, three, four heaping tablespoons into the bottom of the coffee pot and places the blackened kettle onto the cookstove. Flames lick upward and warm the iron surface, and, in turn, the bubbling coffee. Eliza breathes in, a deep, prolonged inhale. She thinks of Shorty up on his claim, and the poor pickings he must drink for his morning coffee, dregs used over and over again. She misses Shorty. No doubt Pearly misses him even more.

After work, Eliza wraps two leftover slices of cinnamon raisin bread and walks to Pearly's. She aims to thank Pearly for her kindness the night before, two slices of yeast bread as an offering. She finds Pearly behind the boarding house in the waning sunlight, a sorry mess of chopped wood at her feet.

"Here, let me," Eliza says.

Eliza takes the axe and swings it upward in a full arc before slamming the axe head on the cordage. The fir splits evenly in two, and Eliza gathers up the split log and stacks it against the back wall. Pearly looks agape at Eliza.

"Where'd you learn to chop wood like that? You'd think you're a woodsman."

"We all of us have our secrets," Eliza says. "Just maybe some have more than others."

She smiles at her friend.

"I'll chop, you stack."

⌒

A SHY THREE MONTHS LATER, "AND NOT A MOMENT TOO soon," Pearly cries, Shorty bursts through the front door of Mrs. Brown's with a smile as big as the sun. He drops his kit and rushes toward Pearly. He picks her up, swinging her around in his bear-like arms. Her dainty boots kick at the air, and her dress swings in wide circles.

He lets Pearly down and kisses her full on the mouth, right in front of Eliza. Eliza blushes and smiles at Pearly, whose lovely face peeks above Shorty's massive shoulder. Pearly looks the schoolgirl, even though she nears fifty.

A foul smell of sweat, tobacco, and dirt envelops the parlor. Pearly doesn't say a word. She nods to Eliza, an un-spoken goodbye. Then she leads Shorty up the carpeted stairway, looking behind her as she ascends every tread so as not to lose sight of him ever again.

26

SEPTEMBER 29, 1898

Overcast, fall chill. Doctor appointment today.

"Another batch of cinnamon buns, and we'll be set for tomorrow," Eliza says.

Eliza wipes her floured hands on her apron and turns to face Rose, whose protruding belly fills out her petite frame. The low sun glints through the grimy plate glass window and sends slivers of sunrays across the dusty wooden floor. In the late afternoon light, Eliza notices infinitesimal sparkles of gold dust, fine as powder, interspersed with dirt locked into crevices of the pocked wooden slats.

Someone's fortune, no doubt.

Eliza reaches for a long handled broom and moves to the front of the café. Her knees ache. She sweeps toward the door. When she reaches the doorframe, she grasps the handle and opens the door out onto Broadway. Horse droppings rim the boardwalk in front of the bakery like clumps of soil. A small brush fire in the lot kitty-corner to the café sends up thick tendrils. Eliza watches the smoke curl up into the cool afternoon air.

Soon I will have to replenish my wood supply.

She shivers.

Must be down to forty degrees. Winter's on its way.

In less than two days they've built another storefront. Two men bandy back and forth, their gestures wide. At the top of the ladder propped against the new storefront, one of the men grimaces as he supports one end of a newly painted sign. The other end of the sign is already attached to the storefront; the side he shores up hangs down at a slight angle. Eliza cocks her head to the left to read the signage: Clease's Stationers. Eliza cannot hear the voices, but watches the scene unfold and imagines their conversations. One man steps to the center of the street and eyeballs the placement. His partner, reaching out at an unlikely position atop the ladder, adjusts the signage.

Clease. Funny name.

A small cloud of dirt mingled with gold dust *poofs* up and out the front door. Eliza makes a second, grander, sweep to disperse the golden dirt off the boardwalk and into the street. She stamps her boots outside the café door and a fine layer of flour descends from her dress and her apron. The railway is nearly finished.

"Rose, it's quitting time!"

Eliza slams the front door shut and bolts the lock. Rose comes out from the kitchen munching a muffin. She unties her apron and plops herself down onto one of the side chairs. She reaches down across her swollen belly and rubs her ankles.

"I don't know how she got herself in this unhappy condition," Pearly had said. "Up the duff and outta the house, that's more the shame. I can see the dollars slipping through my fingers already."

It had been two months since Pearly confided to Eliza about Rose's predicament. Pearly had secured a room for Rose at Captain Moore's.

"He'd take in a stray cat, heart of gold, he's got. Must teach my girls the ways, though. Just no excuse for getting in the family way anymore."

Eliza nearly crashes into Rose at Taylor's Drygoods one late September afternoon. Eliza's basket overflows with saleratus and spices.

"Rose! What are you up to these days? I've not seen hide nor hair of you."

"Been helping Mrs. Pullen with her pies. But it's only two bits a day."

"If you've got the energy for it, I could surely use your help at the café."

"Well, by golly, I could surely use the earnings. Aren't making my usual wages in this here condition."

She pats her growing mid-section.

On her way home from Taylor's, Eliza makes a diversion and follows the footpath over the creek. Eliza marvels over the rhubarb, which grows in large proportions in Alaska's summer, its weighty, feathered leaves the size of a small man. She stops to pick thick stalks of wild rhubarb and adds them to her brimming basket.

ᚲᚾᚲᚾᚲᚾᚲᚾᚲᚾ

RHUBARB MUFFINS

Mix together one-half teacup lard, one egg, two teaspoonfuls vanilla, one teacup buttermilk, and two teacups diced rhubarb. Set aside.

In second bowl, mix two and one-half teacups flour, one-half teacup brown sugar, two teaspoons saleratus, pinch of salt and one-half teacup shelled walnuts, if you choose.

Fold mixtures together and spoon into
greased muffin cups.
Bake until toothpick comes clean.
Serve with jam.

※ ※ ※ ※ ※ ※ ※

AFTER PULLING THE RHUBARB, ELIZA PICKS A BUCKETFUL OF marionberries. They *plink* into her metal pail. She cannot help but gorge herself on berries, and her hands stain a rich purple. Eliza squats by the creek bank and cups her hands. The water runs sweet and cold.

※ ※ ※ ※ ※ ※ ※

MARIONBERRY COFFEE CAKE

Cream one-quarter teacup lard and three-quarters
teacup sugar; add one egg and one-half teacup milk.
Add one teaspoonful vanilla, if you have so.
In second basin, combine two teacups flour, two
teaspoonfuls saleratus and pinch of salt.
Combine mixtures.
Add two generous handfuls berries and fold gently.
Blueberries will do if marionberries are scarce.
Spoon dough into greased baking tin and top with
combination of one-half teacup brown sugar, one-third
teacup flour, and one-quarter teacup butter.
Bake until brown and bubbly.

※ ※ ※ ※ ※ ※ ※

ELIZA, NOT ONE TO BE SMUG, SMILES TO HERSELF. SHE WAS about to steal Rose from Mrs. Pullen. The pleasure of that act diminishes the thought that in doing so, Eliza would be forced to double Rose's pay.

⌒

WITH ROSE JUST OUT THE DOOR OF THE MOONSTONE CAFÉ, Eliza checks her pocket watch.

I cannot be late for my first appointment.

Last week she had scheduled her first visit to Dr. Phillips's office, knowing full well that being a patient of the doctor's and pursuing a relationship with him might cross unspoken lines. The thought had conflicted Eliza, but she decided to proceed with her plan.

Few words had passed between doctor and patient, as Eliza lay prone on Dr. Phillips's medical table. His small brown-papered office boasted meager equipment, and highlighted a framed degree from the Yale School of Medicine, class of 1895.

He must be nearly thirty years old himself, Eliza had thought. *We are nearly the same age, and neither of us now married.*

Dr. Phillips had cleared his throat and raised Eliza's skirt. Eliza closed her eyes to receive the treatment. With a flick of a switch, Dr. Phillips transported Eliza away from the cramped surgery room and caused her body to shiver with previously unknown pleasures. She emitted a sigh so loud she felt embarrassed.

"That's a natural reaction, Mrs. Waite," Phillips had said. "A woman's got tension locked in the womb, and it's only natural to relieve the tension in this way. You should find relief now, at least for several days. Next Thursday, then?"

She makes her four o'clock appointment with Dr. Phillips every Thursday afternoon like clockwork, and is not disappointed with the results. Eliza often stays up nights running her slender fingers over her lily-white skin trying to replicate the sensations she experiences in Dr. Phillips's office.

To Eliza's daily delight, A. J. Phillips, M.D. enters the café. Eliza blushes under her pale skin. Perhaps it is his stature, the cut of his morning coat, his shaven face, and his soft voice. Or perhaps it is the fact that Phillips is "a cut above the rest," as her aunt would say.

More than likely, Eliza thinks, *it's because of our growing intimacy.*

"I'll take another one of the sweet buns," Phillips says, as he peruses the goods displayed on the Moonstone's plank counter. He buys a bun and coffee, and sits at one of the few empty chairs in the café's anteroom. A buzz of male voices, interspersed with laughter and loud burping, delights Eliza's ears.

She remembers what Tuttle had said: *I must say, I sure miss home cookin'. No, men are not the hardest to please. Si Tanner and Jesse Murphy. Frank Clancy. The Sperry brothers. Thank God for my regs!*

Rose holds court over Frank Clancy's table.

"If I knew for certain that he were yours, you'd be walking me down the aisle this very afternoon," Rose says. "Can't rightly say if he's a McDougall or a Janssen, or maybe the babe of one of your friends over there."

Rose cocks her head toward another tableful of men.

"We'll just have to wait and see, won't we? Once I see his ruddy face, I'll know whose bairn he'll be. Now that man better be running as fast as he can toward his Maker, or I'll catch him, that I will."

Eliza tends the counter and slices the last of her apples. She laughs to herself over Rose's comments.

The bakery operates much more efficiently with two people. But in Rose's condition, her energy wanes in the afternoon.

Eliza often sends Rose home mid-afternoon when Rose's ankles swell to the size of melons. Then Eliza closes up shop herself. At the latest, The Moonstone Café closes by four o'clock every afternoon, before the dinner rush at other eateries, The Empire Café, or the popular Arctic Hotel. Once Eliza took her dinner alone at the Arctic, but after four propositions, she refused to eat out alone again. Eliza prefers to stay at home. Plus, she is bone-tired at the end of each day.

So much work! I will have to hire another assistant, once Rose has her little one. I cannot do this alone.

As Eliza rolls out the dough, she wonders how long she can keep up the pace. Business continues at breakneck speed, doughnuts and cakes and pies selling out as fast as Eliza and Rose can turn them out. And bread. Never enough bread. When flour runs low, Eliza makes her cakes and breads just a tad smaller than usual, although she charges the same price. She skimps on butter in piecrusts now.

ᑯᑊᑯᑊᑯᑊᑯᑊᑯᑊᑯ

COUNTRY APPLE PIE

Line uncooked pie shell with five to seven apples, thinly peeled and sliced.

Mix three-quarters teacup sugar, four tablespoonfuls flour, one-half teaspoonful each cinnamon and nutmeg, and pinch of salt.

Add to this one teacup cream or evaporated milk.

Pour over apples and add top crust.

For a sweeter treat, omit top crust and instead top with three-quarters teacup flour mixed with sufficient white and brown sugars crumbled with butter, size of a small egg.

Place topping on apple mixture and bake until filling
bubbles and top is nicely browned.
Best served warm, although can be enjoyed cold in the
morning, with coffee.

ᑦᓀᑦᓀᑦᓀᑦᓀᑦᓀᑦᓀᑦᓀ

IN ADDITION TO ALL THE BAKING AT THE MOONSTONE, ELIZA caters now to the Dallas Hotel, where she delivers hot biscuits every morning at ten minutes before six. Another seven dollars per week. On the day she first clears twenty dollars, she goes to Taylor's Drygoods and orders bleached canvas duck for new aprons. She splurges on new hairpins and new woolen stockings. And she boldly buys a jar of ointment that she intends to use in ways not specified on the tin.

"Necessity is the mother of invention," her aunt used to say.

Eliza thinks back. Her aunt never had an opinion of her own; she let her adages speak for her: "The early bird gets the worm," "Haste makes waste," "A stitch in time saves nine," "Always a bridesmaid, never a bride."

Eliza wonders if she will ever be a bride again. The thought intrigues her. Her first marriage lacked all the trappings of a love-filled union. In fact, Eliza dismisses her first marriage as a union of convenience for her father, with no thought of her own happiness. No, her first marriage had been an utter failure on that count. She knows that her chances of marrying again are slim, especially after she rebuffed Steiner's awkward proposal.

"Rather a beggar woman and single, than married and a queen," her aunt used to say.

Not that there are a dearth of men in Skagway. Eliza encounters half a hundred men a day at the café, and she notices many of them making eyes at her. But of all the men she encounters in Skagway, only Dr. Phillips stirs any longings in her being. And if she isn't mistaken, he makes a special trip to the café every morning.

To see me, Eliza thinks. *It's not just the sticky buns that have got him coming in for more.*

Eliza waits patiently for Dr. Phillips to ask her out walking. She carves out excuses why he hasn't yet asked. But his lack of drive doesn't deter her from walking out on her own, something that ladies don't do in Columbia.

I'm a long way from Missoura.

On Sundays, Eliza closes at noon and takes the afternoons off. Drear days leave her to books and, if the weather dawns clear, a walk up the valley. She notes different animal tracks as she wends up the hillside. The Douglas squirrel's five-toed imprint pales to the larger species she encounters, the wolverine and ·the mink. She strains to differentiate the slender hoof-prints of the mule deer and the moose. There is no mistaking the imprint of the brown bear, and to Eliza's great relief, she spies those prints handily. So far she has not encountered a brown bear in close proximity, and she prays to keep it that way.

On her Sunday hikes, Eliza beats back gigantic mosquitoes as she plods up the well-worn trail north of Skagway. She wears protective netting over her face and hands in response to the blackening swarm. She beats at the swarm instinctively, and swims in a sea of buzzing black. Today, as she nears the ridgeline, Eliza hears a whistling noise. She can't place the sound; it's one she's not heard before.

Coming around a small bend in the trail, Eliza encounters a wizened Tlinget woman bent over at the waist. The woman's basket overflows with roots. Startled, Eliza makes herself known, and continues forward, toward the spot where the woman herself seems planted.

Eliza greets the woman in Chinook, the universal language of Indians and outsiders.

"*Klahowya! Halloo!*"

The woman strains to stand upright and stares at Eliza with small, dark eyes deep set in a weathered and wrinkled face. She is no more than five feet tall. More than a half-minute passes in silence. Eliza swats at mosquitoes. The mosquitoes do not bother the Tlinget woman, although her face and hands meet the elements unadorned. Eliza wonders if the woman will speak in return to her greeting. When the woman does not respond, Eliza decides to plow on, and moves forward on the trail to continue her constitutional. The older woman raises her hand and speaks in clipped English.

"My name Na-Oot-Ka. You are Djiyi'n. Come, child. I know your story."

Eliza, surprised, and tired from her walk, sits on a fir stump, laying her blue plaid blanket on the stump's upturned face, and listens. She thinks of Indian John.

I tell you story.

Eliza remembers the stories of the thirteen moons, beginning with moon of windy time. She tries to remember the order of the moons. In winter and early spring, she remembers, Indian John called them moon when frog talks, moon of whistling robins, and later in the spring, moon of digging time.

A healthy swarm of mosquitoes zings around the netting that protects Eliza's delicate skin from inevitable bites. Their incessant buzzing all but drowns out the wizened woman's words. Eliza leans forward to listen.

"*Orphan girl lives on island by herself. Her name is Djiyi'n. While there, she becomes shaman. By and by, Chief's daughter falls sick and other shamans summoned to heal her. None can help. Finally they call*

Djiyi'n, who knows that wild bird bewitched Chief's daughter. Djiyi'n curses bird and throws it into sea. Orphan girl travels long distances from village to village. Orphan girl use magical powers far and wide."

Eliza cannot speak, cannot think, can hardly breathe. What powers does this old Indian woman have that she can interpret Eliza's story? Of course Eliza is not a true orphan, nor does she consider herself a shaman. But the old woman's words resonate with Eliza. She had lived on an island, and felt urged to leave Cypress. Does she now really possess magical powers?

The older woman nods to Eliza and continues on her own way, stopping to bend over slowly to grasp another gnarled root. An eagle soars above Eliza's head and discharges its haunting cry. Eliza thinks again of Indian John, and the stories he told Eliza. She thinks of the summer moons: moon of salmonberry, moon of blackberry, and moon of salal berry.

If these stories are indeed true—and why wouldn't they be?—I must pay more attention.

Once, Eliza would have dismissed these thoughts. Her strong Christian upbringing laid Native stories fallow. But after living alone on Cypress for so long and being in tune with the melodies of nature, Eliza discounts her skepticism. If she possesses mysterious powers, she is open to their meanings.

Orphan girl use magical powers far and wide.

Eliza realizes at that moment that she hasn't read Scripture since before she left Cypress.

❦

FAR DOWN LYNN CANAL A STEAMER CHUGS AWAY FROM Skagway. From her vantage point, Eliza thinks the vessel looks like a toy boat, its steam stack coughing black coal fumes in its wake. She knows many steamships have not made it out of Lynn Canal. In the short time Eliza has lived in Skagway, the barks *Canada* and *Mercury* have floundered and sank. Most recently the steamer *Whitlaw* disappeared after leaving port. When the craft at the end of her view rounds the end of the canal, Lynn Canal re-emerges in its natural wild and pure state.

Far and wide, Eliza thinks.

Alaska embodies the words. Another eagle cruises overhead, its eyes peeled for vermin.

Eliza hurries downhill toward Skagway, wracking her brain to remember the moons of the fall in order to ward off any fear of predators.

Yes! Moon of silver salmon, moon of elk-mating cry, moon of falling leaves, moon of dog salmon. And then, in the depths of December, moon to put paddles away, and moon of the sacred time.

A smoky haze locks in the cold air at the "V" of the mountains.

That would be White Pass, the route of the almost finished railway.

Eliza stares at the "V" and shakes her head.

Not only steamships go missing, she thinks. *So many men.*

Eliza decides to broach the subject and ask Pearly's opinion of Dr. Phillips. She knows it is a cheap way to find out whether or not Dr. Phillips is a customer at Mrs. Brown's, but Eliza can't think of another way to talk about Dr. Phillips without hinting at her interest in the young doctor. She reframes her questions in her head. Of course, if Dr. Phillips frequents the bordello, Eliza has a good reason to dismiss her amorous thoughts toward him. But Eliza convinces herself that Dr. Phillips would not stoop to visit a brothel. No, it is up to her to use some of the womanly charms she admires in Pearly to lure the doctor into a relationship. She resolves to take greater care with her appearance. She will have a new dress made, and a long-put-off portrait taken. She will buy some rouge, and some new gloves. A new glow settles in Eliza's persona.

I am ready to cast my magical powers far and wide.

The trail widens as Eliza rounds the last curve into Skagway. Her forehead is damp, as are her underdrawers. She hurries to her meager lodgings and changes. In five minutes she will be at Pearly's door, and within fifteen minutes the duo will be settled on the various divans sharing stories and sipping warm aperitifs, cozying into early fall. Her burning question causes her feet to fly down the back stairway, through the maze of muddy alleyways, and out onto Sixth Street. She stamps her boots outside of Mrs. Brown's Boarding House and turns the knob.

∽

27

OCTOBER 5, 1898

Rain. Used last of fresh fruit.
Appointment with Mr. E. A. Hegg.

"Turn your chin a bit to the left," E. A. Hegg says. He removes his face from the voluminous camera drape and motions with his left hand.

"There, that's right. Hold still now."

Eliza sits motionless on the straight-backed chair. She wears a high collared white blouse with a short ascot pinned to her throat by a small gold brooch. Her hair is swept up off her face and she stares into the black box several feet in front of her. Her spectacles attach to her blouse front with a linen loop. She dares not smile, but neither does she set her face in a pout. She cannot keep her thoughts off the news Pearly told her this morning, and what Rose confided to her just minutes before. Eliza tries to concentrate on the moment, but her thoughts crowd her out.

Pearly had sashayed into the café just after nine that morning—*hellos* here and *hellos* there, her wide easy smile captivating the all-male clientele—and pulled Eliza aside.

"I've got to talk to you, and the sooner's the better," Pearly had said.

"I can't slip out now. And I've got an appointment with Mr. Hegg at four-thirty. Maybe at the end of the lunch trade? I can ask Rose to cover for me. Whatever could be so urgent?"

The parlor of Mrs. Brown's had stood empty when Eliza arrived at nearly one. She had closed up her dripping umbrella and left it on the boardwalk under the eaves. She had then peeled off her overcoat and draped it over the edge of the divan.

"First Rose, and now this! I've got half a mind to bolt my doors for awhile."

Pearly shook her head violently from side to side.

"Cilla's made it a habit to take a walk about Skagway every day at noon. 'It's for my constitution,' she says. Well, hogwash! Shorty's been watching her. Got wind that more than once Cilla's gone to Lester Edwards, Esq.'s office when his office closes for the lunch hour. Now that he's back in town, what goes on behind his closed doors is none of anyone's business, but as one of my girls, this situation's every bit my business. Business is business, and it belongs under my roof.

"Looks like I'll be renting out Cilla's room come the end of the year. I'll give her fair warning, but I can't have my girls stepping out."

"Do you have another girl in mind?"

"I never worry about finding a girl. New girls stop by nearly every week. I hate to turn some of them away, but I've only got the four rooms. But I've never had a girl quite like Cilla.

"Cilla's my moneymaker now, entertains six or eight clients a day here, and I have half the take. I know I shouldn't be sharing these details with you, but perhaps you can see my dilemma. Especially with Rose gone now."

"Is this activity—this stepping out—normal?"

"It's a death knell for a working girl. Next thing you know she'll be up the duff herself. Then she'll marry him, and that's the end of that."

The thought of Cilla marrying Lester Edwards, Esq. turned Eliza's stomach sour. But Cilla had her reasons, and a man of means guaranteed a ticket out of the trade. Marriage had its price.

Eliza had scurried back to the café. Just as she opened the back door, Rose pulled her aside, her face flushed and voice excitable.

Later, when Eliza replays the scene in her head, nothing could have steeled her up for this information.

"You'll never guess who's sweet on me!" Rose's flushed face had radiated evident happiness.

"It's Dr. Phillips! He asked me to walk with him after work today. Said he comes in every day to get a glimpse of me, and hasn't had the nerve to talk to me. But with you out today, he didn't have no choice, now did he?"

Eliza had felt an invisible *thwack* to her stomach.

"Dr. Phillips? My, my, Rose. Now there's a gentleman."

Eliza steadied herself and reached for her apron. She tied the loose ends methodically.

Dr. Phillips had arrived at the café at precisely four, and beamed at Rose as she bundled herself against the cold. He tipped his hat to Eliza and then turned his attentions to the lively sprite on his arm, almost half his height and filling out at the waist.

After locking the heavy wooden front door of the café behind them, Eliza had turned and leant against the back of the door. She took a deep breath and hurried through her closing chores: wiping down tables and counter tops, placing chairs upside down atop tables, sweeping and mopping the wooden plank floor, straightening up the small back kitchen, feeding the sourdough.

Dr. Phillips!

She tried not to think of Dr. Phillips and Rose walking arm in arm down Broadway. How could she not realize that Dr. Phillips's attentions were not for her, but instead for Rose?

Rose is a prostitute! And pregnant! What does Dr. Phillips see in Rose that he doesn't see in me? All he sees is Rose. Sweet, sweet Rose. Rose's cheery smile. Rose's ample breasts. Rose's love for life. Rose. Rose. Rose. All he sees is Rose.

Onions sizzle in the heavy cast iron pan. Eliza's eyes well up and she tends the slices in spurts. Cracks an egg, scrambles the yellow yolk and translucent white into the froth, adds the slippery mix into the pan. Swirls the onion and egg. Adds pepper.

Eliza chews a stale crust methodically, crumbs falling past her slender breasts and onto the planked floor.

I feel like crying again, she thinks. *Maybe all the rest of the tears will come now.*

She sits silently in the cramped kitchen, her head bowed toward her lap. In what might have been a minute, or maybe two, Eliza smells the distinct odor of charred eggs.

Damn!

In one motion, she wipes her eyes and moves to the stove, grasps the panhandle with a checkered dishtowel and races to the back door of the kitchen. She leans over the railing on the back porch and tosses the inedible charcoaled mass, pan and all, into the alleyway behind the café. The cast iron pan lands in the center of the alleyway with a loud hiss. A thin curl of smoke circles the edges of pan, its tendrils disappearing into frost. Eliza turns her back on the mess and slams the door shut.

Eliza hurries closing up shop. No time for a long cup of tea and reviewing the day's receipts. She lets herself out of the back door of the Moonstone and hurries up the flight of stairs backing the alley to her cold flat. She blots her eyes and changes quickly. She needs to clear her mind about Rose and Dr. Phillips.

At two minutes past four-thirty, Eliza opens the heavy door to Hegg's studio and calls out a tentative *halloo*. An overpowering smell of sulfur permeates the air. Hegg does not appear immediately, and Eliza wanders around the cramped front room. A curtain separates the front of the studio from the rear, but Eliza hears no movement from behind the curtain.

Eliza admires photos pinned to the wall. She is drawn to myriad images of the human stream of miners summiting Chilkoot Pass, one miner in front of the next, a black ant-like line superimposed on the blinding whiteness of snow. She thinks of so many faces that had stopped in at the Moonstone, never to be seen again. She rifles through stacks of photos on the counter, studying each one, as she waits for Hegg.

A matched team of malamutes leading a rag-tag dogsled pack. Horses stranded on Dead Horse Trail. A blinding snowstorm on the summit of Chilkoot Pass. A hollow-eyed miner reclining on his stash of supplies.

She leans over the glass-topped counter and studies an image of heavily clothed men blasting a cliff's edge, and behind them, a massive locomotive stuck in an immense snow bank. Her eyes fall on another image: a mile-long line of men, dogs, and sleds inching along the banks of a river.

The Yukon?

In another photograph, Eliza makes out masses of boat builders along a treeless shore.

In what God-forsaken place is this?

A loud *slam* indicates Hegg's entrance from the back door of the studio. Eliza lifts her head and arranges herself.

"Mrs. Waite! Sorry to keep you. Right this way."

Eliza follows Hegg to the rear of the studio and settles in Hegg's straight-backed chair. She shakes her head slightly, and finds it amusing to look into the face of a black box and smile. Her mind races. For a moment she thinks the whole endeavor a charade.

Whoever would want my portrait? Certainly not Dr. Phillips!

"I've been admiring your photographs."

"Yes, I'm just back from the gold fields. It's no place for a woman, that I can tell you. But there are some women up there. Beats me why they'd want to go. But it takes all kinds."

"Now, sit straight. Yes, like that."

Eliza sits still, turns her head, and follows through, acquiescing to Hegg's long list of commands. The session lasts an hour, and Eliza goes straight home.

After a sparse supper of cold boiled eggs and cold asparagus, Eliza wraps herself in her blue plaid blanket and reads into the moonless night. She opens *The Awakening* to some of her favorite passages; ones she had underlined in smudged lead, as if she could not get enough of the words etched in black ink and wanted them marked for eternity.

A gasp catches in her throat more than once as she reads Chopin's words. Eliza devours the chapters, again and again, one after another. She sees different meanings in the words, and herself in Edna Pontellier.

"She had all her life long been accustomed to harbor thoughts and emotions which never voiced themselves."

"She was becoming herself and daily casting aside that fictitious self which we assume like a garment with which to appear before the world."

"She felt as if a mist had been lifted from her eyes, enabling her to

look upon and comprehend the significance of life, that monster made up of beauty and brutality."

Eliza marvels that Kate Chopin speaks directly to her own heart. She wonders how many other women, women in St. Louis or Chicago or San Francisco, or in Boston, Charleston, or New Orleans, or even here, on the remote edge of the Alaskan wilderness, feel exactly the same.

◦◦◦

"THERE'S SOMETHING I'VE BEEN MEANING TO TALK TO YOU about," Eliza says to Pearly. The two sit in their usual Sunday spots in the bright parlor at Mrs. Brown's. The electric lights flicker slightly in the cozy parlor.

"I want you to show me how to use your vibration machine."

Pearly smiles, and puts down her cigarette, slowly snuffing out the embers in the amber ashtray.

"Why, my dear Eliza. Of course."

She stands and offers her hand to Eliza.

"No time like the present."

Eliza thought she would be embarrassed by the request, but she finds herself a willing pupil. Pearly leads Eliza again to her boudoir and instructs Eliza to undress behind the screen. Eliza emerges wearing Pearly's cream-colored robe and sits on Pearly's opulent bed. The papered walls and thick drapery enclose her, and she feels warm from within and from without.

This room holds many secrets, Eliza thinks. *Many, many, many secrets.*

Pearly sits near Eliza and switches on the now familiar machine.

"I've been to Dr. Phillips," Eliza confesses, more out of

boredom than titillation. "So the machine is not new to me. I just have never used it myself."

"Well, there's no need for much of a lesson, then," Pearly says. "But I'll get you started."

Pearly turns the vibrator to its lowest setting and hands the pulsating contraption to Eliza.

"I'll leave you to it, then. It won't take long. I would have never guessed that we'd come to this day, the first time we met."

Their eyes lock in unspoken admiration for the other.

"A true friend is the best possession," her aunt used to say.

As if my aunt would know, Eliza thinks.

"Neither would I," Eliza says.

Pearly lets herself out of the boudoir quietly. Eliza closes her eyes, and hesitates for an instant, more of dotted quarter note of an instant, really, a fully infused inhalation of anticipation, and longing, and need, a moment in time but not of time, not just a moment, but her moment, a deep breath before the unknown, before losing herself in what is to come.

28

OCTOBER 10, 1898

Overcast, chance of snow. Check bank account.

On a particularly brisk morning in early October, Eliza hears the familiar tinkle of the bell above the café door. Rose is late. Eliza wipes her hands on her apron.

Tyranny of the urgent, she thinks to herself. *Coffee's boiling, the scones are nearly burning. Attend to customers! Smile! Where is Rose?*

Another coffee and cinnamon bun. Two pioneer cookies. A slice of berry pie. Three coffees, thank you, Ma'am. Another coffee.

Eliza takes Union bills, Canadian coin, and small gold nuggets. The largest nugget she now owns is the size of a pea. Her ornate cash register rings up with firmness and the universal *ch-ang* as the heavy drawer unloads from its casing. Men of all shapes, sizes, nationalities, and languages frequent the Moonstone. Eliza plugs her nose at the stench of some of the miners, and wonders how long it has been since they last bathed.

Thank God pipe smoke covers otherwise unsavory scents.

Others of her clientele groom themselves to a higher standard. She smiles at them all equally. At the end of each day, she totals her take, ten dollars, thirteen dollars, eighteen dollars. She marches straight to First National Bank and makes her deposit.

The morning clambers on, and still no Rose. And no time to look for her.

If Rose's time has come, surely someone will come to tell me . . .

Mid-morning, Eliza looks up from the cash register and stifles a scream. Her eyes widen. A more than familiar face saunters past the front of the café and glances through the plate glass window. There is no mistaking him. The set of his jaw. The long stringy blond hair. His unmistakable build. The slow, sure gait.

Steiner!

He lingers at the window, looks in. Eliza freezes.

This moment was bound to happen, she thinks. *Go away, go away, go away.*

The scene unfolds behind her eyes; she cannot link one coherent thought to the next. Her hand clutches at her breast. Her breathing, short and shallow. Her face, devoid of color.

Rose! Where is Rose?!

Eliza is glad that her customers continue to eat and drink, unaware of her trembling hands and legs. She forces herself to focus on the next customer, and dishes out huckleberry cobbler onto ceramic plates for display.

꙯ꙫ꙯ꙫ꙯ꙫ꙯ꙫ꙯

BERRY COBBLER

Melt butter in baking dish.
Whisk together one teacup of sugar, one teacup of flour, and one teaspoonful each saleratus and cinnamon.

Add pinch of salt and two teacups milk.

Pour into dish with melted butter.

Rinse and pat dry berries. Any berry will do.

Sprinkle berries over batter.

Top with generous handful of sugar.

Bake until bubbly.

Serve warm with fresh cream, if available.

ᑢᖿᑢᖿᑢᖿᑢᖿᑢᖿᑢᖿ

ELIZA HOLDS HER BREATH AND STEALS GLANCES AT THE FRONT window as she ladles the cobbler out of the baking tin. Steiner disappears from her view. She shivers involuntarily and turns to the next customer, a face that—*thankfully!*—she does not know. The fact that Steiner haunts the streets of Skagway congeals Eliza's blood. She does know she will avoid Steiner at all costs, day and night, her senses heightened to his possible proximity.

I will be on guard, she thinks. *It is a gamble I am forced to accept.*

She pats the derringer beneath the counter by the register.

Eliza learns later in the day through Mr. Moore's girl that Rose is now flat on her back, her baby due any day. So Eliza tends the café alone. She wakes in darkness, works in semi-darkness, and retires at the end of the day in even deeper darkness, her feet aching. There is no sign of Steiner. Eliza figures he headed up White Pass before winter socked the Yukon in. If she's lucky, she won't see him again in Skagway until early spring, if at all.

Go away, she had said. *Go away.*

Eliza removes her woolen stockings and massages her feet with peppermint liniment, making small circles with her thumb and forefinger, and working the liniment into her arches. The

smell of peppermint invites tea. Eliza sits in her wing back
chair with peppermint tea steeping in an ironstone mug, her
hands wrapped around the ceramic to absorb the heat.

❧

"IT'S A BOY!" MR. MOORE'S GIRL TELLS ELIZA. ELIZA MARKS
the date, the thirtieth of October, a day shy of Hallowe'en.
Eliza brightens with the news. When Dr. Phillips explodes into
the café at eleven in the morning, his unshaven face beams.
Eliza has never seen Dr. Phillips disheveled, an anomaly to
most of her other patrons. His raw delight escapes from his
otherwise serious countenance; one would think he fathered
the boy himself.

"He's a fine one, is young Thomas," Phillips says. "A
strapping, healthy boy, weighing in at nearly eight pounds!"

"Congratulations, Doc!"

"Time to make an honest woman of your Rose!"

Your Rose.

"Free coffee all around, boys!"

Eliza has never offered free coffee before. In fact, Eliza
rarely leaves the counter, and instead busies herself with
chores behind the safety of the paneled sideboard. If she ever
enters the café's seating area when customers are in, she
hurries to wipe down the tables and bus the dirtied mugs and
plates back to the kitchen. She never stops to chat with patrons
nor serves refills on coffee. Instead, every scruffy man who
enters the Moonstone and approaches the counter for seconds
must *plop* down another dime on the polished wood before
Eliza refills an empty mug.

"And how is Rose?"

Eliza brushes past Dr. Phillips and catches her breath. She

still has fantasies of the doctor when she massages her private parts at night, attempting to climax in paroxysms of wonder. She knows she shouldn't think of Dr. Phillips in this way anymore, after all, he was all but promised to Rose, but the forbidden nature of the fantasy arouses her even more. Now that she knows the pleasures that Dr. Phillips introduced her to, it is difficult to separate her longings from the man who stands next to her.

"Couldn't be better. She was singing like a lark to the young lad. She'll make a fine mother, my Rose."

My Rose.

Eliza smiles. She remembers how she felt when she first saw Jonathan, after his difficult birth in St. Charles. He weighed barely six pounds and mewled instead of bawled. Eliza pictures Rose's boy.

He'll be a bawler, she thinks. *No child of Rose's would mewl.*

Eliza hurries to the Moore's as soon as she closes up shop. She sidesteps dung as she crosses Broadway and steps up on the far side of the boardwalk. She continues up the block, turns right on Sixth, and steps over a large mud hole in front of the Moore house. Mr. Moore's girl answers the door and ushers Eliza into the bedroom.

An infant brightens any day, and this day needs extra brightening, Eliza thinks. *Alaskan days shorten and darken; soon Skagway will be cloaked for six months in darkness for most of the day.*

Eliza cradles Thomas for near an hour as Rose sleeps in the spare room. Rose sleeps deeply, her breathing slow and even. The baby squirms and purses his bow-shaped lips, twists his face into a slight grimace, and then sighs. His fattened cheeks puff in and out as he breathes, and his heaviness settles into the crook of Eliza's left elbow. Eliza's mother heart swells. A tear escapes the corner of an eye. She wipes away the tear with her free hand and turns her thoughts to Rose and the newborn. She pats the newborn imperceptibly and rocks back, forth, back, forth in the caned rocking chair. The chair creaks on the wooden floor. Rose shifts and snores. Eliza hears a distant clattering of horses. No doubt Dr. Phillips returning to his family.

His family, she thinks. *Dr. Phillips, Rose, and Baby Thomas. I wish them every happiness.*

Eliza leaves while Rose still sleeps, and reluctantly hands the baby back over to Mr. Moore's girl. On the way home, Eliza's thoughts race.

I must think of the perfect present.

It has been ages since Eliza has felt any sense of community. Not since she shared private conversations with Ida at the Sunday coffee hour had Eliza felt that she belonged in a certain place. Of course she belonged to a natal family, but that was mere circumstance, or rotten luck. Once Ida, and now Pearly and Rose, these are the people whom Eliza chooses to call family.

I wish them every happiness.

At home, Eliza rips a piece of *The Skaguay News* in two and draws out a rough pattern with a coarse hewn pencil. She adjusts the pattern and carefully pins the newsprint to a piece of new muslin. She carefully cuts out the shape and works a needle and thread through the fabric, each even stitch punctuated with happiness.

A new baby!

Although Jonathan's birth had been under the most trying of circumstances, Eliza knows that every baby brings its own measure of happiness into the world.

Eliza works long into the night piecing together Baby Thomas's gown. First she pieces the sleeves and then attaches them to the body of the garment. Then she works on the hem. As a finishing touch, Eliza works a seam ripper through the collar of her second day dress and removes the lace. Lace falls into her hand one inch at a time. She fashions a collar to the top rim of the baby outfit, and turns the garment right side out. She sets it out to admire.

It is near one o'clock in the morning before Eliza finishes the gown. She touches the collar and laughs aloud. She tries to imagine Thomas's chubby face above the white lace trimmed collar and flowing gown of the cherub costume. She will deliver the outfit tomorrow: Hallowe'en. She laughs again and thinks to herself that tomorrow will no doubt be the only time in Thomas's life that he wears a dress.

29

❧

NOVEMBER 29, 1898

Snow, frigid. Make rags.

By late November, the tide of stampeders changes direction, like the tide. Fewer men head up Chilkoot Pass or White Pass and tenfold or a hundredfold more trudge down. Snow licks the corners of Skagway like a ghost, first like thin vanilla icing and then like whipped sugar piled high, meringue-like, wild and uneven and stiff. The hype of rivers laden with gold has bankrupted the majority of the miners. Instead of returning from the goldfields rich, men pour into town penniless and broken.

Eliza notices a palpable change in the air. Skagway is rife with despair. Although she cannot imagine ever shooting a man, stories of jumped claims and ransom, cheats, and false trustees filter through the Moonstone.

One must be careful.

Eliza keeps her derringer even closer.

I hope I'll only have to use it to ward off hooligans. But if I have to use it . . .

She estimates the inevitable demand for food she'll need

to feed the stream of failed miners re-entering Skagway. She leaves out any day's leftovers on the front stoop, and within minutes of setting the sweets on the stoop, they are gone, eaten as likely by stray men as stray dogs. Not to mention the ragamuffins, the same ones Eliza met briefly when she reached Skagway's wharf less than six months ago. At one time, Eliza may have ushered all the ragamuffins into her care, but those days fall behind Eliza with each passing day. She works to the bone, and alone. Miner's Snickerdoodles become the mainstay of many a failed miner's diet, their heavy raisin and nut-laden dough enough to fill the empty pit of a man's ravenous hunger.

Alms for the poor, Eliza thinks.

༄ໆ༄ໆ༄ໆ༄ໆ༄ໆ

MINER'S SNICKERDOODLES

Cream together one teacup butter, one teacup brown sugar, one-quarter teacup milk, and one teaspoonful vanilla.

Mix well.

Stir in two teacups flour and one-half teaspoonful saleratus.

Add pinch of salt.

Mix in one teacup oatmeal and stir.

Add in generous handful currants and nuts, or dried cranberries, if you have so.

Drop in generous tablespoonfuls onto greased baking sheet and bake until golden brown.

༄ໆ༄ໆ༄ໆ༄ໆ༄ໆ

IF IT WASN'T FOR ELIZA'S REGULAR CLIENTELE, SHE WONDERS IF she could stay afloat. The dynamic has changed dramatically with the death of Frank Reid. Eliza often pictures Reid's masculine presence, even in his absence. Although she cannot put her finger on it, Skagway feels looser, more lawless, without Reid. Dr. Phillips, Lester Edwards. Esq., the newly named U.S. Deputy Si Tanner, and the rest of her regs. These men keep the doors open. And always-new faces amongst the old, the jailer, for instance, whom Eliza only knows as Peterson. Conversation is hushed, eyes dart sideways, men brood. Cold Arctic air moves in and out of the Moonstone.

To Eliza's great surprise, and subsequent horror, Lester Edwards, Esq. propositions Eliza at the end of the month.

"Would you care to accompany me to the Palladium next week? The thespian society is scheduled to unveil a new theatric, *Blue Ticket*, it's called. Vaudeville stuff. Ladies welcome on a Thursday."

Eliza is speechless. She does not want to lead Lester Edwards, Esq. on by accepting his proposal as a formal date, and has no intention of becoming intimate with her landlord. The thought is anathema to her. Eliza knows Edwards frequents Mrs. Brown's, and is especially fond of Cilla. But to turn him down would be unthinkable in her position. Mixing business and pleasure could spell disaster, unless played gingerly.

"That sounds lovely. I'll see if Mrs. Brown and Mr. Richardson would like to attend as well."

The next Sunday, Eliza joins Pearly in the bordello parlor and drinks down a stiff aperitif.

"Whoa, now, hold your horses there, Missy! What's gotten into you? Bug in your bonnet?"

"I've got news," Eliza begins. The duo devises a foolproof plan to thwart any of Eliza's landlord's advances.

Leave it to Pearly, Eliza thinks. *What would I do without her?*

On the frosty night of Thursday, December the tenth,

locals and other colorful folk, among them dancing girls from as far away as New York and Chicago, star in the Blue Ticket presentation at the Palladium.

The theater comprises half a city block, on the southwest corner of Broadway between Eighth and Ninth streets. Electric lights flash on the massive sign: *P-A-L-L-A-D-I-U-M*. The advent of electricity in Skagway brings light into the darkest days.

That electricity has come to Skagway ahead of most of the nation remains a feat of engineering, Eliza thinks. *And magic!*

Eliza marvels at the yellow glow that emanates from the theater sign and sparks into the night air as the yellowed letters blink on, off, against the night sky.

Eliza enters the theater arm-in-arm with Pearly. She wears a brand new fur coat, the first luxurious purchase of her entire life. The pair stands close to one another, for even with fur coats, fur boots, and fur-lined mitts, an arctic chill invades the theater. Eliza's cheeks sport a high glow; one might think Pearly has encouraged Eliza to use rouge for the evening's outing. Lester Edwards, Esq. and Shorty follow the women through the well-lit entry.

The lobby is aglow with flickering electric lights and a buzz rises from the waiting crowd. Eliza and Pearly settle into soft red theater seats. The seats had arrived lately from New York, plush red velvet cushions that hinge on the rear. Eliza wonders if New York has anything on Skagway. She feels a rush of excitement, not unlike how she felt on New Year's Eves in her long-ago childhood, the anticipation of a night of wonders, and all still ahead. She nods to other women in attendance, an unspoken rule of decorum.

So what that I accompany a madam?

Showmen and showgirls, a honky-tonk pianist, and a fire-eating juggler entertain the crowd. There's a trained dog act and a magician. In addition to the professionals, more than a few aspiring locals show off their spectacular talents to loud roars of applause at the Palladium. Never one to shy away from the limelight, the new mayor John Sperry invites members of the audience to join him on stage. This gamble pays off; townspeople flock to the theater not only to see the gregarious Mr. Sperry, but also to see their fellow Skagwayans cavort on the lighted stage.

"C'mon up here, Shorty Richardson," Sperry bellows. "You can't hide in this audience. Plus I know you've got first-hand experience of the gold mining experience!"

Sperry winks at the crowd. Shorty balks, until Sperry shames him into joining the vignette. Normally the center of attention, Shorty shifts uncomfortably on the well-lit stage. If anyone else notices Shorty's wariness, it is drowned out by the audience's loud involvement in the skit. In addition to lengthy monologues and humorous pieces, scantily clad chorus girls pump their limber thighs skyward in the *can-can*. Pearly squeezes Eliza's arm, and turns to whisper to Eliza.

"Next it'll be you up there!"

Eliza dismisses Pearly's comment with a wave.

At intermission, Shorty hurries the foursome out into the chilled night air. He lights a cigarette and offers it to Pearly.

"Never been so hot in my life, all those gas lights flaring," Shorty says. "Good to be outside, it is."

The second act lasts half as long as the first act, ending with the noted Lady Godiva and a flourish of tulle and thighs.

After the theatric, and all requisite *good-byes*, the group again tumbles into the street.

"Anyone for a nightcap?" Pearly asks. She looks straight at Eliza.

Eliza takes her prearranged cue and begs off.

"It's an early go for me in the morning. I'll take my leave here."

Pearly's plan works brilliantly. In this way, Lester Edwards, Esq. would accompany Pearly and Shorty to Mrs. Brown's, and if his luck held, Cilla would be free and take Eliza's place for the remainder of the evening.

A well turned plan, Eliza thinks, and executed perfectly.

☾

THE CHRISTMAS SEASON BOOSTS SKAGWAY'S MORALE, AND invites itself into the lives of the shopkeepers, the drayers, and the stevedores. Even the ragamuffins move with an extra lilt in their step, with full stomachs and a few extra pennies in their threadbare pants pockets. Eliza notices the certain camaraderie.

It is so different from the Christmases spent on Cypress!

Stores put up holiday decor. Wreaths attach themselves to otherwise bland doorways.

Skagwayans breathe a collective sigh of relief mid-month with the welcome headline: *"Fate of Soapy's Gang,"* heralded by *The Skaguay News.* That the scoundrels associated with Smith were tried and sentenced pleases Eliza.

It's about time this town settled down.

Two days before Christmas, Eliza labors doubly hard, turning out a large number of cakes and pies. She aims to take two days off—the first two days in a row she's allowed herself since opening. Flour hangs off her hair in white wisps, and the scent of cinnamon and nutmeg pervades the café.

"It's my pleasure to introduce you," Dr. Phillips says, as he ushers a tall, well-dressed stranger into the Moonstone. The clock has just pealed eleven, and Eliza shakes herself free of flour. The floor around the till is layered white.

"Fraternity brother of mine from university," he says. "The Honorable Joseph Burns, Circuit Court Judge, Seattle."

Eliza wipes her hands on her apron and takes the man's hand in her own.

"A pleasure, Mr. Burns. Please, come and try one of my cinnamon buns. Half price for a friend of Dr. Phillips."

Phillips and Burns sit close; their heads bow toward the other. Eliza thinks the pair more intimate than most. Perhaps once one has spent four years at university living in close quarters with others of the same ilk, a certain degree of brotherliness descends comfortably on their relationship, like fog. She steals glimpses at the pair over her spectacles.

Burns faces Eliza, his back to the window. Eliza feels his gaze before she turns again and notices his glances. He speaks to Phillips, and nods in response to Phillips's conversation. But increasingly Burns looks past Phillips's shoulder and settles his gaze on Eliza.

Eliza, not one for vanity, wishes her first acquaintance with this man of the hour had been more auspicious. Here she is, seven hours into her day, her apron floured and stained, her copper hair escaping its hasty chignon, and her brow caked with damp sweat. Eliza wears the bodice of her waistcoat unbuttoned at the throat. A deep red flush flashes up her neck and into her cheeks. Burns continues his dual conversation, in spoken conversation with Phillips, and in unspoken conversation with Eliza.

Eliza warms to the attentions of Phillips's friend. She takes Burns up on his silent conversation and smiles back at him, coyly at first. After fifteen minutes of this charade, she cannot keep her eyes from his. All the while, his eyes travel up and down Eliza's frame, and return with satisfaction to her pleasant and open face. Phillips and Burns talk in earnest for the better part of an hour at the Moonstone, refilling their coffee twice. When the clock strikes noon, the men slide their chairs backward and prepare to leave. They lumber into their heavy overcoats and retrieve their hats. Burns bows low, and places his hat on his head.

"The pleasure's been all mine, Ma'am. Best cinnamon buns I've ever tasted. Hope it's not too long until our paths cross again."

Eliza never sits that day. By the time the clock strikes four, all her pies and cakes have disappeared, and her kitchen looks like a snow angel's lair, flour and sugar covering the plank table, almost in drifts on the kitchen floor. Usually Eliza keeps careful account of her sugar and flour; today's flurry of baking has left the kitchen in sorry disarray. Her feet have swelled, and the thought of two days off ahead fill Eliza with longing, longing to sit with her feet propped up on the ottoman in front of her chair by the upstairs window, with the soft comfort of her blue plaid blanket wrapped around her.

Just after four, the door to the Moonstone creaks open.

"I wonder if you have but one more of those cinnamon buns for a hungry traveler."

Burns!

"I am sorry to say I have but dregs, sir."

"Dregs it is, then. A beggar cannot be a chooser."

Eliza remembers her aunt proffering the same quotation before Eliza's hasty marriage.

"I am just about to close for the day, no, for two days, actually. A rare treat! But perhaps I can find something to offer you . . ."

She trails off. Burns stamps the snow off his feet and closes the door to the Moonstone behind him. The tinkling of the bell resonates in the otherwise empty front room.

"I'd be obliged, Ma'am. Long day sorting out a legal mess. Old friend of mine, Phillips, he wrote me he had a new son. You've met Young Thomas, have you not? Had to come congratulate the chap. And marry him, the proper way."

Eliza feels an anvil drop in her brain.

Dr. Phillips. Married.

"Why, isn't this sudden?"

"Not so sudden now there's a boy involved. Phillips, good chap, he wants to make this union legal. Says the boy isn't his, but might as well be. Aim to have a private affair tomorrow, just the good doctor and his bride and a witness for each. Everything's settled. Wedding's at nine.

"But after that, will you do me the honor of walking with me tomorrow morning? Show a stranger what Skagway's all about? I've got but another day here before heading back to Seattle. Yes, a stroll would be grand. And then there's a Christmas Eve party I've heard is the toast of the town. Certainly you're going?"

It is just after ten o'clock the next day when Joseph Burns calls for Eliza. He stamps his feet on the wooden boardwalk in front of the shop. Eliza rounds the corner of the building and catches her breath. She wears her new fur coat and mitts. She takes his offered arm, and smiles.

"Up the street is the office of the insufferable Lester Edwards, Esquire," she says, stifling a laugh. "It's true, he knows when a property's open before his renters know. Good thing he likes my sweet buns, or else I might be one of his unknowing victims.

"And this here is the infamous Jeff Smith's Parlor. Surely you heard about Soapy Smith, and the unfortunate incident that befell him this past July."

Burns and Eliza walk up Broadway as far as Eighth, and cross at the old Tivoli Brewery. Eliza surprises herself at her gaiety. Burns smiles at Eliza and squeezes her arm. He asks questions about various proprietors and stops to admire many of the shop windows. At Parnell's Jewelers, Burns pauses and points out a single sapphire ring featured in the window display.

"Now that's a handsome sapphire. I'm quite fond of jewels. Are you?"

Eliza's words catch in her throat.

"Why, I can't rightly say. I've never had a piece. My husband . . ."

She looks down at her feet, and clears her throat.

"My late husband was a minister. Jewels were not a part of the arrangement."

Burns laughs, and surprises Eliza.

"Well, my dear woman, you need to find yourself another 'arrangement,' as you say."

⚯

PEARLY'S POSH PARTY GIVES SKAGWAY AN OPPORTUNITY TO put on fancy dress. Eliza wears Pearly's newest creation, a gown of deep green satin that flows from her shoulders to the floor. The modest bustline enhances Eliza's breasts and the empire sash of ivory satin ties in a sweeping bow in the back. Champagne and canapés flow freely. Eliza has offered sweet treats for the buffet, and for the occasion tried a new pecan tart recipe she found on the pages of *Harper's Bazaar.*

꙰꙰꙰꙰꙰꙰꙰

PECAN TARTS

Prepare simple pie dough and cut into small circles;
place dough in separate wells of greased muffin tin
and pinch crusts.

*Sprinkle dried beans over dough to weight and bake
until light brown.*

Cool completely; remove beans.

*Mix one teacup sugar, one teacup molasses, one
heaping tablespoonful dark rum, one teaspoonful
vanilla, and pinch of salt.*

Stir in three eggs, lightly beaten.

Add one teacup roasted pecans.

Pour into cooled crusts and bake until filling is set.

To test, use back of greased spoon. Cool before serving.

༅ⅅ༅ⅅ༅ⅅ༅

THE TARTS FILL A LARGE PLATTER ADORNED WITH RED AND green doilies. Eliza sneaks a bite of one of the tarts and groans as her teeth sink into the sugary nut concoction. Although she bakes every day, the taste of a new recipe still warms and excites her. She adds another success to her growing recipe file.

The parlor of Mrs. Brown's Boarding House swells to more than sixty people, many spilling out into the street. Pearly pulls Eliza aside.

"You look stunning, Lizzie," Pearly says. "I must say, I never imagined you could be this beautiful!"

Beautiful.

Eliza savors the word. No one has ever called her beautiful before. Eliza blushes at the compliment. Scripture talks about inward beauty; that, Eliza knows, is paramount.

But what of outward beauty?

She catches a glimpse of herself in the parlor mirror.

"Beauty is in the eye of the beholder," her aunt used to say.

Eliza chooses to go without her spectacles tonight, and to let her deep-set green eyes pick up the color of her lavish gown. In order to see herself clearly, Eliza moves closer to the parlor mirror. Her gold locket rests in the center of her meager cleavage, and shines.

Pearly clasps a small package into Eliza's hands.

"Just a little something I picked up for you."

Eliza opens the tissue-wrapped gift.

"But how?!"

"I have my ways."

Eliza looks down at her palm. A small brass pin gleams in her hand. She brings the pin closer to eye level. Eliza runs her finger around the perimeter of the pin and reads aloud.

"National American Woman Suffrage Association. Pearly! I can't thank you enough!"

Pearly takes the pin from Eliza and attaches it to the left side of Eliza's dress, just above the heart. Eliza places her hand over the pin and closes her eyes.

When she opens her eyes, she sees in the background a now familiar figure.

"Pardon me, Mrs. Waite. Is this the same Mrs. Waite as I had the pleasure of accompanying around Skagway this very day? I must say this Mrs. Waite is looking grand this evening."

"Seize the day," Pearly whispers to Eliza.

Eliza turns to face Joseph Burns. She notices the fine cut of his suit, the starched white collar, and the silver tie bar. Eliza piles charm on Joseph Burns, and unleashes a full smile. Color rises on her cheekbones; a gradual warmth works its way from her thawing heart up her neck toward her face. The second person in less than five minutes to call her winsome—this Eliza finds a novelty.

Fueled by champagne, Eliza converses easily. The weather. The party guests. The pecan tarts. Burns steers Eliza to a bench near the front window of the bordello. A halo of smoke encircles

Burns as he exhales a long trail of white. With his second hand, he rearranges a stray wisp of hair that has escaped Eliza's chignon. His hand lingers on her ear. Eliza shivers.

"I've always been partial to redheads. My mother was a redhead. Please, Mrs. Waite, tell me more about yourself. I seem to not be able to get enough of you, just like your cinnamon buns."

Eliza feels a warm rush when Burns touches her back, not unlike the quiver she felt when Pearly brushed her hair. For the first time in her life, Eliza feels genuinely aroused. Her modesty erodes the more champagne she consumes.

Pearly clears the center of the room for dancing. Eliza finds herself caught up in a daze of delight. Burns holds her small waist and whisks her around the parlor like a professional. A lone fiddler plays a brisk waltz and Eliza smiles up at the handsome face that has been paying her such close attention.

I have never been courted, she thinks.

I like it. I like it very much.

Pearly winks at Eliza, and nudges her as she walks by. After a breathless dance, Burns leads Eliza to the green divan, and squeezes in beside her. Cilla and Lester Edwards, Esq. occupy the far side of the divan, Edwards's hand discreetly under the lip of Cilla's gown and Cilla evidently bored with his company, or attentions. The air hangs close, sticky and moist. Eliza smells her partner's sweat. The smell is not at all unpleasant. Burns clears his throat.

"Christmas is always the hardest for me. It's been two years since my wife passed, you see. I've counted the days until I seem to have lost track. Clara . . ."

Stops. Clears his throat again.

". . . that was her name, my wife, Clara. She died on Christmas Day. Terrible, terrible day. Never knew such anguish.

Can't say I revel in the season like before. But now's not the time to be talking about such things."

Burns turns again to Eliza as way of apology. The topic takes Eliza by surprise, but she is not put off.

"It's quite alright, Mr. Burns. I'm no stranger to grief myself. Although it's been much longer."

Jonathan!

Eliza starts to form another sentence, but cannot find her voice.

Burns's eyes burn into the depth of green. He studies her face. For a half minute he holds her gaze, and no words pass between them.

Burns touches the pin attached to Eliza's bodice.

"I see you're a forward thinking woman. I like that."

"Why, thank you, Mr. Burns. It's all I can think about some days."

"Gather around, friends," Pearly says, her voice pitched above the droning hum and the rasp of the warbling fiddle. She stands perched on a wooden chair in the center of the warm parlor. Shorty supports Pearly by the waist.

"We've got much to celebrate tonight! The last of Soapy's louts are now out of town.

"But I'm a bit aggrieved on another subject. By all accounts, it looks like I've lost my Rose for good!"

The crowd sniggers, and Phillips blushes a hearty red. Rose takes the comment in stride. She raises her chin to her new husband.

"And in just a few minutes' time we'll welcome another blessed Christmas," Pearly says.

She eyes the gathered crowd.

"Now I know many of you aren't church-going folk . . ."

Here another round of sniggers.

"But for those of us who remember darkening the door of a country church, well, here's to the reason for the season. And you've still got time to head over to St. Mark's. Heard it'll be a full house for midnight mass tonight."

Pearly lifts her champagne glass in a silent toast, and a chorus of "Merry Christmas" circles through the crowd. Pearly steps down from the chair where she had stood, and signals to the fiddler. He breaks into the silence with a hearty rendition of *"We Wish You a Merry Christmas."* Many voices join the chorus and the parlor rings with circus-like frivol.

Midnight passes, and not many partygoers leave the gathering for midnight mass.

At nearly one Burns asks to walk Eliza home. She says yes without hesitation. Glacial air envelops Skagway, and Eliza steps carefully onto the wooden boardwalk. Her boots crunch the new snow, and Eliza again takes Burns's offered arm as the duo walks the two short blocks to the back of The Moonstone Café. At the foot of the stairs leading to her lodgings, Eliza looks up at Burns, whose head bends down toward hers. Fireworks explode in Eliza's brain.

Without moderating her thoughts, Eliza leads Burns up to her chilly room. Only embers remain in the corner stove. Burns follows Eliza into her lodgings and closes the door behind him with his foot. He turns Eliza around, and backs her up against the door. He looks down at her face.

"May I?"

They kiss at first tentatively, and then deeply. Eliza gasps. Burns slowly disentangles himself from Eliza and removes her coat. He stands admiring her, and traces the outline of her bodice with soft, gentle movements. Eliza stands immobile. Burns moves behind Eliza and steers her around toward the back door. He presses himself up against her back, and cups his hands over her breasts. They remain in this embrace for several minutes in silence, gazing out the back window at the moon.

"Mr. Burns . . ."

"Shhhh . . . Joseph," he whispers.

"Joseph, then. You must think me a good time girl."

"No, on the contrary. I have it on the highest authority that no man has visited you since you arrived in Skagway. I have the utmost respect for you. And for that reason, I think now I must take my leave."

"No!" Eliza startles herself.

With that word, the night descends into intimacies before unknown. Burns lies beside Eliza. They are both fully dressed on her narrow bed frame. Eliza absorbs Burns's warm presence and allows the evening to progress at its own pace, and in its own way. Burns unbuttons Eliza's dress and lowers it, and her camisole, to her waist. He fingers every inch of Eliza's torso with light fingertips, first touching the small space between her collarbones, and running his fingers down and around her now exposed breasts. He takes his time, and Eliza shudders with happiness.

Burns kisses Eliza with latent urgency, and his fingers descend beneath her dress and petticoat, and for the longest and most desirous time, caress her inmost parts. Eliza lets go all sense of modesty, and a warm rising sensation engulfs her. In an urgency she did not previously know she possessed, she arches her back in pleasure, and moans. Burns kisses her again as she climaxes, and whispers in her ear. Burns holds Eliza tightly in a fierce embrace. They lie together like this for most of the night, Burns still fully dressed and Eliza covered with her comforter. She rests her head in the crook of his shoulder. Long into the night, he kisses the top of her head and she murmurs.

"I must go now, Eliza. Not that I want to. You are the first woman I have lain beside in ever so long. I won't soon forget you."

＊

ELIZA WAKES AS IF FROM A DREAM, A SLIGHT HEADACHE NOTHING in comparison to the swelling of her heart. But she knows the previous six hours are far more than a dream. *And quite a lover, too!*

Burns is gone. A slim calling card sits propped on her nightstand: *The Honorable Joseph Burns, Circuit Court of Washington, 14 Pioneer Street, Seattle.* On the flip side of the card, Eliza sees the large masculine hand of the man who shared her bed the night before: *With my deepest regards. Ever, Joseph.*

Eliza swims through many thoughts and emotions toward consciousness. She sits upright and pieces together the events of her awakening. She remembers Mr. Burns whispering into her ear through the night.

If only I could remember his words!

The only coherent sentence she remembers: *I won't soon forget you.*

And now he's on his way to catch the morning steamer, she thinks. *Nine o'clock up.*

Eliza resists the urge to rush to the steamer to see Burns off. Instead, she reclines again on her single bed and wraps herself tightly in the comforter.

What a Christmas, Eliza thinks.

She likens Burns to a present—one she did not have the pleasure of unwrapping.

But—here Eliza blushes, even though she is alone—*Burns unwrapped me!*

She stays in bed for most of the day, wrapping and un-wrapping the night's events. She smells her pillow and detects a faint trace of Burns's cologne, mixed deliciously with his sweat. She feels his invisible fingers roaming over her exposed skin. She pictures his rugged face lying beside her, the deep creases at the corners of his eyes, the slight upturn of his lips as he speaks. She hears his gentle voice.

I will not soon forget you.

Eliza rises from her bed mid-afternoon. She stands naked, and slowly examines herself in the cloudy mirror over the bed stand. She observes every nuance of her body until uncontrollable shivers seize her frame. She grabs her blanket, wraps it around her nakedness, and beats a path to the woodstove to build up a generous fire.

If I had only gotten up last night to feed the fire! But no, I traded one kind of warmth for another kind of warmth, and I would make the same decision again or again not to get up!

Eliza bends and gathers an armload of kindling and places slender pieces crosswise in the gaping iron mouth of the stove. She crumples up two precious pages of *The Skaguay News* and stuffs the newsprint in and under the kindling. With a flick of a long handled match, Eliza coaxes a flame with short puffs of air. Curls of smoke gobble the edges of newsprint; in the process, headlines disappear as surely as all the men who have gone missing in the last nine months since Eliza's been in town.

Eliza inhales the familiar aroma of yellow cedar as flames leap to ignite shards of kindling. She half closes the stove's iron door. She dresses quickly—*oh, how I loved being undressed last night!*—and then returns to tend the fire. It's a good draft by now; the fire pops and crackles as the tinder explodes into flame. Eliza lays a moderate chunk of alder and feeds in additional cordwood. As she grabs another piece, a sliver of cordwood pricks her finger. She instinctively brings her finger to her mouth. She realizes she is positively ravenous.

30

DECEMBER 26, 1898

Partly sunny. Absolutely numbing cold.

The next morning Steiner saunters into the café, his filthy oilskin dragging the floor. He plods to the counter and scans the baked goods. Today Eliza features glazed doughnuts, Miner's Snickerdoodles, and small loaves of currant bread. Steiner's hands, always impeccably clean at Doe Bay, are now grimed with filth. Eliza keeps her distance, does not make eye contact.

If only Rose was back.

Without a helper Eliza cannot excuse herself to go out for a breath of fresh air or to use the privy. Her heart pounds inside her chest. She reaches for her baking cap that dangles from her neck and places it hastily over her hair.

What if he recognizes me?

Conflicting feelings engulf her, and she wraps her apron tighter around her body.

And what of his supposed engagement, she thinks. *And what of Old Steiner?*

Horrified to think that Pearly will spot him on the street,

Eliza catches her breath in an audible short inhale. But Steiner's appearance is much changed as well. After all, Pearly has not seen Steiner in more than thirty years. Eliza wills Steiner to leave the café and hurry to board the next ship south.

It would be better that way, she thinks. *If only he would just get out of town, and leave all the unanswered questions unanswered and unspoken conversations unspoken.*

Steiner approaches the counter and leaves a dime on the counter for coffee. His hollow eyes belie the life he embodied only a year ago. Eliza does not meet his eye, and Steiner takes his steaming coffee to a table less than ten yards away, his back to her. She wonders what she would say if he recognized her. But he won't. For all Steiner knows, Eliza left Cypress for Seattle, or returned to a loveless Missouri. And this handsome woman behind the counter of The Moonstone Café does not resemble the Eliza he knew on Cypress.

How would I explain to Pearly that I know Steiner, and intimately? If I've misled Pearly, that's tantamount to compromising our friendship. No, I will not talk to him.

Steiner finishes his coffee and leaves the café without looking back. Eliza braces herself at the counter. A deep flush creeps up to color her décolletage and neck, and adds rose to her cheeks.

Rose bursts into the café before noon, Baby Thomas wrapped in shawls.

"Why, it's Mrs. Phillips!"

"I've got a letter for you, Eliza. From Mr. Burns. He gave it to Alfred yesterday morning, just before he left on the *Excalibur.*"

Eliza realizes she doesn't know Dr. Phillips's Christian name. *Alfred. Magical counsel, little elf.*

Eliza cannot contain her pleasure, and grabs the letter

from Rose. Of course Rose knows Mr. Burns had not returned to the Phillips's home the night before last. Rose, of all people, knows her secret. Eliza blushes again, and hopes Rose thinks her high color the result of the hot ovens. Eliza slips the letter in her apron pocket.

"And what's your pleasure this morning, dear Rose? A cinnamon bun for you and the good doctor?"

Eliza shutters the shop at four o'clock and hurries up the back stairs to her small apartment. She yearns to read Burns's letter in solitude. Eliza's hand shakes as she dislodges the white vellum from its envelope. She puts a hand to her forehead. She does not have a fever. Instead she feels cold, very cold. She looks for her leather gloves, a new pair lined with the thinnest shearling. She pulls the gloves up to her elbows, wraps her blanket around her shoulders, and peers out the window facing the street. She can see her breath inside the apartment, little wisps of white. She considers putting on her hat.

Large flakes swirl outside the window, cotton balls floating against the pin-dotted darkness. An almost full moon illumines the street below. Men swarm up and down Broadway, like ants. She peers out the front window and squints. From her vantage point, all the men in the throng look the same, their dirty hats pulled low on their heads, and their ill-fitting coats swinging behind them. Try as she might, Eliza cannot make out a familiar face anywhere in the crowd.

When her shaking disappears, she sinks into the armchair slowly and reaches for the vellum. She turns the letter over in her palm and studies the masculine handwriting on the front of the message. She unfolds the letter. She reads the words over and over again.

The next Sunday, Pearly and Eliza sit side by side in the parlor of Mrs. Brown's. Pearly nurses a long cigarette and

Eliza sips her usual stiff aperitif. The antiphon of *Do I? Or don't I?* swirls in Eliza's head.

Should I reveal the last shred of secrecy that stands between us?

On one hand, Eliza knows the confession will act as an ablution. But try as she might, she decides she cannot bridge the divide and will not divulge the fact that she knows Steiner. More imperatively, she will not tell Pearly that Steiner walks the streets just outside the parlor door.

"Cilla out again?"

"The Pack Train. Gotta love her. She's got clients dripping off of her wherever she goes. Even on a Sunday.

"I had a stern talk with her the day after Christmas, though. Did you see the way she cavorted with Lester Edwards at our little soirée? Acting like his wife, she was. Told her it's my house and her stepping out hadn't gone unnoticed. If she wants to be one of my girls, there'll be no more Mr. Edwards. Slime, he is. If she stays here, she's got to earn her keep. And if she has other ideas, well, she'd better get them out in the open."

A slow trickle indicates that Lou luxuriates in the bath. A familiar *whoosh* signals new, warmer water being added to the tub. Eliza considers sharing her news of Mr. Burns, but the subject lurks just at the outskirts of their conversation. Their topics range from the unfamiliar to the almost familiar, but still Eliza does not take the bait.

Just after nine o'clock, Shorty pushes into the parlor, wide-eyed and bloodied. Pearly gasps and rises.

"What in heaven's name happened to you?"

Images of the night of Soapy Smith's murder resurface on the faces of the women. Eliza puts her hand to her throat, and notices a swelling palpitation at the crevice of her neck and her collarbone.

"Big fight over at The Pack Train. Goddamned man nearly killed Charlie Granger. With a broken bottle, no less. Took three of us to wrestle him down. Must've caught a piece of the glass right here."

Shorty holds a bloodied handkerchief to his forehead, and a red streak oozes down the right side of his face.

"Si Tanner's got him now, the bastard."

Eliza stares at Shorty. Her blood runs cold as a wave of adrenaline enters her bloodstream.

Pearly takes the handkerchief from Shorty and continues to press the cloth to his forehead. Shorty winces, but lets Pearly tend to his wound.

Figwort, Eliza thinks. *Indian John would use figwort.*

Pearly stands on her tiptoes in her sleek black buttoned boots and reaches as high as she can. Shorty bends down toward Pearly and looks out from his blackened and swelling eye.

"You're going to have a mighty scar on your forehead," Pearly says. "Make you even uglier than you already are. Now tell us exactly what happened. Every detail, you hear me?"

"Right oddest thing, as the bastard was lying on the floor, he kept pleading for Cilla. Now why would he do that? Cilla was standing right there, just talking to Charlie Granger."

"Cilla! Is Cilla hurt?" Pearly gasps. "And did you recognize the man?"

"Can't rightly say as I know his Christian name, but the barkeep thought his name was Stein, maybe Steiner, couldn't be sure, there was lots of confusion. Cilla's fine, no worries there. She left The Pack Train right away with the others tending to Granger. They're headed over to Bishop Rowe straightaway."

"Stein—Steiner—you say? Are you sure that is what you heard?"

Pearly springs up and walks to her desk underneath the

stairwell. She flips back in the daybook. Pearly's eyes rest on a large, flowery scrawl: A. X. Steiner. It's right there, written in the daybook dated December the twenty-sixth. Day before yesterday. She draws in a sharp breath and looks at Eliza, eyes wide and eyebrows arched.

"It's Steiner."

Eliza registers the name and tries to process the sequence of events.

"You know him?" Shorty asks. "Has he been to see Cilla?"

Pearly covers her shock and emerges from behind the desk.

"Yes, love, he's been to see Cilla. And from what I gather, he's been here three times in the past three days. Wouldn't you know I missed him? Otherwise, I might have recognized the name right away."

Pearly puts her arm through Shorty's.

"Now come upstairs and let's see to that head of yours."

"But first I need to walk Mrs. Waite home."

Shorty glances back over the stair rail toward Eliza.

"Never mind about that, Mr. Richardson. I can make it home by myself. I certainly know the way. Please, not to worry."

Eliza remains amazed at Pearly's poise. Shorty would never know about Pearly and Steiner. And Pearly would never know Eliza's connection to her long-ago lover.

"What a tangled web we weave, when first we practice to deceive," her aunt used to say.

A woman's secrets are buried deep, Eliza thinks. *They're as deep as the gold that waits underground in the frozen Klondike.*

As she walks home alone near midnight, Eliza sees a dim light emanating from the city jail, housed in a corner of Skagway City Hall, a well-built brick structure on the corner of Fifth and State streets. Steiner sits shackled in a tiny jail cell less than fifty yards away. He would never know Eliza walks right by.

Not in a million years, she thinks. *But Skagway's too small for too many secrets.*

Eliza walks as far away from the building as she can, as if getting too close to Steiner would taint her, or, by some force of black magic, draw her into his lair.

A thin skin of circumstance and a matter of days might bring them face to face.

Eliza blanches at the thought.

31

DECEMBER 28, 1898

Overcast, cold. Hike to Pleasant Point today.

At noon the following day, Eliza locks up the Moonstone. In this week between Christmas and New Year's business is slow to non-existent. Eliza leaves the kitchen immaculate. She climbs the familiar stairs to her lodgings and changes into her walking costume. She dresses from the undergarments up, adding layers as necessary.

Now that I have a fur coat, she thinks, *it is high time I got rid of Jacob's coat. It's overstayed its welcome in my life, and that's a fact.*

Eliza walks gingerly through the frozen mud of Broadway and out Third. A lone burning pile smolders at the corner. Eliza hesitates for a moment, glances around. No one is about. She wads the bundle under her left arm into a large, unwieldy ball and tosses the mass into the smoldering fire. The embers lick at the edges of the tattered coat and emit a waft of smoke. Eliza does not linger. In the corner of her eye she sees a whoosh of flame. Jacob's coat, once her only protection from the elements.

Gone.

In the precious few hours of winter daylight, Eliza

continues southeast out of town, and makes her way through the undergrowth and up the well-used trail east of Skagway. The Tlinget people live in the forests east of town, and venture into Skagway. Most come for work, as packers or horsemen. Eliza passes several Tlinget men heading to town. She nods and continues up the well-worn path. She passes no women. Eliza's heart quickens when she spies Na-Oot-Ka at the edge of the burgeoning forest with her woven basket filled with roots. It is Na-Oot-Ka that Eliza has hoped to see.

"Ah, worker of miracles," Na-Oot-Ka says, as she lifts her head to greet Eliza.

"I don't know if that is true, but I appreciate your words."

Words. Words swirl in Eliza's head. Words surround her, convict her, comfort her, instruct her, and uplift her. Words tumble in; words tumble out. She listens to all the words: Jacob's words, harsh and curt; Jonathan's words, pleading and sweet; Indian John's words, instructional and insightful; Pearly's words, frank and pleasant. And all of her aunt's words, those that swirl in and out of Eliza's consciousness, and, try as she may, cannot be snuffed out.

It's odd, she thinks to herself, *how circumstance can change the way words attach themselves. But I know who I am.*

Resourceful, no longer clumsy.

Assertive, no longer quiet.

Beautiful, no longer ugly.

The portrait that E. A. Hegg delivered last week echoed that fact. Eliza had marveled that her likeness stared back at her in sepia tones. Her image is now engraved for posterity. She propped the photograph up on her desk, where she now sees her own likeness looking back at her, and affirming her. She notices the wave of her lovely hair, the curve of her slender neck, and the slight, imperceptible smile.

"You want story?"

"Oh, yes, I certainly want a story."

Na-Oot-Ka straightens her curved back and motions for Eliza to sit. Eliza brushes the snow off a downed log and arranges herself. The Tlinget woman meets Eliza at eye level as Eliza sits. Eliza shivers against the cold seeping through her clothing and onto her bottom. She calculates that she has less than an hour before she is soaked through. Na-Oot-Ka's rheumy eyes stare into Eliza's deep-set eyes. The old woman waits several moments, closes her eyes, and begins the tale. Eliza returns the woman's gaze, shivers again, and listens.

"Today I tell you story of Spirit People.

"In beginning, only night. Always very dark. In quiet part of night, Spirit People hold torches. They wave torches over earth to capture souls of those who die, to lead them over edge of world. All colors of rainbow dance in sky."

Eliza wonders why Na-Oot-Ka chose this particular story, but she listens with keen interest.

"Spirit People lead dead across pathway in sky to land of brightness, where disease and pain no more, and where tables are full with salmon and berries and every kind of food and drink.

"But to this place none but dead and Raven go."

Here Na-Oot-Ka stops for a moment and nods her head, as if agreeing with an inner voice.

"When Spirit People roam sky, they make whistling noise, and Earth people hear them. Earth people run outside and see torches light up night. They see sons and daughters dance in sky.

"Earth people rejoice and dance like sons and daughters. Earth people send message to dead sons and daughters through Spirit People. All colors dance together until morning."

Eliza marvels at the thought of seeing dancing colors in the sky. Seeing such a sight would lighten living in darkness all of the time. It is already dim in Skagway for many months of the year. The unexpected colors of the Aurora Borealis are legend, and Eliza has not seen their magic yet. Eliza craves light, but more than that, she craves communicating with Jonathan.

Could this story be true?

Eliza scolds herself right away.

Of course Na-Oot-Ka's stories ring true, just as Indian John's stories did. Why do I doubt? Especially during this time, the moon of the sacred time?

Na-Oot-Ka bares her gums to Eliza in a crooked smile.

"Is that story you need?"

"It is not me who is a worker of miracles, it is you, Na-Oot-Ka."

"We all worker of miracles," she says. "Now I go feed my husband. He very sick and need my help. Soon he go to spirit world."

Na-Oot-Ka shuffles away into the forest in the growing dark. Eliza knows that Na-Oot-Ka will find her way home, as Eliza will, by following familiar trails, even though darkness envelops the valley. Snow echoes moonlight and lights the trail as she wends her way down the mountain pathway. In contrast to the moonlight, Skagway's newfangled electric street lamps gleam like the sun in the frozen winter night. The night air pricks Eliza's lungs and she rushes toward home.

∽

32

DECEMBER 29, 1898

Steiner lies on a bare tick mattress in his jail cell, a battered man. He has seldom been so cold in his entire life, even counting the treacherous climb up Chilkoot Pass. He actually sweated going up the icy staircase. But here he is too sore to move even one muscle, and he trembles in the dank cell. With the scant dollars left in his pocket, he had aimed to have his share of fun with the cunning demimonde Cilla and drink the nights away before heading south to Seattle at the end of the week. There he might be lucky enough to get his old job back as a barkeep in Pioneer Square. He certainly would not return to Orcas; he'd left his uncle in a tight spot when he pilfered all the money in his uncle's till the day he stiffed his fiancée.

And Jane's father would surely kill me if he ever laid eyes on me again. Couldn't get out of there fast enough, once I knew she was in the family way. Maybe I'll go to San Francisco again, or try my luck further south. Maybe in the City of Angels, or maybe all the way to Mexico. Get myself one of those Spanish vixens. Live out my days in the sun.

He shakes in his thin coat and swears under his breath.

It is blame cold in this hellhole on Earth. And I've been cheated. If there was any gold to be had in these environs, it certainly eluded me.

To keep his mind off his discomfort, he dwells on Cilla.

All that lovely hair. And waif-like, almost like a child.

Steiner grows hard thinking about her. Of all the prostitutes he'd lain with, Cilla possessed skills he never before experienced.

"Shhhh . . . no words," Cilla had said, as she slowly undressed Steiner in her dark blue bedroom. The cold air prickled his skin and Cilla's light touch added to the chill. She had led him to her enormous bed and straddled him, using her hands to arouse him. Cilla held Steiner captive for an entire hour, and spread her waist-long hair over his body as he trembled violently. She had then gathered her voluminous hair in her lovely bird-like hands and moved the damp tresses over her own body, spreading his fullness in a wavy pattern on her paper white skin. Steiner thought she had looked like a butterfly. Steiner wondered where Cilla learned this technique, but he didn't care. All he wanted was to do it again.

Early on New Year's Eve morning, Peterson rustles Steiner.

"Time for the likes of you scumbag shit to be out of here. Boat leaves at nine o'clock sharp. Quite a crowd outside already waiting to see you. I'd watch for flying bottles if I was you."

Steiner turns his bloodied head toward Peterson.

"Go to hell."

Peterson shrugs.

"Suit yourself. Better be ready in ten minutes, or I'll have some of the others help drag you out."

Steiner rubs his head. When he tries to get up from the cot, his bruised ribs ache. It would be a long trip in the brig to Seattle, and then who knows what. Steiner couldn't think that far ahead. He could barely make it to his feet.

Shoulda used an alias.

From outside the cell, he hears a gathering crowd, a murmur that grows louder as he approaches the small cell window. In the muddied street, men and women talk and shift.

He recognizes the tall red-haired man who pulled him from the fight standing high above the crowd and feels the blow to his ribs again. But the blow is nothing compared to the blow he feels when he looks past the man. He squints through the narrow slats and focuses on the face.

Pearly!

Of this he is absolutely sure. She hadn't aged, and Steiner's mind raced to wonder how Pearly landed in Skagway.

Just like I did, he thinks. *She must have followed the lowest common denominator. Some things never change.*

But much has changed, and he shakes his head in disbelief. Here he stands, a bruised and battered prisoner. Pearly, however, stands free, dressed in a fashionable fur coat and an enormous hat, decorated with the head of a red fox, its eyes squinting back at him. Steiner watches Pearly; her mannerisms erase thirty years. He vividly remembers her lying in the clawfoot tub and inviting him in. A lifetime ago.

"Get your sorry ass away from that window," Peterson says. "Time to face the masses."

Steiner steals one more look at Pearly and turns toward Peterson. Steiner dismisses the urge to deck Peterson, the action futile. He barely musters the strength to walk to the near side of the cell. Peterson cuffs Steiner's hands and shackles his filthy boots. The stench emanating from Steiner's grimy, greased trousers almost makes Peterson puke. He stifles the bile that rises up from his gut into his throat and spits on the cell floor. The spit hits the toes of Steiner's boots. The pair exits the cell and shuffles out through the passageway toward the front door

of the brig. Marshall Tanner stands at the door and levels a
steely gaze at Steiner.

"This is it for you, pal," Tanner says. "Get the likes of you
out of Skagway."

Tanner strides ahead of Steiner and Peterson, and stops
short of the boardwalk. He motions with his hands to the
gathered crowd to make way. Once outside, the crowd jeers at
Steiner, many hurling insults his way. Steiner keeps his head
low. He hadn't planned to look at Pearly, but he can't help
himself. When he sees the hem of her long fur coat in the
periphery of his view, he stops for a moment and raises his
gaze. He takes in every detail of her costume, the small black
buttoned boots that peek from beneath the hem, the voluminous swath of the fur coat, her delicate gloved hands, one
resting inside a muff, the other attached to the large man who
dwarfs her, the outline of her robust bustline, the mere hint of
cleavage below the rounded collar, the beautiful, although
somewhat aged, porcelain face. Steiner and Pearly lock eyes.
To Steiner, the moment lasts an eternity, although in common
time, the moment measures two or three seconds. The silent
conversation speaks volumes.

"Get your eyes off the women, you sloth," Peterson says.

"Sorry, Ma'am," Tanner says, as he passes Pearly.

"No, thank you," Pearly says. She looks past Tanner and
stares at Steiner.

Steiner pulls his gaze away from Pearly. The woman next
to Pearly seems familiar, and next to that woman stands Cilla.

Lovely Cilla.

Steiner aches for her. He wrenches his head around to
study the face between Pearly and Cilla.

The eyes, the mouth, the hair. Could it be? No, he says to himself, *no.*

"Move along."

Peterson shoves Steiner on the back and sends him sprawling. As Steiner unfolds himself from the waist up, he looks one last time at the mystery woman. Now he places her.

It's the woman from the bakery. I recognize the handsome face. But still, there is something else . . .

In a fleeting instant, he looks lastly at Cilla. Her eyes register nothing as she looks at him. She stares at him like a stranger.

The crowd lining the street parts as Peterson and the prisoner near the *Rosalie*. Shouts, jeers, and the occasional profanity offend Steiner. He keeps his head low.

At ten minutes to nine, Steiner is none too early to board the ship. He manages to walk up the gangway in small, measured steps; the shackles on his feet hinder his ascent. He shuffles, a slow, dull, *bum-bum*—pause—*bum-bum*, as his boots meet corrugated metal. Behind him, in the sea of faces, he peers over the rail once more toward Pearly and Cilla and the face between them. He lets out an audible grunt when he reaches the top of the gangway.

Mrs. Stamper!

He draws in a sharp breath and exhales despair.

How can that be? She looks so . . . good. How and why has Mrs. Stamper managed to make her way to Skagway? And how has she befriended Pearly and Cilla? Certainly she is not a prostitute? No, she owns a bakery. Why of course! Eliza Stamper who won blue ribbons each year at the Orcas Fair! Mrs. Stamper who I stiffed in favor of that younger, lovelier specimen . . .

Steiner lets out a cynical laugh. Pearly, Eliza, and Cilla, all together in Skagway, a trifecta of women he had cared for in his life. The thought wrenches his soul. In ten minutes' time, he will leave the threesome behind, and probably forever. And now he faces a long torturous ride to Seattle.

His future unfolds behind his eyes, a domino effect that cannot be stopped. He has run from the law for thirty years: countless bar room fights, an unresolved murder and a stolen horse, a near-strangled prostitute. He knows with certainty that his past will finally catch up with him, and he will face the noose.

But seeing those three women at once just a few minutes earlier convicted him more than any legal sentence could ever condemn him. He laughs again, this time at his own expense. He knows beyond any shadow of doubt that he is, indeed, a doomed man.

∽

33

December 30, 1898

Overcast, chance of snow. Send letter.

ime is the father of truth," her aunt used to say.
Eliza struggles against her natural tendency to harbor secrets, especially to a friend.

But some secrets lay safer unspoken.

She seesaws her way through the argument as she tries to warm herself in her chilled lodgings. Seeing Steiner off that morning had shaken Eliza to the core. It was all she could do to go through the motions at work. Now, back in her room above the café, she sits and thinks of all the secrets she hides beneath a thin scrim of deceit.

Gideon.

Steiner.

Phillips.

Burns.

She snorts.

Men! They're all of them men!

Eliza juxtaposes her short list of secrets against those of Pearly's. With that thought, Eliza dismisses any compunction to reveal every last secret she holds inside.

What did she want to remember of Gideon anyway? Like a scab that healed over, only the scar of his memory marked her. And to have traded Jonathan for never knowing Gideon?

Never!

Steiner proves a much more complicated study. His magnetic pull has always confused Eliza, but she knows the further Steiner travels from her she'll be all the more relieved. She doubts she will ever see Steiner again.

And good riddance!

Phillips, Eliza thinks, *now there's a missed opportunity. How could I have misread his cues? Or was I guilty of reading too much into a merely platonic relationship?*

Eliza chides herself for her stupidity.

She turns her thought to Mr. Burns, he who awakened Eliza to the wonders of human sexuality and—*dare she say?*— love. Eliza had scoured the faces of the crowd this morning and wished to see such a face again.

Eliza rises from the wingback chair and stands. She stretches her arms above her head and reaches toward the low ceiling. She moves then from the front of the wing chair to the small desk at the ell of the small lodgings. Eliza settles at her desk and takes a deep breath.

She turns Mr. Burns's calling card over and lingers on the message.

With my deepest regards. Ever, Joseph.

Eliza devours his letter again, whose words she now knows backwards and forwards, like a child's fairy tale, one of the many she read again and again as a child: *The Steadfast Tin Soldier*, or *Sleeping Beauty,* or *Rapunzel.* No matter how many times she heard the fairy stories, she managed to find a fresh kernel, a trace of nuance, a hidden meaning.

My dear Mrs. Waite:

I dread to think on my actions last evening. You must think me a cur. I cannot offer enough apologies to you. I will not endeavor to make excuses for my reprehensible behavior.

If you find any kindness in your heart, I hope you will accept my sincerest apology. I suffer even now as I write to you.

Meeting you kindled a desire I thought long dead. If only we had the time to know each other, and develop a proper relationship . . .

But, alas, I think I have snuffed out any hopes of such a liaison.

You are a beautiful woman, and one of the utmost integrity. If my actions have besmirched your character in your own eyes, or in the eyes of any you know, I will never forgive myself.

Please accept my sincerest apologies. I will not endeavor to contact you again, and understand if your thoughts of me are put quickly behind you.

Wishing you only the best, as you so richly deserve.
Joseph Burns

With resolve, and a heart light and full, Eliza picks up her fountain pen. She dips the nub of her pen into the inkwell and puts nub to paper.

Dear Mr. Burns:

What a source of wonder, wonder and delight, to make your acquaintance on Christmas last. Our precious time together warmed my heart. You misunderstand. I enjoyed our short time together and wish the time could have been doubled or tripled. I am in your debt.

I appreciate your thoughtful words; in this northern climate, warm words are appreciated as much as a warm blanket!

Here Eliza stops. She glances at her bed and recreates the scene, her blanket encasing two bodies locked in passion. She smiles, and tries to remember details of Mr. Burns's face as he nuzzled close to her.

I trust your trip to Seattle proved uneventful. Much excitement has transpired here in this little hamlet since your departure. No doubt you will hear of the scuffle that sent a near murderer out of our midst and to Seattle for sentencing. But perhaps there are many such cases that cross your desk. What drives men to exhibit such lawless behavior? You must scratch your head at times. But I do not intend to bore you with the details of such a trivial matter.

Please let me know if you intend to return to our special part of the world in the coming year. I would love to show you more of what our little town has to offer.

Eliza stops again and blots the ink that stains the cream-colored stationery.

I would love to show you more of what I have to offer, she thinks.

She shakes out her ink-stained hand and continues her message.

I will await your reply forthwith. I send my regards to you, as well, my dear Mr. Burns, and wish you a blessed and prosperous New Year!

Your friend in the North,
Eliza Waite

She waves the stationery in the air and allows the ink to fully dry. She folds the sheet into thirds and pushes the note into an envelope. She pauses and reaches for her small portrait that stands propped on her desk. On impulse, she adds the portrait to the envelope and presses her lips to the seal.

Tomorrow I will post this letter. I will await your reply forthwith.

Eliza quickens to the thought. She cannot imagine her mother, or her aunt, or even her sisters Margaret or Mae, penning such a bold letter.

And sending my portrait to a man!

Eliza sits again in the wing chair and pulls her blue plaid blanket around her. She snuggles into the blanket and rests her head on the back of the wing chair. She remains there until sleep almost overcomes her, and only then does she rise. Her bed frame seems particularly empty. She shivers in the darkness.

I will await your reply forthwith.

Eliza places three large stones on the top corner of the pot-bellied stove. She busies herself with the routine of bedtime: washing her face, letting down her hair, removing her skirt, blouse, singlet, bloomers, and stockings, and then diving into her flannel nightdress. She puts on warm woolen socks and wraps herself again in the blanket. There she sits, lost in a reverie.

A half hour later, she lifts the stones from the stove with a wide pair of tongs and wraps them in cotton rags. She moves the rags from hand to hand and places the rocks at the foot of her bed, under the eiderdown comforter. She shivers again in her nightclothes and dims the lamp. She slips under the covers and settles her feet near the toasty rocks. Waves of heat emanate from the rocks and Eliza begins to warm from the feet upwards.

She raises the nightdress up and over her head and uses her feet to peel down her woolen socks. She lies naked in her bed and thinks of Burns. After many nights of fruitless attempts, Eliza brings herself to full climax. She is both surprised and delighted. She then enjoys a second wave of pleasure. She lays breathless in her bed and throws off the eiderdown. The evening's coolness prickles her body.

She wishes with every fiber of her body that the *Excalibur* would turn about-face in its southerly course—south of Ketchikan by now, perhaps almost to Vancouver—and steam full-on back to Skagway.

But of course it will be more than a week before her letter reaches Seattle and another week before a reply steams northward. Eliza has spent too many winters alone, and longs for Burns's long and lanky body beside hers. His absence magnifies the loneliness of the winter night, and Eliza pulls the eiderdown over her nakedness and invites sleep.

Every day is a day closer, she thinks.

I will await your reply forthwith.

34

∞

DECEMBER 31, 1898

New Year's Eve. Clear. Celebration tonight.

"Quite a night of nights!" Shorty booms. His voice carries down the inlet. Bright stars pin-dot the sky. The glacial air permeates every crevice not covered in fur. Eliza's nose tingles in the cold and she adjusts her woolen scarf. In that split second her hands begin to numb. She quickly replaces her gloved hands into the fur muff and works the lining with her fingers. A thin blue-green wisp wavers across the sky, followed by a halo of orange and yellow, slithering behind the blues and greens, undulating, as if alive, as the Aurora Borealis streaks through the night sky.

Spirit People, Eliza thinks. *They're waving their torches in the sky.*

A quiver runs through her body as she and Pearly walk arm in arm with Shorty. She wonders where Na-Oot-Ka is tonight, and if Na-Oot-Ka's husband is still alive.

Hundreds of people ring the inlet huddling around small and large bonfires. Laughter. A gun shot into the air. Then another. A low hum of voices intersperses with louder voices, and more laughter. The trio scans the assembled crowd, looking for Rose and Dr. Phillips amid the whole of Skagway's cast of characters. Familiar faces gather in an uneven arc around an enormous bonfire at the edge of the mud flats. Eliza spies the Phillips family and steers Pearly and Shorty to the right. Eliza steps gingerly through the muddied flats, her boots squishing into frozen muck.

"Mr. Edwards, Cilla," Pearly says, as the threesome maneuvers through the throng. Eliza echoes the regards.

"You're looking lovely tonight, Mrs. Brown, as are you, Mrs. Waite," Edwards says. He bows to the women in Shorty's tow. Cilla drips in new diamonds, an Alaskan-sized brooch adorning her throat. She holds Edwards's arm like a bird perched on his elbow.

"Why, Cilla, you are looking quite sparkly this New Year's Eve," Pearly says. She moves closer to Cilla and whistles through her teeth as she fingers the brooch. "My, my, now. You've hooked a big one, now, haven't you?"

The men snigger. Eliza nods to Cilla, who turns her head in the direction of Chinese fireworks further down the beach.

"Excuse me, Shorty, Mr. Edwards, Pearly, Cilla."

Eliza extricates herself from Pearly's grasp and moves toward Dr. Phillips, Rose, and Baby Thomas, who sit on a large piece of driftwood not a hundred feet away.

"What a sweetheart!" Eliza says. Baby Thomas, wrapped up so tightly that only his nose protrudes from the shawls, meets Eliza's gaze. Eliza snuggles her face in close to the infant. She whispers and coos. Baby Thomas squirms and smiles.

"OOOO," he says. "OOOO-OOOO."

Eliza positions herself next to Rose and leans in.

"I've posted a letter. To Mr. Burns. We enjoyed a lovely time together just this Christmas last, and I hope to see him again in the not too distant future."

Eliza feels a rush of adrenaline and continues. She leans forward, past Rose and Baby Thomas.

"You wouldn't know if Mr. Burns plans to visit again soon, do you, Dr. Phillips?"

Phillips turns first to Rose and then to Eliza.

"Why, I couldn't rightly say. But an invitation for his return is also in the mail. My Rose, here, she encouraged me to write him. We offered to take him on a train journey up White Pass on his return, and to entertain him properly, now that we've got the space to do so. May we include you in our plans, if Mr. Burns returns to us this springtime?"

Eliza sees Sugi Ito in the periphery of her vision, and watches as Sugi moves through the throng. Her daughters and grandchildren follow her. Sugi stops and looks up at the illuminated sky. She stands transfixed at the edge of the inlet. Eliza thinks Sugi looks like a small tree with her bird family flocking around her.

"Of course you may, Dr. Phillips. I would very much like to be included in your merry band. I've longed to take the railway to White Pass myself. Count me in. Oh! And by the way, you're addressing a now-famous newspaper columnist!"

Rose gasps.

"Is it true? Did Mr. Draper come through on his word?"

Earlier in the day Eliza had held a slightly dated copy of the *St. Louis Globe-Democrat* in her hand, sent by post, as promised, by the intrepid reporter Jack Draper, all the way from St. Louis, Missouri. She smiled to herself, thinking of Draper.

Hail from Missoura, I do, yes.

"*From a Klondike Kitchen: Featuring the Extraordinary Sweets of Mrs. E. Waite, lately of Skagway, Alaska*" had stared out at Eliza from page nine of the twelve-page rag, and she read the piece over and over to see if any mistake had been made. There were no typographic errors. Eliza hugged the newspaper to her small chest and smiled. She wondered if her mother or her sisters, or even her aunt—*God forbid!*—took the *Globe-Democrat*. And what of Mrs. Chopin?!

What a shock to see my name in print! I must write to Mr. Draper to thank him.

Strains of *Auld Lang Syne* waft down the beach. The air bristles electric. If there is ever a time Eliza is excited to take in a breath, it is tonight. The Arctic air makes breathing out like an art form, as puffs of steamed air evaporate into the darkness with each long exhale. Firelight glows off ruddy faces.

"Come, let's move closer to the fire."

As it nears midnight, Eliza takes in the whole scene around her.

"Home is where your heart is," her aunt used to say. For once her aunt was most certainly right.

I belong here. I belong. Here. Yes, here. I belong here.

Eliza accepts a Chinese sparkler from Shorty. Shorty lights the nub end of the sparkler and Eliza holds it alight. She waves the sparkler high above her head and watches its smoky tail winging up to join the Spirit People, the moon, the stars. Eliza tiptoes to the water's edge, her sparkler still aloft.

The Spirit People continue to dance in rolling blues and greens low across the Arctic sky. Eliza looks upwards, mesmerized, and watches as hints of yellow emerge on the underside of the ribbon. Eliza turns and faces down the darkened Lynn Canal, the way from which she'd come nine months ago.

"The water of the Gulf stretched out before her, gleaming with . . . millions of lights . . ."

Eliza focuses now on the lights that dance across the skin of the water.

I will never be able to count that high!

The water hypnotizes Eliza, and she loses herself in its ever-changing movement. The constant lapping of small wavelets brings her out of her trance, and more of Mrs. Chopin's words speak to Eliza as she stands at the water's edge. She listens intently to the *whap, whap, whap* of the waves that threaten to lick her boots.

"The voice of the sea is seductive, never ceasing, whispering, clamoring, murmuring . . ."

Eliza wonders if she'll ever travel south again.

Much depends on Burns's reply, she thinks.

A loud familiar voice booms above the rest.

"Come one, come all!" Shorty yells.

Shorty organizes a rough tug of war under the moonlight, and fireworks explode into the night sky at midnight. Flasks of whiskey and small tin cups of champagne pass thirsty lips. The bonfire's glow settles over the beachfront, illuminating hundreds of hopeful faces. Smaller groups form around campfires and burning barrels; no one wants to leave the revelry. The firelight rings the bay like a lighted necklace.

How coincidental, Eliza thinks. *Here I am standing on the shore of Smuggler's Cove in Skagway, Alaska, when a year ago I stood on the shores of another cove that bears the very same name, more than a thousand miles to the south. What is it about that name? And what have I been smuggling?*

She stops for a moment to answer her own question.

Why of course! Happiness! And miracles!

She smiles internally, and thinks of Joseph Burns. She wonders if her letter has yet reached Seattle, and to what response.

I will await your reply forthwith.

"Eliza Waite! You're looking all dewy-eyed. Come over here; we've got a New Year's resolution to share with you."

Could it be?!

Eliza wonders if Shorty has finally asked for Pearly's hand in marriage. It was an unspoken agreement that linked them together; would Shorty be making Pearly an honest woman after all these years? Eliza looks forward to the imaginary event already. She will make the biggest wedding cake she can afford for her unlikely friends.

"May I guess your resolution?" Eliza asks.

"Now that would be bad luck, especially if you guessed wrong! Here it is, plain and simple," Shorty says. "We've decided to quit this hell hole and try our luck up Nome way. Talk is there's more gold in Nome than ever was found in the Yukon. You're more than welcome to come along."

Pearly nods and smiles up at Shorty.

"Can't stay in one place too long, you know, Lizzie. Gets stale after a while. And Mr. Richardson has asked for my hand, so I can't let him go on alone."

The admission of Pearly and Shorty's impending marriage confirms Eliza's suspicions, but the thought of moving again and losing such a precious friendship takes Eliza back.

So much change, and so soon again.

The choice to stay or go lies firmly within her power.

But tonight is not a night for decisions. For now it's time to offer congratulations all around. Handshakes, hugs, hearty best wishes, that's what tonight's for.

Well after midnight, Eliza bids Pearly and Shorty good night.

Eliza notices the way Pearly and Shorty look at each other.

Why, they must be near fifty!

She wishes Joseph Burns was standing next to her looking at her in the same way.

What a happy evening, Eliza thinks. *In so many ways.*

Eliza takes her time as she walks the six blocks to The Moonstone Café. She passes the wharves, illuminated by the full moon. Water rats scamper under the wharves, their retreating tails their only evidence. Other than the rats, the wharves stand empty. Three vessels are docked at Skagway Wharf. The *SS Superior,* slightly larger than the *Ketchikan,* dwarfs two smaller trawlers. The yawing of the lines creaks and squeaks in the silence. At the end of the pier a young couple stands in close embrace. Eliza yearns for Mr. Burns. She imagines herself as the shorter half of the couple in the distance, and watches as their heads bend to a kiss.

I await your reply forthwith.

Eliza turns up Broadway toward the "V" of White Pass, which is also illumined. All the storefronts stand shuttered against the winter night: E. A. Hegg's studio, Taylor's Drygoods, Clease's Stationers. The doors to the Skagway Livery shut with a *clang*. Eliza sees another solo walker in the distance. A block ahead, a couple steals into an alley away from the cold. She passes a small group of rugged men.

"A Happy New Year to you, Ma'am."

"And to you."

Eliza hums under her breath, an old familiar hymn.

O for a thousand tongues to sing . . .

She climbs the back wooden stairs to the landing of her apartment. She opens the door to her humble abode. She thinks of Pearly's invitation, but sloughs it off. A long moonless winter will unfold ahead before anyone packs up and leaves Skagway behind.

God and I will have a long conversation on this topic!

She undresses slowly and hangs her dress by the door. The full moon gazes through the small window, and Eliza admires the sight. She decides not to cover the window with her dress tonight. The moonlight slides in, her most constant companion, simultaneously tangible and intangible.

Like Jonathan. Tangible and intangible.

Eliza retraces every feature of Jonathan's cherubic face, every curve of his limbs, every nuance of his smile. But she cannot touch him, hold him, or stroke his fine sandy hair. He is as real as any boy, as any of the newsies on the wharf, as any of the boisterous boys running rampant on the moonlit beach. But she cannot talk to him, or offer him comfort or advice. He lives in a photograph, a slim tintype bought for twenty-five cents.

In a feeling that surprises her, the pangs of her despair give rise to a deep satisfaction. The moon, like Jonathan, will be with her always, this Indian John told her. And Na-Oot-Ka reiterated the same.

Spirit People. All colors dance together until morning.

Eliza reclines in her deep featherbed, her arms folded behind her head. She looks up at the ceiling and smiles.

Precious, yes. Each day, each night, precious.

Her thoughts wander, in, out, over, above.

When I wake up tomorrow morning, the calendar will read The Year of Our Lord 1899. And what will the new century bring in a year's time?

The prospect stands before her like the wide and turbulent Gulf of Alaska, always changing, and always to be respected; she knows, instinctively, that like the tides, life will cede and recede, ebb and flow. To try and catch the tide would be fruitless.

As for tomorrow, she thinks, there will be a line formed outside the café just after six in the morning.

My fruitcake will sell out before ten, and then I'll take a long walk up into the valley, as far as I dare go while there's any shred of daylight. I'll take a small picnic and all my memories, and I'll bury the past. I've beaten the devil around the stump too many times; tomorrow I'll do what

I should have done many years ago and put it all behind me. It's time.

And it's time I bought a typewriter. I can well afford it! Perhaps the Jack Drapers of the world ache to see more of my recipes. Why, I could be a syndicated columnist! I can just see my column appearing in newspapers all over Missoura. Or maybe beyond! And who knows who might read my recipes. Maybe Mother, or Margaret, or Mae. Or maybe even Mrs. Chopin!

Perhaps I will finally write to Mrs. Chopin. To thank her for, well, for everything. For her stories. For her words. For the ways she's touched my heart.

The prospect invigorates her, and she finds she cannot sleep, although her body and mind are thoroughly exhausted. She turns onto her side and faces the back door, the bright moon framed in its center window.

"Goodnight, sweet boy," Eliza whispers. "You are never far from my heart."

In the distance, the northern lights dance around the frame of the sky, a fringe of blues and greens receding on the horizon. Eliza sinks into her feather pillow and wishes for a good sleep. Mrs. Chopin wrote about the white light of the moon that fell upon the world *"like the mystery and softness of sleep."*

Ah, sleep, Eliza thinks, *I am envious of sleep. But there is so much to life. Who needs to sleep through it?*

Long about three o'clock, still hours before the dim Alaskan dawn, a sliver of moonlight creeps further into the room and inches its way across the rough pine floor and up onto Eliza's thick eiderdown comforter. It lingers there, and she focuses on the bright moon shadow.

In that moment before sleep, when every movement is exaggerated and intentional, and fueled by an extraordinary effort of sheer will and desire, Eliza reaches for the moonbeam, and falls asleep with it pulsing in her hand.

EPILOGUE

MARCH 6, 1900

The narrow ribbon of blue winds up the landscape, braiding and re-braiding as it passes Channel Town and Swanson and Whitney before it spills into shallow Padilla Bay. Eliza stands by the edge of the slough and dips her bare toe into the swift current. She dislodges a small twig and sends it out, where it swirls clockwise before disappearing in the dirty foam.

She means to sit, but the muddied bank would stain her day dress, and it would take two, maybe three, days to wring it out and dry again. Her feet are swollen and mud oozes in between her toes.

It feels like I'm walking on worms.

Eliza checks her pocket watch: *3:45.* The afternoon is waning and she still needs to walk up the hill before Joseph gets back. In bare feet. She looks around; no one is about. She hopes no one notices that she's not wearing any footwear. There is no way her sausage-like feet will reinsert themselves into her slender boots. She strains to bend over and picks up her boots and stockings.

March is no time for tomfoolery, she reminds herself. *And even if I am heavy with child, I've got no time to waste here.*

An early pang of imminent labor crushes Eliza's midsection. She puts her hand to her side and draws in a deep breath. The Honorable Joseph A. Burns sits in court just two short blocks away at the edge of the hill overlooking Channel Town. It's his eighth trip to Skagit County north of Seattle in the last year. Eliza doesn't accompany him on most trips, but because she's near term, she has chosen to travel with her itinerant husband instead of lying confined in their cavernous Seattle home with only his dead wife's sister as company.

Besides, it's always a gay time in Channel Town, visiting the Conrads and the Johnstons and the Clarks. The food! The wine! The conversation! All of it titillates Eliza, and, in her present condition, takes her mind off the inevitable.

Eliza sloshes her feet in the channel one more time and lumbers up the back way to their lodgings above the courthouse. She passes close to an overgrown patch of salal and catches the lace on her wristlet in the brambles. She disentangles the errant branch and smoothes the lace. A small red gash spouts blood beneath the lace. Eliza brings her wrist to her mouth and sucks at the blood. She continues up the hill, still glancing to see if anyone is following her or coming ahead on the pathway.

If I let myself in the back door, Lettie won't mind the mess. I've never been a front door guest anyway. Better to be a back door guest and share the secrets.

Just nine months earlier, Eliza had disembarked from the *SS Juneau* on Seattle's rough waterfront and had spilled into the arms of her future husband. A hasty wedding took place that evening in the parlor of Burns's Queen Anne home, with another young judge and his diminutive wife acting as witnesses. The newlyweds raced up the stairs after the last of the guests bade their farewells and well wishes. Their insatiability for each other knew few bounds. The summer earlier, when Joseph had visited Eliza in Skagway, they spent four delirious nights making love, without regard for propriety, or gossip.

"I can't wait to make an honest woman out of you," Burns had repeated over and over, as the couple lay entwined on Eliza's feather bed above The Moonstone Café.

"Well. You'll just have to wait, won't you? I've got some unfinished business to attend to, and then I'll be right on your heels. The new Mrs. Joseph Burns, Esquire will arrive in Seattle in less than a month, so hold your horses until then."

Eliza's pregnancy had curtailed their avid love making, but it did not diminish their affection to each other. A pat on the rear. A nuzzled kiss on the ear. A long, tender stroke on the inside of the arm that sent shivers up Eliza's spine.

Eliza trudges up Commercial Street past First and Second. The sun has begun its low arc toward setting, and the channel sparkles with fireflies of light. Tall Douglas firs and cedars dapple the direct shaft of sunlight and Eliza squints toward the west. It's less than ten miles to Cypress Island from where she stands. She wonders if she'll ever go back.

☞

"CHEERS, ALL," JOSEPH TOASTS. THE DINING TABLE IS LONG, AND seats ten comfortably. Tonight the gathering includes Channel Town's highest society. Eliza feels flushed on the warm early spring evening. Her gown is of the highest quality, a rich brown brocade with flattering pleats falling from a high empire waist. Her breasts are swollen due to her condition, and she flaunts them modestly. Pearly's locket hangs in her décolletage and feels cool against her skin. The only discomfort she feels is in her ever-swollen feet pinched into constricting boots. She wishes she was barefoot again.

"And when do we expect the little Master Burns?"

"Mind you, I'm hoping for the little Miss Burns," Eliza says. She looks directly at the mayor.

"I've got a premonition. We'll name her Sarah Pearl, after an old friend."

"You've got your hands full with this one, Joseph," the mayor says. "Not that I'm making any comparisons."

Eliza ignores the comment.

Ass.

She smiles, nonetheless.

"Any bets, boys? My money's on Sarah Pearl, if that's what my wife says," Burns replies.

Eliza does not tell her husband that the labor pangs have started early. She secretly hopes to birth the child away from Seattle so that she does not have to be attended by Joseph's sister-in-law.

"It's too early!" Joseph says, when Eliza wakes him in the dead of night.

"She'll come when she's ready. Quick, wake Lettic, and hurry to Dr. Clark's. We'll be needing him shortly."

Eliza chews on a stick of cinnamon in between contractions. The memory of Jonathan's birth rises to the surface of her semi-consciousness. His had been a long, painful delivery. Eliza prays that she will be delivered of this child in a much shorter time period. When the doctor arrives, the baby's head is nearly crowning and Eliza lets out her first ardent scream.

Eliza hears the steady *clomp clomp clomp* of Joseph's boots on the planked floor of the courtroom below their lodgings as she weathers the last grueling pains of her delivery.

In a flurry of screams and blood, Sarah Pearl Burns makes her appearance at dawn. Eliza glances outside. The sun is just peeking over the eastern horizon. Eliza closes her eyes and notes the date: *March the 7th, 1900.*

Two years to the day since I found the ticket on Seattle's muddy streets. And what a two years it's been . . .

She opens her eyes, takes in a full breath—one to almost overflowing—and turns her attention to her new daughter. She takes the tiny bundle into her arms. Her eyes tear up, and she chokes a suppressed sob.

Eliza clears her parched throat and the corners of her mouth curve into a smile. The baby purses her lips and peers up through the narrowest of slits. Eliza holds the moment for as long as she can, and lets out a long exhale.

"Welcome to the world, Little Pearly."

ACKNOWLEDGMENTS

A mere thank you does not convey the deep gratitude I have for a small circle of family and friends who have supported me throughout writing this novel: Michael Barclay, my husband and confidante, who first brought me to Cypress Island in Washington's San Juan Islands; my parents, Gerald F. Sweeney and Barbara M. Sweeney, whose unconditional support is palpable; and my dear friend Nancy Soderlund Tupper, who read multiple versions of the manuscript and offered invaluable advice and critique.

I also thank supporters from the women's writing retreat center at Hedgebrook on Whidbey Island, Washington, where the kernel of this novel took shape during a week-long master class taught by Jane Hamilton in 2010.

Other thanks go to the staff at the Klondike Gold Rush National Park in Skagway, Alaska, and to the staff at The Anchorage Museum in Anchorage, Alaska; to Catherine H. Spude, Ph.D, for invaluable information about Skagway history; and Jill K. LaPointe for Lushootseed language translations. A special thanks to former Nooksack student Kyle Joseph whose ancestral name, Ts'Qwe-Mit, was used for an important character in the novel. The character of Indian John is a mosaic of several former Native American students who showed much promise as future leaders of their respective tribes. I think of them often and wish them continued success.

Many thanks go to the Wormettes, that zany group of women in my rollicking book and wine club; to Katrina Larsen Groen for her keen-eyed copy edit; to Brooke Warner, Cait

Levin, and the sisterhood of writers at She Writes Press; and to my publicist, Caitlin Hamilton Summie. A thousand thanks!

And, of course, I cannot neglect to add a special thank you to my four wonderful children for believing in me, even when the years and the rejection letters mounted like so many layers on a crooked birthday cake. Here's to you: Chris, Megs, Annie, and John. I love you more than cheese.

Eliza Waite is an amalgam of my imagination. While most of the characters in the novel are fictitious, several historical figures appear, including Jefferson Randolph "Soapy" Smith, Frank Reid, E. A. Hegg, Si Tanner, and Harriet Pullen. All conversations and references linked to these characters are fictional, but I have attempted to stay true to their historical characters. Some historical events, including the release of Kate Chopin's novel, *The Awakening*, which was published in 1899, and the annual Orcas Island Fair, which debuted in the early 1900s, have been accelerated to fit the parameters of the story. The town of Fisher Bay on Cypress Island is fictitious. And while there was no widespread smallpox epidemic in Washington State in the 1890s, smallpox lurked as a feared and often fatal disease at the end of the 19th century.

The Pacific Northwest and Alaska . . . what wild and wonderful places! And to think I planned to visit for only a couple of months when I first visited in the late 1970s.

So glad I stayed. So very glad.

ABOUT THE AUTHOR

A native New Yorker, Ashley E. Sweeney lives and writes in La Conner, Washington. She is a graduate of Wheaton College in Norton, Massachusetts and is an award-winning journalist in Washington State. *Eliza Waite* is her first novel.

REFERENCES

13 Moons: The 13 Lunar Phases, and How They Guide the Swinomish People, Swinomish Indian Tribal Community, La Conner, Washington, 2006.

Backhouse, Frances, *Women of the Klondike*, Whitecap Books, Vancouver, B.C., Canada, 1995.

Becker, Ethel Anderson, *Klondike '98*, Binfords and Mort Publishers, Portland, Oregon, 1949.

Berton, Pierre, *The Klondike Quest: A Photographic Essay 1897-1899*, Boston Mills Press, Erin, Ontario, Canada, 1997.

Bolotin, Norm, *Klondike Lost: A Decade of Photographs by Kinsey and Kinsey*, Alaska Northwest Publishing Company, Anchorage, 1980.

Brady, William J., *Skagway: City of the New Century*, Lynn Canal Publishing, Skagway, Alaska, 2013.

Chandonnet, Ann, *Gold Rush Grub: From Turpentine Stew to Hoochinoo*, University of Alaska Press, Fairbanks, 2005.

Chopin, Kate, *The Awakening*, 1899.

Clifford, Howard, *The Skagway Story*, Alaska Northwest Books, Anchorage, 1975.

Cohen, Stan, *The Streets Were Paved With Gold: A Pictorial History of the Klondike Gold Rush 1896-1899*, Pictorial Histories Publishing, Missoula, Montana, 1977.

Hoffman, David, *An Elders' Herbal*, Healing Arts Press, Rochester, Vermont, 1993.

Mayer, Melanie J., *Klondike Women: True Tales of the 1897-1898 Gold Rush*, Swallow Press/Ohio University Press, 1989.

Meaux, Jean Morgan, ed., *In Pursuit of Alaska: An Anthology of Travelers' Tales, 1879-1909*, University of Washington Press, Seattle, 2013.

Mole, Richard, *Rebel Women of the Gold Rush*, Heritage House, Victoria, B.C., Canada, 1998.

Morgan, Lael, *Good Time Girls*, Epicenter Press, Fairbanks, 1998.

Morgan, Murray, *One Man's Gold Rush*, University of Washington Press, Seattle, 1967.

Murphy, Claire Rudolf, and Jane G. Haigh, *Gold Rush Women*, Alaska Northwest Books, Anchorage, 1997.

Norris, Frank B., *Legacy of the Gold Rush: An Administrative History of Klondike Gold Rush National Historical Park*, National Park Service, Anchorage, 1996.

Ody, Penelope, *The Complete Medicinal Herbal*, Dorling Kindersley, London, 1993.

Orcas Island Historical Society and Museum, *Images in America: Orcas Island*, Arcadia Publishing, Charleston, S.C., 2007.

Pandell, Karen and Chris Stall, *Animal Tracks of the Pacific Northwest*, The Mountaineers, Seattle, 1981.

Peterson, Gary and Glynda Schaad, *Women to Reckon With: Untamed Women of the Olympic Wilderness*, Poseidon Peak Publishing, Forks, Washington, 2007.

Ritter, Harry, *Alaska's History: The People, Land and Events of the North Country*, Alaska Northwest Books, Anchorage, 1993.

Spude, Catherine Holder, *The Mascot Saloon: Archeological Investigations in Skagway, Alaska, Vol. 10*, National Parks Service, Anchorage, 2006.

Stewart, Hilary, *Indian Fishing*, University of Washington Press, Seattle, 1977.

http://www.ctgenweb.org/county/cowindham

ELIZA'S RECIPE FILE

Kudos to recipe testers: Marilyn Allen, Jeany Aupperlee, Eve Boe, Wendy Dahlgren, Janelle Draayer, Vanessa Finch, Debbie Galbraith, Janet Gifford, Cate Grinzell, Megan Groen, Anne Hays, Karen Kapovich, Madra Likkel, Sue Likkel, Blair Sweeney Maurer, Lisa O'Brien, Susan Olsen, Ruth Posthuma, Krysten Reimann, Esther Templin, Monica Todd-Klopfer, and Nancy Tupper. Your comments about creating 19th century recipes in 21st century kitchens have been entertaining and valuable, and the results have been surprisingly tasty. A special thanks to a project sponsored in Windham County, Connecticut chronicling newspaper recipes from the late 19th century where some of the following recipes that appear in the novel originated.

꙳ꙩ꙳ꙩ꙳ꙩ꙳ꙩ꙳ꙩ

FISH CAKES

Take cold boiled fish, either fresh or salt, remove the bones and mince the meat; take two-thirds as much warm mashed potatoes as fish, add a little butter and sufficient beaten eggs or milk to make the whole into a smooth paste, season with pepper, and make into cakes about an inch thick; sprinkle them with flour and fry brown in butter in cast iron pan.

꙳ꙩ꙳ꙩ꙳ꙩ꙳ꙩ꙳ꙩ

EGG TOAST

Beat an egg smooth with half a teacup of evaporated milk.
Dip slices of stale bread in this and fry a nice brown in butter.

If for "the men," add a pinch of pepper and salt to the egg. For children, omit these and give them honey or syrup with it.

⸞⸟⸞⸟⸞⸟⸞⸟⸞⸟

CHOW-CHOW

In the evening, soak two heads of cabbage for two hours in scant amount of water and a generous handful of salt.

Rinse cabbage and add two onions, a half-dozen green peppers, one dozen cucumbers, all chopped fine; sprinkle another generous handful of salt over mixture and let sit for two more hours.

Lastly, add two quarts tomatoes and let sit overnight.

In the morning drain off the brine, and season with one tablespoonful of celery seed, one ounce of turmeric, half-teaspoonful of cayenne pepper, one teacupful of brown sugar, one ounce of cinnamon, one ounce of allspice, one ounce of black pepper, one-quarter ounce cloves, vinegar enough to cover, and boil two hours.

Process in water bath for ten minutes.

Store in cool, dark place.

⸞⸟⸞⸟⸞⸟⸞⸟⸞⸟

POTATO OMELET

Take five ounces of potatoes mashed, pepper, salt, and a little nutmeg; mix in with five eggs previously well beaten separately. Squeeze in a little lemon juice, and fry nicely in pancake-sized rounds.

Add any herbs as you have so, or top with cheese if serving for company.

⸞⸟⸞⸟⸞⸟⸞⸟⸞⸟

FRIED POTATOES

Take raw potatoes, peel, and cut in rings the thickness
of a shilling; throw slices into cold water until you
have sufficient; drain on a cloth; and fry quickly in
plenty of hot fat in cast iron pan; dry them well from
the grease and sprinkle with salt.

When nicely done, and piled up properly, they make a
fine side dish, which is always eaten with great relish.
Or cut a potato lengthwise the size and shape of the
divisions of an orange, trim them neatly, and fry them
with or without sliced onions; they are an excellent
garnish to pork chops, sliced cod, red herrings, or with
a rasher of bacon.

꒯꒰꒯꒰꒯꒰꒯꒰

SCOTCH BROTH

Put a teacupful of pearl barley into four quarts of cold
water, let boil, add two sliced onions, two diced
turnips, two carrots cut in slices, and one carrot
grated; add any meat bones—mutton, beef, or ham hock
—and herbs, if available.

Boil slowly for three hours; do not rush the boil.

Add generous amount of salt and pepper to taste before
removing from fire.

꒯꒰꒯꒰꒯꒰꒯꒰

JULIENNE SOUP

To make this soup, cut carrot, potato, turnip, and
celery root into neat bits and fry them thoroughly in
butter, partly boiling them first if old and tough. Add
them to some clear vegetable broth just before serving.
Season with salt and pepper and any fresh or dried
herbs as you have them.

꒯꒰꒯꒰꒯꒰꒯꒰

WHITE VEGETABLE SOUP

Boil two carrots, two turnips, two onions, three stalks
of celery, three potatoes; add half a pint of split peas,
boiled and rubbed through sieve; then pass all the vegetables through the sieve; add one quart of good vegetable
stock, and half a pint of cream or good milk; season to taste.

༺ೲೲೲೲೲ༻

GREEN PEA SOUP

Take one and a half pints of green peas, boil them in
water with salt and a little mint; when thoroughly
cooked, pound them and pass them through a sieve.

Put a pat of butter into a stew pot; when melted put in
an onion and a carrot cut in thin slices, fry until they
begin to color.

Add a quart of stock, a little salt, pepper, and a pinch
of white sugar. Leave it to boil for a quarter of an hour,
then stir in the puree of peas, let it come to the boil.

Serve with a small slice of bread fried in butter.

༺ೲೲೲೲೲ༻

WELSH RAREBIT

Melt three tablespoons butter with three tablespoons
flour, whisk over low heat until a roux forms.

Add one teaspoon of dry mustard to roux and whisk
quickly.

Add one large stein of beer, at room temperature, and
continue to whisk until mixture thickens.

Add a hefty portion of grated cheese and one-half
teaspoon prepared horseradish; mix with a wooden
spoon coated with lard. Add black pepper as desired.

For those who refrain from alcoholic beverages, sub-
stitute ginger beer; the taste will be somewhat different,
but will not cause distress. Serve over toasted bread.

ᑯᕐᑐᑯᕐᑐᑯᕐᑐᑯᕐᑐᑯᕐᑐ

OX-TAIL SOUP

Take two tails, wash and put into a kettle with about one gallon of cold water and a little salt.

Boil, then simmer.

Skim off the broth.

When the meat is well cooked, take out the bones and add a little onion, carrot, and tomatoes, if you have any. It is better made the day before using, so that the fat can be taken from the top.

Add any combination of chopped vegetables the next day, and boil for a half-hour longer.

Topics and Questions
for Discussion

1. How does the title frame the reader's experience of the novel?

2. How do Eliza's thoughts toward men evolve through the story? Where do you see a turning point in her feelings?

3. Describe Steiner's positive qualities and Eliza's negative qualities. How does looking at these qualities change your perception of either character?

4. What role does weather play in the novel?

5. What is the significance of the recipes peppered throughout the novel?

6. Who is Pearly? What do we know of her from fact versus the reality she's created for herself?

7. Why do you think Dr. Phillips chooses Rose to be his wife?

8. How do you feel about Cilla's decision to marry Lester Edwards? What other decisions do women in the novel make that please you or bother you?

9. Discuss surprises in the novel.

10. What is your favorite Kate Chopin quote? Why?

SELECTED TITLES FROM SHE WRITES PRESS

She Writes Press is an independent publishing company
founded to serve women writers everywhere.
Visit us at www.shewritespress.com.

Lum by Libby Ware. $16.95, 978-1-63152-003-7. In Depression-
era Appalachia, an intersex woman without a home of her own
plays the role of maiden aunt to her relatives—until an unexpected series of events gives her the opportunity to change her
fate.

Little Woman in Blue: A Novel of May Alcott by Jeannine Atkins.
$16.95, 978-1-63152-987-0. Based on May Alcott's letters and
diaries, as well as memoirs written by her neighbors, Little
Woman in Blue puts May at the center of the story she might
have told about sisterhood and rivalry in her extraordinary family.

A Cup of Redemption by Carole Bumpus. $16.95,
978-1-938314-90-2. Three women, each with their own secrets
and shames, seek to make peace with their pasts and carve out
new identities for themselves.

Shanghai Love by Layne Wong. $16.95, 978-1-938314-18-6. The
enthralling story of an unlikely romance between a Chinese
herbalist and a Jewish refugee in Shanghai during World War II.

The Black Velvet Coat by Jill G. Hall. $16.95, 978-1-63152-009-9.
When the current owner of a black velvet coat—a San Francisco
artist in search of inspiration—and the original owner, a 1960s
heiress who fled her affluent life fifty years earlier, cross paths,
their lives are forever changed . . . for the better.

The Vintner's Daughter by Kristen Harnisch. $16.95,
978-163152-929-0. Set against the sweeping canvas of French and
California vineyard life in the late 1890s, this is the compelling
tale of one woman's struggle to reclaim her family's Loire Valley
vineyard—and her life.